Paul N

∾

"The greatest imaginative novelist
of our generation."
E.M. Forster

"Lawrence, who brought to consciousness and
formulated so much that was coming
to life in the country as a whole, is
blended into the cultural air we breathe. It
is not easy to know what is our own,
and what came through him."
Ted Hughes

"The greatest writer of the century."
Philip Larkin

"He's an intoxicator... Has there ever been
anyone like him for bringing places and
people so vividly to life?"
Doris Lessing

Paul Morel

D.H. Lawrence

Text Edited by
Helen Baron

ONEWORLD
CLASSICS

ONEWORLD CLASSICS LTD
London House
243-253 Lower Mortlake Road
Richmond
Surrey TW9 2LL
United Kingdom
www.oneworldclassics.com

Paul Morel first published in 2003 by Cambridge University Press
© 2003 by The Estate of Frieda Lawrence Ravagli
This edition first published by Oneworld Classics Limited in 2009

Reprinted October 2009

Printed in Great Britain by CPI Antony Rowe

ISBN: 978-1-84749-119-0

Contents

D.H. Lawrence (1885–1930)

Lydia Lawrence,
D.H. Lawrence's mother

Ernest Lawrence,
D.H. Lawrence's brother

Jessie Chambers

Frieda Lawrence

Nottingham Road, Eastwood, *c*.1900. D.H. Lawrence was
born in Victoria Street, off this main road, on the right

D.H. Lawrence's birthplace
in Victoria Street, Eastwood

The chapel designed to house
D.H. Lawrence's ashes

Oh dear no: the conversation was Paul's. at Nether Green. She wanted from him a some sort of acknowledgement of his love. She knew he loved her, but she wanted him to acknowledge it himself. Men are so blind, and they run so to futility, in their blindness. The second self that watches things was beginning to rouse in Paul; these remarks were some kind of justification of himself.

"You know" he was saying ponderingly "I think if one person loves, the other does."

"Ah!" she cried, "like mother said to me when I was little 'Love begets Love.'"

"Ye-es — something like that. — I think it must be" he said. Her hesitancy hurt her. She no. Miriam verily noted again: you see, at this time, the balance of strength was on the edge of Miriam, so that she was great reserve strength. While Miriam knew it was a personal question between them and had not grown beyond herself — nor beyond her control. It was not until it became "defie so — because if not, love ought be very terrible" she replied, invested with solemn like religion. and not believing it the whole force of the will a love that the denial of it was.

"Yes, but it is: at least with most people" he answered. And, not reading her reservation aright, she was assured Nay— Miriam knew that Paul spoke for his own assurance.

She always regarded that sudden coming upon him in the lane as a discovery. It revealed to her a part, that she thought, with some justice, nobody had never seen, and that he himself did not suspect. She held it very precious, this finding out that he was lonely, as she termed it. He had so many friends, such a rattling host of affections, that it seemed a splendid paradox for her to make Paul very human knowledge alone, that he was lonely. There was a suggestion

Paul Morel

Note on the Texts

The text of *Paul Morel*, as presented here, is an edited transcript of the second and the third in a series of manuscript drafts of the novel that became *Sons and Lovers* at the fourth writing. The first manuscript draft is lost. Lawrence wrote the second draft from around 13th March to mid-July 1911, when he left it unfinished. The first seventy-one pages of the manuscript are now missing. Lawrence worked on a third draft of *Paul Morel* from 3rd to 15th November 1911, but then he fell ill and stopped writing, having completed only seventy-four pages. Lawrence appears to have discarded the opening pages of the previous draft as he wrote the third draft, copying with revisions onto fresh paper.

For the present volume, the logical sequence of the two surviving drafts of *Paul Morel* has been restored (i.e. the text of the third draft comes before that of the second draft), as the text of the second draft follows naturally on from where the text of the third draft leaves off, although there is some overlap and a few inconsistencies, such as the name "Eastwood"/"Eberwich".

Lawrence went back to the third draft of *Paul Morel* in February 1912 and completed it in April the same year. Most of the latter part of the third draft is now lost, so it is not possible to know how long it was when completed.

As it was an abandoned working draft, the errors in *Paul Morel* were left largely uncorrected by Lawrence. On 29th May 1911 he posted a "mass" of pages to Louie Burrows, claiming it was a quarter of the book, and asking her to "correct it and collect it". This explains a number of corrections by her, which are listed in the Textual Apparatus of the Cambridge Edition of *Paul Morel* (2003).

Some silent emendations and regularizations – such as omitted full stops, quotation marks, apostrophes and irregular titles (e.g. Mr./Mr) – have been made by the editor. A full list of emendations, substantive errors and author's manuscript revisions is included in the Textual Apparatus of the Cambridge Edition of *Paul Morel* (2003).

3

Chapters 1–4
(Third Draft)

Chapter I

ANTECEDENTS

"The Breach" succeeded to "Hell Row". It was a natural sequence. Hell Row was a block of some half dozen thatched, bulging cottages which stood back upon the brook-course by Greenhill Lane. The row was burned down in 1870, and shortly afterwards, near its site was erected the camp of miners' dwellings known as the "Breach."

Eastwood had scarcely come to consciousness when the notorious Row was destroyed. The parish was strewed with groups of dwellings which scarcely made a village. Since the Seventeenth Century the people of Eastwood have scratched at the earth for coal, and here and there, amid the pasture of the hillslopes, were many little gin-pits, perhaps twenty yards in depth, employing each some dozen or score of men. Hell Row was built to accommodate the miners of the two gin-pits that stood in the field at the end of Greenhill Lane. Other such rows, old and thatched, were stranded beside the three highroads, of Nottingham and Derby and Mansfield, whilst odd cottages, and pairs of cottages were strewed lonelily over the parish. Such, with a few farms, was Eastwood sixty years ago.

Then the great coal and ironfield of Nottinghamshire and Derbyshire was discovered, and Eastwood issued forth from its larval state, astonished. Lord Palmerston formally opened the first colliery at High Park in a corner of the great wood where Robin Hood had a settled home, beside a spring which still bubbles up, keen and cold among its mosses and liver-wort, well within hearing of the whirring chuff of High Park colliery. Down the long valley, the brook hastens from out of the woods, filters through Nethermere, tumbles and tosses its way to the Erewash, that twisting tiny river which separates Nottinghamshire from Derbyshire, then tumbles into the Trent. Down the long valley comes the colliery railway, from Watnall pit on the highlands among the woods, through the cutting of red sandstone, under the oak trees; crossing, on its embankment, above the beautiful meadows of the Carthusian monks, past the high, ruined prow of Beauvale Priory, to High Park pit; then past the woods again to the great mine at Moorgreen; then on again, across the brook, and over the wheat-fields of the hillside facing Eastwood, to New England Colliery hidden in the coppice; then it branches to the north, runs through low-lying, snug Brinsley, up the long hill to Selston, whose colliery and village stand naked on a hill-top, starkly looking over at the hills of Derbyshire: six great mines like black studs in the valley, linked by the fine chain of the railway.

To accommodate the new regiments of miners, the Colliery Company built the 'Squares' on the hill-brow at Eastwood: two great quadrangles of dwellings with a street all round, which arose like barracks on the hill-slope, to face the pageant of sunsets among the Derbyshire hills. From the Squares, downhill, runs the chequer of the allotment gardens right down to the valley bed where the 'Breach' was built.

The Breach is an oblong of miners' dwellings, six blocks, two rows of three, like the dots on a blank-six domino. At the back of the Breach comes the scarp slope, from Eastwood town: in front the great beautiful opening of the dipslope, like the climb of a cockle shell, like a convex clamp shell sloping upward to the far-off pivot of Selston headstocks.

The dwellings themselves were substantial, even handsome: tall, solid, respectable houses with a neat garden in front. The fronts faced outwards, so that one could walk all round, seeing little plots of pinks and sweet williams on the sunny side, and saxifrage and auriculas in the shade: seeing little porches, and neat front windows, and high dormer attics. The backs, however, were less inviting. The kitchen windows looked down the narrow back gardens to the ash-pits. Coming up the back-garden path, one had a view of all the dozen back-yards in the block, and of all the dozen women at gossip or at work. Then, through the back-garden gate, one was in a very ugly alley, lined with ash pits, whose square, evil-smelling doors were level with one's knees, or with one's head, as the land rose. In this nasty alley the children played, the hucksters bawled, the women came out and gossipped, the men not at work lounged in gangs, just as in any slum.

It was no wonder Mrs Morel was bitterly chagrined at having to move into the 'Breach'. Hitherto she had managed to keep out of the miners' dwellings. Now at last, after eight years of marriage, she descended to the 'Breach'. To be sure, she had an end house: Number 52, on the top block, beneath the sharp slope of the short hill. The end houses were rather larger than the rest in the blocks, had side porches, so that the front door did not open direct into the sitting-room; and had long side gardens, so that there was a strip of garden on three sides of the house. Moreover, the rent being 5/6 per week instead of 5/-, occupants of end houses enjoyed a kind of aristocracy in the Breach. But it was a kind of aristocracy Mrs Morel did not seek.

She was thirty-one years old, small and delicately made. She had come down to the Breach in July. In September she expected her third baby. Her husband was a miner. On the August Bank Holiday he had gone off early in the morning. His wife had done her work as usual, had sent the children off on a picnic into the meadows by the brookside, had spent the rest of the day sewing. She was alien to the women of the Breach, who spoke the broad Derbyshire accent, and had ways broad and uncouth to her. Therefore, at evening, when the children were in bed, and the light was going, when Mrs Morel could sew no more, when she was restless, and the old forlorn ache came creeping in upon her, she had nothing to do but to think, nowhere to go but to the door. Glancing out of the side window she saw the people returning from pic-nics, climbing tired but happy up to Eastwood. She saw the women of the Breach at the corners of the alley, watching the beautiful weather. Then there were gangs of youths lounging and remarking on the passers by. It was fading dusk, and she was intensely lonely.

She went out into the front garden. It was quite a tiny square with a privet hedge. Opposite the red gate was a stile, through which the path climbed, shaded by a tall hedge, with the cut pasture burning gold at the hill top. The glow sank quickly, and the fields and the tall hedge smoked dusk. Only the sky overhead throbbed and pulsed with light. Over the hill-top, towards the east, stood an immense red moon, bare, and exposed in its flushed nearness. The west was warm and brilliant on the one hand, the moon hung soft and flushed and enormous on the other. Between, down the trough of the path under the overarching hedge, the men lurched home, brimmed-up, ghoulish black shadows stumbling down the dusk, and singing drunkenly. And far-off, here and there far off in the distance, could be heard the shouting and singing of the drunken miners, who were drifting out into the close of the beautiful hot day.

Mrs Morel remembered that somewhere, among these lurching shouters or singers, her husband's voice was upraised. It made her heart stand still. After all this time, she had not got used to it. To be married to a man who was staggering in the under-dusk of the evening, bawling with drunkenness, made her feel as if she were in some painful dream, as if it could *not* be true. Yet his children slept upstairs, and another stirred within her. It could not be true. Some things happen in life, and carry the body along with them, accomplish facts, and make one's history, and yet are not real. Mrs Morel felt that her inner life denied her experience, said "It is a battle field: my flesh is a battle field where aliens fight. But underneath and untouched the spirit is waiting, lying dormant. My life is not of me, it is only upon me. This is a vast echoing and action all round me. I am within, untouched, folded in silence, waiting for ever. I do not live, I wait."

Away on the hill brow there were three oak trees, side by side, which had been killed by the digging away of the yellow clay for bricks. The trunks stood gaunt, spreading twisted arms. It reminded Mrs Morel of Calvary. Down the Breach, drunken men were sitting on the doorsteps singing "Lead Kindly Light" with much pathos. Quite a young voice, somewhere, sang tipsily the children's hymn "There is a green hill far away."* Mrs Morel quivered. She looked at the three trees, at the darkened, mown hill, she listened to the sounds of the full dusk.

"Not so very far away, my Sirs," she said to herself, half in wonder, half in bitterness. She began to realise the Crucifixion. She herself was being slowly crucified. She was waiting, all the time in pain, to say "It is finished"*: and then she could be free, and she could do.

She watched the black swifts, that the children call 'devilins,' dart to and fro like black arrow-heads just above her, veering round the corner of the house, flying in at the broad eaves, then slipping and darting down the air again, all silent and belated. A man came down the steep bank-slope of the hill-foot at a run, crashing into the stile. Mrs Morel shuddered. He swore low and evilly: a swift cut by just close to her face. She was afraid of the terrible dusk.

Turning, she saw the stone-crop by the path was crushed and trodden. She crouched and brushed it up with her hands. It was a relief to do so small a tender thing. She loved the pitiful little stone crop, that was littered with fallen white rose-leaves, from the big old bush that flowered so thickly and smelt so sweet. She caressed the flowers one after another: she must have something to caress.

At last she passed indoors, straightened the house, lit the lamp, mended the fire, looked out the washing for the next day, put it to soak. She had plenty to do.

Mrs Morel came of a family noted for many generations for its handsome, overbearing men and women. The Coppards had been among the gentry of Nottingham in Henry the Eighth's time: they had fought hard with Colonel Hutchinson and Cromwell, and had been famous Independents. They lost their standing after Waterloo. George Coppard, Mrs Morel's father, was the first of the family to work as an artizan.

He became an engineer. A fine, handsome, haughty man, his poverty galled his fibre. He became foreman of the engineers in the dockyard at Sheerness. Mrs Morel—Gertrude,—was the second daughter. She favoured her mother, loved her mother best of all: but she had the Coppard's clear, defiant blue eyes, and their broad brow. She remembered to have hated her father's insolence towards her gentle, humourous, kindly-souled mother. She remembered running over the breakwater at Sheerness, and finding a boat. She remembered to have been petted and flattered by all the men when she had gone to the dockyard, for she was a delicate, very refined child. She remembered the funny old mistress, whose assistant she had become, whom she had loved to help in the pleasant private school. And she had the bible that John Field had given her. She used to walk home from chapel with John Field, when she was nineteen. He was the son of a well-to-do grocer, who had been to college in London, and who was to devote himself to business.

She could always recall in detail a September Sunday afternoon, when they had sat under the vine at the back of her father's house. The sun came through the chinks in the vine-leaves, and made beautiful patterns, like a lace scarf falling on her and on him. Some of the leaves were clean yellow, like yellow flat flowers.

"Now sit still," he had cried. "Now your hair, I don't know what it *is* like! It's as bright as new money, and as red as burnt copper, and it has gold strands, where the sun burns on it. Yet they say it is dull brown. Your mother calls it mouse colour."

She had met his brilliant eyes, but her clear face showed none of the elation which rose within her.

"But you say you don't like business," she pursued.

"I don't—I hate it," he cried hotly.

"And you would *like* to go into the ministry," she half implored.

"I should—I should love it, if I thought I could make a first-rate preacher."

"Then why don't you—why *don't* you." Her voice rang with defiance. "If *I* were a man, nothing would stop me."

She held her head erect—he was rather timid of her.

"But my father's so stiff necked. He means to put me into the business, and I know he'll do it."

"But if you're a *man*—!" she had cried.

"Being a man isn't everything," he replied, frowning with puzzled helplessness.

Now, as she moved about her work at the Breach, with a working knowledge of what being a man meant, she knew that it was *not* everything.

At twenty, owing to her health, she had left Sheerness. Her father had retired home to Nottingham. John Field's father had been ruined: the son had gone as a teacher in Croydon. She did not hear of him until, two years later, she made determined inquiry. He had married his landlady, a women of forty, who had money.

And still Mrs Morel preserved John Field's bible. She did not now believe him to be—well, she understood pretty well what he might or might not have been. So she preserved his bible, and kept his memory intact in her heart. To her dying day, for thirty-five years, she did not speak of him.

When she was twenty three years old she met, at a Christmas party, a young man from the Erewash Valley. Morel was then twenty-seven years old. He was well-set-up, erect and very smart. He had wavy, black hair that shone again, and a vigorous black beard that had never been shaved. His cheeks were ruddy, and his red, moist mouth was noticeable because he laughed so often and so heartily. He had that rare thing, a rich, ringing laugh, like the clapping of glad bells. Gertrude Coppard had watched him fascinated. He was so full of colour and animation, his voice ran so easily into comic grotesque, he was so ready and so pleasant with everybody. Her own father had a rich fund of humour, but it was satiric. This man's was different: soft, non-intellectual, warm, a kind of gambolling.

She herself was so different. She had a curious, receptive mind, which found much pleasure and amusement in listening to other folk. She was clever in leading folk on to talk, being bright, sympathetic, and of quick understanding. What she loved most of all was a discussion on religion or non-technical philosophy or politics, with some educated man. This she did not often enjoy. So it was her constant habit to have people talk to her.

In her person, she was rather small and delicate, with a large brow, and dropping bunches of brown silk curls. Her blue eyes were very kind, and very seeing. She had the beautiful hands of the Coppards. Her dress was always very subdued. She wore a dark blue silk dress with a peculiar silver chain, of silver scallops. This, and a heavy brooch of twisted gold, was her only ornament. She was still perfectly pure in soul, deeply religious, and full of beautiful candour.

Walter Morel was rather timid of her. She was to him that thing of delicate mystery, a lady. When she spoke to him, it was with that southern pronunciation and that purity of English which thrilled him to hear. She watched him. He danced well, as if it were natural and joyous in him to dance. His grandfather was a French refugee who had married an English barmaid—if it had been a marriage. Gertrude Coppard watched the young miner as he danced, with a certain subtle exaltation like glamour in his movement, and his face the flower of his body, ruddy, with tumbled black hair, and laughing alike whatever partner he bowed above. She thought him rather wonderful, never having met anyone like him. Her father was to her the type of all men. And George Coppard, erect and dignified, of leisurely movement, who preferred theology in reading, and who drew near in deep sympathy only to one man, the Apostle Paul; who was harsh and austere in government, and in familiarity even only playfully ironic; who in his pride ignored all sensuous pleasure—he was very different from the miner. Gertrude herself was rather contemptuous of dancing: she had not the slightest inclination towards that accomplishment, and had never learned even a Roger de Coverley.* She herself lived mostly within the white light of her own consciousness. Therefore the dusky, golden softness of his sensuous flame of life, that flowed from off his flesh like the flame from a candle, not baffled and gripped into incandescence by thought and spirit as her life was, seemed to her something wonderful, beyond her.

He came and bowed above her. A warmth radiated through her as if she had drunk wine.

"Now do come and have this one wi' me," he said, caressively. "It's easy, you know. I'm pining to see you dance."

She glanced at his laughing deprecation, and smiled. Her smile was wonderfully beautiful. It moved the man so that he felt dizzy.

"No, I won't dance," she said softly. She minted her words as clean as new coin.

Not knowing what he was doing—he often did the right thing, by instinct—he sat beside her, inclining reverentially.

"But you mustn't miss your dance," she reproved.

"Nay, I don't want to dance that—it's not one as I care about."

"Yet you invited me to it."

He laughed very heartily at this.

"I never thought o' that. Tha's soon taken the curl out of me."

It was her turn to laugh quickly.

"You don't look particularly lank or limp," she said.

"Like a pig's tail, I curl because I can't help it," he laughed—rather boisterously. She found him very piquant.

13

"Aren't you having anything to drink?" he asked.

"No thank you—I am not at all thirsty."

He hesitated—divined that she was a total abstainer—and felt a rebuff.

Then he pursued a number of quite polite, interested questions. She answered him brightly. He seemed quaint.

"And you are a miner!" she exclaimed in surprise.

"Yes. I went down when I was twelve."

She looked at him in wondering dismay.

"But don't you feel stifled?" she asked.

"You don't notice it. You live like th' mice, an' you pop out at night to see what's going on."

"It makes me feel blind," she shuddered.

"Like a moudiwarp!"* he laughed. "Yi, an' there's some chaps as does go round like moudiwarps." He thrust his face forward in the blind, snout-like way of a mole, seeming to sniff and peer for direction. "They dun though!" he protested naively. "Tha niver seed such a way they get in. But tha mun let me ta'e thee down sometime, an' tha can see for thysen."

She looked at him startled. This was a new half of life suddenly opened before her. She thought how brave and reckless he must be, how noble: the pit would be madness to her. He risked his life daily, and with gaiety. She looked at him, humbly, and appealingly.

"Shouldn't ter like it?" he asked tenderly. "'Appen not, it 'ud dirty thee."

She had never been "thee'd" and "thou'd" before. It was strange, rather thrilling.

The next Christmas they were married, and for three months she was perfectly happy: for six months she was very happy.

He had signed the pledge, and wore the blue ribbon of a total abstainer: he was nothing if not showy. They lived, she thought, in his own house. It was small, but very convenient, and quite thoroughly furnished, with solid, worthy stuff that suited her honest soul. The women her neighbours were unintelligible to her, and his mother and sisters were apt to sneer at her lady-like ways. But she could perfectly well live by herself, so long as she had her husband close.

Sometimes, when she herself wearied of love talk, and tried to open her heart seriously to him, she saw him listen deferentially, but without understanding. This killed her efforts at a finer intimacy, and she had flashes of fear. Sometimes he was restless of an evening: it was not enough for him just to be near her, she realised. She was glad when he set himself to little jobs.

He was a remarkably handy man, could make or mend anything. So she would say:

"I do like that coal-rake of your mother's—it is so nice and handy."

"Does ter, my wench. Well, I can make thee one."

"What—why it's a steel one—!"

"An' what if it is!—tha s'lt ha'e one very similar, if not exactly same."

She did not mind the mess, nor the hammering and noise. He was busy and happy.

But in the seventh month, when she was brushing his Sunday coat, she felt papers in the breast pocket, and, seized with a sudden curiosity, took them out to read. He very rarely wore the frock coat he was married in: and it had not occurred to her before to feel curious concerning the papers. They were the bills of the household furniture, still unpaid.

"Look here," she said at night, after he was washed and had had his dinner. "I found these in the pocket of your wedding coat. Haven't you settled the bills yet?"

"No—I haven't had a chance."

"But you told me all was paid. I would never have thought it of you. I had better go into Nottingham on Saturday and settle them, I don't like sitting on another man's chairs, and eating from an unpaid table."

He did not answer.

"I can have your bank book, can't I?"

"Tha can ha'e it, for what good it'll be to thee."

"I thought— —" she began. He had told her he had a good bit of money left over. But she realised it was no use asking questions. She sat rigid with bitterness and indignation.

The next day, she went down to see his mother.

"Didn't you buy the furniture for Walter?" she asked.

"Yes, I did," tartly retorted the elder woman.

"And how much did he give you to pay for it?"

The elder was stung with fine indignation.

"Eighty pound, since you're so keen on askin'" she replied.

"Eighty pounds! But there are ninety two pounds still owing!"

"I can't help that."

"But where has it all gone?"

"You'll find all the papers, I think, if you look—beside ten pound as he owed me, an' six pound as the wedding cost down here."

"Six pounds!" echoed Gertrude Morel. It seemed to her monstrous that, after her own father had paid so heavily for her wedding, six pounds more should have been squandered in eating and drinking at Walter's parents' house, at his expense.

"And how much has he sunk in his houses?" she asked.

"His houses—which houses?"

Gertrude Morel went white to the lips. He had told her the house he lived in, and the next one, was his own.

"I thought the house we live in—" she began.

"They're my houses, those two," said the mother-in-law. "And not clear either. It's as much as I can do to keep the mortgage interest paid."

Gertrude sat white and silent. She was her father now.

"Then we ought to be paying you rent," she said coldly.

"Walter has been paying me rent," replied the mother.

"And what rent?" asked Gertrude.

"Six-and-six a week," retorted the mother.

It was more than the house was worth.*

"It is lucky to be you," said the elder woman bitingly, "to have a husband as takes all the worry of the money, and leaves you a free hand."

The young wife was silent.

She said very little to her husband, but her manner had changed towards him. Something in her proud, honorable soul had crystallised out hard as rock.

When October came in, she thought only of Christmas. Two years ago, at Christmas, she had met him. Last Christmas she had married him. This Christmas she would bear him a child.

Being of a deeply sympathetic disposition, she never repelled an honest woman's advances, though she herself never sought friendship. So she got into the habit of talking with the neighbouring women. They were always rather deferential to her, and they liked her.

"You don't dance yourself, do you Missis?" asked her nearest neighbour, in October, when there was great talk of opening a dancing class over the "Three Tunns Inn", at Eastwood.

"No—I never had the least desire to," Mrs Morel replied.

"Fancy! An' how funny as you should ha' married your Mester. You know he's quite a famous one at it."

"I didn't know he was famous," laughed Mrs Morel.

"Yea, he is though! Why, he run that dancing class in the Miners Arms Club-room for over five year."

"Did he?" Mrs Morel was very cold.

"Yes, he did." The other woman was defiant. "An' it was thronged every Tuesday, and Thursday, an' Sat'day—an' you could hear 'em when they come out, shoutin' and carryin' on, for a mile round."

This kind of thing was the bitterness of death to Mrs Morel, and she had a fair share of it. The women did not spare her, at first; for she was superior, she could not help it.

He began to be rather late in coming home.

"They're working very late now, aren't they?" she said to her washer woman.

"No later than they allers do, I don't think. But they stop to have their pint at Ellen's, an' they get talkin', an' there you are!—Dinner stone cold,—an' it serves 'em right."

"But Mr Morel does not take any drink."

The woman dropped the clothes, looked at Mrs Morel, then went on with her work, saying nothing.

Gertrude Morel was very ill when the boy was born. Morel was good to her, as good as gold. But she felt very lonely, miles away from her own people. She felt lonely with Morel now, and his presence only made her lonely, rather unhappy life harder.

The boy was small and frail at first, but he came on quickly. He was a beautiful child, with dark gold ringlets, and dark blue eyes, which changed gradually to a clear grey. Mrs Morel loved him passionately. He came just when her own bitterness of disillusion was hardest to bear; when her faith in life was shaken, and her soul felt dreary and lonely. She made much of the child, and the father was jealous.

Then at last Mrs Morel finally despised her husband. She turned to the child, she turned from the father, in contempt. He had begun to neglect her, he wearied of domesticity. He had no religion, she said bitterly to herself. What he felt just at the minute, that was all to him. He would sacrifice his own pleasure never, unless on an impulse, for he had plenty of impulsive charity. But of the deep charity, which will make a man sacrifice one of his appetites, not merely one of his transitory desires, he was quite unaware. He was strictly irreligious. There was nothing to live for, except to live pleasurably. She was deeply religious. She felt that God had sent her on an errand, that she must choose for God from her sense of right and wrong. So she kept undaunted, her sense of duty and responsibility bearing her onward.

There began a battle between the husband and wife, a fearful, bloody battle that ended only with the death of one. She had his soul in charge.

Like a sheep dog, she tried to keep him from straying. She barked in front of him, she fought with him. In two words, she turned the point of one of his own petty meannesses back into himself. He could not endure moral suffering: it drove him mad.

While the baby was still tiny, the father's temper had become so irritable that it was not to be trusted. The child had only to give a little trouble, when the man began to bully. A little more, and the hard hands of the collier struck blindly at the child. Then Mrs Morel loathed her husband, loathed him for days: and Morel went out and drank: and Mrs Morel cared very little what he did. Only, on his return, she scathed him with her satire.

The estrangement between them caused him, knowingly or unknowingly, to grossly offend her where he would not have done. William, the baby, was just a year old, was just beginning to toddle, and to say pretty words. He was a winsome child, still with a little mop of boy's curls, darkening now to burnt gold. He was fond of his father, who was very gentle, infinitely patient and full of ingenuity to amuse the child, when it pleased him. The two played together, and Mrs Morel used to wonder which was the truer baby, though she knew which was the purer. Morel always rose early, about five or six o'clock in the morning, whether holiday or work day. On Sunday morning he would get up and prepare breakfast. The fire was never let to go out. It was raked just before going to bed. That is, a great piece of coal, a raker, was placed so that it would just be nearly burned through by morning. On Sunday mornings, the child would get up with his father, while Mrs Morel lay in bed for another hour or so. She was then more rested than at any other time: when father and child played and prattled together downstairs.

William was only one year old, and his mother was so proud of him, he was so pretty. She was not well off now, but her sisters kept the boy in beautiful clothes. Then, with his little white hat curled with an ostrich feather, and his white coat, he looked very bonny, the twining wisps of hair clustring in a rich aureole round his head. Mrs Morel lay listening, one Sunday morning, to the prattle of the two. Then she dozed off. When she came downstairs, a great fire glowed red in the grate, the room was hot, the breakfast was roughly laid. And seated in his armchair, against the chimney piece, sat Morel, rather timid: and standing between his legs, the child,—cropped like a sheep, with such an odd round poll—looking wondering at her: and on a newspaper spread out upon the hearth rug, a myriad of crescent-shaped curls, like the petals of a marigold reddened in the reddening firelight.

Mrs Morel stood still. It was her first baby. She went very white, and was unable to speak.

"What dost think on him?" Morel laughed uneasily.

She gripped her two fists, lifted them, and swept forward. Morel shrank back.

"I could kill you, I could!" she managed to articulate. She glared at her husband in hate, her two fists uplifted.

"Yer non want ter make a wench on 'im," Morel said, in a frightened tone. His attempt at laughter had vanished.

The mother looked down at the jagged, close clipped head of her child. She put her hands on his hair, and stroked and fondled his head.

"Oh—my pretty—" she faltered. Her lip trembled, her countenance broke, and, snatching up the child, she buried her face in his shoulder and cried dreadfully. She was one of those women who cannot cry: it hurts them more than it hurts a man. It was like ripping something out of her, her sobbing: like the rip and tear of the feathers plucked in handfuls from the body of a bird. Morel sat with his elbows on his knees, his hands gripped together till the knuckles were white. He gazed in the fire, feeling almost stunned, as if he could not breathe.

Presently she came to an end, soothed the child,—and cleared away the breakfast table. She could eat neither breakfast nor dinner but went about her work pale and very quiet. Morel was subdued. He crept about wretchedly, and his meals were a misery that day. She spoke to him quite civilly, and never alluded to what he had done. But he felt something terrible had happened.

Afterwards, she said she had been silly, that the boy's hair would have had to be cut, sooner or later. In the end, she even brought herself to say to her husband, it was just as well he'd played barber when he did. But she knew, and Morel knew, that that act had caused something dreadful to take place in her soul. She remembered the scene all her life, as one in which she had suffered the most intensely.

This act of masculine thoughtlessness was the spear through the side of her love for Morel. Before, while she had striven against him bitterly, she had fretted after him, as if he had gone astray from her. Now she ceased to fret for him: he was an outsider to her. This made life much more bearable.

Nevertheless, she still continued to strive with him. She still had her high religious sense, inherited from generations of Puritans. It was now a religious instinct, and she was almost a fanatic. If he sinned, she tortured him. If he drank, and lied, was often a poltroon, sometimes a knave, she wielded the lash unmercifully. No man can live unless his life is rooted in some woman: unless some woman believes in him, and so fixes his belief in himself. Otherwise he is like a water plant, whose root is detached: floating still, and apparently flourishing, upon the river of life, but really decaying slowly. Morel decayed slowly.

It was a great tragedy, and it is the tragedy of many a man and woman. The pity was, she was too much above him. She could not be content with the little he might be, she would have him the much that he ought to be. So, in seeking to make him nobler than he could be, she destroyed him. She injured and hurt and scarred herself, but she lost none of her nobility: she had the children.

He drank rather heavily, though not more than a large proportion of miners, and always beer, so that whilst his health was affected, it was never injured. His habit was to spend all Friday and Saturday and Sunday evening in the Miners Arms: Monday and Tuesday he gave himself some three hours: Wednesday and Thursday, less or none, according to his humour. He practically never had to miss work owing to his drinking.

But although he was very steady at work, his wages fell off. He was blab-mouthed, a tongue-wagger. Authority was hateful to him, therefore he could only abuse the pit-managers. This braggart abuse, uttered in a public house, went home to its object. Consequently, Walter Morel, although he knew as much about the pit, and about coal-mining, as any man on the job, gradually came to have worse and worse stalls, where the coal was thin, difficult to get, and came down small. So that, whereas when he married he often made four or five pounds a week in wages, he came later on to count two pounds a good week, and in summer, when the pits were turning badly, he often drew a mere sixteen or twenty shillings. Of this he kept a small part. From forty shillings, he kept ten: from thirty, he kept five: from twenty, he reserved two. This was for tobacco and beer. With the rest, Mrs Morel had to provide everything—rent, food, clothing, clubs, and insurance. It was wonderful how she managed, with three children: for Morel never had a penny; instead, it would fall to her to pay his debts. Yet all her life she kept clear, and the children had a good home, and proper meals. The way in which the women of England do this is wonderful, and terrible to think of, because of the stress it occasions. Sometimes, when she had four children, and Morel gave her fifteen or sixteen shillings a week for five or six weeks running, Mrs Morel used to feel as if she would go mad. She had every morsel of responsibility.

Their second boy, born two years after marriage, died at the age of two. Morel sadly wanted a girl. But when the little Annie came, when William was four, he turned against her from the first. She was rather peevish: she would not let him handle her: she would not play with him.

"Oh you whining, twisting little thing," her mother said to her. And she was as stubborn as a rock: she had not a trace of Morel's fluent nature. The father did not care for her.

Annie Morel was four years old when, in the July, the family moved down to the Breach. At that time Morel was working badly. It was a hot summer, and hardly any soft coal was being turned. For the Bank Holiday week, Morel had given his wife a guinea. She was trying to save against her confinement, so that the knowledge that he had kept five or six shillings for pleasure galled her. Gradually her delicacy had been worn down. To live at all, she had to harden and roughen, outwardly at least: otherwise she would have broken. Often, dreadful combats took place between them.

When Morel began, on the Monday morning of the holiday, blithely to bestir himself for his outing, Mrs Morel felt that she could not bear herself. A naturally vain man, he had shaved his beard, keeping a heavy black moustache. He was still ruddy and handsome, a little inflamed in countenance, perhaps; and, during the ten years of marriage, there had come a look of peevish, stubborn defiance. The black eyebrows arched upward, narrowing the insignificant brow. There was a resentful score down each ruddy cheek, ageing the man surprisingly. His old, fine swagger had degenerated into a petulant kind of stiffness, and only showed now and then when he was in high feather.

This was one of those occasions. He whistled, and joked with the children. He was jaunty and cocky as of old. But now it only irritated Mrs Morel past bearing. At ten o'clock he began to get ready. The old 'beau' was to be furbished up. He shaved himself with evident satisfaction; he parted his waving, glossy black hair very scrupulously. When he was dressed there was about him a perkiness which Mrs Morel loathed. He gave the two children a half-penny each. That was their share of the holiday, for their mother had not a penny to spare. William and Annie thought him generous. They got more pennies from him than from their mother, who was rather stern in the matter.

At half past nine, Jerry Purdy came to call for his pal. Jerry was Morel's bosom pal, and Mrs Morel's contemptible enemy. He was a tall man, thin as a lath, with a weevilly, 'cute face that never could grow a moustache. He walked with a stiff, brittle dignity, as if his head was on a wooden spring. By breed, he came of the sewer rat type. He was, however, cold-blooded, and very intelligent, though vulgar to the last fibre. Apparently he found particular pleasure in the red-blooded Morel, and, a veritable bottom-dog, tasted with savour the proximate refinement and culture of Mrs Morel.

She hated him. He was a widower whose eldest daughter kept house on pinched money, though Jerry himself was never short.

"A mean, wizen-hearted stick!" Mrs Morel sneered.

"Jerry's not mean—he's as good-hearted an' open free handed a chap as you'd find, look where you may for the next," Morel retorted. He had caught many a trick of his wife's speech.

"Good hearted to *you*, he may be. Such good-heartedness is part of his common viciousness."

"Ah, it would be, it would be, if it was for *me*," Morel retorted, hot and bitter.

Jerry befriended, treated, and domineered over the domineering Walter Morel.

"Mornin' Missis—Mester in?" Jerry asked from the threshold.

"Yes, he is," was the unwilling answer. Jerry entered unasked, and stood by the kitchen doorway. He was not invited to sit down, but he stood coolly asserting the rights of men and husbands.

"A nice day," he said to Mrs Morel, whose blood boiled at his insolence. "Yes."

"It's grand out, this morning," he insisted. She refused to answer.

The two men set out, both glad, Jerry however calm and dignified, Morel laughing, making a display of spirits. They preferred to walk to Nottingham, ten miles away: going across the fields. They climbed the hillside from the Breach, mounting gaily into the morning, Mrs Morel watching them from the front window. At the "Three Tunns" they had their first drink, their second at the "Old Spot." Then a long five miles of drought, to raise a delicious thirst to carry them into Bulwell. But they stopped in a field with some haymakers whose gallon bottle was full, so that, when they came in sight of Nottingham, Morel was sleepy. The town spread away before them, dimly smoking in the midday glare, fridging the crest far away to the south with spires and factory bulks and chimneys. In the last field Morel lay down under an oak tree, and slept soundly for over an hour. At one o'clock, when they rose to go forward, he felt queer and dizzy. A little brandy soon put that right.

They dined down in the Meadows, at Jerry's sister's house. Then they repaired to the "Punch Bowl," where they mingled in the excitement of pigeon-racing. Morel played his favourite skittles, and won half a crown, which restored him to solvency. By seven o'clock the two were in goodly condition. They caught the 7.30 train home.

Mrs Morel had been unaccountably depressed all the day. William, a bonny lad of seven, very thoughtful for his mother:

"Should I stop with you, mother?" he asked.

"Stop with me, child,—what for?"

"Well—aren't you going out nowhere?"

"I shall take Annie a little walk this afternoon."

He looked at her wistfully, helplessly, then departed with his playmate on a picnic.

In the afternoon, the Breach was intolerable. Every inhabitant remaining was out of doors. The women, in white aprons, talked in twos and threes at the garden fences, the men having a rest between drinks lounged at the end of the alley. The place smelled stale in the arid heat. The black slate of the roofs glistered.

Mrs Morel took the little girl down to the brook, to the meadows which were not more than a hundred yards away. The water of the brook ran quick and bright over coloured fragments of pot and smooth stones. Mother and child leaned on the weather-grey rail of the sheep bridge, watching. Up at the dipping hole, far up the rank meadow, Mrs Morel could see the naked forms of boys flashing round the deep, yellow water, or an occasional bright figure darting glittering over the blackish-green meadow. She knew William was at the dipping hole, and it was the dread of her life that he should get drowned.

Annie played under the lofty hedge, picking up the black little cones of last year, which had fallen from an alder, and which she called currants. The child required a great deal of attention, and the flies were very teasing. Mrs Morel, who always bore the heat badly, panted in distress.

The children were put to bed at seven o'clock, after which time she worked whilst waiting for her husband.

When Walter Morel and Jerry arrived at Langley Mill they felt a load off their minds: a railway journey no longer impended, so they could put the finishing touches to a glorious day. They entered the "Lord Nelson" with the swank of returned travellers. Mrs Morel, laughing, said that a collier's rosary was a string of public houses: bitterly, that it wasn't far from her husband's heaven to hell: only from the public house, home—and there was only a long lurch between.

Nine o'clock passed, and ten, and still the "pair" had not returned. Morel had at last quite quenched the spark of uneasiness that lingered within him. Meanwhile Mrs Morel sat at home churning her bitterness. As she sewed the baby-clothes, she cast her thoughts backwards and forwards, like a shuttle across the years of her life, weaving her own philosophy from the yarn of her experience. She was able to do this the more, as she was not identified with her own living, but remained a good deal outside it: a good part of herself was left, like an artist, uncaught by life, watching. In this she was very different from most women, who are the subject matter of life, therefore, 'in esse', not philosophers or artists, who weave up for presentation what is produced. And women have submitted so wonderfully, because, being the subject-matter, the stuff of the Tree, they will come to fruit whatever the wind and weather. They take a man almost as a flower takes a bee: and if he be a fly, a drone, a creeping insect, a mere despoiler, they reject him and starve him. Out of the very sap of life they bring, like blossoms, the nectar and beauty and pollen. And all this they wish to give to the man, who can lay up honey of beauty and wisdom from them, to feed the next generation. Walter Morel had given his wife children, according to the doctrine of Schopenhauer.* But he would not take from her, and help her to produce, the other finer products, blossoms of beautiful living, of which he might make wisdom like honey, and dreams like worship. Therefore she refused him: also, fearfully, she combated him. She was too much of a woman, too much of the stuff of life, to despair for herself. She was still fast producing life, and religion of life for her children.

The kitchen remained maddeningly rigid. The stiff, dark wooden chairs, and the podgy little dresser stood against the walls like menacing hieroglyphs. The firelight shone on the white hearth, now littered with bits, and on the bright steel fender, that had two dull spots where drops of water had fallen. The table, with its red cotton cloth, and the rather stately sofa, that had a scarlet chintz bed and cushions, both looked, along with the hearth, very cosy. But Mrs Morel did not feel cosy. She felt as if this close cosiness shut her in, as if she were a wild fish stifled in the warm room. As she sewed, the lamplight from overhead fell on her brown hair, that was now taken straight back to a knot that only needed four hairpins. She was already beginning to grow grey, though she was only thirty two years old. As the child stirred within her, she straightened herself, and sighed. On the fire, a large black saucepan bubbled slowly, and the room was full of the scent of boiled hops and dandelion.

"Eleven!" said Mrs Morel, aloud, and she braced herself up to bear the shrill striking of the clock-bell. The baby clothes were resumed.

Three men sat on three front doorsteps, singing "Lead Kindly Light" as they faced the moon. In spite of herself, and though she had heard the drunken men serenade their own tipsiness with that hymn dozens of times, she bubbled with laughter, and then immediately burned in hate of the fools. There was a quarrel somewhere,—there was brawling. And from the top of the hill, from under the moon, the little sound of shouting as the "Three Tunns" turned out. And from down the valley, towards the darkness, the nearer roistering from the "Palmerston Arms." And far-off shouts from the Mansfield high-road, as the men came out of 'Bostock's'. Mrs Morel listened to the shouting and chanting as the men descended the hillside straight upon her house. She looked up. It seemed they might burst in. The brass candle sticks shone complacently. She resumed her sewing.

It is a question whether she was more intoxicated with suffering than her husband with drink. He came at about twenty past eleven. He was not drunk, but in that wound up state of intoxication whose precious calm and equipoise is easily shaken, when a little readjustment is irritating to make, when real thwarting maddens. He was perfectly lovable and serene when he got to the garden gate. But the latch was hard to find, and then it was stiff, so he swore viciously. He was sufficiently drunk to be oblivious of everybody save himself.

There was a step up from the scullery to the kitchen. The kitchen door was open. He entered the scullery, a kind of porch, quite decently, but he stumbled up the step into the living room, into his wife's presence. She started up, a wave of madness going over her like flame.

"A nice way to come in—!" she cried.

"They shouldna put the fool's step there!" he shouted.

"It's not the step—it's the drunken nuisance that falls over it," she vibrated.

"Who's a drunken nuisance?" he resented, bullying.

"Why, say you're not! You haven't been boozing all day with that other drunken dirt, without being."

"No, I haven't been boozing all day."

"Ph—!—It's very evident what you've been doing."

"Oh is it—Oh!—Oh, is it!"

"Goes out at nine in the morning, and comes tumbling in towards midnight—what else have you been doing? You and your beautiful Jerry, it's all you're fit for: a drunken, filthy scum!"

"Who are you callin' a drunken scum—What?"

"You can find money to bezzle* with from dawn till midnight—"

"I haven't spent a two-shilling piece all day," he cried, with peculiar proud glee. He had won another half-crown, so it seemed to him the day was all assets.

"Don't lie to me," she cried in contempt. "You don't get as drunk as you are on nothing—And—" she flashed— "If you've been sponging your Jerry—let *him* look after his motherless children."

"'Let 'im look after his motherless children!'—Why, yer nasty little bitch, what children's better looked after than hisn?"

"My Sirs, not yours, it's true, if you had the looking-after them. A man as can afford to swill from the beginning of the day till midnight—"

"What does it matter to you," he shouted, "what I do, so long as it costs you nothing?"

"Costs me nothing!" she cried in bitterness. "It looks as if it cost me nothing . . . a lousy twenty one shillings to pay for everything with, while he can go jaunting off for the live-long day, and come home rolling drunk at midnight—"

"Shut your face, woman!" he bawled. "I've had enough of it."

"And so have I, and more than enough. You've had enough of it, my lord?—and so have I. Nothing but struggle and scrape, and barely enough to feed the children on, and then to have to sit pedgilling* away till midnight, waiting for a man who's been out on the spree, swilling and carousing all day—to come home rolling drunk, and then expecting to be made a fuss off."

"I expect nowt from you, you mingy— —What are you talking about, woman?" he suddenly exploded in fury.

They were now at battle pitch, both. Each forgot everything save the strife with the other. She, who, in other circumstances would have been a proud, sensitive, *man's* woman, fought with him here the common battle of blood. They fought wildly, with brutal words, till he called her a liar.

"No," she cried, starting up, scarce able to breathe. "Don't call *me* that—you, the most despicable liar that ever stepped in shoe-leather." She forced the last words out from suffocated lungs.

"You're a liar!" he yelled, banging the table with his first. "You're a liar, you're a liar."

She stiffened herself, with clenched fists.

"I'd smite you down, you cowardly beast, if only I could," she said, in low, quivering tones.

Then, in the next wave, came out her passionate loathing of him. He raged at her, and banged the table till the house rang, while she poured over him all her disgust, contempt, hate of him.

26

"The house is filthy of you," she cried.

"Then get out on it—it's mine. Get out on it," he yelled. "It's me as brings th' money whoam, not thee. It's my house, not thine. Then ger out on't—ger out on't!"

"And I would," she cried, suddenly shaken into tears of impotence. "Ah, wouldn't I, wouldn't I have gone long, long ago, but for those children. Ay, haven't I repented not going years ago, when I'd only the one—" suddenly drying into rage. "Do you think it's for *you* I stop—do you think I'd stop one minute for *you*—"

"Go then," he shouted, beside himself. "Go!"

"No!" she faced round. "No," she cried loudly, "you shan't have it *all* your own way: you shan't do *all* you like. I've got those children to see to. My word—" she laughed, "I should look well to leave them to you."

"Go," he cried thickly, lifting his fist. He was afraid of her. "Go!"

"I should be only too glad—I should laugh, laugh, my lord, if I could get away from you," she replied.

He came up to her, his face, with its blood-shot eyes, thrust forward in frenzy, and gripped her arms. She cried in horror of him, struggled to be free. Coming slightly to himself, panting, he pushed her roughly to the outer door, thrust her forth, slamming the bolt behind her with a bang. Then he went back into the kitchen, dropped into his arm-chair, his head, bursting full of blood, sinking between his knees. Thus he dipped gradually into a stupor, from exhaustion and intoxication.

The moon was high and magnificent in the August night. Mrs Morel, seared with passion, shivered to find herself out there in its great, white light, that seemed to fall cold on her inflamed soul. She stood for a few moments helplessly staring at the glistening great rhubarb leaves near the door. Then she got the air and the calm into her breast. She walked down the garden path, trembling in every limb, while the child boiled within her. For a while, she could not control her consciousness; so that mechanically she went over the last scene, then over it again, certain phrases, certain moments coming again like a brand red hot, down on her soul: and each time she enacted again the horrible hour, each time the brand came down at the same points, till the mark was burnt in, and the pain burnt out, and at last she came to herself. She must have been half an hour in this almost insane state. Then the presence of the night came again to her. She glanced round in fear. She had wandered to the side garden, where she was walking up and down the path beside the currant bushes under the long wall. The garden was a narrow strip, bounded from the road that cut between the blocks, by a thick thorn hedge.

She hurried out to the narrow garden to the front, where she could stand as if in an immense gulf of white light, the moon flying high in face of her, the moonlight standing up from the hills in front, and filling the valley where the Breach stood, almost blindingly. There, panting and half weeping in reaction from the stress, she murmured to herself over and again: "Oh—what has he done to me—what has he done to me!"

In her weariness she wished she might never see him again, that she might be spared henceforth the sight of him. This time, her loathing was the mechanical loathing of self preservation.

She became aware of something about her. With an effort, she roused herself, to see what it was that penetrated her consciousness. The tall white lilies were reeling in the moonlight; and the air was charged with their perfume, as with a presence. Mrs Morel gasped slightly in fear. She touched the great, pallid flowers on their fleshy petals, then shivered. They seemed to be yawning lasciviously in the moonlight. She put her hand into one white bin: the gold pollen scarcely showed on her fingers by moonlight. She bent down, to look at the gold within the bin: but it only looked dusky. Then she drank a deep draught of the scent. It almost made her reel.

She looked round her. The yew hedge had a faint glitter among its blackness. Various white flowers were out. In front, the hill rose into indistinctness, barred by the big high black hedges and nervous with cattle moving in the dim moonlight. Here and there the moonlight seemed to stir and ripple like water.

Mrs Morel leaned on the garden gate, looking out, and she lost herself awhile. She did not know what she thought. Except for a slight feeling of sickness, and a second consciousness in the child, her self melted out like scent into the shiny, pale air. After a time, the child too seemed to melt with her into the mixing-pot of moonlight, and she rested with the hills and lilies and houses, all swum together in a kind of swoon.

When she came to herself, she was tired for sleep. Languidly, she looked about her; the clumps of white phlox seemed like bushes spread with linen; a moth ricochetted over them, and right across the garden. Following it with her eye roused her. A few whiffs of the strong scent of phlox invigorated her. She passed along the path to her beloved rose-bush of common white roses, the sweetest of all. She smelled them, and caressed their cool ruffles. They refreshed her like a draught of water. She smiled on them, put her mouth to them, and turned home. She was tired, she wanted to sleep. In the mysterious out-of-doors she felt forlorn.

There was no sound anywhere. Evidently the children had not been wakened, or had gone to sleep again. A train, three miles away, roared across the valley. The night was very large, and very strange, stretching its hoary distances infinitely. And out of the silver-grey fog of darkness came sounds vague and hoarse: a corncrake not far off, sound of a train like a sigh, and distant shouts of men.

Her quietened heart beginning to beat quickly again, Mrs Morel hurried down the side garden to the back of the house. Softly, she lifted the latch: the door was still bolted, shut hard against her. She rapped gently, waited, then rapped again. She must not wake the children, nor the neighbours. He must be asleep, and he would not wake easily. Her heart began to burn to be indoors. She clung to the door handle hysterically. Now, it was cold: she would take a chill, and in her present condition!

Putting her apron over her head and her arms, she hurried again to the side garden, to the side window of the kitchen. Leaning on the sill, she could just see, under the blind, her husband's arms spread out on the table, and his black head on the board. He was sleeping with his face lying on the table. Something in his attitude made her feel pitiful, and contemptuous. The lamp was burning smokily, she could tell by the copper colour of the light. She tapped at the window more and more noisily. Almost it seemed as if the glass would break. Still he did not waken up.

After vain efforts, she began to shiver, partly from contact with the stone, and from exhaustion. Fearful always for the unborn child, she wondered what she could do for warmth. She went down to the coal-house, where was an old hearth-rug she had carried out for the rag-man the day before. This she wrapped over her shoulders. It was warm, if grimy. Then she walked up and down the garden path, peeping every now and then under the blind, knocking, and telling herself that at last the very strain of his position must wake him.

At last, after about an hour, she rapped long and low at the window. Gradually the sound penetrated to him. When in despair she had ceased to tap, she saw him stir, then lift his face blindly. The labouring of his heart hurt him into consciousness. She rapped imperatively at the window. He started awake. Instantly she saw his fists set and his eyes glare with wrath. He had not a grain of physical fear. If it had been twenty burglars, he would have gone blindly for them. He glared round, bewildered, but prepared to fight.

"Open the door Walter," she said coldly.

His hands relaxed—it dawned on him what he had done. His head dropped, sullen and dogged. She saw him hurry to the door, heard the bolt chock. He tried the latch. It opened—and there stood the silver grey night, fearful to him, after the tawny light of the lamp. He hurried back.

When Mrs Morel entered, she saw him almost running through the door to the stairs. He had ripped his collar off his neck, in his haste to be gone ere she came in, and there it lay with bursten button-holes. It angered Mrs Morel.

She warmed and soothed herself. In her weariness forgetting everything, she moved about at household duties, raked the fire, and went to bed. He was already asleep, as fast as if he were dead. His fine black eyebrows were drawn up in a sort of peevish misery, into his forehead, while his cheek's downstrokes, and his sulky mouth, seemed to be saying: "I don't care who you are nor what you are. I *shall* have my own road."

Mrs Morel knew him too well to look at him. As she unfastened her brooch at the mirror, she smiled faintly to see her face all smeared with the golden dust of the lilies. She brushed it off, and at last lay down. For some time her mind continued snapping and jetting sparks, but she was asleep before her husband awoke from the first sleep of his drunkenness.

Chapter II

BIRTH AND DEATH

After such a scene as the last, Walter Morel was for some days abashed and ashamed, but soon he regained his old bullying indifference. Yet there was a slight shrinking, a diminishing in his positivity. Physically, even, he shrank, so that his fine, full presence waned. He never grew in the least stout, so that, as he sank from his jaunty bearing, his physique seemed to contract along with his pride and moral strength.

But now he realised how hard it was for his wife to drag about at her work, and, his sympathy quickened by penitence, he felt she was heavily burdened. He came home earlier from work, he stayed in at evening.

"Dunna thee ma'e th'beds, leave 'em for me," he would say as, in his pit-clothes, with a red scarf knotted round his neck, and his tin bottle rolling in his jacket, he went upstairs at a quarter to six in the morning, to say something to her before departing to work.

"All right," she answered coldly. She longed to have him out of doors. When she heard the door bang behind him, heard the heavy slurr of his pit boots over the yard, heard the receding thud of his feet down the garden, she settled down to *rest*: really to rest, in the atmosphere of her own home, to which he did not belong.

He was good to her, at such times as she was ill. He would*

* * * *

and went upstairs Hearing him coming, Mrs Morel sighed, and stiffened herself, as if to bear something.

He was quite black from the pit. She could smell him of the pit: she could see where the sweat had trickled in the coal-dust on his forehead. His eyes seemed startlingly pale in his black face.

"An' how are ter feelin' by now, lass?" he asked in a tone of extravagant tenderness, that she found very hard to bear.

"As well as you can expect," she said.

"Ay—ay."

He stood gazing down on her face, sentimentally. He would have liked to kiss her, to shed a few tears over her. But she was so impassive. To escape his emotional gaze, she turned down the sheet from the infant. Morel leaned over her. She felt unbearable.

"Ay, bless 'im, the darlin'," he said, and the tear she had been expecting rose to his eyes. He wiped it off with the back of his black, hard hand, and sniffed. Mrs Morel felt sick. She turned her face away. He gazed awhile longer, then, so fondly, he smoothed the sheet over her shoulder, leaving grimy marks on it.

Then he went downstairs, where he sat for a time, his chin in his hand, gazing miserably, or pathetically into space. After which he ate a very good dinner, and waxed surprisingly cheerful.

Mrs Morel had a visit every day from the minister of the tiny chapel of Moorgreen. The clergyman was a young man, of about thirty, who, as the colliers said, was only half there. They meant he was almost imbecile. He was the son of a well-to-do tradesman, and drew no income from the church.

Mr. Revell was short and thickly built, yet he stooped, walked almost in a rambling fashion. He had a large head, and his black hair stuck out like a ragged haystack. His face was long, pale, and very heavy, and he had a trick of cocking his head to one side, nearly shutting his eyes, and of musing quaintly. He was fairly well read, and had his B.A. degree.

The clergyman was scoffed at everywhere by the miners and tradespeople. He was 'batchy', 'balmy', he was 'touched', he was 'something short'—'not quite there'—and so on. Add to this that he was extraordinarily sensitive, and it will be clear that he was not a great success as a minister.

He often came, rather forlornly, to see Mrs Morel. She perceived his sensitive soul, his helplessness, and she mothered him. When he found her in bed, very pale, he was startled. She thought his bewildered brown eyes rather pathetic.

"Are you very ill?" he asked.

"No, I am not," she smiled. But she was.

He knit his brows, cocked his head on one side in a puzzled fashion, and considered.

"Are all women as ill as you?" he asked, still puzzling.

"Most," she answered.

He reflected still longer, then he looked at her rather pathetically:

"My mother died when I was born— —I never thought— —" he faltered. She saw in his eyes pre-natal sorrow.

"What kind of a woman was she, do you think?" she asked.

"I don't know. I—I believe she played the piano very well."

Mrs Morel did not smile. "A little more," she thought, "and this man would have been a great musician. There's just a little flaw in his machinery—otherwise— —"

"You are not like your father?" she asked.

"Dodda?—I don't think I am. He is a business man."

Mrs Morel thought of that woman's son—would her's be the same? She looked at the child. It had a certain heavy-lidded look, of startled wonder, but wonder at pain: as if pain had startled its consciousness over early. She felt her heart bowed very gravely.

"Can I look at it?" Mr Revell asked.

He was always very delicate in his human intercourse. He put his head on one side like a listening bird.

"Is it a boy?"

"Yes."

"It makes you shudder to think we all have to be born," he said.

She smiled very winningly on him.

"It wouldn't, if you were a woman," she answered.

He did not understand.

"Should I say a prayer?" he asked.

"Do you wish to?"

He cocked his head like a doubtful bird. Then he said, quite simply: "Yes."

"Pray for us then," she said.

He said a brief prayer. He was so clumsy in his speech, she had to divine what he meant. That, she knew, was beautiful. When he arose from his feet, she asked:

"Will you be my baby's god-father?"

"How?"

"His godfather. To watch that he lives well, and to teach him."

"Do you think I could?"

"I want you to."

They called the child Paul, after Mr Revell.

The minister used always to come to see Mrs Morel on Thursday afternoons. She would have finished work if she could. But while Paul was a little baby, she was often behind-hand. Then she left the ironing till Mr Revell's visit, because she could iron and talk.

They used to discuss what he wanted to say in his sermon, and she would try to express for him what was in his heart. The baby was five weeks old when the minister came for the first discussion after Mrs Morel's illness.

"I don't think I ought to be a minister," he said wistfully. Evidently he had been brooding.

"Why not?"

"I have preached bad sermons while you have been ill."

"Nonsense," she smiled. But she was very pleased.

"And I ought not to preach *your* sermons."

"You are talking rubbish, you know."

She gave the iron a little bang on the table.

"You are very clever," he said to her, wistfully. "You haven't been to college, have you?"

"No—nor am I clever." But it pleased her to hear him say so.

Before she had finished her talk with him, the children came in from school. The baby lay in the cradle. Since he was nominated God-father, Mr Revell took a peculiar interest in the child. The other two children were no more to him than two moths which might flutter from place to place. They were alien to him, he could not understand them.

Paul began to cry. Then William, a growing lad, sat on a small stool by the fire, rocking the child. Annie, four year old, put out knives and spoons from the table drawer, while Mrs Morel beat up a batter pudding. All seemed very strange, almost wonderful, to Mr Revell, who had always lived secluded, waited on by a servant. Particularly wonderful seemed the way in which Mrs Morel clapped the heavy, sulphur coloured liquid, held the basin sideways, and beat the stuff with a clocking, liquid sound, without spilling a drop.

"Put baby in the cradle, and mend the fire, William," said Mrs Morel.

"Can't I do it?", said Mr Revell eagerly.

"William will do it."

So Mr Revell leaned over the big wicker cradle, that had a great wicker hood, like a half dome.

"It's like the early Britons," he smiled. It was very rare for him to come so near a joke.

Presently Mrs Morel had to lift a heavy saucepan from the fire. She was still frail, and her hands were small and white again. Mr Revell was startled when he saw her take the large black pan by the handle.

"You're not going to carry it," he said, alarmed.

"I must strain the potatoes," she smiled, setting herself to lift the pan. He was at her side quickly, much perturbed for her. She had to work far beyond her strength.

"I'll do it," he said. "You oughtn't to do things like this."

"I do much heavier work," she smiled. "I lift the wash-tub—and that *is* almost too much for me—"

He looked at her, much troubled. Then he bustled out into the scullery with the pan. When he set it down, he turned to her with bright, excited eyes. She took the lid of the pan, trapped the potatoes, and tilted the pan on its side. He watched the yellowish liquor gush steaming out.

"I say," he said with enthusiasm, "isn't that a neat trick!"

She laughed heartily at him. He mused awhile.

"Don't you think you have a lot of nice things in your life?" he asked, quizzically, his head on one side.

"What kind of things?" she laughed.

"Why—!" he stumbled and fumbled for words. "There's always something to watch. It is like a play at the theatre."

"I don't see it," she laughed.

"Well—how you iron: you spit on the hot iron. And then you beat that stuff in a basin. *I* couldn't."

She laughed, did not consider him seriously.

The two sat at tea, the children waiting. Mrs Morel had made the table look nice, as still she could. She talked brightly, with extraordinary enthusiasm discussing the next Sunday's sermon. Her genuine warmth of interest kindled the faltering parson, till he was quite lucid. Mrs Morel was living for a moment, her own life, not sacrificially.

Then, of course, Walter Morel came in.

"Of course!" she exclaimed in bitter exasperation, as she heard his step. He was rather earlier than usual.

Walter Morel was tired and bad tempered. As a matter of fact he was sickening for an illness. He entered the kitchen, glowered at the two people seated at table, turned, and put his tin bottle on the dresser with a bang, not having said a word. The children stopped chattering. Then their father went back into the scullery. He returned coatless, the sleeves of his singlet—a flannel chemise—leaving his arms bare from above the elbow; bare, and speckled black with coal-dust.

"Hanna yer got owt ter drink, for a man as comes home barkled up wi' pit-dust?" he said, in a bullying tone.

Mrs Morel knew he had drunk already at the 'Palmerston Arms'. This was his bluff and his disagreeableness. Without a word she poured him out his tea. He emptied the cupful into the saucer, and sucked it up as noisily as possible. The clergyman looked at him as if he had been a gorilla, or some such wild beast. Mrs Morel felt her anger run through her veins like fire. Morel panted after one drink, blew his saucer, and sucked again. Mr Revell watched in amazement. Morel set down his cup and saucer with a bang, sucked the drops from his moustache, dragged his chair to table, and sat down. His mouth showed very red and bright in his black face.

"A man gets his throat clogged up, all the hours he's down in the pit," he said sententiously to the minister. Mr Revell said, 'Yes, he was sure he must.'

"On'y them as goes down th'black hole knows what it is."

Mrs Morel knew her husband was quite as much at home in the mine as in his own house: that he liked the pit. This was a piece of sentimental play-acting that disgusted her. He sprawled his black arms over her clean, best cloth.

"Look at my cloth!" she cried.

"Am I to go i' th' yard, like a dog?" he shouted.

"There was no question of the yard," she said in cold contempt.

The little clergyman, bred up in the most clean and colourless fashion, was astounded.

"Why, a man as 'as been dinging away at th' coal-face, and rock all day, he's that tired he doesn't know *where* to put his arms," explained Morel. The minister looked pitiful. It did not occur to him that Mrs Morel was so tired at night that she scarcely knew where to put her body, and that it was not necessary wilfully to soil her table cloths. But the woman scorned to make her side good.

After a time, Mr Revell, in great uneasiness and distress, said he must depart. Morel was sitting with his hands under his chin, his great moustache sticking out, his red mouth pushed forward beneath it. So, he looked uncouth and brutal.

"Can ter tell me owt as'll do my 'ead good?" he asked, sentimentally of Mr Revell.

"I'm afraid I don't know," fluttered Revell.

"Drink less, and keep your liver in order," said Mrs Morel coldly.

"I'm sure tha'll ha'e ter put thy spoke in. *Tha'd* ha'e th'doctor runnin' in two or three times a day."

Mrs Morel looked down at the baby, which she was suckling.

"Do you expect your children to be born without a doctor?" she flashed.

Mr Revell looked at her, frightened. He glanced at her breast, then did not know where to put his eyes. He was unutterably startled and shocked by the violence of their life. He had scarcely the presence of mind to depart.

An atmosphere of irritation reigned in the home. William, aged seven, hated his father for the time being. Annie hung on to her mother's skirts whining.

"Shut thy face, tha snivellin' little stinkpot," shouted her father, whereat she grizzled the more. As Mrs Morel cleared the table, she referred to the great smudges of dirt on the cloth.

"You mun keep th'cloth off then," he bawled. "Ah'm non goin' ter sit danglin' my hands down'ards, not for nobody."

"You have arms to your chair."

"It doesna matter a—!" he swore, and bullied. The baby, on William's knee, began to cry in a wailing fashion. In her agitation, Mrs Morel knocked Annie on the head with the saucepan which she was lifting from the hearth. Annie lifted up her voice loudly.

"Goodness me," cried Mrs Morel, "what were you doing there in the way, then!"

Annie wept louder.

"Shut it up—shut it up," bawled Morel, frantic with rage.

Annie wept in a paroxysm.

Then the baby cried loudly in concert.

"Oh goodness," exclaimed William, the nurse. "You needn't cry an' all," and he plaintively tried to hush the child.

Morel rose in fury, sent his chair over with a bang. Mrs Morel rushed in from the scullery, and gave Annie two sound smacks.

"Now stop!" she said. "Now stop!"

"If 'er doesna—" threatened Morel, speechless with fury. In the momentary lull, William, seated on the hearthrug, looked up and read the text that hung over the mantel.

"God Bless Our Home!"

Mrs Morel, beside herself for the moment, flew at him, and spanked him soundly on the shoulder.

"*What* have you to say!" she panted.

Then immediately, seeing him duck his head between his shoulders, the comic side of the scene struck her. She sat in her rocking chair and laughed aloud, threw her head back and laughed, laughed and laughed uncontrollably. The husband and the children looked on in awe and discomfort. Then came a long hush in the house.

To quiet herself, Mrs Morel went out a while later, to the cricket ground which lay over the brook course, two hundred yards away. She went out of the Breach, skirted the gardens on Greenhill Lane, crossed the sheep-bridge over the lazy water, and a corner of the great meadow,

37

that seemed one space of ripe, evening light whispering with the distant mill-race; then through the stile into the cricket ground. Under the alders, she sat upon a seat with her baby, and fronted the evening. Behind she could hear the water run through the shadow. Before her, level and solid, spread the big cricket ground like the bed of a sea of light. Children played in the bluish shadow of the rustic pavilion on her left hand. Many rooks, high up, came calling home across the softly-woven blue of the sky. They stooped in a long, drooping curve, down into the golden glow, concentrating, cawing, wheeling like black motes of some force round the dark core of a tree clump upon the shining slope of opposite pasture.

A few gentlemen were playing a lingering last game of cricket. Mrs Morel could hear the chock of the ball, and the voices of the men suddenly roused: could see the white forms of the men flit over the intense green, upon which already the under-shadow was smouldering. She could see the great grey stacks of hay at the grange, one side lit up, while a high wagon of sheaves rocked into the melting yellow light.

The sun was going down. It is a countryside famous for its sunsets. Every open evening, the hills of Derbyshire blaze up like a beacon. This night Mrs Morel watched the sun sink from the glistening sky, leaving a soft, flower-blue overhead, while the western space went red, as if all the fire of the day had swum down, leaving the bell cast flawless blue. The mountain-ash berries across the field were like coals among the dark leaves, that were overcast with crimson. A few shocks of corn in the corner of the fallow uphill stood up as if alive; she could imagine them bowing. Away to the east, the mirrored sunset floated like a cloverfield opposite poppies. The great haystacks uphill abutted into the glare, as a man who stands fierily in a furnace door.

Mrs Morel watched it all passionately. Now and again a swallow cut close to her. Now and again Annie come up with her handfuls of alder 'currants.' The baby was restless on his mother's knee, clambering with his hands at the light. He was plump, but pale, with a good deal of brownish gold hair. Mrs Morel looked down at him. She felt very strangely towards the baby: not a delighted passionate love, such as she had felt for William, but rather a hurting love, that she did not call love. She had discovered a peculiar little knitting of his forehead, a sort of tiny, scarcely noticeable knot of pain and perplexity on the infant brow. His mouth opened wistfully. Suddenly it occurred to her she would call him 'Paul.' As she looked at him, her usual feeling of anxiety and presentiment, that he caused her, flew into a pang of passionate grief.

She bowed over him, and a few tears shook swiftly out of her very heart. The baby put his fingers on her face.

"What, my pet!" she said, with a heart-break.

She herself never understood the peculiar feeling that oppressed her, a feeling of guilt, and of awe.

The baby was gazing full up at her. He had blue eyes just like her own. His look, however, was heavy: conscious, almost, with a steady, heavy look as if they had realised something.

"Oh dear!" she whispered in her heart. "Oh dear, oh dear!" She would have given anything to have that dark look of knowledge removed: it hurt her too much. She felt that he looked into her. There was a thrill in that. But the sense of guilt was most oppressive. She hid him against her bosom, pressed him there, feeling that she would weep if it were of any use. She felt the child's consciousness close to hers, like a mate's. But the sense of tragedy was greatest. How terrible for the child to come into life thus heavily laden—with what, she knew not! She pressed the baby to her breast.

Then, as the sun on his way came full face to face with her, between two black clumps of trees, she held the baby up.

"Look!" she said. "Look how pretty!"

She thrust the infant forward to the level sun, which, full of crimson, throbbing liquid that clotted round the rim, throbbed opposite. She thrust the child forward as if she would dip him in the red well of fire. Looking at him, she saw him all rosy with reflection, staring eagerly round, the red light glittering on his eyes.

"I will call him Paul," she said. "And then, if he lives, he will perhaps be a great man."

Thus she solaced herself as she put him again in her bosom, and after a while, she went home. A fine shadow was flung over the deep green meadow, darkening all.

As she expected, she found the house empty. But Morel was home by ten o'clock, and that day at least ended peacefully.

Walter Morel was, at this time, exceedingly irritable. His work seemed to exhaust him. When he came home, he did not speak civilly to anybody. If the fire were rather low, he bullied about that; he grumbled about his dinner; if the children made a chatter, he shouted at them very disagreeably.

"You have no need to shout their heads off," Mrs Morel would say. "We are none of us hard of hearing."

"They'll get 'em knocked off," he would bawl.

If, whilst he was washing in the scullery, anyone entered or left the house:

"Shut that doo-er!" he shouted, so that he could be heard down the Breach.

"It's a pity, poor nesh* creature!" Mrs Morel sneered.

"I shonna ha'e my ribs blowed out o' my sides wi' that draught, for nobody!" he would shout. Whenever he was angry, he bawled.

"Goodness me man," said Mrs Morel at last in contempt. "There isn't a bit of peace while you're in the house."

"No, I know that. I know you're niver right till I'm out o' your sight."

"True," she said calmly to herself.

"Oh I know—I know what yer chunterin' 's about. You're niver satisfied till I'm down pit, none on yer. They owt ter keep me theer, like one o' th' 'osses."

"True," said Mrs Morel again, under her breath, as she turned with a sneer on her tight-shut mouth.

He hurried to escape from the house, thrusting his head forward in determined rage.

"I'll pay the b— out!" he said to himself, meaning his wife.

He was not home by eleven o'clock. The baby was not well, and was restless, crying if he were put down. Mrs Morel, tired to death, and still weak, was scarcely under control.

"I wish he'd come," she said wearily to herself.

The child at last sank down to sleep in her arms. She was too tired to carry him to the cradle.

"But I'll say nothing, whatever time he comes," she said wearily to herself. "It only works me up, I won't say anything." She did not trust herself, however. Time after time she had said the same, determined to refrain, and then her sudden anger had flashed out. She wished, with the loathing of weariness, that she might be spared seeing him when he came home. The reason she would not go to bed and leave him to come in when he liked—let any woman tell.

"I know if he does anything, it'll make my blood boil," she said pitiably to herself.

She sighed, as she heard him coming, as if it were something she could not bear. He, taking his revenge, was nearly drunk. She kept her head bent over the child as he entered, not wishing to see him. But it went through her like a flash of hot hate when, in passing, he lurched against the dresser, setting the tins rattling, and clutched at the white pot knobs for support. He hung up his hat and coat, then returned, stood glowering from a distance at her, as she sat bowed over the child.

"Is there nathing to eat in the house?" he asked, insolently, as if to a servant. In certain stages of his intoxication he used the clipped, mincing speech of the towns. Mrs Morel hated him most in this condition.

"You know what there is in the house," she said, so coldly, it sounded impersonal.

He stood and glared at her without moving a muscle.

"I asked a civil question, and I expect a civil answer," he said, affectedly.

"And you got it," she said, still ignoring him.

He glowered again. Then he came unsteadily forward. He leaned on the table with one hand, and with the other jerked at the table drawer to get a knife to cut bread. The drawer stuck, because he pulled sideways. In a temper, he dragged at it so that it came out bodily, and spoons, forks, knives, a hundred metallic things flounced with a clash and a clang upon the brick floor. The baby gave a little convulsed start.*

* * * *

profusely. As she glanced down at the child, her brain reeling, some drops of blood soaked into its white shawl. But the baby was at least not hurt. She balanced her head to keep equilibrium, so that the blood ran into her eye.

Walter Morel had gone pale. He remained leaning on the table with one hand, looking forlorn. When he was sufficiently sure of his balance, he went across to her, swayed, caught hold of the back of her rocking-chair, almost tipping her out. Then, leaning forward over her and swaying as he spoke, he said, in tone of wondering concern:

"Did it catch thee?"

He swayed again, as if he would pitch onto the child. With the catastrophe, he had lost all balance.

"Go away!" she said, struggling to keep her presence of mind.

He hiccoughed. "Let's—let's look at it," he said, hiccoughing again.

"Go away," she cried.

"Lemme—lemme look at it lass—do now."

She smelled him of drink, felt the unequal pull of his swaying grasp on the back of her rocking chair.

"Go away," she said, and weakly she pushed him off. He stood, uncertain in balance, gazing upon her. Summoning all her strength, she rose, the baby on one arm. By a cruel effort of will, moving as if in sleep, she went across to the scullery, where she bathed her eye for a minute in cold water. But she was too dizzy. Afraid lest she should swoon, she

41

returned to her rocking chair with the baby, trembling in every fibre. By instinct, she kept baby clasped.

Morel, bothered, had succeeding [*sic*] in pushing the drawer into its place, and was on his knees, groping with numb paws for the scattered spoons.

Her brow was still bleeding profusely. Presently Morel got up and came craning his neck towards her.

"What did it do to thee, Gerty?" he asked, in a very rare intimate tone. She did not answer. He stood, bending forward, supported on his arms, which grasped his legs just above the knee. He peered to look at the wound. She drew away from the thrust of his face, with its great moustache, averting her own face as much as possible. As he looked at her, cold and impassive as stone, with unflinching mouth shut tight, he sickened with feebleness and hopelessness of spirit. As he was turning drearily away, he saw a drop of blood fall from the averted wound into the baby's fragile, glistening hair. Fascinated, he watched the heavy dark drop hang in the glistening cloud, and pull down the gossamer. Another drop fell. It would soak through to the baby's scalp. He watched in horror, feeling it soak in, as if it were on his breast. Then, finally, his manhood broke.

"What of this child?" was all his wife said to him. But her low, intense tones brought his head lower. She softened,

"Get me some wadding out of the middle drawer," she said coldly. He stumbled away very obediently, presently returning with a pad, which she singed before the fire, then put on her forehead, as she sat with the baby on her lap.

"Now that clean pit-scarf."

Again he rummaged and fumbled in the drawer, returning presently with a red, narrow scarf. She took it, and with trembling fingers proceeded to bind it round her head.

"Let me tie it for thee," he said humbly.

"I can do it myself," she replied, very cold and distant. When it was done she went upstairs, telling him to rake the fire and lock the door.

In the morning, Mrs Morel said:

"I knocked it on the latch of the coal-place, when I was getting a raker in the dark, because the candle blew out." Her two small children looked up at her with wide, thoughtful eyes. They said nothing, but their parted lips seemed to express the unconscious tragedy they felt.

The women of the Breach said among themselves:

"We know who did it—no coal-place latches. Er'll be scarred for life. He ought ter feel mighty proud of hissen when he sees it."

Walter Morel lay in bed next day until nearly dinner time. He thought of anything but of the previous evening's work. He avoided thinking of the affair as a dog that has been thrashed avoids the place where he got the thrashing. So Morel never acutely suffered anything, and was the nobler for it. Suffering destroyed him. Nothing could prevent his inner consciousness inflicting on him a dreariness and an oppression which ate into his spirit like rust, and which he could only alleviate by drinking.

He was unwilling to get up, because he feared to have to face his wife and her bandaged head. Moreover he had himself violent pains in the head. It was Saturday. Towards noon he rose, cut himself food in the pantry, ate it with his head dropped, then pulled on his boots and went out, to return at three o'clock, sober, but relieved; and once more to depart straight for bed. He rose again at six in the evening, had tea, and went straight out.

Sunday was the same: bed till noon, the 'Palmerston Arms' till 2.30, dinner and bed; scarcely a word spoken. When Mrs Morel went upstairs, towards four o'clock, to put on her Sunday dress, he was fast asleep. She did not notice him, or trouble about him. His part of her was numb.

The family began tea. Sunday was the only day when all sat down to meals together.

"Isn't my father going to get up?" asked William.

"Let him lie," the mother replied.

There was a feeling of misery all over the house. The children breathed the air as if it were morally poisoned, and felt dreary, ailing. They were rather disconsolate, did not know what to do, what to play at.

Immediately Morel woke he got straight out of bed. That was characteristic of him, all his life. He was all for trivial activity, as a substitute for thought. The prostrated inactivity of two mornings was stifling him.

It was near six o'clock when he got down. This time he entered without hesitation, his wincing sensitiveness having hardened again. He did not care any longer what the family thought or felt.

The tea-things were on the table. William was reading aloud from "Little Folks," Annie listening and asking eternally 'Why?' Both children hushed into silence as they heard the approaching thud of their father's feet, and shrank as he entered. Yet he was usually an indulgent father.

Morel made the meal alone, brutally. He ate and drank more noisily than he had need. No one spoke to him. The family life withdrew, shrank away and became hushed as he entered. But he cared no longer about his alienation.

Immediately he had finished tea he rose with alacrity to go out. It was this alacrity, this vulgar haste to be gone, which so sickened Mrs Morel. As she heard him sousing heartily in cold water, heard the eager scratch of the steel comb on the side of the bowl, as he wetted his hair, she closed her eyes in disgust. As he bent over, lacing his boots, there was a certain vulgar gusto in his movement that split him off from the quiet, reserved, watchful family as much as some coarse trooper quartered on a refined household would be excluded and alien from those with whom he sat at board. The children waited in restraint during his preparations. When he had gone, they were glad.

When he closed the door behind him he was glad.

Chapter III

AFTERMATH

During the next week Morel's irritable temper was almost unbearable. He drank a great deal, and on coming home from the pit, complained lamentably of pains in his head.

"Shouldn't drink!" said Mrs Morel shortly, accustomed to his complaints. Morel would curse her hardness of heart as he dolefully leaned with his head in his hand. Like most working men, he was a great lover of medicines. Usually, however, he only swallowed such useful beverages as wormwood tea, rue tea, hyssop tea, horehound tea.* He kept great bushes of these herbs hanging in the attic, and had usually a big jug of one or other decoction standing on the hob, from which he swallowed long draughts in the morning. But this time neither wormwood nor rue, hyssop nor horehound, marsh mallow nor parsley purt nor dandelion would remove the headaches. These medicines, which he loved, and which he would tell the children were: "Grand, child—grand! Come and taste a sup"—failed, so he tried the druggist.

He had caused an inflammation of the brain by sleeping on the ground on the August Bank Holiday. This fever had been consistently aggravated. Now he fell seriously ill.

For a fortnight he lay very sadly stricken. With her baby at her breast, Mrs Morel attended to him, and did everything. But the doctor forbade her to suckle the child. The neighbours did what they could for her. Often a woman would send in for the children, to give them dinner, and so to save Mrs Morel the trouble of preparing a meal. Another woman would prepare and bring in the baby's food, another would come and do an hour or two of housework in Number 52. Her neighbours were very good to Mrs Morel. And she had twenty five shillings a week from clubs, while Morel's fellow butties, very generously, would put aside every week six or seven shillings from the profits of the stall, for her. So she managed. But for days, she never took off her clothes nor went to bed. It was a dreadful, hard struggle.

The weeks passed, Morel pulled round, almost against hope.

"Well, resuscitated man!" said Dr Barber cheerfully. The doctor himself, a brilliant fellow, was sadly given to drink. "Well, resuscitated man, you've only got your wife to thank, that you're not prisoner at the bar up aloft there, at this minute. She's saved you, not me."

Walter Morel was profoundly thankful that he was not: "prisoner at the bar up aloft there." He had a vast dread of any such thing. For the moment he was deeply grateful to his wife, and inclined to weep as she moved about silently at her nursing. He wanted her to be tender to him, to fold him to her breast, to lavish a little softness on him. She was gentle enough, for that matter, but she never indulged his sentimental cravings.

Of all his pals, Jerry alone, besides his butties, came to see him.

"Has so-an'-so axed owt about me?" Morel would inquire plaintively.

"He hasn't. Nobody's been but your butties, and Jerry," she answered; and scolding in a kindly tone: "It shows what your pals care about you, when you can't get out to the public house."

He sighed, arched his eyebrows, lifted and dropped his hand pathetically, like a man disillusioned.

"Ay," he would sigh, sigh very heavily.

But Jerry came. Perhaps he alone dared face Mrs Morel. He had, as she said, the cheek of forty folk. At any rate, he turned up regularly every Sunday morning.

When she saw him, on Sunday at about ten o'clock, advancing up the path with his usual staccato brittle dignity, she was wild. She hated him: all women hated him; he was too cold blooded, he disliked the opposite sex. As he drew near the house, his thin dry body jerking like a stiff dry reed, Mrs Morel shut the door in his face. Then he went to the scullery window, whence he could see through into the kitchen. Mrs Morel could not bear to have him craning his neck and watching her. He would *not* knock. She had to open at last, pretending she did not know he was there:

"Oh, it's you! I never heard your knock."

"Good mornin' Missis. How's mester shapin' by now, like?"

It was Jerry's unabashed, insolent familiarity that annoyed Mrs Morel so much.

"He is improving."

Jerry relished the unusual distinction of this English.

"An' does he seem pretty middlin', then?"

He remained calmly standing on the doorstep. Mrs Morel was reluctant to answer.

"Yes," she replied.

"Ah. E's not sittin' up a bit?"

"No, he isn't."

"Ah!"

A pause. Neither moved. Jerry looked down the garden. Mrs Morel's mouth was shut tight.

"'E's able to talk a bit by now, they'n bin tellin' me," said he.

Mrs Morel was silent. Carlin, one of the butties who had paid Morel a visit, had evidently told Jerry.

"I browt him," the man said, still easily, "a few mushrums as I seed in a shop i' Nottingham."

Mrs Morel did not answer.

"They very scarce now," he persisted.

There was a tone of question.

"Yes, they are," she replied.

"Yes.—An' I know he's fond of a bit of a mushrum."

"Yes."

Jerry took out the bag. But he was not defeated yet.

"'*As* 'e much of a happetite?" he asked.

"He eats as much as one can expect."

"Nowt to brag of, like? No, I's warrant not."

Mrs Morel bristled with hostility. He was so easy and so subtly insolent. She felt insecure.

"'Appen I could ta'e 'em up to 'im mysen."

She could not deny him.

"I suppose so, if you don't talk too much," she said, as she turned to lead him upstairs.

"No, you'll not catch me sayin' a deal, if it's goin' ter harm him," Jerry answered with equanimity, glancing at the kitchen as he crossed it.

When Walter Morel heard the voice of Jerry downstairs, he settled himself in a strewn, pitiful attitude on the pillows, and put on a worn expression. He had been roused on his elbow listening to the beat of a spoon downstairs, betokening egg and milk. Now his whole attitude betrayed unspoken suffering.

"Well lad, I dunna like findin' thee like this," said Jerry brokenly.

"No, an' I wish tha could ha' found me different," faintly answered Morel.

Mrs Morel grinned to herself. It really amused her to hear the one man cading, the other pulamiting.* Jerry stood beside the bed, looking down at the sick man. Morel grasped faintly at the eider-down quilt, then his head sunk wearily to one side:

"Sit thee down," he murmured.

Jerry's tears rose. He seated himself beside the bed, and sniffed.

"Tha's 'ad a near touch." he said, snuffling.

"Ay," sighed Morel. "It's a'most kippered me."*

Jerry sniffed sharply into his white handkerchief.

"An' dost think tha'rt mendin'?" he queried plaintively.

"I dunno," said Morel, with dreadful pessimism.

"Why he's a lot better: he's a king to what he was," said Mrs Morel rather scornfully. Neither man took any notice.

"Ay, it's been a rough journey for thee," sighed Jerry, suddenly wiping his eyes. Morel put out his hand, now pathetically white and shapely, upon the red flowered silk of the quilt. It was a touching invalid gesture. Jerry was suitably impressed.

"Tha's gone off to next to nowt" said Jerry.

"An' I'm twice of what I have been—" said Morel.

"Why he's wasted very little—very little, considering," Mrs Morel exclaimed. "It stands to sense, it's not an ailment that wastes you."

"I browt thee a few mushrums," said Jerry, ignoring the woman. "I thowt as 'appen they'd tempt thee. Dost think as tha could fancy one?" Jerry put the bag on the little table. It bore the name of a high class fruiterer of Nottingham.* Mrs Morel admired Jerry's courage, for not many colliers dared have gone into such a shop for a pound of mushrooms.

Morel put out his hand. He wore a white night-shirt with a turned-back cuff. Jerry, he knew, had not dreamed of such heights of refinement as a white, feather-stitched night-shirt: and somehow Morel was aware of how this refinement fascinated his friend. The miner took out a small mushroom, and put it into the sick man's hand with tenderness.

"Isn't it a little beauty!" said Morel, eyeing the mushroom bud. "It's as white as a bit of pear-blossom."

Jerry was touched. "Yes," he said fervently, "they was two shillings a pound, but I said to myself—'If 'e'd like one, 'e s'll 'ave one!' Price was no consideration."

"Eh, tha's pleased me as much as if tha'd gen me a sovereign!"

"He'll not cease to think about them till he's eaten them," laughed Mrs Morel.

"I shonna that," replied Morel, quite gaily. "She'll 'appen put 'em under th' meat for me, they grand that road."*

Jerry handed the bag to the wife. She thanked him, and accepted her dismissal. As she went downstairs she heard Jerry say blithely:

"I feel fair set up ter think as tha'll relish 'em."

"It'll be th' first thing as I *have* relished for many a day," Morel replied pathetically. Mrs Morel laughed at the impudence of the fib. She felt rather disgusted and rather amused at the fondling, lavish affection displayed by the two men. Such, she said, was the true plane of their loving.

Morel's black hair looked well on the pillow, and the great moustache, being so strangely out of place above the bed clothes, had an emotional value. He had an actorly instinct. He felt the superiority of his position. The room was darkened, but not too much to hide the solid mahogany furniture, which was better than most colliers could boast, and for which Mrs Morel had paid so bitterly. Then the old, silk-covered down quilt was a comparative rarity at that time. It was a gift from one of Mrs Morel's sisters. Finally, there was the nightshirt with the Byronic collar, which suited Morel, and showed him handsome. Jerry would be suitably impressed. On the strength of all these things, he would pay court and stand treat for many a day.

They discussed the illness, every symptom, every detail of pain, with gusto. Jerry related tales of other people who had had brain fever. One man's hair had gone quite white.

"Mine hasna turned?" asked Morel.

"No, thine's all right."

"Tha'd find plenty of grey in it, if tha looked."

Jerry did not press the point: it was too dark to look.

Mrs Morel, below, wondered what interest they could find in one another. What could they find to talk about?

In the midst of their discussion of the malady, Jerry lowered his voice.

"I'n got a drop of Ellen's best," he murmured.

"Tha what—?" Morel started softly.

"Ellen's old brown."

Ellen was landlady of the 'Raglan.' Jerry took a flat bottle from his pocket. Morel felt a shock as he looked at it. All along, he had felt a low quiver of excitement and anticipation. Now he felt like a lover whose mistress yields. He was impatient to have the beer in his throat.

"Durst ha'e a drop?" whispered Jerry.

"Ay lad!" replied Morel eagerly. He leaned on one elbow. Keeping a keen ear on the sounds below, Jerry silently uncorked the bottle.

" 'Er wanted to fill it wi' whisky, but I said no, tha'd rather ha'e th'old brown. It's a vittle."

Holding the flat rum-bottle, which contained about half a pint of brown liquid, carefully pitched, Jerry leaned forward to his friend. Morel held his mouth open. It was a moment of intense emotion. Putting his trembling hand half over Jerry's, Morel adjusted the bottle to his mouth. He took a throatful, detaining it, slowly squeezing it down, extracting from it the last drop of relish. Then he pushed the bottle back, and sank down on the pillow.

"Grand!" he whispered faintly. "Grand!"

"I thought on thee," said Jerry.

"Grand!" murmured the other, as he lay back, deliciously suffused by the old liquor. Jerry, holding the bottle as if in some religious ritual, leaned forward over his friend, like a lover.

"Thee drink!" said Morel faintly.

"Nay lad!" Jerry protested. "This is thine."

"I s'll non—be able to manage—all that," murmured the other.

"There's nowt but a thimbleful," Jerry tenderly protested.

"Ay—but I durs'n't."

"Tha durs'n't!!"

"Me 'ead!" murmured Morel. "Me 'ead!!"

Tears came to Jerry's eyes. He dropped his head. In a moment he raised it again to have a pull at the bottle. His adams-apple went up and down twice. Then he sighed, wiped the neck of the bottle on the palm of his hand, surveying the swaying beer in despair. He was too full to look at Morel. So he fidgetted until, by inspiration, he began to poke the fire, thus venting his emotion.

Presently he put down the poker and turned to Morel. The latter had brisked up considerably. One eye was cocked upon the bottle.

"Come," said Jerry tenderly, "'a'e just another drop."

Morel summoned his energy, took one crushed throatful, drooped, then, making an effort, took another. Pushing away the bottle he sank back.

"How dost feel?" inquired Jerry anxiously.

"Grand!" murmured Morel.

Jerry was suspended over him, waiting.

"Finish it," whispered Morel, who lay with closed eyes.

As he gazed at the silent face of his friend, Jerry drew out his pocket handkerchief, softly wiped his nose and his rather red eyes, then suddenly gulped the remainder of the beer, after which he thrust the bottle into his pocket. Thence, he sat with his arms dejectedly on his knees, watching the silent countenance of his friend. Presently:

"Walt," he said. "Walt lad?—art bad?"

Morel opened heavy eyes upon him, saying:

"Me 'ead's that wattery!"

Jerry's eyes watered in sympathy. He wiped them on the back of his hand as he drew from his pocket two sprigs of parsley.

"Walt lad, dost think tha could chew this?" he said, holding the curled green leaf near the great black moustache of the other man.

"I'll try," murmured the sick man, looking down his nose at the sprig. Jerry carefully picked off the stalk and put the leaf between Morel's red lips. He watched his friend slowly chew. Presently he spat his own leaf into the fire, carefully burning all vestige of the stalk. Meanwhile Morel had swallowed his parsley.

"Now let me smell thee," said Jerry, putting his sharp nose to Morel's great moustache.

"Tha'rt all right, lad," he said. "Let her have a nose as sharp as a needle, 'er'll non twig* that."

Morel put his hand out from the bed and laid it on Jerry's.

"Tha'rt a blessin', Jerry, tha art!" he murmured.

Jerry sniffed aloud.

Presently Mrs Morel came up. She glanced keenly at her husband, went up and put her hand on his head.

"I suppose you've been talking too much," she said.

"Nay Missis, that we 'aven't!" replied Jerry. "Neither him nor me's spoke above six words for the last twenty minutes."

"At any rate," said Mrs Morel. "He is excited."

Jerry sighed deeply.

"Ay, he's in such a weak state!" he deplored.

"Well, he'd better be left quiet now."

Jerry rose, walked stiffly but silently downstairs and out of the house.

Morel grew rapidly better. He had a fine constitution, so that, once on the mend, he romped back to recovery. Soon he was downstairs, pottering about.

During his illness, even his wife had spoiled him, petted him, caded him a little. He loved such treatment, so was unwilling to be established well again. Frequently he put his hand to his head and shammed a pain he did not feel. There was no deceiving Mrs Morel. At first she merely smiled. Later she said:

"Goodness man, don't look so lachrymose."

As he did not know exactly what she meant, he need not feel offended. The lesson was not severe enough. At last she had to say:

"I wouldn't be such a mardy baby."

He dropped his head, cursing her under his breath. Mrs Morel was not one to tolerate sham or sentimentality, neither would she moulder in resignation. Her swift flashes of anger kept her heart fresh.

For some time, Mrs Morel hoped that the state of peace might continue, refusing to see that only his feebleness made him tolerable to her. However, almost a year of peace in the house was secured by the exercise of some forbearance.

At first, Morel had to be a total abstainer. Then his wife noticed a growing restlessness. Going counter to her fierce high principle, she ordered a case of beer. It was a great concession, but a useless one. His restlessness was not quenched.

She hated to hear him crackle the liquor in his throat as he swallowed. He would sit rustling, struggling through the newspaper, while she worked of an evening, and all the time she dreaded to see his hand go to the glass, because of the noise that got on her nerves. He would read her an item, slowly pronouncing and delivering the words like a man pitching quoits. It was a painful process, but she listened patiently. If she hurried him on, supplying him with a phrase, he took her words and repeated them humbly, whether they fitted the sense or not. Then she would smile quietly to herself.

But the children must not make any noise at play whilst he was in. Mrs Morel would have liked to hear the children's noise: that would have soothed her. But he had his head as an excuse.

The silences between them were peculiar. There was a will to friendliness on either side, but the presence of each hampered and strangled the natural progressive flow of the other's life. Mrs Morel, at last began to feel as if she were stifling in his company, while he suffered almost as badly.

It was the baby who shook this artificial equipoise. At ten months old, he had a gathering in his ear. The mother was distracted between a baby convulsed with real pain, and a querulous husband. Her nerves were inflamed, so that she felt her irritable scorn longing to burst into fire against her husband, as he sat looking piteous, and petulantly jerking the newspaper, because the baby cried. She exercised at these times some heroism of restraint.

The child would not be nursed by him. It would stiffen in his arms. Although a quiet baby on the whole, Paul would scream, would draw back wildly from his fathers arms. Morel saw the small fists clenched, the baby face averted, the wet blue eyes turned back wildly towards the mother, and he would say, in a kind of despair:

"Here, come an' ta'e him."

"It's your moustache frightens him," she said. But she would press the child on her bosom, as it clung to her neck, cleaved to her. And Morel was afraid of the baby. For it, if for anything, he would have sacrificed himself.

Meanwhile another child was coming, fruit of this interval of kindliness between years of aversion. Mrs Morel had more grief in her heart over Paul than she would have cared to admit. If she had worked it out, she would have found it was because she felt the child was wronged of her. The same feeling, stronger, was in Morel's heart. When Paul was seventeen months old she handed him over to the nurse who came to take charge of the house.

"To think," said the mother to the nurse, "that he should be pushed aside so soon."

The woman looked at Paul Morel. He was not pretty: plump, pale, with heavy eyes, and the peculiar slight knitting of the brows that persisted in him, and which was noticeable in Annie Morel. His eyes, however were different from his sister's: still, with a heavy, abstract look.

"Poor lamb!" exclaimed the nurse, kissing him. The baby took no notice, only began to cry as his mother went away.

The new baby also was a boy, fair, and bonny. After a week or two, he was ravishingly pretty, with a mop of yellow curls, and large blue eyes. He took to his father. Morel was delighted. They called him Arthur. William Morel, who loved his mother devotedly, was again a slave and a nurse to her. But still, in her heart, she wished this last baby had never been born, and might die.

Chapter IV

GLIMPSES OF EARLY LIFE

The new baby flourished. He had a crown of brown-gold curls, and dark blue eyes. Everyone found him charming. He was spoiled by the whole household, particularly by his father. Walter Morel had returned to his old ways, but was not very bad. He had always a warm place in the house: the baby loved him. Whenever Morel was in the house, the child put out its arms to him, an appeal he could not resist. So the two formed a close alliance.

This was a joy to the miner, who was all for easy, sensuous love. One of his great grievances had been that everybody shut up and darkened as soon as he entered the house. Now one bright blossom, the beauty, the baby, radiated at the sound of its father's footsteps. Morel was delighted and Mrs Morel, relieved by this child's gay, happy disposition, even indulged it.

Meanwhile Paul, colourless and quiet, struggled through various illnesses. His fair hair turned darker, his blue eyes turned grey, he grew slimmer. By the time he was three he was a light, quick child; all day long he ran like a fawn at the heels of his mother, chattering to her endlessly, for he was very quick at speech. He was exceedingly sensitive to her. If she were quiet, brooding, the tiny child would ask:

"Are you poorly mother—are you?"

"Poorly—no child."

"You haven't got toothache, have you?"

That would have been the maximum of sorrow. Mrs Morel suffered a good deal from neuralgia when the children were little, and it fretted them, particularly William and Paul.

As he grew up a little, before he went to school at all, Paul had charge of his younger brother. Arthur was wilful, and inclined to mischief. He loved to sit in the coal-house down the garden, among the small coals. When at last he came back to the house with Paul, and their mother saw the young child quite black with sucking coal, his hair full of slack,* she would make that quick "tut-tut-tut-tut" with her tongue, which always distressed Paul.

"Well, he's only little, mother," he said.

"Little! He's a little smut! Ah you dirty little wretch, now you'll have to be bathed again."

"He's only little mother," pleaded the five year old.

Then Mrs Morel would laugh.

Paul was naturally very active, both physically and mentally. He trotted about the whole day long, very observant, chattering to his mother. Then, while still quite young, he would have fits of despondency, days when he would sit heavy-eyed, watching anything that moved, saying nothing. Sometimes he would begin to cry for no reason at all. Then Mrs Morel would knit her brows.

"What are you crying for?"

"I don't know."

"Well whoever heard of such a thing—crying for nothing! I wouldn't be such a baby."

Sometimes she could neither shame him nor interest him nor scold him into stopping. He cried on—a miserable thing. If the father were in, he would go almost into a frenzy. Then the mother would carry out the little chair, walk out the child, seat him beside the rhubarb bed, saying:

"Now cry there, you miserable child."

Perhaps a butterfly on the rhubarb leaves would attract him, and he would sit perfectly still and heavy, watching it. Perhaps he would cry himself to sleep. However he ended, he left his mother with a very sore heart.

Walter Morel often stayed at home on Tuesday, Wednesday, and Thursday evenings, when he had no money. Then, it being dark outside, the family would cohere happily. The lamp lighted, parents and children were busy.*

Chapters 3–9
(Second Draft)

[Chapter III]

the nightshirt with Byronic collar.* Jerry, shrewd rat from the lowest stratum,* had an appreciative eye for these refinements. Morel understood it by instinct, and enjoyed the fine impression he made.

They discussed the illness, every item, every symptom, with gusto. Mrs Morel, below, could not imagine what offal of interest they could find to gorge together, two old crows that they were. Jerry related tales of others who had had brainfever.* One man's hair had gone white.

"Mine hasna* turned," Morel half asked, half asserted.

"No, thine's all right," Jerry assured him. It was black as bootblacking. Morel resented its not having gone white.

In the midst of the discussion of the malady, Jerry lowered his voice.

"I've got a drop of Ellen's best* in my pocket," he said.

"Tha* what—?" Morel fairly started.

"Ellen's best home-brewed," repeated Jerry softly. Ellen was landlady of the "Fleece." Jerry took a flat bottle from his breast pocket. Morel felt a shock as he looked at it. All along he had felt the low quiver of excitement and anticipation, wondering if Jerry would be faithful. Now he felt like an aching lover whose mistress has at last whispered 'Yes'. He lay back on the pillow, really overwhelmed by the nearness of the delicious trespass.

"Durst ter ha'e* a drop?" Jerry asked.

"Just—a drop," said Morel, whose heart was beating, who could scarcely speak.

Jerry kept a keen ear open for the sounds below. He uncorked the bottle silently.

"Ellen wanted to fill it wi' whisky when 'er knowed who it was for, but I said no, tha'd better ha'e beer. It canna hurt thee, this—it a vittle—"* He spoke very low. Holding the flat rum-bottle, which held about half a pint of brown liquid, carefully pitched, he leaned forward to his friend. Morel held his mouth open. It was a moment of intense intimacy, excitement, and pathos, for both men. Putting his trembling hand half over Jerry's, Morel adjusted the bottle to his mouth. He slowly, caressingly took a throatful, detaining it and squeezing from it the last drop of relish. Then he pushed the bottle back, sank down on the pillow.

"It's grand," he whispered faintly.

"I've thought on thee," said Jerry.

"Tha has!" murmured the other.

It was an intense moment in the lives of both men. Morel lay back, deliciously suffused by the one throatful. Jerry, holding the bottle as if in some religious ritual, leaned forward over his friend, like a lover.

"Thee drink," said Morel weakly.

"Nay—nay lad!" Jerry protested in a low, serious voice. "I brought it for thee."

Morel lay still a moment or two.

"I s'll non—be able to manage all that—" he said pathetically.

"There's nowt but a thimbleful," Jerry tenderly protested.

"I durst-na," whispered Morel.

"Tha durs'n't!" exclaimed Jerry.

"No—me 'ead!"* murmured Morel.

Tears came to Jerry's eyes. He dropped his head. In a moment, he raised it again, to have a short pull at the bottle. His adams-apple went up and down twice. Then he sighed; he wiped the neck of the bottle on his red handkerchief, surveying the swaying beer in despair. He dared not look at Morel, for fear of bursting into tears. So he fidgeted, until, moved by inspiration, he began to poke the fire, and thus give vent to his deep emotion. Presently he put the poker down, to look at his friend. Morel had brisked up considerably. One eye was cocked upon the bottle.

"Come," said Jerry tenderly, "'a'e just another drop."

Morel summoned his energy, took one crushed throatful, drooped, then, making an effort, took another. Pushing away the bottle, he sank back.

"How dost feel?" inquired Jerry anxiously.

"Grand," murmured the other.

Jerry was suspended over him, waiting.

"Finish it," whispered Morel, who lay with closed eyes. As he gazed, Jerry drew out his pocket-handkerchief, softly wiped his nose and his already sore eyes, looked at his friend, then suddenly gulped the remainder of the beer, and thrust the bottle finally into his pocket; after which he sank dejectedly, arms on his knees. He watched the silent face of his friend for a few moments. Then he said, alarmed:

"Walt—Walt lad, art bad?"

Morel opened heavy eyes upon him, and said:

"Me 'ead's that wattery—!"*

Jerry's eyes watered in sympathy. He wiped them, then drew from his waistcoat pocket two sprigs of parsley.

"Walt lad," he said, "dost think tha could chew this bit o' parsley."

"Eh!" murmured Morel. The other repeated his question.

"I'll try," said the sick man.

Jerry carefully picked off the stalk, then put the curled parsley leaf between his friend's lips. He watched his friend slowly chew. Meanwhile he chewed his own leaf awhile, then spat it in the fire, carefully burning every fragment of stalk. He returned to Morel, who had swallowed his leaf.

"Now let me smell thee," said Jerry, putting his sharp nose near Morel's great moustache.

"Thou'rt all right lad," he said. "If 'er's a nose like a needle 'er'll never know."

Morel put out his hand from the bed, and laid it on Jerry's.

"Tha'rt a blessin' to me Jerry, thou art an' all!" he murmured. Jerry sniffed aloud.

Presently Mrs Morel came up. She glanced very keenly at her husband, then went up and put her hand on his forehead.

"I suppose you've been talking too much," she said gently.

"Nay, we haven't, Missis," said Jerry, quiet and calm. "He's not spoke above six words for twenty minutes—nor me neither."

"At any rate," Mrs Morel answered firmly, "he is more excited than he should be."

Jerry sighed deeply.

"He must be in a low weak state," he said desperately.

"He'd better be left quiet.—Are you feeling worse?" she asked her husband. "Will you have your egg and milk?"

"I'll rest a bit," he murmured.

She drew down the blind. Waiting, she saw her husband dropping off to sleep.

Jerry rose, walked stiffly but silently down the stairs and out of the house.

Morel grew rapidly better. He had a fine constitution so that once on the mend, he romped back to recovery. He was soon downstairs, pottering about. During his illness even his wife had spoiled him, petted him, caded* him. He loved to be made much of; he was unwilling to be established well again. Frequently he put his hand to his head, arched his eyebrows, pulled down the corners of his mouth, and shammed pain he did not feel. There was no deceiving his wife. At first she smiled and said nothing. At last she had to say:

"Goodness man, don't look so lachrymose!"

He understood her intent, not her word, so he need not feel offended. The lesson was not severe enough.

"I wouldn't be such a mardy* baby," she said later. He dropped his head, cursing her under his breath. Mrs Morel was not one to moulder in resignation: she had not that feminine weakness. Her swift flashes of anger kept her heart fresh.

For some time Mrs Morel hoped faintly that the amicable state of affairs might last, forgetting or refusing to see that it was only his weakness made her cherish him. However, almost a year of peace in the house was procured, by some exercise of forbearance. For a time, Morel was a total abstainer. Then his wife noticed a growing restlessness. Making a violent effort, she went counter to her fierce high principle, and ordered a barrel of beer to come into the house. It was a great concession. Morel drank moderately: but the restlessness did not go.

She hated to hear him crackle the liquor in his throat as he swallowed. He would sit rustling, struggling through the newspaper, while she worked of an evening, and all the time she dreaded to see his hand go to the glass, because of the noise that got on her nerves. He would read her an interesting item, slowly pronouncing and delivering the words like a man pitching quoits. It was a torturesome process, but she listened patiently. If she hurried him on, supplying a phrase, he took her words and repeated them humbly, whether they fitted his reading or not. But the children must not play with any noise: he had the excuse of his head: they must be like mice. Mrs Morel would have liked to hear the children's noise; that would have soothed her. His clumsiness worried her. The silences between them were peculiar. There was a will to friendliness on either side, but the presence of each restrained and hampered the activity, the peaceful progress, of the other's thought or drifting muse. Mrs Morel felt relieved when her husband, towards nine o'clock, stumped off to bed, leaving her with her work and the slumbering Paul. Morel was certainly glad to get to sleep.

It was the baby who shook this artificial equipoise off the balance. At ten months old, he had a gathering* in his ear. He was not naturally over healthy. The child screamed with pain. The mother was distracted between a baby convulsed with real pain, and a husband pulling mournful, self-pitying faces. Her nerves were inflamed, so she felt her irritable scorn longing to fasten on her husband, miserable object that he was. She exercised some heroism of restraint at these times, when he sighed, pulled down the corners of his mouth, and petulantly jerked at the newspaper, upset because the baby cried.

The child would not be nursed by him. It would stiffen in his arms. On the whole a good, quiet, sad-looking infant, it would cry and press back from its father's hands, straining like a young hare. Morel felt the tiny hands pushing away at his chin, saw the baby's face averted, the wet blue eyes turned back looking piteously for the mother, and he said, troubled:

"Come an' ta'e him, quick."

"It's your moustache frightens him," she said. But she would press the child on her bosom, and, as it pushed its face between her chin and her throat, snuggling up to hide in her, clasping her neck with small arms, she had much ado to prevent herself sobbing bitterly. Morel grew to be afraid of the baby: he winced before it.

Meanwhile another child was coming, fruit of the interlude of gentleness between years of aversion. Mrs Morel had more grief in her heart over Paul than ever she admitted in her thought. Among her deep feeling for him was a grain of fear, as if in him was to be seen a judgement on her. Morel's feeling would have worked down to the same: "In this child I am judged and condemned." When Paul was seventeen months old, Mrs Morel handed him over to the woman who came to take charge of the house.

"To think," said the mother to the nurse, "that he should be pushed aside at that age."

The woman looked at Paul Morel. He was not pretty: plump, pale, with heavy eyes, and the peculiar, tormented puckering of the brows that persisted in him, and that was slightly noticeable in Annie Morel. Paul's eyes, however, were different from his sister's. Hers were rather fretful, and restless; his were still, with a heavy, abstract look.

"Poor lamb!" exclaimed the nurse, kissing him a large kiss. The baby took no notice, only stiffened and watched as his mother went away, the tears slowly shaken from her eyes.

The new baby was also a boy, also fair, also bonny. Mrs Morel lay and looked at the newcomer. His eyebrows, slightly arched, were serene. After a few days, his beautiful blue eyes were already candid and debonair, to the mother's thinking.

"He will be like his father," she said, and somehow, the thought set her heart at ease. Morel came upstairs. He fumblingly picked up the baby and kissed him.

"Bless thee, my little duck!" he said.

The infant wrinkled its nose on account of the moustache, but waved a small fist friendlily.

"He takes to you," said the mother indifferently.

"Eh my little man! Eh my little beauty!" cried the father, dandling the small child.

"Don't shake him about," said the mother, wearily.

"Dost feel owt like,* lass?" asked Morel, lowering his voice. He was really fond of his wife, really moved to see her lying there. Once out of the house, though, he would have forgotten her; which she knew.

"I feel quite as well as I can expect to feel," she replied.

"Um," he sounded regretful, sympathetic. She half closed her eyes and averted her face to escape the lavish, maudlin pity of his gaze down on her. He remained for a few moments in this trying, touching attitude of downward gazing pity and sorrow.

He was roused by the entrance of Miss May.* She was a lady of thirty odd years. She had perfectly white, wavy hair, thick dark eyebrows, a strong pleasant mouth, and wore spectacles.

"Well, Mrs Morel," she said brightly, "another boy!" She went over and pressed the hand of the mother.

"Ah, a dear little fellow! What are you going to call him?" She turned from the mother, flashing with a smile at the father. He was always much taken by Miss May. She was such a lady, so polite to him.

"I'm sure I don't know—can't you suggest something for us, Miss May?" replied Morel, bowing slightly by instinct. He was born a gallant. Perhaps it was the French strain.*

Miss May looked at the mother. Mrs Morel looked at Miss May. The latter's eyes saddened, her face stilled.

"Call him Arthur,"* she said.

"We will," replied the mother.

"It's a name I like in particular," said Walter Morel. Mrs Morel looked at the other. The two women were of the same age. But Miss May's eyes had a sad look of disappointment. Mrs Morel's eyes had an infinitely sadder look of disillusion. But disillusion can afford to pity disappointment. Mrs Morel pitied Miss May as the maiden lady named a child, not her own, Arthur.

Presently Mr Revell* entered. The minister was still at Morven,* and was a frequent visitor at 52, The Breach.* It had become customary with him to come to discuss his anticipated sermon with Mrs Morel. Then he would make notes which the woman would revise, and from these he compiled his sermon. Mrs Morel finally collected* his sentences, strung his clauses into shape. She saved time from her household work to do this. The minister profited immensely thereby. He learned his sermons nearly off by heart, until at last he acquired quite a reputation as a preacher.

"Is it right, do you think, for me to preach as my own sermons you have helped so much in?" he would ask of her, wistfully cocking his head to one side and blinking at her. She laughed.

"Is it right, do you think, to dig a heavy, rich soil, and to lighten it with sand—?—or should we scatter the seed on it just as the Lord or the weather left it?"

Her robust authority easily satisfied him.

Miss May, being of Eberwich,* did not know Mr Revell personally, only esteemed him as a preacher. He was shy with her. Not so with Mrs Morel. He bent over the mother, his shy brown eyes troubled.

"Are you sorry?" was his question. He had not known she was with child.*

"Eh, what's the good of being sorry!" she laughed.

Miss May stood aside.

"But the other—!" The parson screwed up his eyes musingly, as if uncertain.

"Ah this is a bright baby, a beautiful baby, not like Paul," cried Miss May, flashing her smile and her spectacles. The minister looked at her, flushed, bowed, then turned nervously to the mother. She was as a mother to him.

"But Paul is—Paul is a nice baby for us," he said.

"Poor little fellow," said Miss May.

Mrs Morel did not answer. The minister watched for her look. Anyone else was an impertinence to him while she was near. He drew as close to the bedside as possible. Yet he could find no word to say. His brown eyes, childlike, did not disconcert Mrs Morel, rather rested and gratified her. She saw he was struggling to say something.

"Shall I pray?" he asked doubtfully, flushing.

"If you wish," she answered softly.

He prayed that she might grow strong, strong enough to do her work, so that she would not be so tired again as she had been before; he prayed to God not to let her be so tired, to take some of her work away, to send her help: then that God would open people's eyes, so that they would see how she suffered too much, and worked too hard; would see how fine her spirit was, would see how, like one of God's queens,* she was noble in all her soul's bearing; and then, if they saw this, people would be humble to her, would understand, and would bend their heads to her good wish. He prayed briefly for Paul to be made healthy and bright. That was all.

Miss May looked at him with her fine, fearless grey eyes.

"He has a beautiful soul," she said to herself.

Mrs Morel sent them both downstairs, then she wept bitterly into the pillow. Not that she cared for the young parson, other than in a motherly, protecting way. No doubt it did her good to weep—it was unusual to her.

Chapter IV

PAUL MOREL'S FIRST GLIMPSES OF LIFE

The new baby flourished. He had exquisite dark-gold curls and dark blue eyes. Everyone considered him exquisite. As he grew a little older, he was spoiled. Walter Morel had returned to his old ways, but was not outrageously bad. He had always a warm place at home: the new baby loved him. The child wanted his father whenever Morel was in the house. Consequently the two struck up a close alliance. Arthur could do no wrong in his father's eyes.

When this pet was a year old, he was master of the house. Beautiful, curly-headed, imperious, everyone went under to his whim. Immediately Morel entered the house, he must take Arthur. This was a source of great pleasure to the miner. One of his known bitternesses had been that everybody shut up and darkened as soon as he entered the house. Now one bright blossom, the beauty, the baby, radiated at the sound of its father's footstep. Morel was delighted. And Mrs Morel, relieved by this child's gay, winsome disposition, loved it with demonstration.*

Meanwhile Paul, colourless and sad, struggled through various illnesses. His fair hair turned darker, his blue eyes turned grey, he grew slimmer. By the time he was three, he was a slim tall child, light, quick, and quiet in his movements, an endless chatterer to his mother. All day long he ran like a sickly fawn at his mother's heel. He was very quick at speech. When he was quite tiny he could converse childishly with his mother, and almost his earliest phrase was: "Are you tired, mother?"—or, "Have you got toothache, mother?"

Mrs Morel suffered a good deal from neuralgia* while the children were young. Paul was endlessly solicitous concerning her. Also, at the age of three he was nurse of Arthur, guiding that wilful yearling's steps. Paul was only four, Arthur two and a half, when the elder would say to his mother, hearing her exclaim at some mischief of the young one's:

"He's only little mother; well, he's only little."

Four-year-old was so conscious of his superior age, so willing to have his mother overlook the pretty brother's fault, since the baby was "only little."

On the whole, Paul was endlessly active, a great talker to his mother, very quiet in his ways otherwise. Sometimes he would be very still, apparently playing, making no sound for an hour, yet not notably occupied. Again, he would sit on the sofa, close his fists, and, with broken breath, begin to whimper, then to cry. As his weeping increased into sobs, Mrs Morel would ask: "What are you crying for?"

The small boy would sob convulsively at this. The mother repeated her question, and insisted:

"Tell me what you're crying for."

"I don't know," the child replied.

The mother's face underwent a swift tightening.

"Then," she said gently, but firmly, "you must not cry for nothing."

He would stop after a while. But if Walter Morel happened to be in when one of these crying bouts came on, there was a storm. The father, getting into such frenzy that he could hardly bear himself, would shout at his wife:

"What's he crying for then, if there's nowt up wi' him?"

The boy's sobs shook more. The mother had enough to bear, without her husband's bullying frenzy being added thereto.

"Now Paul," she would say, kind but strict, "if you don't stop crying I shall put you out of doors."

Then, if the melancholia* of the child did not pass off, if his quiet crying continued, she would carry him into the garden, set him on a seat by the rhubarb bed, where perchance a butterfly would distract him, whence he would no longer drive his father to a point near madness. This kind of thing continued till the boy was about six or seven, and had learned more control.

It became usual for Walter Morel to stay at home on Tuesday, Wednesday and Thursday evenings: when he had no money. Then, it being winter, the family occasionally experienced the full joy of family life. The lamp lighted, parents and children set about amusing themselves. The father either cobbled the small boots, singing lustily as he hammered away upon the old-fashioned hobbing iron, that was set in a rough trunk of wood; or he soldered kettle or lading-can; or he made fuses.* Whenever actively employed, he sang, and he had a good baritone voice, and he knew unheard-of old ballads about tailors or gipsies. He was quick and accurate in his movements, he was very ruddy and black, and to be in shirt-sleeves with waistcoat unbuttoned suited his debonair way, so that it pleased folk to see him pleasantly at work.

Paul preferred his father to make fuses. Then the lamp would be set on the mantel-piece, and a heap of gunpowder put in the middle of the white boards of the table. Walter Morel brought down a sheaf of long, sound wheat-straws, which he cleaned with his hands till they shone like gold tubes of lacquer, while Paul sniffed the sweet scent. Having cut the straws into six-inch lengths, Morel would lay down his murderous clasp-knife, and proceed to stop with soap such straw-tubes as were unnotched, open at each end. Paul seized the straws already bunged by a notch, proceeding to fill them, taking a little palmful of powder, letting the black grains trickle gaily into the tube till the six-inch length of gold reed was full, whereupon he dug with his thumbnail a plug of soap from the moist lump in his saucer, and with this plugged up the fuse, which he popped in the iron powder-tin ready for his father to take in the morning to the pit. Paul loved to watch the race of black grains of powder into the straw, to see those that escaped gaily peppering the white-scrubbed board of the table, loved finally to plaster up the mouth of his fuse so that not one grain might escape.

Meantime Arthur, a lad of four or so, stood at his father's elbow. The conversation was between the two all the time.

"But tell me," said the child, "about your horse down pit."

"Why," Morel would continue, "there's one name Taffy. He's a little 'un, he is, but force—he's a force little jockey* if you like—"

Morel put stores of interest and excitement in his voice. The children thrilled at the sinking and sudden rush of the sound.

"What colour?" Paul, silent and very busy, would interrupt to ask.

"Brown—as brown as a nut, my darling," Morel would reply, in a different, more endearing, but less free and easy fashion. Then he would resume, with the old extravagant 'colouring' of tone, to Arthur—

"And 'e's comes into th' stall wi' a rattle, but when you're not looking, he slives* an' shoves his nose in your jacket pocket where it hangs up, an' he snuffs, an' snuffs—" here Morel snuffed with his nose at Arthur, who rippled with laughter, till his mother smiled— "an' he snuffs till he finds a bit o' bacca, an' then he'll chew it, an' lift his head up an' chew—an' if it wor* wrapped in paper, spit it out—" Morel did the action. Arthur again rippled with laughter: he had beautiful eyes. Paul would hold himself up and think:

"But is it nice—tobacco? How does it taste?"

"Bitter—not at all nice," his father replied, with the subtle change of voice. He was politer, used better English, to Paul.

"Then why does he eat it?"

"Eh, I don't know, my laddie: 'cause he likes it." Before he went to bed that night, Paul had nibbled a bit of tobacco from his father's pouch. Then he wondered and wondered what the pony's feelings could be as it ate such stuff.

"But if Taffy can't find owt in your pocket," Morel resumed, "—all of a sudden, you feel him blowing warm in your neck-hole, an' he shoves his nose again your face, an' he fair talks to you. But he ma'es you jump sometimes, an' you shout 'Get out!' Then he tosses his head up, as mad as owt, an' happen gives you a nip with his teeth. Oh, he's a tanger."*

Mrs Morel would listen, delighted. At such times she was fond of her husband—at such times Paul liked his father. Annie played everlastingly with little dolls: William* was usually out of doors, being a wild active boy: the mother was always busy.

"What else, Daddie, what else," Arthur cried, dancing with excitement.

"Why, he'll come behind you, and nudge you with his head, an' shove you. Then you say 'What dost want, Taffy?' an' he lays his head again you. When he's had a bit of bacca, he puts his head down to his knees, and chews, and puts his head till his nose nearly touches the coal, and chews—he does enjoy it."

The children always remembered these tales of their father's: but the stories from Andersen* their mother told them, they forgot. Paul was very happy on these evenings, but it was partly the happiness of relief.

Often, on Saturday or Monday evenings, he would be waked from sleep by the sound of fierce quarrel below. The heavy booming of his father's voice, that sunk into sullen level, then raised at a rush till it was almost a yell; the sudden bang of his father's fist upon the table; the wrathful, but piteous sound of his mother's voice, which always seemed to Paul so hurting to hear, because it voiced so much suffering; the occasional terrible crashes, the sometimes sudden intense silences, which Paul knew were the silences of blood; all these, sometimes, not infrequently, made hell in the child's soul as he lay, very straight and tight clenched, listening, while the blows on the table seemed verily to fall on him.

Such were the bad nights. And, when the father was out, the children always mounted the stairs for bed with heavy hearts, lay down anxiously, unwilling to go to sleep, lest something might befall the mother, sitting down there below, on the return of the father, drunk or half-drunk.

"Lord, make my father not drink," Paul prayed, time after time each night, for twenty years, adding occasionally, "or else let him be killed at pit." He knew if his father were killed in the mine, there would be some sort of pension.

However, to return to the happy evenings. Towards half past seven the children were put to bed. Arthur would cry: "Can I go with my Dad?"

Mrs Morel would reply that the father did not want to go to bed so soon, but Morel answered:

"Ay, I'll go wi' thee, my beauty!"

He was delighted that the boy wanted him.

"I'm afraid he gets cold, being carried from our bed fast asleep," the mother said.

"Not him—he'll none catch cold—shall ter,* my darling."

"No mother—" and Morel pottered off to bed with his boy.

Paul slept in the attic with William, who was not sent to bed till later. The boy lay alone at the top of the house, listening to the sounds of the birds in the eaves, watching the shadows which the miners, going on for the night shift swinging their torch lamps, sent sprawling across the ceiling. Paul was sometimes very much afraid of the dark, sometimes not at all. He did not trouble his mother with fears. When he was sure the dark shadow, where the roof sloped, swung about and was alive, he resolutely closed his eyes, saying to himself: "Now I'll say 'A dear little girl—'."* With his heart beating fast, with his fists tight shut, he would repeat steadfastly to himself:

"A fair little girl sat under a tree

Sewing as long as her eyes could see— —" Having finished that, his favourite piece, he turned to hymns. Thus he succeeded, at the age of six, in overcoming himself, putting himself to sleep; unwilling, small though he was, to disturb anybody, or to obtrude himself anywhere.

William Morel was too big to make much of a companion of Paul. The eldest lad was tall, well-built, with a roughly-carved, freckled face, and 'ginger' hair.* He was spirited, active, and on the whole, good humoured. Though very fond of his mother, he often hurt her a good deal by his carelessness, his thoughtlessness. When she was really grieved, he was heartbroken, and, great lad that he was, retired to weep into the roller towel behind the scullery door. For the rest, being companion of lads older than himself, he scarcely considered Paul, six or seven years younger. Paul, then, was thrown into the charge of Annie. She grew up a tom-boy, with wild dark hair. Like William, she preferred companions older than herself. Unlike him, she was passionately attached to Paul, and would have the boy with her at all times. This led him into strange ways.

Mrs Morel had no pride of class sticking to her. She did not hob-nob with the women of the Breach, simply because of a discrepancy between her mind and theirs; she was friendly with most of the women, however, and was esteemed by all. This was because, though much more refined and superior by nature and nurture, she acknowledged herself intrinsically to be just the same as the rest. Therefore, Mrs Morel never patronized, never inclined graciously towards anyone: it was either friendship on a frank footing of equality, or else enmity.

And the Morel children mixed with whomsoever they liked, ran the streets at night and holiday, where they would. When Paul was six years old, Annie nine, the latter had a 'gang' of wild girl friends in the Breach. To this gang, Paul was admitted as a silent attaché. The girls, ranging from nine to thirteen years, kept an exclusive herd antagonistic to the boys. The young amazons* were just as wild and harum-scarum as their brothers, but they had different interests, which they hid from the young males. Paul was whisked about by "that screech-owl, Annie," as the mother called her. He was light, quick, quiet, and very adaptable, could run as fast as his sister, could enter into her game as if it were his own. So he played, vicariously. On winter evenings, the gang of girls rushed about at their games of hiding, danced backward and forward to "Three Men from Lincolnshire",* scoured the dark wilds of the Breach like real savages: and everywhere, along with the impetuous Annie, Paul flew, excited, his young heart beating. It happened that sometimes these young Bacchantes,* in mysterious mood, would agree to have tale-reciting evenings. Then, as many as could, obtained a candle or a piece of candle. The miners, at that time, used in the safe workings, emerald blue dips which they bought by the gross. Some girl would steal three or four of these; another, counted wealthy, might procure a wax candle; the rest filched odd inches of tallow* dip. Fortified with these, and a box of matches belonging to some bold old girls—it must be said that the Morel children never filched from home—the gang retired to an out house, either a pig-sty temporarily unoccupied, or a tool-shed, or a coal-house. Gathering round the one, or two candles, according as the supply allowed, the girls began the story-telling. Each member must contribute one tale. Paul, however, was not counted. The girls generously overlooked him at their round games, but they resented his intrusion into the tale-telling circle. Annie Morel, however, held him close and declared she should not come without him, so he stayed, the only male allowed near such a conclave; the fact was, Annie Morel was stocked with invaluable 'Ugly Duckling' and 'Little Folk' stories, and she was glib to a fault,* therefore indispensable.

The tales the girls told were largely of the common run, but some, lurid and ghastly and 'wicked', must have been the products of vicious childish imagination. There is a little stock of these brutal, ugly stories, and they are handed down. Grown-ups never hear them, for they are impossible to grown-up ears. The children themselves forget them after a certain age, as being tales too extravagant, perverted. But among the young, presumably, they persist. It was a great shock to Paul's young masculine mind—boys' tales, their secret tales, are different from those of the girls—to hear these stories. Standing at the back, on the edge of the candle-light, never attracting any attention to himself, he would watch the big, brutal girl repeating her story, while the others listened furtively, shrinking yet enjoying, till it seemed to him this girl was a monster, and that every girl had some violent depths of monstrosity hidden away deep down in her.

When the boy's mother found from him that he had attended these secret tale-tellings, and learned what girls had recited, though the lad said nothing of the stories that to him were shameful, yet Mrs Morel began gradually to wean him away from this society. He was very quiet, too observant, too self-mistrustful to mix readily with boys. He was much attached to young Arthur, but did not provide great amusement for that lively and exacting boy. So Paul played a great deal alone, one of his favourite occupations being to draw, on a slate, imaginative scenes.

In summer, when quite a tiny,* he liked to wander from the house, some half mile up Engine-Lane, to the railway crossing near Morven pit. At the level crossing was a wide stretch of metals of the colliery-railways, eight or nine tracks. There the trucks always stood in ranks: there the little colliery engines were always passing from the pits at High Park and Watnall down to Brinsley or to the Great Northern Railway, drawing their trains of trucks. There, the engines shunted backwards and forwards; there, they were filled with water from the leathern pipe which dangled like an elephant's trunk from the tall iron scaffold beside the squat, tiny signal hut: Paul loved and trembled to hear the water gurgling rushing into the belly of the gasping, arrested engine; there, enormous horses were used for shunting, and Paul gripped his fists as Nero, the great grey, hitched on to three or four empty trucks, set himself against the sleepers,* threw his great weight on the breast-band, and pulled till it seemed the chain must burst, till at last the trucks rolled off, to the shouting of the shunters, while Nero strode panting and majestic beside. Beyond the crossing was the woodyard for the collieries, with its stacks of timber and its tree-trunks lying; also stables for the farm horses and some pit horses. Always, across the uneven metals, high wains of hay went rocking, drawn by the splendid horses of the Company; and wagon loads of mangolds, and sacks of corn. Also, carts were loaded with coal from the trucks, and rolled off down Engine Lane.

Paul loved to sit on the bank where dirty, dusty stitchwort grew, and watch, hour after hour, this pageant of industry. When he was only five, he would run from home to sit here and watch, so that soon the carters knew him, and would tell Mrs Morel: "There's that lad o' yours, Missis, right up at Morven crossing; he'll be getting killed yet." Mrs Morel, busy at home, anxious, begged the man to send him home. When the carter spoke to the boy, Paul turned pale and shrank away, never answering. He would not be put for a ride in the coal cart, but ran swiftly home. As a rule, he alternated between a dreamy dawdle, and a light quick run; it depended what was his end.

The winter of Paul's sixth year* was remarkably severe. The alley between the Breach was frozen stiff for two months. William Morel, then thirteen years old, was a tall rawboned boy, generous, impulsive and hasty, very active. He was the only fair haired child; Paul's hair had turned to a warm chestnut colour, was very thick, while his eyes were of light forget-me-not blue. He was becoming a rather pretty boy; but his full mouth hung slightly open, as if already unstrung by sorrow, while his eyes, set deep, had a heavy stubborn look, sometimes anxious, sometimes suffering, sometimes pleading, but always stubborn.

William promised to take Paul to Nethermere,* a long lake half a mile wide and twice that length, which lay in a pretty valley by the woods a mile from the Breach. William was going to skate, Paul to slide and see the ice. Paul loved to see things, cared little for doing things. He envied the skaters when he saw them skim beautifully, but he would not mix with the boys; nor would he do anything in public which he could not do well, preferring to remain passive and ignorant rather than appear clumsy or stupid. The lads had sandwiches of bread and butter sprinkled with brown sugar. Paul was carefully wrapped up, because his health was very fragile, and was solemnly entrusted to William's charge.

It was a beautiful morning, the sun illuminating a crisp frostmist. The lads stopped continually, first at the old sheep bridge, where Paul found strange pleasure in seeing a bit of his own blue pot frozen and inaccessible beneath the water. The next halt was at the mill-dam, which spread out beside the road. William slung off down the slide, Paul wandered, full of wonderment and delight, to the edge of the sluice. The gate was down, the water frozen at the fall. The boy looked at the ropes of ice that crawled and slid up and down the race like serpents. It seemed an awful thing to him to stand on the brink of what was really a raging cataract. He stamped his foot: supposing the ice burst, and the whole crashed out into the meadow twenty feet below; he stamped again, and shuddered. Then he looked over the wide, alluvial meadows, frost-seared, where winter-ruddy, velvety horses wandered disconsolate. He liked to see the earth wan and stupefied in a stern grip: it pleased him that the earth, the vaunter,* could be seized thus helplessly by the invisible. He saw the bushes sealed within the water, grasses set in the solid. The truncated cone of the mill-tower, where his father, then a boy, had brought his gleanings to be ground, stood dark beside the ice. Paul thought the days of his father's boyhood must have been wholly delightful.

The brothers proceeded to the crossing. Under the tank where the engines filled, an enormous naked fire was blazing. The boys warmed themselves thereat. Paul watched the heat wavering up to the tank. He imagined it tickling, rubbing on the base of the iron, the water within stirring uneasily at the warmth. Meanwhile William hunted for nuts of coal and chips of wood to feed the blaze. The man from the signal hut—the points were all pulled from levers beside the metals—came out to look at the boys.

"Let us go," said Paul.

He dreaded acutely being accosted by anyone; rather than that the man should shout at him, he would have foregone all the pleasure of the fire.

In a moment or two, William was opening the grease-boxes on the axles of the truck-wheels.

"This," said he, "is truck butter. If you're starving you can eat it."

Paul looked at the dirty, rancid butter of palm-oil, trying to imagine himself biting bread spread therewith.

"You could eat dry bread," he replied, wondering that William should take pleasure in foisting a disagreeable notion on himself. At that moment, the man from the hut did shout at them. Paul started, curled inwards, longing to obliterate himself. And he hated the man, who merely roughly bawled at them to clear off; he hated the man, would have slain him if wishes could have killed; nor did he forgive the fellow, not so long as his boyhood lasted. The child also felt a sullen dislike, for the moment, for his brother, who, by clumsy meddlesome interference, had submitted them to the bullying of the watchman. William knew nothing of his brother's feeling, and only jeered at the man.

From the hill-top the boys looked at the mine.* It was a large one, with two shafts. Raised on its black bank, it balanced in silhouette upon the golden, wintry mist. High up, cresting the headstock, the four wheels that carried the ropes spun quickly, twinkling their darkness, resting, and twinkling back the other way. The driving engines sent up great, splendid columns of steam that swung white like plumes reaching high above the shafts. The pit was shimmering with dark activity, re-echoing with hollow sounds, while all around it stood tall, broadening columns of icy steam, blue upon the goldish mist, and swaying as if alive, things between earth and heaven.* The large pit hill, with its sheer end jutting the high heaven, the whimsey, or pond, at its foot far below,* loomed like a mountain on the mist, and Paul watched tiny figures, shadows, a man, a horse and wagon, toil up the dip slope, poise small on the crest of the sheer fall, a minute human drama of labour such as the Gods may see, diminished as we are in their sight; then the boys heard a faint noise as the rubble rattled downwards, saw the shadows of smoke where the great hill burned, saw the little, shadowy man and horse return. They were so tiny, as they crept down the slope from heaven, that how could such animated specks be counted by the far-off Gods. Yet if that one speck on the pit hill fell with its load of rubble, it were counted an irreparable tragedy. The pit panted, roared, and shuddered with rhythm like music. In the midst of its black, organised movement, one could see the great fans spinning softly, insidious black things, could see the chair appear suddenly above the ground, and small men move off, over the upper earth. Paul loved to watch; he could stand for an hour gazing at the same thing.

But William's skates clinked impatiently. Presently the boys were out on the white high road half way between Nottingham and Alfreton.* Heavy with frozen dust, the road was; the trees stood tall and utterly still on either hand.

From the round top of the road, between the delicate lines of ash boughs, the boys saw the ice, like a vacant grey piece of sky dotted over with rooks, placed among the low meadows and woods. Paul fluttered with excitement, William set off at a run. It was a fine square mile or thereabout of smooth ice. On the right rose the black, shaggy woods, on the left rough meadow-hills and, far away, a scoop of black-rimmed upland, topped with forest.

"You," said William Morel to his brother, when the skates were firmly fixed; "you have a look round, and a slide, while I have a skate. You can watch me if you like."

Paul watched the evolutions of his brother, till the latter, touched by the forlorn aspect of his charge, came up and said:

"Why don't you slide, or do something."

Paul obediently wandered off. He dared not slide on the big slides; he shrank more than ever from accosting, or from being accosted by, strangers. So, getting out of range of his brother, he watched a young, wiry-headed urchin of his own age performing on a slide.

"Now see me," cried the urchin, and he sailed down the slide on one leg. Some big fellows applauded, amused by the youngster's cheek.

"Go it, Ginger!"* they cried.

The 'ginger' seven-year-old squared up to them.

"All right, juicy noses," he retorted.

Paul Morel bubbled within himself; the louts roared; Ginger tried another feat. He 'croodled', sat down on his heels, hugging his knees, as he whirled along the slide. Somebody nudged him over, so he spun like a top. But in an instant he was up again, defiant.

"Ho, Feet!" he jeered, "th'ice is bending under your black pasties!"*

He yelled with laughter, pointing at the large ungainly feet of the youth, and, still laughing, the urchin set off down the slide again, this time cracking nuts: that is, he stamped one heel as he slid on the other foot. But he was too clever for himself; over he went. He raised a great howl. "Me arm, me arm, me arm, me arm!!!" Lying on the ground he kicked wildly into the air, as he yelled for ever "Me arm, me arm!"

He was raised and led away, still yelling.

"Me arm, me arm—OOOO me arm, me arm, me arm!"

Paul Morel, much distressed by this event, found himself near a roped-in enclosure. The ice had been sawn away about ten feet square, for the fishes to breathe. The black water was skimmed over again with ice. A swan sat out unhappily on the icy border of the hole. Paul felt some sympathy with the bird, that turned miserably from time to time, as if its feet were cold. He looked across the wide, bleak expanse of ice, and shivered inwardly.

Presently a lady skated up, and held on by the rope.

"Paul Morel—what are you doing here all alone?"

It was Miss May. Presently, Lucy Staynes,* a tall high-school girl of fifteen, swung up beside her former governess. She had pale features, long fair hair.

"Are you resting then?" asked Miss Staynes.

"No. This is Paul Morel."—Lucy was not interested. "He mustn't stop here, a child with a weak chest," continued Miss May.

"Oh, look at that poor swan," cried Lucy. "Poor thing."

"Your father is coming," announced Miss May.

There approached a tall, thin, dark man, with mutton-chop whiskers. He was pushing a chair on runners, in which sat a little girl, about six years old, a ruddy complacent child, whose eyes wandered calmly from object to object. Mr Staynes skated slowly, in a genteel manner. Behind him came a lady in a dark veil. Mrs Staynes* was a frail body whose every movement was timid.

"This is quite a study in attitudes!" Staynes began, in loud, urbane tones, immediately he could pull up. He spread forth his hand oratorically in the direction of the swan. "There, you have the outcast, excluded from his element, indifferent to everything—" The swan turned its back impatiently. "Then, this child, abashed like a stray fawn-kid"—he laughed—"You won't think me descending into slang!—I mean the infant animal of the fawn—"

"Do you know the child?" interrupted Mrs Staynes, in a low, musical voice. She was turned to Miss May.

"It is Paul Morel—you have heard me speak of Mrs Morel," the governess replied.

"He is cold, poor child," said Mrs Staynes in her plaintive, musical way.

Paul Morel wished he might sink through the hole in the ice.

Mr Staynes waxed suddenly magnanimous.

"Ah, let me see if I haven't a good plan—"

Mrs Staynes, however, again interrupted. She went awkwardly forward to the child.

"But you are cold, dear." She put her hand on his arm, tried to take his fist. He knew his nails were dirty, and had doubled up his fingers. "You are stone cold! Ah, your poor mother!"

"Miriam!"* declaimed Mr Staynes, calling attention by his tone, "I am sure you will say to that little boy, 'would you care to have a ride with me, and to warm yourself under my warm rug.' I am sure you will say that, if I suggest it. Eh?—What?"

Mr Staynes was a prominent Christian.*

"Would you like a ride?" asked Miriam, surveying the boy with all her mother's solicitude, though, perhaps, having in her manner a touch of her father's patronage. He was an odd figure to her, with his thick grey scarf hanging down to his knees.

Paul Morel wiped his nose. His handkerchief was a red one, with which he had previously cleaned his slate. He became aware that the rag was offensive, and blushed deeply. Miss May lifted him gently into the chair. He shrank away from Miriam, who leaned over him, conferring her tender young patronage, offering a biscuit. He turned his face away and snuffled slightly, aware that he must not expose his handkerchief again.

"Have you ever been in a sleigh before?" asked Miriam.

Paul Morel looked at her with his heavy, calculating gaze.

Miriam was slightly agitated. She tried to make him speak.

"What's your name—tell me, won't you? What's your name, eh?" She put her gloved hand on his shoulder as if she were many years his elder. The boy looked at her again, and again the slow, heavy, unwavering look, as if he were holding her in a balance.

"It's Paul Morel," he said.

She was still more agitated. He was uncomfortable in her presence, she knew, but that only because he would rather be alone, would rather she were removed. This piqued her, young as she was. She took off her glove to feel in her pocket. In rummaging, her warm hand touched his cold one. She shivered, he drew away. The sleigh moved.

"My nice rug will soon warm you," she said, with lavish childish tenderness. He shrank away from her.

"Do you like it?" she asked, anxious to be able to confer her patronage.

"Doesn't it go any faster?" he asked.

"It does if my father likes," she said.

The speed was increased. Paul still found it slow.

Miriam, her eyes dilated, laughing at once from excitement, looked anxiously at the boy to see if now he appreciated.

"It's not very fast," Paul said.

Miriam called for more speed. She was frightened. She nervously gripped Paul's arm. Mr Staynes was on his rare metal. He would show himself remarkable even here.

"Now then, young people!" he cried. "How is this!"

"It's not half as fast as a cart," said Paul.

Mr Staynes skated at top speed. They were nearing the narrow end of the lake, where the woods stood in the water. The runners of the chair whistled; some black-necked geese, scared, rose clacking in heavy flight. The nervous man swerved. Miriam was pale and tense; Paul smiled slightly, his eyes at last open and bright. The little girl glanced humbly at him. Suddenly Mr Staynes caught sight of a black bough raised like a snake from the ice. He veered wildly. The chaise careered on one runner, described an elegant curve, then twisted the man smack onto the ice, while itself slid on its side. Miriam rolled out over Paul. Mr Staynes skimmed like a figure of X.

Paul Morel got up as soon as he could. Miriam lay as if she were dead; her eyes were fixed with nervous horror. Mrs Staynes, who had followed apprehensively in the rear, pressed her hand to her heart. She tottered on her skates, came to a standstill with feet spread apart, lifted her hands helplessly, about to faint. Lucy, skimming after her mother, lowered the delicate woman onto the ice. Miss May hastened, hobbled to Miriam. Mr Staynes, raised his lugubrious head from the ice, like a lizard looking round. Only Paul Morel was erect. He might have exclaimed with his patron:

"This is quite a study in attitudes."

However, the boy was too much aghast at the general wreck, of which he felt himself the cause. Miriam was trembling too much to stand. Mr Staynes, white to the gills, and peaked, nervously hovered, incapable of doing anything but hover, making a tremulous fuss.

Paul Morel drew away from the catastrophe he felt he had wrought. His head sang, the blood ran from a slit over his brow, and trickled into his eye. Worst of all, he felt a sickly sense of guilt. Therefore, in a half dazed condition, he wandered away towards home. He plodded forward, having, when he was dazed into unconsciousness, a stubborn will which superintended and carried him along mechanically. Every now and then he wiped his eye with the offending red handkerchief.

Near the centre of the lake he met William. The latter skated up anxiously.

"What has ter done to thysen? Hast fell down?* I've been hunting thee everywhere."

William took hold of the lad in great concern, carried him off to the hole. There, the elder knocked a hole with his heel in the skim ice, and bathed the boy's brow. It was only a small, clean crack in the skin. But the application of ice-cold water to the brow was stunning. Paul was pale and trembling, breathing through parted lips. The mile home was very long and arduous. Neither brother spoke.

It was only half past twelve when the two arrived in the Breach. The morning was crisp and beautiful. Mrs Morel had been cleaning upstairs, whence she could see across the bluish valley the yellow corn-stacks at the Grange Farm* glimmering their warmth in the wanness of winter. She was in a bright mood. Annie and Arthur, playing together on the hearth-rug, heard the unwonted sound of their mother's soft singing to herself as she worked. A ray of sunshine, and the chatter of the children near the fire, woke the canary into a shrill winter song.

Hearing the clack of the yard-gate, Mrs Morel went to the bedroom window. She saw the white, expressionless face of Paul, the guilty mien of William, and instantly her old tension of anxiety tightened up. She hurried downstairs.

"Now what's the matter?" she asked sharply.

"He fell down an' cut his forehead a bit," William replied, preparing to be resentful.

Mrs Morel saw at a glance that Paul was going to be ill again. He had that heavy, indifferent look.

"Eh dear!" she exclaimed, "if I'm not sick and surfeited! However did you do it?"

With a weary gesture, she took the lad and put back his hair from his forehead. Paul loved his mother very much. He left himself in her hands, not wincing when she pressed his bumped forehead. The touch of his mother's fingers was the only thing he cared about, all he wanted.

"Where hurts you?" she asked.

"Nowhere," he replied. Sensitive and therefore bilious by nature, he trembled uncontrollably.

His mother sighed as she took off his cap and scarf.

"I'd no business to let you go," she said grievously. "I might have known our William would not look after you."

Whereupon William went out and wept into the scullery towel. Annie and Arthur looked on with solemn eyes.

"Tell me where hurts you," Mrs Morel repeated.

"I feel—sick," he replied tremulously.

His mother's eyes contracted with irritable distress.

"Eh child," she said, "I shall have nothing but trouble with you as long as you live."

Which Paul Morel implicitly believed.

Suddenly her manner changed.

"Come and lie down," she said, very gently, soothingly. She beat up the bed of the sofa, and soon Paul was curled up on the chintz-covered cushions he knew so well and liked so much during childhood. Mrs Morel rebelled no longer. She moved about quietly getting the children's dinners.

After a while Paul went to sleep. Whenever he was not well he made small moaning noises as he slept, a sound trying to bear by anyone but his mother; her it did not irritate. All the afternoon Mrs Morel was ironing, and the boy was vaguely aware of the clatter of the irons as they were put to the red fire, of the clink of the iron-stand, of the thud, thud, thud upon the table; of the dry scorched scent of garments and linen. When he opened his eyes, he would see his mother turn, her dark blue eyes meeting his: and comforted, cradled as it were in her gaze, he went to sleep again. Once, half awake, he caught the sound of his own throat. Then, looking through his sleep he saw his mother standing on the hearth-rug with the hot iron near her cheek. Her still face, listening as it were to the heat, with its firmly closed mouth, was very sweet to him. She looked her best when she was quiet, so brave and rich with life. She spat on the iron,* and the little ball of spit bounded, raced off the dark glossy surface. Mrs Morel kneeled, rubbed the iron on the sack lining of the hearth-rug vigorously. She was ruddy in the firelight, her movements were light, accurate as the dip and tilt of a gull; the room was warm, full of the sweet scent of ironed linen. Paul went gratefully to sleep again.

Later on, the parson came. Mr Revell had stayed at the little chapel, although he was not popular. But he drew only a very small income, being now master of a hundred and fifty* a year. He was very much attached to Mrs Morel, would watch her wistfully while ever she was in sight. For her part, she treated him as if he were a big child of hers; indeed he seemed so. Instead, as he grew older, of becoming more virile, he grew still more dreamy and speculative, so that all the common people said he was 'dotty', 'batchy',* 'not right', 'touched'. Mrs Morel was very sorry for him, but often she found him wearisome. Herself, she thought steadily, never resting till she had come to her conclusion; therefore his vague fumblings among speculative thought tired her. Dimly, he was aware of this, and longed to do something for her, to establish his claim to her acquaintance, which he felt he could not live without: he must have support.

"Aren't you disturbed when he makes that noise?" said Revell, referring to Paul. Mrs Morel stood still at her ironing, looked at the boy.

"He always does it when he is not well," she answered.

"It makes me feel—" Revell blinked, dreamed; Mrs Morel went on ironing, paid slight attention to him.

"It makes me feel queer,"* he finished.

Mrs Morel did not reply.

"Is he your favourite son?" Revell suddenly, and startlingly inquired. Mrs Morel laughed.

"I don't know. One does not have favourites among one's children, Mr Revell. But he gives me most trouble, so perhaps—"

"Could I do anything for him?" Revell asked, wistfully. It was for the mother he wanted to do something. Mrs Morel smiled.

"You shall be his spiritual father," she said.

"Shall I?" said he, accepting her. He put his head on one side and began to dream.

Chapter V

ACQUAINTANCES

Paul Morel had an attack of bronchitis after his adventure on the ice. On the whole he did not mind being ill, as he was passive, could lie and dream for long hours. Annie Morel, faithful in her love, gave him her every spare moment. She was a glib reader and tale-teller; so she spun stories, read stories, and recited to her brother, unweariedly. He enjoyed her gusto: she was so unhesitating, so sure and uncritical, so unlike himself. Arthur also played with his elder brother; but Paul had to make the play, deferred everything to the whim of his spoiled little brother, petted the child, and wearied himself. He was happier alone, with a couple of earthenware cows, which he made to roam over the wide pastures of the sheets, up the hills of the pillows. Also he used to draw. But he had no confidence, no self-esteem, qualities indispensable to the making of pictures. Therefore he was disappointed with the results of his work, and never took up a pencil without having decided on failure; which naturally produced failure.

But this taste for drawing had two results. 'Ginger', the boy who had tumbled on the ice, proved to be a neighbour of Paul Morel. His name was Alec Richards. His father had married again, and come to live in the Breach.* Alec's arm was broken by his fall. He found his way to Paul Morel's bedroom, somehow or other, and, having a whole right arm, and seeing a slate and pencil, he instantly drew a house and a woman jumping out of the bedroom window in her sleep. This was to illustrate a recent catastrophe in the Breach. Paul Morel admired Alec's success, gave way before the other's energy, allowed the obtrusive boy to obtrude to his heart's content, to put him, Paul, into the utter shade; from which shade Paul watched with steady eyes, until he should have estimated the soul-power of Alec. When the latter had gone, Paul also drew the woman jumping out of the window, first copying, then altering, and, to his own thinking, vastly improving on the first sketch of the plausible 'Ginger'.

Miss May also came to sick-visit, bringing Miriam with her. Miriam wore beaver hat and furs, was ruddy, had short revelling curls of black silk, had beautiful dark eyes. Paul looked at her for a long time. At last he said, in his quiet critical way, to Miss May:

"Hasn't she got nice eyes!"

"I suppose she has," replied Miss May, laughing.

Paul was silent again for a time, all the time watching the little girl, who, like a shy robin, sat silent.

"Was she hurt when she fell out of the sledge?" he asked.

"Frightened more than hurt," replied Miss May, stroking the hand of her charge.

"It would be sure to frighten her," he said, condoningly.

Miss May laughed brightly.

"You are a queer boy," she said.

He looked at the lady, as if to ask why.

Miriam was earnest and intense by nature. She had no friend but Miss May. Paul Morel started in her a slight attraction towards him.

Thus the boy began two of his life-intimacies.

As for himself, people came and went, he was interested and moved, but after a while, he forgot, nor would he have cared if none of these were ever seen again. Only his mother's step he listened for on the stairs, only her opening the door would quicken his heart.

He loved the evenings, when the children were in bed. Then he would have the light put out, so that he could lie watching the fire-flames spring out into the dark, could watch the huge shadows waving and rocking over the walls, till the room seemed full of great presences which combated around him, and the unknown shapes of the dark, which made his father drink, which made his mother love him, played a great drama in his presence. Sometimes he would be afraid, sometimes there would come back bouts of his congenital melancholy, when he would hide his face in the pillow and cry. On the stay-at-home nights, Walter Morel, retiring to bed in the back-room before eight-o'clock, would come in to see his son. He stood at the side of the bed, looking down pityingly on the boy. Paul, hiding his tears under the bedclothes, would lie quite still.

"Are ter* asleep, my duckie?" Morel would softly enquire. Paul had not sufficient hardness to remain silent.

"No Daddy—where's my mother?"

This instant, and plaintive question, cut the father, affectionate as he was, rather sorely, and always in the same place.

"She's folding the clothes, my darling. Do you want anything?"

"No—Will she be long?"

"I don't think so. Shall I get you a drink?"

Morel had instinctively left the vernaculer, in which he had begun.

"No.—I wish she'd come," sighed the child.

"Shall I stay with you, darling?"

Paul did not answer, not having the hardness to say the "No" he intended. Morel walked round to the fire, stood hugging the warmth, his shoulders hunched against the cold. He crouched up at the touch of a chill air. The father waited ignominiously on the hearth-rug, an intruder in his own bed-room, intruding on his own child. And it was the same with the other children, except young Arthur. The penalty was hard and ignominious.

"I wish she'd come," Paul sighed, at the end of half an hour, oppressed by his father's presence. Then Morel went to the top of the stairs, calling softly:

"Are you coming, Bertha! This child is fretting for you."

When the mother came up, Paul turned his face hard away from his father, afraid of being kissed by that great moustache. Morel looked at the child a moment. Then he stumped slowly from the room, with a gentle, submissive "Goodnight, my son," to the child, and an embarrassed "Goodnight!" to his wife.

"Goodnight," the two replied, indifferently, and the man retired, blotting himself out, as they wished.

The boy was always glad when his father was gone to bed, and his mother was come upstairs. No anxiety, no stress for his mother, no turbulence on his father's part, but submissiveness rather. Paul never knew a finer bliss than to have his mother lying beside him, while the night was still young. "She won't be tired, she'll rest a long time, she'll go to sleep when she's with me," was the thought that gladdened him. Mrs Morel was a bad sleeper, who ordinarily lay awake for hours. Paul, in the excitement of sickness, would lie listening, and when he thought his mother was asleep, he exulted within himself. Then, on the border of a sick-sleep, he would be dimly aware of the red-and-black shadow-ridden room, that bloomed with magic, as if the red, passionate throbbing of life, and the dark shapes that guide this blind hot throb, were here together and amicable. Paul loved the night that was at rest, and amicable; he loved to think that round him and his mother, round his father, and all the house, was a lovely, warm, ruddy-shadowy long night, which no strife would shake or scar, which like a shawl folded the household together in sleep; and those who sleep together love one another. It was worthwhile to be ill, at the price.

And getting better was pleasant to Paul, more than to most children, as he did not chafe. In convalescence he would sit up in bed, see the people pass up and down the hill in the snow, watch the miners troop home heavily, black, slow figures trailing slowly in gangs. Then he lay and dreamed of the darkness that came up in dark blue vapour over the snow, thickening upon the woods right away.

Paul Morel, when a young child particularly, loved to watch things. As if initiated, he saw the wonder actively present in all life. The snowflakes, suddenly arriving on the window pane, clung there a moment as swallows cling to the eaves, then changed into a crawling drop of water. They were dead. In flight, the snowflakes whirled round the gables of the house as seagulls screaming stream past a jut of rock, out whirling to sea. It was the magic made life so charming. Satisfaction of young appetites counted for little with the boy.

At seven he went to school. Then, the trouble of his life began. He had a horror of being thrust into public, and a horror of being presented with a task. The first trouble he said little about; but over the second, he wept, unwilling to be submitted. He did not want to go to school.

"I can't do the things they do," he cried to his mother.

"But they don't expect you to be able to do them—they want to teach you."

It did not matter. The teacher would present him with a task he could not do, which terrified him. He did not want to fight among the rest, nor to achieve, nor ever to win victories. He wished to advance by his own way, unnoticed. The pleasure of a fight was gone for Paul before life began in him. Instead of such quick triumph, he had the sureness of tenacity and patience. And he was remarkably quick in intelligence. He could read well at eight years old, could draw passably. When so tiny, he said to himself: "My mother says she would be well off with a steady thirty shillings a week. When I am a man, I shall be able to earn thirty shillings a week, and if I have a wife a bit like my mother, then I shall be safe all life, and happy." He dreamed a great deal, but was never the heroic figure of his own dreams.

The ginger boy, Alec Richards, however, became his friend. The two were utterly different. Alec was vainglorious, inclined to be vulgar; Paul was refined, and very shadowy. Yet the two remained friends. They often went out together early in the morning, either in the fields to find mushrooms, or along the roads to gather the horse-droppings. Paul loved to find something, something he was free to take, that no-one had lost. It seemed a treasure straight from the hand of Nature, or from God. Moreover, it was something for his mother. No tribute on earth was ever brought more gladly, no offering ever laid before any altar

87

with finer ecstasy of love and gratitude, than were the mushrooms, the blackberries, the coltsfoot flowers for beer, or the horse-manure for the garden brought by Paul Morel to his mother. They were his offering to her.

He loved to go horse-manuring, with young Arthur rather than with Alec Richards, who excited emulation. The two brothers would take a little barrow and set off at seven o'clock in the morning, down Greenhill Lane to Nethergreen.* Along Greenhill Lane was a wild cherry tree that glistened. At Nethergreen the road swung into a hollow and over the brook. There, great trees stooped their great green shoulders, leaned together as if they were talking: and Paul recognised the individuals by their brilliance and softness. "He's a beech, and he's horse-chestnut stuck all over with white feathers like a savage." At the same time he glanced swiftly down the scoop of grey road, that lay, its heavy morning dust splashed with patterns of shadow and light, colonnaded like a cloister with gloom, everything perfectly still as if in a picture; and he looked to see if there were any droppings. Then the boys raced down, sniffing the breath of leaves that seemed to be talking. The brown manure was not a whit unpleasant to their thinking, no more than the drift of bright brown waste from the beech trees, a rubble of discarded silk wrapping of young leaves that lay over the dark green mosses on the park wall, and on the grey dust.

With their little barrow, the lads went what seemed to them far afield. There was the adventure: to climb, before any shutter was taken from the shops, the steep hill to the tiny market place,* there to stand and glance swiftly towards Derby first, and then towards Nottingham. From the Market Place the road sweeps down-hill, past hawthorns white and heavy with flower, sheer into a very black cave of trees at the bottom. And if there were nothing for the barrow in sight, then, far over the trees lay Heanor, its clock-face like a chalk dot on the tower set small and very high; all the hills of Derbyshire spread away to the right.

Paul loved these high-roads very much in the early morning, when old red walls burned dark, when green of spring was very flame of green. But if his barrow were empty he was disappointed. With Arthur, who did not care a rap whether they returned home loaded or empty, the lad would hurry downhill.

"Lord!" Paul would pray, in his naïve, intense fashion, "Lord, let there be a big tod* in the shadow, when we get down to the trees."

And if there were, when it was safely, heavily, richly bestowed in the barrow, Paul turned his head aside, looked deep into the trees where the gloom was thickest, and nodded thanks, just a trifle confusedly, to the Lord.

The boys loved to see the wagons come laden with flour from the mill at Langley Mill, toiling up the ascent to Nottingham. There would be four wagons in a train, two horses in the shafts, and in front of one load, a leader horse. This leader would help all wagons, one after the other, up the last stiff pull, under the hawthorns. The boys would stand aside, watching the three great brown beasts struggle, almost prancing upwards, the skin on their haunches furrowed as they pressed from the great hind feet, their fore feet plunging to the cry and crack of the driver, as the load toiled upward, the round scotch* rolling and bobbing excitedly behind. Then the team came to a standstill in the market place, just beyond the Statutes ground, panting, almost leaning their great bodies against the chemist's corner door, safe on the little plateau on which the town is built.

Once, when the flour wagons had just gone by, and the boys were toiling uphill with their load, it happened they saw William coming down with a fellow clerk. William was just installed as a young clerk in the offices of the Colliery Company.* He was reputed very clever. He was very jolly, debonair, popular; very fond of his young brothers, who admired him immensely, and who stood this morning at rest to greet him as he passed by on his way to work.

Paul looked hard at William. But William looked hard away from Paul, not wishing to recognise in these two young scavengers, brothers who would shame him in the eyes of the senior clerk. Paul watched William go by, watched the handsome form of the lad get less, and he wondered. "He wouldn't look at us!" was the first amazed thought. "I suppose it's because we're horse-manuring," was the next. "Does it matter if you go horse-manuring when you're little?" he then wondered. "I suppose it does matter," he concluded. "We won't come this way any more."

Arthur, who did not mind in the least since Paul did not care, chattered away as gaily as ever to his elder brother.

Other adventure which Paul loved was 'foalfooting'—that is, gathering colts-foot flowers to make herb beer. When the engines ceased running on Saturday afternoons, Annie and Paul and Arthur Morel set off up the colliery railway lines to pick these early flowers. This task was one also, that belonged to Good Friday. Then the children took dinner, and went a long way. They would scramble over the pit workings at Morven, peeping down the shaft, dropping down a nut of coal and listening awed to the reverberation as it hit and hit and hit again the sides of the great hole in falling. They spun round on the turn-tables, where the little trucks were turned, great discs of iron at the nodes of little tram-lines. They peered at the hosts of safety lamps in the lamp cabin, that smelt so sickly of oil. They peered through at the great driving engines lying now still and religious as if in a chapel, since it was holiday; whereas the donkey-engine* kicked, or thumped with its long arm continuously, driving the fans; which, enormous, dark, insidious, hollow things, flew round ceaselessly, bringing up the foul air.

The railway ran along an embankment, raised above the meadows. Down the banks the foalfoots grew, like sovereigns shining on stems. Paul would dart up and down like a lizard, after the flowers. At any pursuit that pleased him, he was tireless, seemed to have an exhaustless store of energy. The three would try and break into the tiny tool huts sunk in the bank, imagining them to be cabins of misers, robbers, or wicked lonely folk. They would peer through keyholes ardently, thrilling at the sight of a murderous pick-axe.

They passed the ruins of an old Carthusian priory, whereupon they sat down on the bank facing it, eating their food, whilst Annie romanced* to the best of her ability. She was a splendid companion, so enthusiastic, such a one for yarning. Paul sat and listened, looking at the farmstead in the meadow below him, and at the large grey, ragged-edged shoulder of wall, a great sweep of ivy hanging as if it were a folded mantle from one side, away from the big ruined window through which birds flew, and wind drifted. Paul listened, accepted and rejected his sister's tales as she told them, gathering something more fitting, something more true and sad from the rag of remaining ruin. He, moreover, took into count the great wood which, like a rocky shore, rose up a long scarp hill from the level meadow, not far from the foot of the Abbey Farm. The wood was part of Sherwood forest.* It was larches just near the railway cutting, but oaks all the rest.

When the children returned home, and Paul saw his yellow tribute spread out on a black tray to dry, he said: "They're not worth much, mother, are they?"

"I suppose not," she said.

"Two-pence?" he asked.

"Perhaps," she replied.

Then he wondered, to think that he should have grieved his heart so when no foalfoots were on the banks, should have been so anxious, with his prayers: "Lord, if there'd only be a cluster, fifty, on the other side!"—and all for less than two pence. Had it been for anyone else than his mother, he would not have troubled for two pounds. But he passionately hunted even the little yellow flowers, so that he might spread them out for her. It was only such things as these he could offer up to her. If he had any money, he counted it hers, as money, mere augmenting of his father's wages. But a handful of foalfoots was his own tribute.

Meanwhile Paul's education was not neglected. He attended the board school, where he was always second or third from the top of the class; rarely first, rarely fourth, rarely remarked by his teacher. Such was his talent for passing unobserved, as great as his will thereunto.

But Mr Revell became of some use at last to Mrs Morel. The poor gentleman, now about thirty-eight years of age, was upon the point of resigning his position in the little chapel where he had preached for ten years. For ten years he had come twice a week to see Mrs Morel; for ten years she had revised, shaped, and, towards the end, almost written the man's weekly sermon. Now he wandered too much, his health was waning, and the congregations were too small; he was about to resign. For some time he had given his Saturday mornings to teaching the boy some French, German, and a little Latin.* Now, freed from church work, he was going to consider himself tutor of Paul, although the lessons were still to be confined to Saturday.

Perhaps more important to Paul Morel were Miss May's lessons in painting, which he received on Saturday afternoons, when, going up to the Staynes' house in Eberwich, he learned how to copy a little picture in water-colour, or to paint poppies and corn.

When Paul Morel was about eleven years old, his father, coming home from work one morning—the pits were turning slack time—brought in a very small wild rabbit.

"Look ye here," he said, holding the small ball of fur between his blackened hands. Paul looked. The rabbit shrank up, and was perfectly still.

"It's a wild one. There it was on a path across the closes, sitting fair dazed, and its mother lying dead just against it, and its two little brothers an' all. It never offered to move when I come up, an' it's never moved in my pocket, no more than now."

The tiny rabbit sat in a small bunch, ears flat and still as two long leaves, eyes alone showing life, glistening very dark.

"What had killed them?" asked Paul, quivering to tears, for pity. Arthur was already brimming.

"Eh, I dunno—a dog perhaps—perhaps a horse. There they lay in the path, close against a stile, all spread out, all dead but this one. And I thought I'd bring it you."

"Yes," said Mrs Morel, "and you *know* it'll die."

"Ay, I expect it will, lass," assented the man.

"Why?" asked Paul.

"It will pine for fear and strangeness," said the Father.

"Yes, and think of the bother when it does," continued the mother. "There'll be weeping and wailing,* till we shall wish you'd never seen the little thing."

Paul took counsel of his mother: what would it eat?—It would eat nothing, but would pine from fear. At this prospect the boy was aghast. He took the rabbit into the front room, warmed a cloth, and laid the creature thereon, in a dark corner under the sofa arm.

"He'll think, perhaps, that it's his mother made the duster warm," he said.

Then he heated milk to lukewarm, and put the saucer near the rabbit. After which he sat for a quarter of an hour, gently stroking the little creature's head and back with the tips of his light fingers, talking to it very low now and then. The rabbit, brown, warm little object with glistening black eyes made no response, only its heart beat quick like the soft ticking of a watch. Finally, Paul left it. He kept guard, allowing no one near the room. By teatime the rabbit had drunk some milk. It was very tiny.

Next morning, when Paul investigated, he heard a wild scuffle behind the chiffonnier. With most delicate tact, he tamed the rabbit. It was called 'Adolphus'. Presently, it was so tame, it would fly round the house like a little spirit, only two weeks old. One moment, it would be scuffling among the boots under the sofa, the next, flinging like a ball out of the door, Paul in mad pursuit. He was terrified lest the neighbouring cats should get poor Adolphus. The rabbit knew the boy, and sometimes would fly to him like a missile, if danger threatened. At tea-time and breakfast it became the custom to have Adolphus on the table. Mrs Morel objected, but Paul persuaded her.

"Well mother, don't you want to see him, how pretty he is?—Just look!"

Adolphus, the friskiest atom, would give a wild start at the jam, turn, dart six inches, then reconsider himself. He climbed with his fore-feet on the rim of the sugar basin, and helped himself to a lump; this before he had been in the house a week. He would sit and grind the sugar for a moment, putting his head on one side and—"Just look at him glegging* at me out of the corner of his eye, mother!—he wants to see if I'm after him." Then, dropping the sugar, with a bolt and a tumble he was rolling wildly in Paul's knee. Adolphus ousted the gold-fish, given by Miss May, a pair of fine, large, black brindled fish which Paul insisted on having before him at meal-times, so that he might consider them. They were called Anthony and Cleopatra;* because they were swarthy, and fiery, and golden: and Anthony had a black moustache.

On the Saturday morning Paul had two mishaps with his pets, which were more anxiety to him, as his mother said, than a family of children was to most men. The gold-fish globe had been broken on the Wednesday. Mrs Morel, ironing at the long bench, let the iron slip. It touched the bowl, and the heat broke the thin glass. So Anthony and Cleopatra were relegated to a large stew-jar. On Friday night Anthony bethought himself to jump out of the stew-jar, and was found in the morning limply gasping on the floor. Restored, he lay on his side. Paul's heart closed tight, and he felt the acute, almost deathly horror to which he was liable, coming over him. When Mrs Morel saw the child's mouth and eyes come open, saw him go pale as death, she was angry.

"Oh, you silly!" she cried. "The fish will be all right." Whereupon she rudely poked Anthony with her finger; who, like a Roman, struggled valiantly into a perpendicular. Cleopatra floated callously below.

"Will he mother—will he be all right."

He was all right.

But, returning home from his French lesson from Morven, with the verb 'to be' chasing round his brain, Paul received another shock. Adolphus had been in the maw of a ravening cat, only rescued by the faithful Annie, who, when she heard the poor pet's squeal, rushed wildly out, Indian scalp-lock flying,* as her mother said, and frightened the cat out of its wits. Adolphus, sulking and trembling, sat in a corner. Paul breathed hard as he heard the tale. He vowed, in his own heart, never to leave Adolphus in a precarious state again.

That afternoon, however, he had to take to Miss May his painting of some wall-flowers; Adolphus should go with him.

Miss May lived with the Stayneses still, although she no longer acted in the capacity of governess. Mr Staynes had inherited from his father a large grocery business, and had acquired with his wife the old-established chemistry and pharmacy store in Eberwich. The family lived in Mrs Staynes' large house in the main-street,* the chemist's shop once having formed the front. But Staynes had been a speculator, and a gentleman. He had been superior to retail business, consequently his fairly substantial fortune had declined till now the grocery shop was sold, and the remnants of his stock brought into the chemist's shop; which had become a kind of odds-and-ends store. The house was his own, through his wife.

It was a large building, with enormous gloomy rooms. Since Staynes' prosperity had dribbled away, along with his virility, Mrs Staynes had become an invalid, suffering with her heart; Lucy Staynes was away, living with a well-to-do aunt, who was determined that the 'chances' of a girl 'so refined' should not be spoiled. So the great, dark house was only half inhabited. A woman-servant of about forty-five years did all the work, also waited in the shop should Mr Staynes happen to have run down to the little Conservative Club,* where the old and the idlers spent their time, for a game of chess. Miss May had become a peripatetic teacher, who went here and there to the daughters of tradesmen, teaching music and painting. Miriam, attached to her mother, but forced to be subdued and restrained in presence of her illness, loved Miss May, who was almost mistress of the house in which she stayed only for the sake of the child and the suffering mother.

The front door of the house was the shop door. Paul never entered that way. It was the dreariest shop, very spacious, but half empty, giving the impression of a lumber room that needed straightening. The boy went round the back entry, between great bare walls. Thus he came to the yard, that was piled with empty boxes, which seemed to make a light in the dark-blue tiled place. In this yard again were two doors, one very large, opening into the hall; one, smaller, down a dark passage, being the scullery door. Paul usually went to the scullery door, as he belonged to the common order. This afternoon he carried a large bunch of purple and white lilac, which nodded in his hand. Mr Revell had sent it to the invalid lady; rather, Paul had suggested to the parson that he should send it. Then the boy carried his painting block under his arm, while he kept his left hand in his pocket, soothing Adolphus, who, as soon as the hand was removed, peered perkily forth. While Paul opened and shut the heavy yard door, Adolphus danced around and snuffed the air. Paul captured him just in time. With beating heart, the lad stood in the yard, between the great high walls, and listened. The piano was going in the drawing room, where he could hear Miss May's voice counting very sweetly "One two and three four, one two and three, one and two and three four," while young hands played a tune. Miriam was having her lesson. Paul went to the scullery door.

Mr Staynes happened to be running away from the shop: he opened to Paul.

"Well, little man!—Ah!" he lifted his hands, "lilac blossom, how very pretty! I think, you know, that lilac blossom is the most sumptuous flower.—Do come in.—Laburnum, now, that is graceful and—er— exquisitely dressed, shall we say—quite ladylike—" he preceded Paul through the big scullery, that was piled with unwashed pots of good china, while copper pans stood under the silver taps on the sink, and uncleaned boots stood under the table—"the Germans call it 'Golden Rain',* very apt, I think." He bowed brightly, questioningly, to the boy.

Paul gazed with serious, heavy-browed eyes on the man, admiring infinitely the grace, glibness, and poetry of his speech.

"Take a seat, do—while, if you will excuse me—" he spread out his hands with an ironic gesture, as he asked a mute shy collier's boy of eleven years, a boy wearing nailed boots and corduroy breeches, to excuse him. In a moment he had flitted away, and was calling softly, in a voice that startled Paul by its very softness and music:

"Mrs Langford!"—"Mrs Langford!"

He re-entered into the kitchen, followed directly by a short, stout woman, whose round smooth face, rounded eyebrows, half-shut eyes, and covert sneering expression, reminded Paul always of a cat. "Pussy Langford," he called her to himself.

"What do you want?" asked the woman, in a quiet but very grating voice, also cat-like.

"Will you find me a bowl suitable to contain these flowers, Mrs Langford?" the man asked, sweetly.

"You'll find one in the china closet; all the flower-vawses* is there, on th' third shelf, Mr Staynes."

Paul watched her; there was something he could not understand about her. Her manner of voice was deferential enough, but the body of her attitude was contempt for her master. Paul could not quite analyse so far. He gazed heavily at the woman. She glanced back quickly, with a flicker of hostility, towards his penetrating stare.

"On the third shelf in the china-closet—?—Thank you, then I shan't need you any further—" The woman's mouth sneered as he played master. "Except," he added, "that I may be called out in a while, for half an hour or so."

"Well I can't look after the shop," the woman answered. "I can't be trapesing up an' down stairs every minute, I s'll never be done as it is." She looked at him through her narrowed eyes. He bowed his head with dignity.

"I will wait till you are at liberty, Mrs Langford."

The woman went out. She hated the man. Paul heard her boots click on the tiled hall, but then the sounds ended altogether, the house was so solid, and heavily carpeted.

Mr Staynes found a bowl to his taste, a majolica with a rich luscious glaze, in which dark colours mingled.

"I almost think," he said, "that a dull surface would have been better; you have seen glass the sea has thrown up, so smooth that it is like a green grape dimmed with bloom—"

However, having arranged the flowers, he raised the bowl.

"Shall we now carry in your offering?" he said.

They went to the wide, barren hall, that reminded Paul of the deserted temples of Egypt, and thence, softly, into the morning room. This apartment, heavily and stuffily furnished in red woollen brocade that was fading brown, whose padding and cushioning seemed all to be sat* hard and unyielding, was scarcely occupied by Mrs Staynes.

The sick woman, spread in her invalid chair, was so lonely and at such low ebb of vitality, that the room seemed almost unoccupied when she sat there alone. Her face was pale and impassive, as if two hands were placed expressionless across it. Only her brown eyes, turning slowly and indifferently as the door silently opened, startled the child; he could imagine he looked into still brown water and saw in the deep shadow on the floor of the pool, dead beautiful things, dead children, dead swallows, and dead men of heroic cast.

"Is not this beautiful!" exclaimed in soft tones the husband, a tall, slight, grizzled man. Throwing himself back in half ecstatic, Bacchic* attitude, he held out the bowl to her.

"Oh, how lovely!" she murmured. But her voice was tired, as if she did not enjoy the flowers, and her eyes did not gain any life.

"The lilac is the most sumptuous, yet virginal flower, I have been saying," he began. Mrs Staynes did not listen as he went on, but looked down at the flowers as if she pitied them their praise.

"I hope I have arranged them to your taste," he concluded, delicately placing a spray.

"They are very charming," she replied in her dead voice, that never sounded more than a murmur.

He went on to muse of how he would like to have set them for her, in what dream of a vase, in what dream of surroundings. She closed her eyes wearily. And now he had talked himself out.

"Is there anything I could get you?" he asked tenderly.

"Nothing," she replied.

He suggested a dozen things—nice things, Paul thought. This was evidently a kind of ceremony between them. When the husband wanted to flit away and enjoy a glib hour here and there,* drone bee that he was, he outwearied his wife with solicitude. She consented to have a piece of orange. He brought it, perfectly set, with a silver spoon, and a bright little bowl of fine sugar, everything exquisite. Then he fled. He fled, though he went reluctantly, saying:

"Tell Mrs Langford I am called out for half an hour, will you, if she should happen to ask for me."

Mrs Staynes merely lowered and raised her eye-lids in answer.

Paul was left alone with the sick, hopeless woman. He put the knees of his corduroy breeches together, and hid his hand.

"Did you bring the flowers?" Mrs Staynes asked, with the tone of pathos and sympathy she always used towards children.

"Yes, I asked Mr Revell for them for you.—You never go out, do you?"

"Not now," she said.

"For how long?"

"For two years now I have not been out."

"Don't you get lonely?"

"No, I am never lonely. I don't know what it means."

"And don't you want people to come and see you?" He put the question with misgiving. She smiled sweetly, catching his fear.

"I like *you* to come."

He was silent for a while. She watched him all the time, smiling. He had heavy, serious brows, and full lips parted in sorrow that was half-unconscious, sorrow innate, that he knew nothing about. Consciously, he was very bright.

"Don't you want to go out?" he asked.

"Do you mean, 'do I fret to go out?'—I don't."

He told her how beautiful the spring was, describing in a hot, blundering, passionate fashion. He felt grieved and passionate about something, something of which he wanted to convince her.

"Yes," she said, only smiling patiently in the end. "I know it is very beautiful, very beautiful."

She put out her tiny, frail hand, heavy with rings that had come through generations of well-to-do ancestors, and touched the lilac.

"And don't you want to go out and see it?" Paul urged.

"Not now," she smiled.

He was very deeply troubled: she did not want to see the spring come in, she did not want to see people. How different from his own mother, who welcomed with enthusiasm every living interest. His mother seemed so rich in comparison. He looked round wistfully.

"Does it ever sunshine in here?" he asked.

"I think not," she replied smiling. She said she liked the shade, it was stiller. Then she made him tell her all the boyish, childish things: what other boys said to him, how the common children played with him, what he saw, what he learned at school and with Mr Revell. She did not weary of his talk of childhood. He told her about Anthony and Cleopatra, and she was delighted. At last, encouraged, he told the tale of Adolphus. She was interested as he—anything that was really of children stimulated her, and only that.

"And have you really brought him?" she asked.

"Should I show him you?—he's bin asleep for a bit, but he's just woke up, I can feel."

Adolphus sat between Paul's two hands, while the boy kneeled by the invalid chair, at the side of which stood the untouched orange; and Mrs Staynes, murmuring with trembling lips, touched Adolphus' shrinking brown head with her finger-tips. Paul remained quite still, holding his little offering. She, catching her breath with tears, leaned forward in her chair and softly touched the balled rabbit, which pressed back its young ears of oil-silk, and kept its young eyes wide-aglisten and alert. It was not trembling or afraid.

All the time, the piano-playing had continued in the drawing room across the hall. Presently it stopped.

"Why 'Adolphus'?" Mrs Staynes asked, regaining her composure, though she still trembled.

"I don't know—it came to me. You never know why you call things things, do you; why you call them the names you do?—Doesn't it suit him?"

"Very well," the invalid answered, smiling.

Just then, the door opened softly, and Miriam entered. She was growing tall. Her hair was still twining in black silk curls, her eyes were soft dark blue as ever; but her face was changing to oval from its ruddy roundness, and she had learned a trick of nervously drawing in her underlip. She hung in the doorway, looking at the two. Paul stood up.

"Did you hear me, Mother?" Miriam asked softly.

"Yes dear—you played very nicely."

"Did you hear me too much, Mother Dear?" the little girl asked, going forward with pleading look to the invalid.

"Not too much dear," the mother replied.

"Has it seemed a long time without me?" the child faltered, wistfully. She was hungry for love.

"You see, I've not been alone, my pet. I've had Paul with me quite a long time.—Yes, I missed you, Darling.—But see what Paul was show-ing me."

Miriam, a naturally rapt, unobservant child, had not noticed the rabbit. Paul had remarked, as soon as she stood in the doorway, that she wore a tortoise-shell band that took her hair straight back from the forehead: which did not suit her; also that she wore a beautiful dress of cream lace over a silk slip. This he admired very much, not knowing how old-fashioned the garment was. Everything was the same in Belfast House: fine and in good taste, but obsolete. Miriam turned to look at the rabbit, but first met Paul's stready and admiring eyes. She flushed, became a trifle confused and affected.

"What have you got?—Oh, the dear little thing! What is it?—Is it a rabbit? Oh mother, isn't it pretty."

"It's name is Adolphus," said Mrs Staynes.

"Why?—Adolphus is a silly name," Miriam said scornfully to Paul. Paul flushed and shut his young mouth.

"He knows it now, though," he said decisively. It was a passage of pride-in-arms* between the two whenever they met. Miriam wanted to hug Adolphus; she wanted to cuddle him, to put him under her chin, to crush him, if need be, for very love. Paul watched her and was angry that she should make such display of tenderness. He winced at her lack of reserve, being himself undemonstrative. Adolphus squirmed out of her arms, fell, fled under the couch.

Miriam stood petrified at once, looking at her mother to see if the invalid had received any shock. Paul had known too great shocks to be an alarmist.

"He's not hurt," he said, "and I can easy catch him."

Mrs Staynes was not upset. Miriam wanted to see Adolphus eat. As the tiny rabbit put his two paws in the saucer, twitched his velvet tiny nose over the milk, or rubbed the moisture with his fore-feet from his whiskers, Miriam was breathless with excitement. She even wept for pleasure to watch him.

"He's a little fairy prince who was enchanted— —" and she rambled into a fairy tale. Paul thought it twaddly—* the iridescence of his fancy had been stained with blood. He told the story of the destruction of the rabbits, concluding:

"but he enjoys himself ever so much, bangs the boots about like anything. When he's big my mother won't have him in the house, and I shan't have him in a hutch, because he sets off at the scullery and flies off through the kitchen and passage into the parlour* like a shot. Then he pretends to hide a second in the parlour curtains where they hang on the floor, and then he shoots back—as quick—before you know where you are. So he'd never live in a hutch. So when he's big I s'll take him to the wood and let him go. Only perhaps the other rabbits won't have him, because they'll sniff him and he smells strange. Do you think they would? Do you think they'd give him great kicks and clawks* with their hind legs? They can do, because my white doe used to do me when she didn't want me to bother her. What would he do if they all turned on him like that? And he'll not know his way about, because rabbits have roads. And he'll get all ravelled up in the bushes.—But my mother won't let me keep him when he's big. Besides, the cats 'ud get him— —"

This was so much more vital, and so much more painful, and so much more interesting than Miriam's fairy princes, that the young lady hung in deep consideration. She didn't like Paul, he was too scornful of her bubbles. But his method of marching right up against facts, standing there at challenge, fascinated her.

"At any rate," Mrs Staynes said, "you can't say that he will not be quite happy. And if he is not, you *won't know*—."

Miriam was very anxious that Miss May should see the "dear little beauty."

"I'm sure Miss May doesn't want bothering," said the invalid, and this was the first sign of pettishness.

"Oh yes Mother!"

"Why aren't you content to be here with Paul and me, without vexing your soul with Miss May?"

"But," Miriam's eyes grew large and startled, her under lip quivered: "But she wants to know Paul is here—she doesn't know." Miriam loved her mother. But as Paul heard the invalid, he pitied the girl; Mrs Staynes was so different from his mother. Between Miriam and Mrs Staynes was always a cold, chill shadow; between Mrs Staynes and everything was the same, an estrangement. The lady had not been able to see herself set at nought, sold to a man she despised, brought to be a mere tiresome cipher, without revenging herself by despising all things. Miriam loved Miss May better than her mother.

After a while:

"Go along—go to Miss May," the invalid said. "I want to rest. I have been excited."

"Can I do anything for you, mother? Can I bring you a pillow? Let me raise your feet— —"

Paul thought of Mr Staynes. But Miriam's was a real wound that made her hands tremble.

"Leave me, dear," said the mother.

Miriam kissed her, clung to her a moment, and went, along with Paul, Adolphus, and the saucer of milk.

Miss May was upstairs, tidying the bedrooms. Poor Mrs Langford was called down to the shop. The stairs were very wide, with a heavy rail, and carpeted with thick, oriental carpet that twenty years had not more than flattened. But it was very dark everywhere.

The governess was in Miriam's bedroom. Paul also loved Miss May. She had hair perfectly white, and abundant, coiled in a thick knob at the back. Her brows were black and firmly planted; her grey eyes, behind the spectacles, were very shrewd and very kind. There were laughter-wrinkles at the corners of her eyes. She was only forty years old.

"Well Paul Morel," she asked brightly, "and how is the painting?"

He showed her the bunch of wall flowers, done in water colour.

"What did your mother say to this?" she asked.

"She said she thought it would do for you."

"Would do for me," Miss May laughed. "I think it very good indeed."

Paul looked at her with quiet, unbelieving eyes. Miss May laughed.

"Why do you look at me like that, you quaint boy? As if I should tell you just to flatter you. They are very good, your flowers—admirable."

Miriam, anxious to see, tiptoed over to her governess.

"They're rather blotchy," she said.

Miss May laughed again.

"Rather blotchy, are they? Perhaps they are. But they have something about them—a kind of glisten in their darkness—quite a touch of genius, Paul."

Paul coloured, was very glad.

"If I am a genius," he thought, "what will my mother say. That will be the thing she'd like most, to have a genius for a son."

Whereupon he fervently hoped he were a genius, although he was convinced that, of himself, he was nothing of the sort. Perhaps, though, he might be turned so as to catch the light of God at an angle sometimes, and the light would break into colours. They went to a table in the great window of Miriam's bedroom, and there Paul had his lesson, while Miriam listened.

The room was very high and spacious. In the days of his betrothal, whilst still rich, and grand in his ideas, Mr Staynes had had built the furniture for the two best bedrooms, so that now Miriam slept in an

[One page of manuscript missing]

"We reckon Adolphus is a hedgehog. You cake him right up in clay— a towel will do—and put him under the pillow to bake. When he's done, and you pull the clay off, his skin comes off as well: 'cause the hair sticks in, you see."

This realism was new and shocking to Miriam.

"No," she said, "we can't cook Adolphus."

"Yes," he said, "we can."

He caught the rabbit, which was hobbling and sniffing curiously over the counterpane, wrapped the little creature in a towel.

"No," cried Miriam. "No, don't do it."

"Shall I hurt him! What's the good of playing if we can't do it proper. Make the oven."

"No," said Miriam, and now she had begun to tremble slightly. "No, I don't want to play at that."

"Then I'll play myself," he said.

He took the pillows and piled them up.

"If you're the wife," he said, "you ought to make the fire."

She put her head down and hugged the rabbit.

"You shan't be baked, darling, shall you?"

The rabbit wriggled away from her.

"You frighten him," said Paul coldly.

She looked at the lad with dark, wounded eyes. He captured Adolphus, who had lobbed to the edge of the bed and was peering over, twitching with excitement.

"Come on, hedgehog," said Paul. "Come and be wrapped in clay, like a ball."

"No!" cried Miriam.

Paul looked at her in scorn, then laughed. He picked up Adolphus, folded him quickly again in the towel, and put him among the pillows.

"You won't hear him sizzle," he said, "because clay keeps the juice in. He'll be done in five minutes."

"Ah, you are horrid, you are horrid!" panted Miriam, her blue eyes dilated, her little body trembling with distressed excitement. Paul looked

back at her with cold eyes, and eyelids tilting with amused contempt.
He was a boy of middling stature, delicately made, with dark chestnut
hair, and eyes the colour of a thrush's egg.* His mouth was red, his face
very pale.

"What a fuss!" he said.

Meanwhile Adolphus, very lightly wrapped, very loosely bestowed
among the pillows, had suddenly bolted. The young rabbit found himself
slipping over the edge of the table-land. He hung back, but in vain, went
sliding down the counter-pane. Paul turned quickly, and his face went
dead pale.

"He's fallen," he said quietly.

Miriam, awed by the quiet despair in his tone, hung upon the boy's
look. She longed, first impulse, to comfort his white despair. Paul looked
quietly over the edge of the bed, expecting to see Adolphus stretched
out. The rabbit sat, somewhat astonished, resting after its fall, the young
nose twitching in surprise. Paul slid down the bed to him. As soon as
Adolphus saw his master, he scampered off.

"He's not dead!" cried Paul in joy, and he went after him. Miriam
slid down also.

Then began a wild chase. Adolphus whizzed about like a little demon.
He tore round the room, in and out the furniture, flashed across the
floor, and hid. The two children had a mad and delicious chase. It was
some time before they captured the rabbit. Paul caught his pet by the
ears, and brought the kicking, plunging little rebel to his knee. There
he soothed him. Miriam stood and watched.

"What, my little!" the boy crooned, in his infinitely tender voice
that thrilled the girl. "What my little precious, has it hurt you! Has
it frightened you, pigeon—my little chick!" Then suddenly Paul
raised serious eyes to Miriam, and said, normal voice: "His heart *does*
beat!"

Miriam was quite upset by this tragic information.

"It fairly tickles, it goes so fast," Paul added, suggestion of tears in
his voice this time. He bent his face to the rabbit to hear and listen.

"You won't go and die of fright, little, will you—say no." But the
rabbit, instead of saying 'No', spurted out of the lad's arms, giving him
a keen kick with the hind leg. Paul started, his hand to his cheek. Then
he laughed.

"He's only having me on," he said, looking round.

"He's scratched you ever so," said Miriam.

"He's that frisky," laughed Paul, very much relieved to know that
Adolphus was sound.

"He might have scratched your eye out," said Miriam. Paul shrugged his shoulders. Miriam came up, unable to refrain from touching the boy's face.

"It must be sore," she said, in low, vibrating tones of sympathy.

"It's not—it's nothing," the boy answered, drawing back his head. Miriam hung upon him with her serious, wide look.

"Let's see if he'll come for calling," said Paul, and again he started the chase.

After a time Miss May came in. She laughed at the children's sport, finally settled down to talk to Paul concerning the painting. The conversation drifted to Mr Revell. Miss May was very much interested in the parson: she had taken a kind of shelter-mother rôle* upon her. Mrs Morel was not unwilling to free herself of the burden of the helpless parson, and to interest her friend in him. The little man irked Mrs Morel by his over attachment to her. She was sorry for him, but she set no store by the ineffectuals. Gradually, she weaned away the minister, substituting Miss May. As Mr Revell got more dreamy, Miss May gained greater ascendency over him; but he adored Mrs Morel.

The two children and the governess sat in the large window looking down into the main street of the mining town-let. It was sunny, the shops were shaded by blinds, women were shopping in a pleasant, unhurried fashion, whilst almost every tradesman was leaning against his doorway in amiable conversation with an acquaintance. At the Market Place corner, which they could just see, miners, twenty or more, were sitting crouched on their heels, smoking and talking all day long. Occasionally one or two crossed the sunny road, went up two white steps into the Lord Nelson,* and were lost to sight. Occasionally, men issued from the public house, and walked totteringly home. Richmond, an enormously stout policeman, joked with every tipsy miner, and laughed wickedly in sympathy.

Presently, stumbling down the steps of the 'Nelson', came two men, hanging on to one another. One was Walter Morel. He had a red scarf round his neck, and was drunk, as Paul knew in an instant.

"I tell thee thow'rt a liar—and tha sees that—?"—Morel suddenly showed his fist. Then he ran, in a flash, and struck the other, bigger man.

"Tha sod," roared the other. In a moment the two were fighting. Miss May watched with clouded brow.

"That's my father," said Paul, in a quiet, normal tone. "I wish the other man would kill him." He expressed a wish simply.

"Oh hush dear!" said Miss May.

Miriam looked at the boy. He was very white, but appeared impassive. His eyelids hung rather low and sullen over his eyes, his mouth was shut: that was all. No one would have known he was much moved. Yet he trembled inwardly with violence. Miriam was afraid of him. He seemed to her a galvanic,* pale thing, full of sudden energy like lightning.

The men fought for a minute. Then Walter Morel went rolling in the dust.

"I knew he'd be beaten," said Paul, in utter contempt. "He always is."

Richmond, the fat policeman, came up.

"Now then, now then, now then, now then!—come, come, come, come, what are you doing of, do you think! Get up, Walt. Why don't you wait and settle it by morning."

The men, muttering, were separated. They staggered off home.

"He'll be fit to devour himself when he knows you've seen him," said Paul to Miss May. Walter Morel had a profound respect for the bright, generous, clever lady.

"You won't tell him, dear, will you," pleaded Miss May.

"I shall tell him, then he'll perhaps remember another time," said the boy.

He was not ashamed for himself; he was too contemptuous of such a scene, of such protagonists, to derive shame therefrom. But he knew that his mother was shamed to her last fibre, which knowledge he could not endure. Save on his mother's behalf, Paul felt no very violent feeling for his father, either way.

The boy stayed to tea, as he had done several Saturdays. He had no heart to remain; he wanted to be off and see how things fared at home. "But," he said to himself, "if I go home, my mother will say 'Didn't they ask you to stay to tea today, then?', and she will think they don't want me, and she will feel a bit mortified." So he stayed as long as was necessary.

The meal was served in the morning room, where Mrs Staynes sat. Paul thought it very beautiful to sit perfectly at peace, in a quiet room, taking tea with people all of refined manners: no dinner boiling on the hob, no miner eating dinner noisily while other folk had tea, no jumping up and down to serve vegetables and puddings, no discord, no hopeless scotch in the conversation, no spots on the cloth. The boy looked at the fine linen and china, at the glisten of silver and of flowers; he noticed the quiet, refined accent of everybody, and thought:

"When I am grown up, this is how my mother shall sit at tea. But she had it so before-hand;* what a cruelty to come to our roughness."

It was the one ambition of the boy, to provide a home for his mother, wherein there should be an atmosphere of flowers, of quiet, and of harmony. To this end he would dream and dream of a wrestle with the future, and a victory. When he dreamed of himself, it was in a future with which he did not wrestle, but which he accepted: a passive, small life, poor, but lovable.

As soon as he could, with politeness take his departure, Paul did so. Then, tucking Adolphus safely in his pocket, the boy hastened off. Since he had seen his father stumble homewards his heart had not lightened from a heavy anxiety. He crossed the 'Square', an open space stuck with many line-posts,* and shut in by the backs of four great rows of high dwellings, miners' houses built by the Company when the pits were opened. The rough, sharply sloping square was play ground and drying ground to the tenants of the quadrangle. It was about a hundred yards from corner to corner. Paul dared not run across, for fear of attracting attention. The 'Square' urchins, some of whom knew him by name, jeered him, because, they said, he was 'proud'. Proud he was; he would have run them over into the sea, like the swine of the parable;* every one of them. But, perforce, he paid no attention to them, crossing their area not too fast nor too slow, afraid for Adolphus.

Once in the common gardens, he ran down the black path* of the sunny hill-side, home. The front gardens of the Breach were full of pink daisies and London Pride* and pansies. The hedges on the hill were white with may. Pigs squealed gaily in the sties on the common gardens. Paul noted these things as he ran swiftly home.

He went up to the door slowly. His mother and Arthur were alone in the kitchen.

"Has my father come in?" was Paul's first question.

"He has," replied the mother curtly.

"And is he in bed?"

"He is—there let him stop."

"Was he drunk?"

"What need to ask? After being out from nine o'clock in the morning till six at night—what need to ask if he was drunk!"

"Was he disagreeable?" Paul was determined to know.

"If you were not in, what do you want to know for?" Mrs Morel asked.

"He shouted as hard as he could shout," said Arthur. And the boy, his father's favourite, a child already as tall as Paul, gay* and light by nature, set wide his beautiful blue eyes in anger and animosity. Paul looked at his brother.

"Well, it's no good getting into a flaring temper," he said. Arthur flashed at him, that he hadn't heard, or he would have been in a flaring temper. Paul's heart hardened afresh against his father.

"Well, he's in bed now," he said, "so we needn't bother." Then he passionately told his mother what he had seen; he could keep nothing back from her. She was very angry: but the boy's wrath and hate were so childishly extreme that she forgot her own in moderating his.

Then he showed her the painting, told all Miss May had said, talked to his mother earnestly of the things that had interested him: of Mrs Staynes, of the furniture of the bedrooms, of Miriam. Mrs Morel was very interested herself in the boy's observations.

"Yes," she said, "Mrs Staynes may well have a sad face. He's a man that must sadden God himself, such an unstable, feathery good-for-nothing."

Then Mrs Morel talked to the boy, gave him her answers to the things that puzzled him. He listened devoutly, and talked with her.

Chapter VI

LAUNCHED

Paul Morel remained at the Board School until he was thirteen years of age. All this time he continued to study under Mr Revell's faint direction. The latter had resigned from his ministry, and spent his days in wandering round Morven, or in playing his own dreamy nothings upon the organ of his own chapel, an organ which he had bought himself, which, therefore, the deacons could not withhold from him. Once a week, still, he visited Mrs Morel, and, profound egotist that he was, talked to her of nothing but his own nebulous states of soul, all of which she heard reiterated with much patience, since Paul could now read a story in French, recite a ballad of Uhland, or quote hesitatingly from Virgil.*

The boy made great progress in languages, having a passion for foreign literature. In his turn he taught Alec French. The two boys, the one lusty, big-limbed, clever but unimaginative, the other delicately made and delicate of growth, wonderfully perceptive, remained firm friends. At first, Alec was controller and patroniser, since his was the superior strength and physical energy and enterprise. To all of which Paul submitted, which he even encouraged. But gradually the balance shifted. Alec abated himself without knowing it. He resigned his leadership. Instead of: "We are going for a swim in the morning," it was,

"Shall you go for a swim, Paul, or don't you want to?"

If the two boys went for a swim, then again Alec resumed his superiority.

"Don't you go and get a cold; don't you go and do too much, or you'll be badly," he would say. And then: "Can I swim across this lake and back?"

"I don't know," Paul replied.

"I'll bet you I can. You sit there and watch me." Having done the deed, Alec never wearied of vaunting himself. Paul heard without listening. A feat of arms had no value for him, unless it were imaginative. He played cricket without caring vastly who won. If he ran a race, ten to one he walked the last lap, indifferent, although he was fleet of foot.

"I don't care whether I'm first or last. I don't care whether Alec does things better than me. I don't care if everybody does. What does it matter?"

This modern and decadent contempt for action separated him from the mass of boys. He had always a few friends who were attached to him, the rest regarded him coldly, with hostility, or contempt. None of which troubled Paul, he merely went unperceived on his own way.

If, however, it were a question of imagination, Paul ran with the best. When the Breach fought the Square in snowball fights, Paul Morel was always in front. A fight, when it was in a common cause, and not for his own rights or his own glory, delighted him. Danger, on such occasions, always made him laugh. He would laugh as he raced after the 'Square-dogs', even though they put stones in their snowballs, would run forward in the thick of their shower, laughing with a tighter mouth when cut on the brow.

Yet nothing could persuade him to fight in his own cause. In the first place, he had not the English fisticuff instinct. The great grudge his school mates had against him was that he was proud. Once, the bully faction, which he scorned, avoiding them, who in turn did not remark on him, were set upon him because of the respect or consideration shown him by one of the teachers. They attacked him first with the sleering, coarse abuse of a gang in cry. He made no answer, merely looked away. Meanwhile his heart was boiling with hate. Then they took offence at the bow of black ribbon his mother tied him for a tie. The biggest bully tore it off. Another ripped his collar.

Paul did not move, only to stiffen back his neck against the tugs on his clothing. He did not speak, nor moved a muscle of his face, only his eye like a mad thing's flashed from neck to neck of the bullies.

"If," he said over and over again in his heart, "If I had a knife, I would stick it there, and there, and there," glancing his eye from throat to throat, looking always at the big vein. "If I had a knife, if I had a knife—"

Then, as he imagined the difficulty of pulling a knife out to strike the next blow, the delay thereof, he changed his glance, looked intensely between the eyebrows of the lads, whose faces he saw not.

"If I had a revolver—there, there, there," he counted in a flash, "with five chambers, I would blow their brains out, one after the other."

He chose the spot, felt his fingers stiffen to the trigger.

"Though," he said to himself, "I'd rather have the knife, to strike, to strike in their necks."

As it was, having no manner of instinct to use his fists, he allowed the boys to do what they would. They soon began to feel uncomfortable.

"Look at his bull-eyes," became their cry. They drew off.

It was the only time in his life Paul was ever assaulted by a gang of boys.

He was very passionate, but being exceedingly gentle, and very indifferent to what lads whom he considered clowns should say to him, he rarely, very, very rarely, became enraged: sometimes, with his father, once, with Alec, and rather often with a girl friend of Annie's.

The occasion when he was enraged with Alec* occurred when both boys were thirteen. As a rule, Alec was the soul of generosity and consideration. Paul, on the other hand, was inclined to be sneering. Alec had had a braggart fit; Paul had cut him to the quick. Alec spoke of fighting; Paul turned up his lip.

"You've never fought in your life," jeered Alec.

"I never made a fool of myself, so I never needed," Paul replied.

"Who's a fool!" cried Alec, in hot wrath, pushing up near his friend. The other nudged him contemptuously with his elbow, turned aside his face, with a sneer of contempt.

"Mind who you're shovin'!" Alec warned, white hot.

"Then get away," said Paul, giving him another push back as he edged up, and lifting his lip with a hateful expression as though his friend's proximity disgusted him. At the blow of Paul's elbow, Alec sent his fist in the other's eye, where it did very little damage, owing to the thickness of the lad's brows. But Paul drew his breath with a hiss, and fused molten hot. It felt just as when the soft body of powdered borax, on charcoal,* is caught by the blast of the blow-pipe and springs instantly into a molten, mobile, white-hot thing. Paul lost consciousness in a flux of passion.

He was a mere wild force as he flung himself on the antagonist.* The two lads went down with a crash. Straight, like lightning, like a ferret, Paul made for his goal: he set his hands in steel on the other's throat. Alec tore and beat him.

Paul came to himself suddenly, when he caught sight of his friend's horror-opened, frenzied eye. He relaxed limp in an instant, and was kicked off the body of Alec. The next moments of anguish were very dreadful. The fierceness of his passion had almost shattered him. He laboured for breath, his heart choked and plunged, his soul was sick with a dreary disgrace.

The boys never mentioned this again. But whenever Paul was in a passion of rage, after this, he recognised the steely hardening, and the inclination of his hands. Men, however, soon lost the power to rouse him to such pitch, only women could put him in a real passion. He early learned their capacity for so doing. Martha Sharp,* Annie's friend, a reckless, mobile girl, had only to set herself to taunt him, with feminine subtlety snicking his vanity, when he felt himself getting blind-enraged. Once he hit her across the mouth, once he took her by the hair and knocked her head against the wall; to his everlasting shame.

Paul Morel had, then, under all his quietness, his submissiveness, and notwithstanding all his affectionate gentleness, blood as sudden as a Spaniard's. He was, however, so schooled by sorrow, with which his very flame of life was lit, that he was temperate and docile more than most moderate English. He always understood the hurt he might give, so he usually refrained, and rarely blundered. Himself he subordinated often and ever, rather than give the hurt his own way would have exacted.

When he was turned thirteen,* Paul had to look out for a job. Mrs Morel had vowed her sons should not got into the pit. William, by reason of his cleverness, had got into the offices of the Colliery company.* There was no one enthusiastic on Paul's behalf, as the schoolmaster had been on William's. The eldest son of Mrs Morel was born to succeed. He was frank, merry, very intelligent, and lacked penetrative insight. Everyone liked him, no one was jealous of him. At seventeen years of age he was earning eighteen shillings a week; which he gave to his mother with pride. All Mrs Morel's children were passionately devoted to her.

Paul hoped to be like his brother. He was not, he knew, so clever, nor so taking; yet he hoped to get a situation such as his, a situation so genteel and lucrative. But Paul was not made for success. No one was ever enthusiastic on his account; there was an uncomfortable atmosphere about him, which disturbed folk. He hunted in the newspapers for advertisements. This he loathed bitterly. There was a reading room attached to the Cooperative Stores. Paul would reluctantly climb the stairs, listening as he went to discover if anyone were in the room. In presence of an occupant, he would not scan the advertisement column, but sat in the window seat, pretending to read the news of the day; in reality, watching the sunflowers stare, over the wall of the cottage garden opposite, inquisitively down on the heads of those who passed along the pavement; watching the woods on the far-off hills, and wishing he were a wild animal to wander about, to race through life, and be shot, all without care; watching the great brewers' wagons come rolling up from Kimberley, enormous barrels like beans in an open pod, and a giant of a wagoner enthroned aloft, rolling in his seat, his round red face with its bleached moustache balanced sleepily, and his thick, naked red arms covered with reddish hair rocking idly on his sack apron. Paul wished he were a brewer's wagoner.

"Why can't I go rolling, red and massy, through a sunshine scented with beer! Why should I be hunting here, like a dog kicked out, for the scraps flung in the street! Why am I worth nothing, why does nobody want to use me, why am I nothing but an expense to my mother."

A series of 'why's which he never answered, and which, with most other queries, time taught him at last not to bother about. But he would not copy an advertisement while anyone was there to see him; it mortified too much his pride.

In the end he was bidden call on Mr Thomas Jordan, manufacturer of surgical appliances, at 21 Friar Lane,* Nottingham. Mrs Morel was all joy.

"Why!" she said, "you've only written four letters, and here the third is answered. You are lucky, my lad, I know you are lucky."

Paul did not tell his mother what a torment this business of offering himself as a servant was to him, but she guessed from his silence.

Mother and son set off together one Thursday morning. It was August, and blazing hot. They went up the gardens, through the town, the long mile and a half to the station. Paul, highly nervous and bilious organism, simply held himself in a grasp of control all the time. He was in such a seethe at being thus thrust out of his old routine, he was in such an inflammable flux of excitement, as to be a mere chaos of surcharged emotion. Yet no one would have known, save from his pallor, his bright eyes, and tight lips, that he was moved at all. He kept himself in perfect control, chatting to his mother, pointing out things to her. She was almost gay. She made plans for him, anticipated good fortune for him, was so bright and interested that Paul would have died rather than disappoint her. As he watched her take the two return tickets to Nottingham—they were one-and-eightpence each—as he watched her small hand in its wrinkled black glove take out the silver from her purse, he felt as if surely, should the man refuse to have him, his heart would burst. Mrs Morel, however, was not troubled by doubt.

"If you don't get this—well, you don't *expect* to get the very third place you apply for. But I believe you will, for all that."

Mrs Morel smiled into the eyes of her son. She had the most winning, gay way of smiling, so confident, so intimate, withal, it seemed, so adventurous, that Paul felt his heart flutter, his eyes dilate, his face flush. Mrs Morel chattered away. It was a long slow journey, sixteen miles by train. Paul's eyes were full of torment, save when his mother looked at him, and he smiled.

"If I get this place," he thought to himself, "I'll stay there all my life; I shan't move; at any rate I shall earn there enough to keep me."

They arrived in the old station at Nottingham. Paul had been to the town only a few times before. The station was very dark and dirty.

"I wish," he said to himself, "that my mother had let me go down pit. I should have known folk there."

He was a boy of middling stature, delicate, with dark, thick, chestnut coloured hair, and light blue eyes that seemed, usually, to sulk under the heavy brows. He was pale at all times.

Mother and son hastened down Station Street, dreary as prison, into Carrington Street, that is one of the arteries of the town. The street crosses the canal. Paul looked down at the gaudy red and yellow barges sprawled on the black water, saw the men on the barge roofs recklessly moving about, while babies played by the red and yellow doorways.

"This is like Venice," he said to himself. "How fine to be a barge baby, to come through our meadows right to here."

They crossed the road to see the other side. There again, down below, men were moving about, women in their floating houses were making dinner. It was like a theatre, to hang over the rail of the roaring street and see these people in their quietness busy upon the water, in the cool shadow. Looking down the canal, Paul could see the Castle* standing up to heaven on its bluff of gold-coloured rock. The grey, square castle, the golden rock shining piled up in the sunshine, a medley of dark factories and buildings beneath, very lowering after the glinting green bushes on the scarp; last, the sheer cliff of wall dropping deep to the dusky, flickering canal, on which the barges sprawled gaudy and black, all fascinated Paul.

"I shall be able to come here, mother, at dinner time," he said, with wide eyes of anticipation. She smiled again upon him.

They passed along, and Paul loved the town. The glass in the shop windows flashed, the brass ledges blazed, the shadows of the sheltered side were full of colour and movement of people. Paul walked under the lime-trees and admired the grass with its daisies, round the alms-houses. He had a drink at the monumental Fountain.* All the time, he felt himself in two portions: one was a coiled, shuddering mass of suspense, the other an alert, vivid intelligence, that held down the riot of emotion, and at the same time explored the new sights. It was eleven o'clock by St. Peter's Church.

"We shall be there in three minutes," Mrs Morel said. Instantly all Paul's energy was concentrated in keeping a calm control.

They turned up a narrow, dark lane that climbed up to the Castle. Mrs Morel hunted about for Thomas Jordan's. It was up a dark, wide passage, a board informed her. The passage opened into a gloomy, dark blue yard, where were several doors. This was a common yard to several little industries. Mrs Morel found Thomas Jordan's door: the glass was barred across; it was very dirty. Pushing it open, she saw a flight of narrow, wooden stairs, with bare walls. This again was rather dirty. At the top was another door. Mrs Morel pushed this open, then stared about in pleased surprise.

She found herself in a large, oblong room, evidently the warehouse and clerking floor of the establishment. It was lighted from above. Looking up, Mrs Morel found that each floor was only like a wide balcony: she could see, through the big, oblong space in the ceiling, the heads of women moving beyond the low wooden wall of the room above. A woman appeared at the fence, leaned over; then a small goods-lift came rattling down its shafts, passed the warehouse, and vanished towards the ground floor. There was a great babel of little noises, from above, from all around.

The walls of this, the second floor, were padded deep with parcels in strong, glossy, creamy-yellow paper. There must have been thousands of these pale parcels in the racks against the walls. Large, broad counters formed the inner rectangle of the room, counters which backed upon the hole or shaft. The entire building was lighted from the ceiling. Between the solid counters and the walls of parcels, was a floor-space for two to walk abreast. This went all round the room, and there was no more floor than this. Right at the far end of the room was a glass office, wherein the gas was lighted. In the office, a white-bearded man raised his ruddy face and looked from afar off, upon the entry of the woman and boy. There were six clerks in the room, all busy at their various portions of the counter, with parcels and pale coloured goods. The nearest clerk showed Mrs Morel into a waiting-room that was at her left hand. It was a dingy apartment, upholstered in black American leather, very shiny. Two bulging arm-chairs glistened, as Paul thought, with excess of vulgarity. On the table was a pile of trusses, in their new yellow wash-leather, gripping each other, a sinister medley. Paul sniffed the odour of chamois leather,* wondering what the contorted things were. He was so much excited as to feel scarcely able to stand; he shuddered so he could hardly conceal it.

There entered the little, stout, salmon-coloured man with white whiskers.

"Goodmorning," he snapped, keeping his hands ready for action, in a business-like fashion.

"This is my son, Paul Morel," said Mrs Morel, in her sweet, slightly deferential way, the way of a woman who knows she has not the where-withal to command respect from a man at sight, of a woman conscious that she is neither young, nor any longer 'lady-like'; who has yet a favour to ask.

"This is my son Paul Morel; he has an appointment with you—"

"Yes—yes—Oh!—Sit down!"

He hastily, almost irritably pointed to a chair, then turned sharply to the boy, pulling out of his pocket at the same time a letter which he read, bending forward to it in the same irascible fashion, as if he were going to snap at it. Then he looked with a jerk at Paul, who stood trembling, and who felt his bowels melt within him at this sudden irascible stare.

"Did you write this letter?"* the little man snapped.

"Yes," said Paul, and immediately his heart said back to him, "That's a lie. William wrote it, you only copied it: and in a villainous hand, at that."

"Hm!" said the little man doubtfully. He considered the letter again.

"You say you know French?"

"Yes," replied Paul, to whom this was acute torture.

"I didn't write that letter," his heart chanted persistently inside him, doing away with the vestige of his self-confidence. The little man pulled out another envelope. There was a crackling and Paul was handed a large sheet of foreign note-paper, upon which were written, in a thin, pinched foreign hand, half a dozen lines of French.

"Can you read that?" asked Mr Jordan.

Paul took the paper. He managed to keep one spark of calm intelligence afloat on all the seething turmoil of his emotion. The handwriting was very foreign, very difficult indeed to a child. Paul began to pant lest he should fail. He suddenly got hold of the first line and gasped out "'Dear Sir, Please send me'—er—er—er—I can't tell that—er—er—'two pairs of grey thread stockings without fingers'—er—I can't read the—I could read the *French*—I can't tell the—"

The word 'handwriting', or even 'writing', failed him utterly. "I can't read the—" and there was a blank space where 'handwriting' should have come in his mind.

The little man, seeing him stuck, snatched back the paper.

"'Grey thread stockings without *toes*—'" he snapped, and was going muttering through the rest of the translation when he was interrupted by Paul.

"Well, it means fingers usually—'doigts' usually means fingers—"

"Fingers to stockings—!" said the little man, not unkindly, though he had worked his voice to a snappy, grating intonation he could not now avoid.

Paul hated him, he could cheerfully have murdered him where he stood. To tell the truth, throughout all Mr Jordan's subsequent gruff, but real kindness to Paul, the lad never forgave him this first disgrace. Paul Morel had been made to look clumsy and asinine before his mother, and this by a little common man who spoke bad English. Paul Morel never forgave his employer, never could bring himself to be other than repellant towards the little man.

The upshot of it all was that Paul was engaged at eight shillings a week.

"There my boy," said Mrs Morel, as soon as they got to the bottom of the hollow wooden staircase—"There my boy," she said gaily. "Didn't I tell you we should get it!"

Paul was gladder than he had ever been. He could have wept for joy to see his mother so pleased, so elated that the world esteemed him thus much as to engage him at eight shillings a week, on the third application. He went down the dark yard that smelled of straw and crates, lifting up his heart with joy and gratitude. Like any devotee, he thanked Almighty Heaven for this great beneficence. He was of worth in the world; his mother had at last a real champion now, who would buckle to the fight for her. The boy felt no doubt, no misgiving concerning his life in the dim, close warehouse, it all seemed a highly desirable adventure. He walked on air, his face shone with gladness, he looked up at the sky that shimmered blue above the vast market-place, praising God in his heart.

Mother and son had a little dinner in a tiny, ancient, dark eating-house, whose upper storey overhung the pavement in Bridlesmith Gate. Mrs Morel was acquainted with the proprietress, who, for two years, had been her mother's servant in Mansfield. Now, however, 'Minnie' was 'Mrs Kirk'; she was better-off than Mrs Morel, whom now she treated with just sufficient familiarity to show that she knew her own value, but whom she warmly liked, nevertheless.

Paul had a little kidney pie with potatoes, his mother the same. They sat together in a dark corner of the dark place: it was tremendously exciting. Paul's only grief was that it cost his mother her bit of money. If he could have conjured up the shilling to pay the bill, he would have been at the pitch of happiness. But his mother was quite reckless of her money. She made him have a little currant tart, because he was fond of such.

"No mother, no," he pleaded.

"Yes," she said, her blue eyes bright and alert. Then she asked of the serving girl, always in the same quiet way, as if she asked a favour:

"Will you bring him a currant tart?"

Mrs Morel had not a grain of vanity: when she asked even for goods in a shop, it was as if she asked William to do some task for her; when she chid a beggar at the door, it was as if she scolded Paul: she was deeply respected, and liked.

Such a little outing, alone with his mother, was for Paul the keenest of happiness; while she enjoyed it just as much. She was as enthusiastic, nay, far more enthusiastic than the boy; there was between them that love and intimacy which makes the mere walking down the street together a glorious adventure, an experience. They were as happy as the day together, and neither knew it. When he got home in the evening, and not till then, Paul was ill from the stress of the day.

He started work on the morning of the Monday following. Rising at a quarter to six, he caught the 7.15 train to Nottingham. His mother packed his dinner in a little, brown shut-up basket. He pulled a white, half-opened rose from off the great bush as he passed. His mother came to the gate with him. There she stood, in the dewy, early sunshine, smiling bravely at him. He smelled his rose, smiled back at her with his eyes, then turned nervously along the top of the Breach. The cool, rich air was tinged with the scent of pinks and white lilies.

"Oh I don't want to go," his heart cried. "Oh, if I could stop here, in the Breach that lies so low and quiet in the sunshine."

He turned and waved to his mother, smiled at her gaily. She watched him out of sight. Never a condemned creature walked more wretched and unwilling than Paul walked towards Nottingham and the torture of new experience. No one knew, however. He pretended to be gay even in sight of strangers.

At eight o'clock he walked up the stairs of Thomas Jordan's 'Surgical Appliance' factory. His hours were from eight in the morning till eight at night. Only two clerks were punctual. One of these took Paul round to his corner in the spiral department. There, in the very dark corner, Paul sat on a high stool at the counter, and waited for Mr Pappleworth.

Thomas Jordan made trusses on the top storey, wove flat indiarubber stockings on three frames which stood in the top room of an adjacent building, while on the ground floor he stored raw material, and had his 'spiral' rooms. The 'spiral' rooms were two long wooden apartments forming a right-angle. Fixed to the benches that ran along these rooms—rooms that always reminded Paul of a green-house with its benches—were eight or nine little round machines that wove the spiral, seamless stockings. There were eight girls in this room. Upstairs, hung outside the wall of the main building, as a studio is often hung out, was another room, much like a small carpenter's shop. The door of this room opened out of Paul's corner, and six steps plunged down from the main floor to this 'finishing room', where sat some five girls, stitching and finishing the 'spiral' goods.*

Mr Pappleworth came at 8.20. He was a thin, rather frisky man, proud of his clothes. He had a very thin dark moustache on a pale face, and very often chewed chlorodyne gums.* His manner was breezy, the "Hello—I say!" manner of the saloon bar of a public house.

"Hello—and are you my new man!" cried Mr Pappleworth, pulling off his coat with much activity, turning back the green and white striped cuff of his shirt, showing a thin arm with veins swelling, and covered with black hairs. He chewed his sweet, bustled into an old jacket, then turned again to Paul.

"Ha, well, come on then," he said, in quiet, friendly tones. All his movements were quick, and he seemed in a great haste. Mr Jordan had appeared at his desk, had opened most of the letters, had sent down a handful to Paul. Mr Pappleworth was the oldest clerk; he was about forty years of age, and had been with Mr Jordan for twenty five of these years. Therefore he had much licence; still, for appearance sake, and because it was the nature of the man, he must bustle.

"Come on then here—What's your name?—Paul! Come on Paul. Look here, I'll show you what you want to do."

He pulled out a thin ledger from the rack that rose behind the desk.

"You want to copy these orders in here—look—see? You can begin as soon as you like, if I'm not here—see? That's the ticket, my son. Well, you begin then—"

He sniffed, chewed his gum, dodged away to a very big ledger. After a while, he came to see how the boy was getting on.

"Oh, you'll do fine, you will. But look you here, put the number on there, and the date, see—and—" he hastily explained.

"Now you've got it, eh, Paul? We s'll get on like man an' wife, I can see. Hurry up, my lad."

Mr Jordan came up to see. He watched apart like a general. Paul had to go to Mr Pappleworth.

"Pen in your ear, pen in your ear, if you're a clerk," snapped old Jordan, in his grating voice. Paul picked up his pen from the counter, stuck it behind his ear, flushing.

"He's shaping A.1."* said Mr Pappleworth to his employer. Mr Jordan stared authoritatively about.

"He'll have to learn to make haste," he said, and the little man, having demonstrated his own importance, stumped off.

Paul very quickly settled down at Jordan's. In a fortnight he was quite at home there, and quite happy. Everybody was kind, as working people are one to another: the beauty of the long, laborious days which occupy a man's life, is in the comradeship which folk who share the same work enjoy. At work, a man sinks his own claims, strives no longer with his fate, has no personal object to secure. In this submissive state of soul he, normally, feels a genuine sympathy, a glad, boyish sense of comradeship with his mates. As soon as work is over, a man becomes again the egoist; his aim, his personal desires, submerged in the work-shop, renewed as soon as he reaches the street, separate him from his fellows of the day-time: he seeks a fresh mate, begins a fresh life. So that a man's individual life may be very unhappy, his work-life, very happy.

Paul Morel, along with all the men at Jordan's, and probably the great majority of workmen everywhere, was very happy at work, rejoiced particularly by this comradeship with the other men, which was a new thing to him, and a great discovery in life. Mr Pappleworth, always late, generally in a bustle, was rarely irritable or ungenerous. Sometimes, however, he was sallow and inclined to spurt.

"Haven't you done that yet?—Go on, be a month of Sundays! I could have eaten it by now."

Paul, a laborious writer, ducked his head and scrawled on the ledger with great contempt. Mr Pappleworth was silent for ten minutes, after which time he had digested his spleen.

"I'm going to bring my best little Yorkshire terrier down this afternoon," he said. "I'll show her you: she's worth seeing."

Paul stuck his pen in his ear, looked across at his chief, thoughtfully.

"Is it very silky, colour of metal, steel and gun-metal and tarnished silver?"

Mr Pappleworth rested a moment in amused wonder. Then: "That's it!" he said with enthusiasm. "A pure-bred, weighs fifteen ounces. You must see her afore the man comes for her—"

Mr Pappleworth was sometimes paternal—he was old enough to be Paul's father—sometimes simply friendly, as if he were a lad like Paul, or as if the boy were a man; sometimes irritable; sometimes the knowing vulgar man of the public-house winking on the hidden side of his face at this delicate, sensitive, virgin boy—never the superior; Mr Pappleworth never affected that moral and psychic superiority over his subordinates, which makes the rule of women so detestable. The two talked awhile as they worked, until the elder said:

"We'd better get on. Dolly's here this morning."

Dolly was Miss Dorothy Jordan,* who came down on occasional mornings to attend to her father's foreign correspondence. She wore shirt blouses with man's collar, did her hair on top, and moved as if she were infallible. For the rest, she was thirty five years old, and, casting her critical eye over the clerks, was wont to comment on their appearance, their show of industry, and so on.

Mr Jordan came and examined Paul's ledgers at the end of a week. They were execrably written, badly ordered without being exactly un-tidy, and there were several glaringly mistaken entries ruled across. The little, stout man slowly turned the leaves, considered the work, then closed the book. He did not say a word. Paul was blushing to the roots of his hair, gazing all the time at his employer. The boy had this uncom-fortable knack of gazing persistently and impenetrably on his interlocu-tor. He was saying in his mind—"He's quite common, he's as common as anybody, although he is the master. He'll be disagreeable in a minute. I hate to see old men talk when they're ill-tempered. They seem to spit words about as if they were spitting bile, I suppose they've got no teeth."

Paul, however, did Mr Jordan an injustice. The old gentleman had been a workman himself, so was inclined to domineer and snarl and snap unbecomingly. But this was only because he occupied, and must justify himself in, his trying position of master. He did not speak a word of censure. He looked at the boy.

"Hold your back up," he snapped. "You'll be as round-shouldered as you can be by the time you're thirty. Look at me!"

The stomachy little man carried, of course, square shoulders. He strutted off down the room. Presently he called, from the glass office:

"Mr Pappleworth—send Paul Morel here a minute."

Paul went. Miss Jordan was in the office.

"Take your coat off," said Mr Jordan.

Paul blushed. The old man fussed round with a tape measure, measuring his shoulders.

"Why don't you get some flesh on your bones," he said.

Paul held his head erect. He was rather thin, he knew. Miss Jordan saw that he had a wonderfully white skin, a white, round stalk of a neck supporting a well-shaped head, whose thick chestnut hair grew low. His red mouth shut close, his look was inscrutable, rather wistful. His appearance made an advocate on his behalf of this managing woman. Mr Jordan fitted Paul with some of the special supporting braces made on the establishment.

"I did him an injustice," the boy said to himself. "He's good-hearted. But for all that, I don't like him."

The truth was, the old man pricked Paul's overweening pride too often.

The work was not arduous at the 'Surgical Appliance Factory'. Paul arrived at eight. The old chief clerk, or Mr Jordan, sent him the letters, and he copied the orders. This was usually done, or well on, before Mr Pappleworth arrived. From the order-book Paul copied orders, on long strips of yellow paper, for the 'spiral' girls downstairs. There would be commands for silk elastic stockings without foot, thread stocking with foot, knee-caps, thigh hose, all kinds of weird, woven, elastic goods that could be produced on spiral machines. These orders Paul took down to the girls of the spiral room.

There were four, five, six or seven of these girls, according to orders. Frances was the overseer. She was a small, sharp, highly-coloured woman, very neat and pleasing in appearance. Her age was between thirty and forty. The other girls were younger. They were all soon friends with Paul, who was very gentle, very courteous to women, frank, gay, ingenuous, and of perfect purity. Paul was pure in fibre, from his great and intimate love with his mother. The girls were ordinary working girls. Yet not one of them ever flicked the least spot of dirt on the boy. Paul liked them all very much, they were all fond of him.*

It came to be that, when he took down the orders in the morning, he sat on one of the high stools and gossiped for a quarter of an hour. Frances was very much an elder sister to him. She condescended to him, keeping just a little stiffness in her manner, as became an overseer so proper. Little by little, she taught Paul how to make the elastic web, how to narrow for the ankle, how to take the spiral machines to pieces, all the ins and outs of her business. He was interested in everything. It was one of his chief attractions, his ready and absorbed interest in things. When there was a grievance between the girls, or between Frances and a girl, Paul was sure to hear both sides. Then he made excuses from one to another, till harmony was restored.

Often, whilst Paul was downstairs in this long workshop, bare dry board everywhere, with little round machines being ground by the girls, who were always neat and pretty, whilst one would often sit like Gretchen at the Spinning Wheel,* winding the pale tinted elastic, blue, or white or heliotrope, into balls, there would come the shrill of the speaking tube whistle. Frances would go to the tube and listen. She would instantly turn and repeat what she had heard, laughing at Paul.

"Is that young Paul down there?"

All the world heard her answer calmly—"He is."

Then she listened again. Turning away from the tube:

"Ask him how much longer he's going to be."

Paul flew upstairs, laughing.

"What yer been doing?" Mr Pappleworth enquired, impatiently.

"Putting stitches on for a knee-cap."

"You'd better go and be a spiral girl straight-off."

Paul did not mind being invited to be a spiral girl. He smiled, continuing his work at the main ledger, or making invoices.

Dinner was from one o'clock to two. Mr Pappleworth lived at the far end of the town, so he was never back till towards three o'clock. All the clerks went home to dinner. At first, Paul used to sit in his corner and eat his meal, then wander round the streets. As the weather grew colder, however, it became the custom for Frances to hot him up, or cook, whatever food he had brought, then he dined down in the spiral room with her and Connie. Connie was a very beautiful girl, like Rossetti's 'Beata Beatrix.'* She was just Paul's age. Her hair was like flamy clouds, her face like apple blossom. An orphan, she lived unwelcome with a poor aunt, since her father, a doctor, had died of consumption. She was a very quiet girl, spoke rarely to anyone. It was her habit to sit and listen to Paul, who was an inveterate chatterer when a woman was near, glancing at him from time to time, and smiling. Miss Jordan, who was an amateur painter, had Connie up at her house in the Park, making Rossettian copies of the girl.*

"If I had time, I would paint you," said Paul.

He knew he could not have made anything like a portrait, but he would have tried. His painting was neglected since he came to Jordan's, as he had only Monday afternoons, and Sundays, at home. He had made very fair progress. His mother had several little studies, quite good, that the boy had made from bits of scenery. Landscape attracted him most, and particularly trees. He would stand for an hour looking at a tree, communing with it.

"I always think you can talk to trees better than to people: they speak low, and never say the things that aren't worth hearing. They don't read newspapers—" he said to his mother, after they had both been bored by a discussion on politics, very tedious.

Still, wherever he went, he watched the trees. To see the lime trees listening to the traffic, flicking the lamps and nestling round the light at night pleased him infinitely.

At two o'clock, Paul usually went up to the finishing room that was lodged, like a studio, just behind his corner of the great warehouse. Not many girls were in this room. The overseer was Fanny, a hunchback. She would sit, a short, hunched little body on a high stool, her long legs reaching nearly to the ground, sewing deftly, and talking a great deal in her contralto, complaining voice. She was very moody, often despondent. Her face was long, heavy, and pale, with a large nose. Her eyes glanced quickly, then shrank away. She had a wealth of beautiful brown hair, which she coiled round her head in thick plaits. Immediately Paul saw her thin, flat arms and nervous fingers sewing swiftly, he felt his heart melt with pity. Fanny came from a poor home, and her people were common. She herself was of the naïve common type, unreserved, easily offended into hate, easily won back into lavish friendship, suspicious, carping, but very generous on appeal. Every day Paul listened to her grievances: Frances had snubbed her, the girls had laughed at her, she had had to do the work over again, and so on. She was indeed very trying to the girls, taking offence at nothing, flaring into rage immediately. Sometimes she would weep bitterly. She was twenty nine years of age.

"But," Paul would say, "Frances didn't mean to be nasty. You know she didn't."

"She thinks I'm dirt," wept Fanny.

"No she doesn't," Paul insisted. "She said at dinner, 'Oh dear, Paul, Fanny *does* make me mad. I told her she never was satisfied without she was ticking and tanning and snagging with somebody. She did get in a tear.* But I wish I hadn't said it: you do say things when you're mad'."

Paul comforted Fanny, and appealed to the other girls.

"She doesn't feel very well, you know," he said to them.

"Oh but it's sickening," they replied. "We don't see why we should put up with it."

Nevertheless, in the afternoon, when Fanny was sitting glum and wrath, wordless, the girls would address her pleasantly:

"Fanny, who do you think I saw— —"

And Fanny was soon mollified, and so glad to have friends again.

Fanny told Paul all her history—which was sad enough—and he told her all about his mother. He was so clever, so gentle, yet so unaccountably passionate; so considerate, yet so vastly contemptuous where other folk were respectful, that he became a hero to Fanny.

"I think you have very beautiful hair," he said to her once. "It must look lovely spread out."

Instantly she took the pins from her hair, and with thin, nervous fingers, pulled the plaits untwined. She shook her hair behind her, so that it fell, a rich glossy brown, all around her stool. There were only two other girls in the finishing room that day.

"My!" said Susan. "You look just like an ordinary girl sitting drying her hair. It hides you."

"Shouldn't I be proud of it," said Louie.

Whereupon Fanny wept uncontrollably, and Paul fled into the dark basement to struggle with his own few difficult tears.

"What did that fool want to say she looked like an ordinary girl because it hid her, for," Paul said fiercely to himself. He never cared for Susan after that.

One other thing Fanny did to please Paul was to sing. She had a very good contralto voice. Her stock of songs was limited, chiefly old music-hall songs, and a few ballads. She sang very well, so that soon it was an acknowledged thing that Paul was given two songs after dinner. If Fanny were in a happy mood she sang 'Oh, Flo, why do you go—'* and so on; if she were sad 'Ye Banks and Braes O Bonnie Doon',* and sometimes, she would not sing at all, nor even speak. Then Paul either made sketches for her, on the yellow order paper, or he told her a story: a sad one, because, when they had all been sad together, she cheered up the quicker. The other girls, also, began to teach her songs, so that there was always sound of singing from the finishing room. Occasionally, Mr Pappleworth would put his head through the door, and looking down at the girls, say:

"Hey there, just a bit quieter, folks'll think we keep cats."

Paul ran up to work at about a quarter to three. Afternoon was usually a slack time. At five o'clock, all the men met at the long table on the ground floor, next the spiral room, for tea. Each had his own little teapot, which one of the girls filled, whilst the baker left rolls. The men were always jolly among themselves: they never quarrelled, like the girls. There were seven clerks down to tea.

"It is like having seven brothers," he told his mother. He talked to them very little. Only to Mr Pappleworth, when they were upstairs, and sometimes to Mr Weston, he chattered freely.

The evening was a very busy time, when the goods had to be got off. From six to eight it was a rush. Paul loved it, it was so exciting. The gases were lighted, the men called from floor to floor, the girls brought the finished goods, there was a sound of voices checking orders, of crackling paper, of dictating of addresses, of the clink of weights on the scales, of the calling to know the price of stamps for foreign parcels. All this slacked off at a quarter to eight, when the postman came in, joking and laughing. He seemed so ruddy and fresh from the air, that to Paul he felt like a piece of the weather entering.

At five to eight, the boy ran off with his basket to the station. From the train he watched the lights of the town, little lamps thick on the hills and melting together in a blaze in the valleys; he saw the great patch of lights at Bulwell, like petals shaken from a bush of fallen stars; he saw the red light of the furnaces,* away off, playing like hot breath on the clouds; then the train ran through the woods and the cuttings. Paul had to walk from Kimberley Station, two miles and a half. Often he was very tired. The road goes up two hills, and down two hills; but Eberwich is much higher than Kimberley. So he would count the lamps that curved and climbed to Hill-top,* saying "Seven more—five more—one more."

From the top of the hills he would look round. In the pitch-dark nights, the villages four or five miles away seemed like brilliant masses of stars. Marlpool and Heanor clothed the far-off, black hill with glittering: between was a great valley-space filled with darkness, traced, violated occasionally by a great train rushing south to London, or north to Scotland. The trains rushed like projectiles level down the darkness, fuming like burning arrows, making the valley roar and clang with their passage. They were gone, and the lights of townlets and villages glittered in silence. Over the hill-top, was a wide, black world of shadow, spaced with only three clusters of lights, three pits that sparkled like three small fairs. The rest was the blackness of hills and woods and water reflecting the night: save that, away back, Underwood scratched the horizon with sparks of lamps. Paul would plunge into the darkness of this side of the hill, gratefully. He knew each stone, each rut in the field paths down to the door. The Breach lay like a big home, silent, very dark. Paul saw the light of the side window, and lifted up his heart. He was indoors, in the snug, bright kitchen, his mother was making his coffee, and smiling, while at once he began to tell her all the news of the day. She shared his life to its smallest, interesting, detail: which was her heart's desire.

Chapter VII

LOVE

At Christmas Paul's wage was raised to ten shillings. Mr Jordan was certainly very good to him. He always paid the lad with four half crowns. Paul was very glad with the money. The first time he gave his mother his wages, he was quite shy. It was four florins. He had walked home on the Saturday night, elated to a seventh heaven of pleasure to have so much silver to give her. It was a quarter past nine: only Mrs Morel was in the kitchen. He set down his dinner basket.

"Look Mother!" and he put the four florins on the table. Mrs Morel picked them up.

"Well," she laughed, "it's no more than we expected, is it."

He did not answer, but gazed at her with beaming eyes while she put the money in her old black purse.

"It makes your purse a lot fatter," he said.

She laughed again, amused by his self-gratification.

"It's a fatness that'll soon go off," she said.

"Will it keep me?" he asked.

"And clothe you, and buy your season ticket—?" she replied. "Eight shillings isn't all the world, my dear boy."

"But it'll help," he pleaded.

"It will pay rent and insurance."

Paul's four florins ceased to look so magnificent.

"Well, I s'll get more later," he persisted.

She laughed, and laughed again at his determination to figure largely in the family finances.

"Come and get your supper," she said, "without bothering about money."

The next morning as he was whistling at his painting, and his mother was cooking, she said, smiling brilliantly:

"It's nice to have you at home again: you are away so late."

That was a rare piece of demonstrative affection from her. Paul hid his face over his painting, and winced. Their love would not brook the least display of affection.

Meanwhile Arthur Morel was growing up. He was a quick, clever boy at school, whilst in appearance he remained the flower of the family, being tall and graceful, with fresh colouring, dark hair, and exquisite deep blue eyes shaded by silky lashes. As the boy grew up, however, his light-hearted carelessness passed away. He was still mercurial, swift and enthusiastic, but sometimes there came a baffled, hesitating expression on his face, and often he flashed into irritable temper; especially if thwarted, he was insolent and fierce.

"This is the fruits of your father's spoiling," Mrs Morel would say to him, after one of his displays. Then the boy would turn in superb contempt from his father.

Walter Morel wore badly. When his pride in himself as a handsome animal died out; when, gradually, he came to know that at home no one respected him, then he ceased to hope for admiration; when he ceased to hope for admiration, he ceased to try for it. His fine manners, his fairly good English, wore off him as silver plating wears away. Then the actual base metal of the man was brought out. He was very vulgar in his personal habits, disgusting the rest of the family. At table, he made them revolt. He was often coarsely, brutally ill-tempered, bullying children and wife and flourishing his fists. As the children passed through the crucial state of adolescence, when they were nervous and susceptible and highly-strung, the behaviour of their father was like venom in their changing blood.

Arthur suffered worst, perhaps. This terrible irritant in the family had not troubled him during his childhood. It attacked him first when he was about eleven years old. About that time, Walter Morel, abandoned to a kind of inner, subtle despair, but fierce in his belief in his own satisfactoriness, was at the pitch of brutality.

"There's not a man in the world tries harder for his family. He does his best for them, and then is treated like a dog. But I'll not stand it—I'll not."

Then he would thump the table till the house rang, and bawl again.

After all, the final lesson of life is honorable self-sacrifice. It was a lesson Walter Morel would never learn. Mrs Morel sacrificed herself utterly, and the children often put away themselves. But Walter Morel would repress not one inclination for the sake of the others. It is true, he was impulsively generous: if by wishing he could have made his wife and his children happy and wealthy, he would have done so; but not at his own expense. He never said, to one of his lusts or his desires "You must die for their sakes." No—always the phrase of his soul was

"They'd stop me doing this; they'd stop me doing that, but I'll show 'em."

He did show them. He became disgusting and dirty in his habits, so that he violated the children's deepest and most delicate instincts. Infinitely vulgar himself, he shocked and vulgarised their young, forming souls.

Arthur Morel was very sensitive, and the most spoiled member of the family. He was not accustomed to submit. As he grew older, the shocks of disgust he received from his father, the insult, and the degradation, gradually inflamed in him not the slow, steady dislike of the other children, but a vivid, quivering inflammation of hate.

William Morel remained in the office, where he did well. He brought his mother a sovereign a week by the time he was eighteen. Annie Morel, who grew up quiet, very much like Paul, without the boy's perspicacity, was put to dressmaking. She worked very earnestly, so that at sixteen she brought in ten shillings per week. Then there was Paul's eight a little later, so that Mrs Morel was fairly well off. Arthur, the darling of the family, even Mrs Morel's darling—Paul was too much to her to be that—was sent to a private school when he was eleven. At the age of twelve, he won a scholarship for the High School at Nottingham.*
Mrs Morel was very proud. The boy, with refined instincts, acquired a gentlemanly demeanour quickly. To be a gentleman was a passion with him. Consequently his father was to him the gall of bitterness, so that soon there was antagonism between the two, a writhing, tortured contempt on the boy's part, and brutal resentment on the side of the man. In his heart, Mr Morel was proud of the child: but he knew the lad's flickering, fiery nature, volatile and changeable, so he was not abashed by him. The father had always faltered before Paul, and was considerate of him, if of anyone.*

Thus, when the financial tension was relieved for a time from Mrs Morel, the stress of family discord became greater. Paul escaped a great deal, being away so much. William left home when he was twenty, to go to a more lucrative post in London. Always he seemed to be doing very well. He was passionately attached to his mother; but it now took all his resources to keep himself. His money was sadly missed. However, Mrs Morel contrived to keep up the new condition.

The family had moved from the Breach to a better house newly built on the hill-top* a furlong away, a house which looked over the chimneys of their old home, at a great sweeping horizon, blue on the left with the last spurs of the Pennine Chain. Paul loved the immense sky of the

129

hill-house. At evening he would sit under the ash-tree in the field before the home, and watch the immense flamboyant sunsets silently change their vast array.

He had Sunday and Monday evenings at home. Monday was a half holiday. It was his custom sometimes to visit Mr Revell, sometimes Mrs Staynes and Miriam on this afternoon. He stayed with his mother till tea-time, when his father would be coming home to dislocate the harmony; then he went out on his visit, returning to be with his mother again about seven o'clock. Sometimes he spent the evening with Alec.

It happened, however, that important changes took place among Paul's friends as well as home. Alec went into the coal-mine, but he continued his painting all the same: it was a means of vaunting himself; he was regarded as a prodigy. Paul painted very little, having no time. Then, when Miriam was fourteen, and Paul fifteen years old, Mrs Staynes died. Six months afterwards Miss May married Mr Revell. The poor gentleman had got very lonely, even despondent. He clung to Miss May for support. Mrs Morel, the mother of three active, adventurous sons, wearied of the helplessness of the wistful parson. She tried to shake him into activity, and succeeded only in wounding him. The poor fellow became afraid of her, whom he loved with reverence. He would hesitate on the threshold, to know if he were welcome, and it was quite pitiful to see his eyes wistfully, timorously watching her. She was not sorry when Miss May married him.

Mrs Staynes was dead, Mr Staynes was, after a decorous interval, paying attentions to a spinster who lived in a pretty cottage down Church Street. Miss May married Mr Revell. She was too wise to ask to be allowed to take Miriam with her. The child was left at home with the father, whom she troubled by her forlorn appearance. After a while, Mrs Revell asked Miriam to visit her in her cottage at Morven. Miriam went, and stayed, much to her joy, and to the joy of the Revells.

Mr Revell's health, however, did not improve. He began to waste, so that it was feared he was in consumption. His wife decided to move to a roomy cottage that stood high on the hill near Willey Woods, in a corner that was thick with pine trees. This was when Miriam was fifteen, and Paul sixteen years of age. Paul had continued to visit his old tutor, though irregularly. He had also become a close friend of Miriam. But the removal to Herod's Cottage,* three miles from the Breach, interrupted these visits for some time, until, one spring, Miss May begged Mrs Morel to journey so far. Mrs Morel knew that Paul would enjoy such an excursion, so she proposed to him, that, the next afternoon of his holiday, they should go together. Paul was delighted.

Mother and son set off together. They passed Morven colliery, over the hill to the side of Nethermere, and near High Close house,* left the high-road and entered wild, hilly meadows. There was scarcely any track. Paul was delighted. These meadows, never mown, whose lowest edges ran down to the lake, were haunted by peewits and waterfowl. Higher up, a few Scotch cattle* stood and stared at the invaders. The path was no more than a rabbit-track. Mrs Morel and her son stood looking round. Below was the long blue lake, backed by a great wood, in which hid one house called Woodside. The wood dropped towards the upper end of the water, so that, through the great loop of opening, Eberwich could be seen afar off, its great squares leaning on the side of the hill making it look like a fortified or a barracks town, while its church tower and a chapel spire of grey stone gave it some nobility. Very far and blue at the back, rose hills higher than the high, dwarfed hill of Eberwich. Paul and his mother were delighted. They were out on an adventure together again, this time in the midst of most beautiful, lonely country. It was the happiest day of Paul's life. They espied a white gate in the wood's edge before them, and soon were in a broad green alley, old oak wood dipping down and up on the left hand, thick plantation of firs and birch trees on the right. In the path, purple self-heal stood stiff in ranks among the lush grass. There was a scent of wood-ruff, that they call new-mown-hay, and down the oak glade the blue-bells stood in pools of blue among the new green of hazels and the rich brown of the loam. Paul was in an ecstasy.

"Look mother! You see that ash-trunk—shouldn't I love to get it, out of the ultramarine of those blue-bells. It's a perfect grey, almost like flesh."

His mother recognised the artist's enthusiasm, and her heart was elated with pride.

They climbed the stile at the end of the path. To their left was still a wall of ancient oak wood: to the right, naked, rounded fields that dipped away-off down to a valley. Across, in the distance, were hills crested with woodlands. In front, two fields away, was a low heap of brilliant red farm buildings. Paul led his mother there, along the wood's edge. Flush with the wood was the orchard where the apple blossom was falling on the golden-coloured grindstone. At the end of the orchard was the farm yard. The pond was under the oak trees of the wood. On the other side of the yard, fronting the sun, was a long red line of buildings: cowsheds, stables, Herod's farm, and Herod's Cottage, all in one line. The farm was a small one. It was asleep in the sunshine. But there, in front of the cottage, dozing or dreaming in an invalid chair that stood on the grass before his door, was Mr Revell. At the foot of the garden, tall and threatening, rose the pine-trees.

"How gloomy they are," Paul thought, "and ill-fated, like Birnam Wood* on one's doorstep! They are almost like blood in their bodies, and for the rest they are black as if they hid their faces in a mantle. Yet the house shines in the sun like a marigold. How they front one another, the gay, bright little house, and the black wood sinister as fate."

Mr Revell rose slowly and doubtfully. He had gone thin, but still his jowl was heavy. He cocked his brows, smiling in his old manner as of a bird that listens and is uncertain.

"Is it really you?" he asked.

"It is really me," Mrs Morel laughed. "But it is not you in so much reality, for you're only half yourself."

She pressed his hand, smiling upon him. He turned away, flushing. Paul looked at his mother, and saw in her smile that she was much moved.

"We are so happy up here," the sick man said.

Miss May came out, delighted to see her friend. Paul wandered curiously indoors.

He found himself in a red-tiled kitchen that was all corners. It was very small, furnished only with a table a sofa, and some chairs. The stairs were taken out of the room, so that there was a recess at the back, under a round archway, and in this recess, at a let-down table, a girl was cutting bread and butter. Everything seemed very rosy, very sunny, clean, and silent. But Paul was afraid of the country girl who was cutting bread and butter.

He turned, saw to his surprise that, behind the pushed-open outer door, was another doorway, which was three-parts obliterated every time one opened the kitchen door. Through the space remaining, Paul could see into the next room. It was a step higher than the kitchen, was long, having two windows facing the wood. Through these two white framed windows the sunlight streamed upon a piano, a dark-stained floor, and on Miriam, who stood with her arm on the sill of the far window, as if she had been looking out, though now she was turned to Paul. Her face was startled, her mouth open, her dark blue eyes dilated as if she were almost afraid of the youth. She stood in the blaze of sunlight, her richly coloured face and her curls like soft black flowers lit up. Her eyes were watching Paul as if she were afraid of him, and loved to be afraid. The boy felt himself start. He felt a warmth reach deep in him, as if, flowerlike, he had just opened to the sun. His blue eyes opened and danced with a laughing pride of power. Miriam trembled and was dazed as if his eyes were lightning, that made her half lose consciousness.

"Miriam!" he said, in wonder and pride.

She did not answer, but looked at him instead, with large pleading eyes. Her hands trembled.

"I never thought I should see you," he said, as if something wonderful had taken place.

"No," she replied, in a low, long note. She had a rarely musical voice. She too was breathless with wonder: and she was afraid.

He came forward. He was seventeen years old, slim, but, it seemed to Miriam, full of force as an electric wire. She trembled and drew away as he touched her in leaning on the window-sill beside her. He looked through the small panes into the splendid silence of sunlight that stood between the house and the wall of woodland, saw his mother smiling at Mr Revell as Mrs Revell teased her husband. Mrs Morel was delicately, gracefully made. Her brown hair was turning grey, but her face still was fair in its complexion, and her smile was wonderfully winsome. Instantly, Paul's love for her, that was born of pain, leaped in his breast.

"She does think it's beautiful up here," he said. "I wish she could live here, as well."

Miriam looked swiftly at him. He was watching his mother with such grave eyes of love that the girl felt a sudden tightening at her heart.

"I wish she could," she added.

But Paul took no notice. He was dreaming of what he should do for his mother. Meanwhile he felt more peaceful and happy than he had ever been, in the sunshine, at the window with Miriam, watching his mother who was smiling and looking with delight at the woods and flowers.

Presently Mrs Morel entered the house.

"Why Miriam, you do look well! You will be in your element here, with the wood and the fields."

Miriam was very nervous. Mrs Morel seemed to her so capable, so managing.

"Isn't it lovely!" she exclaimed, with a thrill in her voice. Mrs Morel objected to the thrill.

"It is very pleasant," the other replied, rather coldly, seeming to disapprove of the girl's raptures.

Paul was delighted with the situation of the cottage. It was so wild and obscure. All week long he remembered the woods where he had walked with his mother, and the cherry trees that waved white behind the house. Next Monday he went again, this time without his mother, for whom the distance was too great. Miriam took him over the farm that adjoined the cottage. Paul was eager to sketch the cattle, and the fowls: he sat on the cart shafts working swiftly, while Miriam stood near. All the time he worked he whistled low.

"Why do you whistle?" she asked

"I don't know—perhaps because I feel happy."

He glanced up at her and laughed. He had a way of laughing with his blue eyes, so that she felt herself thrill. She hung her head, nervously plucking at a straw that lay on the ground.

"But," she said, "what do you whistle?"

"Anything," he answered, drawing assiduously.

Then he told her about Fanny, who taught him songs. Miriam felt she could score a point. She trembled, hid her face, and asked:

"Why don't you whistle Schubert's songs?"

"I only know 'Du bist wie eine Blume',"* he replied wistfully.

"I know a lot," she said.

"Sing me what you like best then," he said, resting from his drawing, to watch her with serious eyes. She was startled, laughed in great trepidation, shook her head so that her curls danced, then hid her face.

"But," he said, wondering, "anything dare sing. Listen! And I will draw for you. Look, I can't make this hen's walk look right. What shall I do to it? Isn't it awful?"

She shook her head again in confusion. To her, the hen he had drawn was perfect.

"I think it's ever so good," she murmured.

He looked up at her with a flash of laughter.

"Do you?" he said. "Well, it isn't! See—" He pointed exactly what was wrong. She was astonished at the artist's insight.

"There!" he said. "I do things all wrong, because I can't do them any better, and I let you see. Now sing to me, and teach me."

She cleared her throat, bowing her small head. She was terribly afraid, and she trembled, but at that instant she was willing to sacrifice a great deal of herself for him. He looked at her keenly, then continued his drawing, making quick, sharp lines as if disappointed. The sight of his hand, that was shapely and very decisive in its movement, urged her.

"He thinks I am stupid," she said to herself. "He would do it for me. He wouldn't be afraid of *me* laughing at *him*."

She cleared her throat, turned away from him, and began to sing. Her voice was low, trembling, and had a crooning, sad note, as if she were lonely. Paul stopped drawing. He looked at her swiftly, feeling a sadness start at the sound of her. She held her face averted as she sang. Her profile was beautiful, her lips moved with hesitancy, she seemed submissive, and sad, as one who was destined to lose in life. Paul saw her rather red hands gripped till the knuckles stood out white. The tears almost came to his eyes. She seemed like one of those haunted, wistful angels that have taken refuge in heaven. Paul turned quietly away, continued his drawing in slow, thoughtful strokes. When she had finished:

"You are so different from Fanny," he said slowly.

"Why?" she whispered.

"You haven't, no, not a bit of roughness. You're like the wind that goes looking for something at night."

She laughed within herself—why, she knew not.

"Did you like the tune?" she struggled to say.

He would have her teach it to him, phrase by phrase.

Music was Miriam's pull over Paul. The two wandered out in the open till it grew dark. Then, in the low, long parlour, she lit the candles on the piano and played to the lad. Her touch was never decisive: she never showed mastery of a piece.

"You make me think," Paul said, "of a moth fluttering at a light, when you play music."

Nevertheless, it was from her he learned to understand that music had a meaning. And two people who keep company in an atmosphere of music arrive at a subtle intimacy.

It was the place, he thought, that charmed him. But when he arrived one day and found Miriam gone in the farmer's gig to Nottingham, he was vastly disappointed. In the second spring of their new acquaintance, it became his habit to walk up to the Cottage every Monday afternoon. All morning long, in Nottingham, he would watch the weather, because if it should rain his mother was angry at the thought of his tramping the three long miles. But when it was fine, he ran gaily through the streets of the town. Mentally, he performed the journey beforehand. "There's the train, through the tunnels and over the viaducts—then uphill and through Eberwich, everybody asleep in the sun—then dinner—then down-hill to Nethermere, and over the rough meadows. Perhaps she will meet me at the wood-gate." As he ran into the dark cave of a station his spirit was greeting Miriam by the wood fence, out of sight of any house.

He was eighteen years, and she seventeen, when their intimacy was at its perfection. Paul was late developing towards physical virility. He was always light, very slender and pale, yet extraordinarily active. He went incessantly in search of things. At eighteen the lad was perfectly chaste. Miriam, for her part, was one of those spiritual women whose passion issues as a prayer, becomes a religious service, rather than a carnal thing. She was born to be a nun: the flesh was too violent and shocking a thing for her. Nevertheless she wanted him to kiss her; she often ached for him to kiss her with a long, sweet kiss, a kiss unsullied by desire. And at that time, he did not want to kiss anyone, in love, save his mother. Many a light, flying kiss he gave to the girls at Jordan's: but he never touched Miriam with his lips, feeling too deeply towards her, to kiss her lightly, and unable to meet her mouth in love. When he kissed his mother, it was as if his heart rose and filled him with the strong blood of love, so that his kiss was close and rare and sacred. He kissed other girls just as he touched flowers with his fingers, a thing he liked to do. So long as Miriam did not touch him, he was admirable towards her.

It was her habit to roam the woods, the warren, the meadows, to find the beautiful bits for him. This was her service. Through the week she was uplifted if she had discovered some new, rare charm, that she saved for him, so he might kindle it for her.

In the very early spring, she had come upon a fine treasure. Monday broke fair and blue, with a quiet wind. Far away, over the great iron valley, the atmosphere was blackened heliotrope, but shiny, suggesting gun metal. And right deep in this distance, far-off full-blown clouds hung like gold roses, still, poised at eye-level, but beyond the ordinary borders, in another, darker atmosphere. From these suspended roses steeped in gloom, came a procession of clouds, purplish gold, pale lavender, and then, round close about, clouds like masses of white lilac blown from the bough and floating under the bright blue air. Miriam stood and worshipped before this vast sky. She was through the wood and at the wood gate, on the hill, with the valley opening to the heart of the midlands. She knew she was half an hour too soon, so she had leisure to exult in the beautiful country. Nethermere stretched shining in changing colours, blue and white, below the meadow and the tree clumps. Miriam laughed as if she performed an altar ritual, as she swung along the path.

Paul was under the oak trees, between the oaks and the willows of the water's edge, when he saw her coming. She wore a crimson tam-o-shanter, and walked with a long, ecstatic stride, bending her head as if she exulted and would fain not show it. Being short-sighted, she did not perceive him till she stood on the turf bridge among the rushes. Then her heart leapt, and she waited.

Paul did not greet her save by raising his cap. His eyes were shining: he was alive with happiness.

"Aren't I early!" he said.

She dilated her magnificent eyes in joy as she looked at him. At this time, Miriam was ruddy and wild. She had naturally a rapturous look. They talked a great deal by direct looks into each other's eyes. As they walked together along the narrow path that was made only by the rabbits and by Paul, they started naturally into conversation.

"I've brought you *Jane Eyre*," he said.

It was the custom for him to supply her with books.

"I bet you it's the best novel you've ever read," he added.

"Ay!" she said, wondering, and glad.

"I think," he said, "that I shan't fall in love till I'm about forty—like Rochester."*

"No?" she said.

"I don't believe I shall. I *like* heaps of women—all those at Jordan's—oh ever so much. But I shan't fall *in love*, not for ages and ages—not till I'm really old and getting thick—you know—till you feel stable and solid."

She looked at him and laughed in her heart: when would he be stable and solid? Yet he puzzled her.

"I shouldn't wonder," he said, "if I never married."

"Why not?" she said.

"I don't know. I feel as if I could live by myself; and I don't think I should worry about comfort. Lots of men marry for comfort. I could do without it—I believe I could do without being married. You only marry because you'll be all-in-all, life, and death and God and everything, to your family—or you think you will be. I don't care whether I'm indispensable or not—"

He spoke in such perfect good faith and innocence—he was so ridiculously naive, that Miriam took him seriously: it might be unconscious prophecy, she thought.

"Perhaps so," she assented, bowing her head. But in her heart of hearts she said: "How blind he is—how blind he is."

"I don't know," he continued—"when I look at married folks—at my mother—marriage seems like a millstone round your own neck, and round somebody else's, even the children's."

Miriam assented, moodily biting her forefinger. He often spoke in this strain, quite unconscious in his cruelty, and perfectly sincere. He was very egotistic, therefore very naive, too egotistic to be vain.

They came to the wood-gate. He helped her over the fence, laughing because she gripped his hands so tight. She sprang beside him, rather heavily, laughing in a peculiar low fashion; she had so nearly fallen on his breast. He was quite oblivious.

"I never knew anybody more excitable than you are," he said. "You are purely emotional. Emotion sweeps you backwards and forwards, and you can no more help it than the sea can help swinging and fuming about, always unsteady.—I can get an ice footing out of my brain any time, sure as rock."

It was the remarkable truth of these observations, which he flung off in natural conversation with her, that so fascinated her and made her fear him. Yet she was continually angry with him. He was so blind with his heart, if perhaps wonderfully 'seeing' with his brain. At once he could analyse and perceive her emotional character, but he could not understand or sympathise with the emotion itself. He never *understood* how she loved him: his eye was too quick and critical.

"Come," she said, rather muted, "Come this way."

He was going up the broad path towards the cottage. Divining that she wanted to keep him all to herself, he smiled rather mockingly and ironically.

"Why?" he asked.

"Come—I want to show you—"

In an instant he was with her, so that she had no need to name her treasure. They were between the plantation of fir-trees and the hedge, in a broad rough road of grass. It was early spring: the grey-green rosettes of honeysuckle danced, the elder buds were opening blackly on the pale, flesh-like wood. Turning a corner, Paul sniffed the air.

"Ah," he said—"Scent! Nearly like Custard Powder!" He sniffed again. "It's lovely and rich—but—not quite subtle enough—sort of fla-grant, common scent. But I like it, it scents the sunshine."

They went on round the corner, where was a magnificent tree of yellow willow-catkins. At a distance it looked like a great pale puff of yellow dust hanging—as smoke hangs over a gun—from the black edge of the wood, towards the sun and space of the down-hill meadow.

"Ah lovely!" cried Paul, arrested.

It was for these sudden passionate acclamations that Miriam loved him. He was silent for a few minutes. Then he advanced, much elated.

"Now I'll bet you, that's a 'Passover', I mean a 'Tabernacles' remembrance: I'll bet you, when God appeared in a fiery bush to Moses,* it was just like that. What sort of a scent do you think the fiery bush had?"

He demanded an answer with startling rapidity. Miriam shook her head, trembling, half with joy, half in fear: she was utterly incoherent, incapable of thought, but simply flushing and waving with emotions.

"*It* would have a harshish, rather cruel scent that made you afraid: and this has a tang of it. Hark—there's some bees in among the yellow. You might say the bush was talking. By Jove, Miriam, what if I was Moses and you Rebecca."*

The incongruity of the names puzzled Miriam: and Paul was usually accurate. But he was looking at her with daring brilliant eyes, and she was trembling.

"Yes, it is beautiful," she murmured with a choked throat.

Feeling giddy, she went near to him, leaned slightly against his shoulder. That was delicious, and he did not move away. She knew she was making a mistake, yet she could not refrain from timidly sliding her hand into his arm. He drew away, almost unconscious: his instinct was to keep himself alone, intact. This is the instinct of a man in love, when he is away from the beloved. Miriam noted with bitterness the withdrawal, whilst he was serenely unconscious. So that, whilst the harmony between them seemed to him, save for indistinct moments, perfect, for her there was always a discord and a sense of strife.

"Shall we get some?" he asked her, glancing from the bush. She recognised his delicate scruple in violating the tree, and loved him for it. Nevertheless she wanted some of the blossomy dust balls: she wanted it close, to touch, to bury her face amongst, to caress and caress as if she would eat it, as if she would absorb it, the radiant stuff. She looked across at him, quickly lifted her eyelids in daring, and nodded—as if she incited him to a wrong-doing for her. Paul leaped, straight and light as a jet of water. He caught the bough, bringing the tree down with him. The bees hummed louder in anger, a fine, wrathful mist sprang into the sunshine, the blooming yellow buds danced in soft myriads just over Miriam's face. She laughed low in the fulness of her heart, caught the willow boughs against her cheek, in a passionate caress. Paul was rather startled by her low, passionate, caressing laugh. It made him wince and shrink. He quickly scanned over the bough, selected the thickest sprays

139

of soft yellow, and broke them off for her. She plucked at random, gathered with difficulty where she could, her own bouquet.

"Enough?" he asked.

She looked at him. She was not nearly satisfied. Herself, she could have torn down the tree in her love of it, in her passion to possess it. Her glance at Paul was half-pleading.

"Enough!" he said. "It's a shame to break it."

This detached, artist's judgement which he exercised so often hurt her.

"He would not break any more for me—he would not even let *me* break any more," she said to herself, for Paul had let go the bough, and it swung out of reach.

He had no idea that she was offended. To him, all things had their rights, and Miriam was to be hurt rather than the tree, because she was responsible. Notwithstanding he smiled at her very gently as she stood, just a bit disconsolate under the blooming, golden tree.

"Let me look," she said, raising his bouquet which he held forgotten. She put their two bunches of yellow palm side by side. His was full and soft and unified, the lowest balls just ripe, standing out with sulphur-tipped silk, the upper balls having beads of ruddy-gold set in their fine velvet. It was a handsome, rich bunch. Hers was wild and twiggy, very uneven, the sprays ragged in bloom, the balls often over-ripe, having long, shrivelled filaments like damp hairs. It was she who loved to make this comparison so disparaging to herself. He would rather the difference had gone unnoticed.

"You should always be careful, when you're gathering flowers, not to have even one, even one lowest, shrivelled. One withered bit makes the whole rest look blowsy."*

He said this merely, in a quiet voice, then sunk his bunch. She, however, drew it back beside her own, glorying in the discrepancy.

"What a difference!" she said.

"Ay," he laughed. "Even when we are not conscious of it, I am selective and critical, and you're blind emotional."

She laughed, dropped his hand, not liking his explanation.

So the summer went on. The wind-flowers came on the highest slopes of the wood. There, among the fallen trees and the great rough stones, stretches of wood anemones lay white flecked on a level green, reminding one of white crow-foot floating in open bubbles on a pond. It was very cold. Paul stood near the top end of the wood, looking north over the table land, beyond the wide mow-closes of chill, intense green, to the mining village and the church that stood out stark. The wind broke into the wood and pressed upon the anemones, that undulated under it like virgins it raped. Paul sniffed their tiny scent, which reminded him of apple-blossom petals, when you pick up a handful of blown fragments, pink and white.

"I sometimes think," he said, as he stood gazing from the cosy wood out over the rain-cold, green-and-grey world, "that it is so much easier to die young, like the ladysmocks," (wood anemones are so called in the midlands) "than to be forced through a torment of green fruiting, and then ripening to fall, like may-blossom, for instance, and its haws.—Do you know, Miriam, I often dread growing up. I do. I am so young, aren't I?"

He turned to her with a bright, self-mocking smile. In spite of himself and his portentous talking, he *was* exceedingly young, as the woman, his junior, well knew.

"You are," she asserted with earnestness.

"But I don't care—I'm as wise as most old folks," he declared. Whereat she smiled to herself. It was such youthful presumption on his part.

The blue-bells arrived. Paul, coming one Monday early in May, could scarcely understand how it had happened.

"You'd think," he said, "that they'd flown and settled like a swarm of blue locusts—or butterflies, if you like. But no!—there they are, erect and rooted and shaking with blue."

The wealth of colour moved him to a passion. He thought the very top of life was on the brim of the hill, very high, where a wide path slipped downwards, and the hazels were thin. There, like a living shifting flock were the blue bells, a dense blue deposit that almost flamed on the clear broad path, that sunk and stretched farther and lower under the hazels and oaks till Paul believed they dripped, like a Greek ocean, over the edge of the world.* He was too much moved to speak. Miriam watched his face, as he stood, upright, with open lips and eyes, seeming in a wonder. She thought he looked as if he had a vision, and she humbled herself before him, leaving him alone.

Later, he must make a painting. The sketch succeeded very well, conveying some of the rapt, splendid stillness of the blue wood.

"I must show it my mother," he said, as the sunlight faded and he surveyed his work. "My mother will like it—she'll perhaps say it's too blue, but she'll like it, I know she will. I must take it to my mother."

On the Sunday he succeeded in bringing his mother to see the wood. Then he delighted in her delight. He watched her keenly to see if she saw: he pointed out this beauty and that, with artistic discrimination.

Mrs Morel felt the tears in her eyes—she thanked God for the scene. Paul saw her, and clenched his fists, and stood still.

"She loves it—she'll not be tired—she'll not feel old at all—she'll feel as young as me—she loves it," his heart repeated.

He no longer revelled in his own delight. His joy was in his mother's joy.

The bluebells faded out, the forget me-nots, like fine broken spray flew palely along the paths, and in the wood bottoms shone like luminous mist rising from among the felled trees, whose stumps put forth bronze-leaved, tragic shoots. Paul and Miriam made bouquets, which she contrasted.

"I think I am cruel," he said. "I don't care a bit about the bluebells. I loved them while they were here—but they're gone, and I don't need them any more. I don't care that they're gone."

"I wish they were here yet," said Miriam, in her deep, earnest tones.

"Well," he said, "if you can extract the meaning of things in the once while they're here—they're barren flowers after. I'm like a bee: if I visit a flower once, I explore it, and get all I want out of it, then I've done with it."

"Yes, you *are* like that," Miriam very sadly assented. It did not occur to her to answer, "Yes, but the flowers come next year with new honey, and people who are living and growing blossom afresh with new meaning every day."

She, instead, took it to herself that when he had explored her and extracted her flavor he would fling her aside uncared-for.

"I loved the bluebells," he said. "And loving them got out of them their secret—then they're not interesting any more. They can go."

And she had not the wit to remind him of Lord Tennyson's famous dictum,* nor the presence of mind to clip his vanity by telling him that one secret discovered filled him up and made him insensible to the five million remaining. No. She accepted him, and saw the time when she was discarded.

The blue flowers all drifted away, then, in the clearing where the trees had been felled, there appeared a cloudy, pink wrack of rose campions, very startling as seen issuing from the sombre brownish deeps of the wood. The wood was silent and fruiting: the rosy misty heaps of campion mounted in soft puffs of pink, warm, almost like a flush of 'pudeur'.* Paul felt the secret shame of things.

"I don't care for the wood now," he said. "There is a sense of nakedness about it, and swollenness, as if it were with young. It makes you feel queer."

Miriam was startled, shocked, and thrilled. Paul led her out. They waded through the high pink froth of the campion wrack, towards the other, south-west gate of the wood. There the field was wild and dotted with gorse. Still a few gorse blossoms smelled of flesh and hot oranges. The louse-wort was pink in the turf, the milk worts purple; there came with the wind a scent of wild thyme. In the hedges the fox gloves waited and exposed themselves like harlots.

Paul lay down in the hot evening, on the dry short grass. He talked very little. What he said was low in the throat. He lay and watched the flaming sun go down, watched a snipe over-head fly round in immense, flickering circles, listened to its complaint. He felt ironical: his blood was turning thick and red. The bird cry-crying overhead irritated, even maddened him.

"What do you look so downcast about," he said roughly to Miriam. She was downcast because he took no notice of her and was harsh.

"I didn't know I did look downcast," she said.

"You look like a miserable beggar waiting through eternity at the door of heaven," he said brutally.

"I don't know why," she said coldly.

"Good Lord—I can't bear plaintive folk. I like wilful folk who have their fling, and bruise the face of those that deny 'em."

Miriam bowed her head and said nothing.

"Pitiful, plaintive, pleading folk," he said, "make you feel cruel. You feel as if you'd put your foot on their throats for the horrid pleasure of hurting them."

His eye was dark, dancing cruelly, his lips curved in almost savage irony.

"What is the matter with you tonight," she said, very low, trying to draw near and soften him. He kept sharply away, and said cruelly:

"Why should it always be *me* there's something the matter with. Hark at that blooming bird up there cheep-cheeping as if it would weary the very stars out, whining for something it can't get. Why ask what's the matter with *me*? Isn't it such-like and it, that are a-matter."

"And I thought it would be so beautiful, this evening, the sunsets being so rich," she said piteously.

"Pah!" he retorted brutally. "What do you mean by beautiful!—a bloody red sun tramping and trampling something to death, a bird with a snake—its bill looks just like a snake—hanging from its neck— a black sulky wood, gorse like hate, and a marsh raw with passion— pah!"

She could make nothing of him: he could make nothing of himself; they were merely at a deadlock when he felt his blood reddening and thickening and growing hot.

For his mother began to grow jealous of Miriam. At first she said nothing, yet he felt her displeasure. He became faltering. If, on Sunday afternoon, he went out to meet the girl, he said only to his mother.

"I'm going a walk, mother. I may as well, mayn't I—I don't get out very much—?"

"No, you don't get out very much," his mother merely assented. She divined in an instant, by his rather appealing tone, what was his errand, and she was hurt. But it was a point of delicacy not to know what he did not wish her to know: such was the woman's fine flattery of the lad she loved. Paul, nevertheless, felt contrition as he went along the road. Mrs Morel did not speak to him about Miriam. He was himself slightly contemptuous when he spoke of the girl in his mother's hearing, and if Miriam and Mrs Morel were both present, then Paul was winsome with his mother, cold, almost insulting in his studied neglect of the maid, who could not help following him with great, sad, appealing looks of love. Miriam's hands always began to tremble when she was with Paul and his mother: they both seemed so united against her, and so cruel.

Paul loved to talk about books and life and philosophy and religion, with Miriam. Till he was eighteen he had developed entirely under his mother's influence. But now he began to assert his own individuality. He had to thresh out his own pulse of truth, he would be no more fed by hand. Miriam was invaluable. She was the switch which connected Paul with the current of life, and set concepts, thoughts, ideas flowing through him in a prolific and conscious stream. Paul's mother, whom he loved, could never have this value to him. It needed someone soft, unformed, subservient, who would be a medium to him rather than a force directing him. Miriam was this medium, and a wonderful medium.

"Nobody, nothing can make me think, and see things, and say brilliant things, like you. You are really like a touch-stone to me. I'm dumb and stupid and I can't understand things. Then you come, or I think of you, and things seem to throng in my brain, and I teem with living—at least, with being. With you, I begin wonderfully 'To be'. 'To be or not to be—'* that is to have you to talk to or not to have you."

Paul had touches of inspiration. At eighteen, with Miriam, he occasionally said profound things. And, having a rare psychic energy, he was ceaselessly active in drawing life within his net, in sifting it, sifting it down, to store his soul with understanding. His untiring activity frightened Miriam.

"Will you never *rest* with me?" she asked pathetically.

"Rest?—why rest? You might as well be dead. I can rest while I'm at Jordan's, and in the train—"

This was by no means Miriam's idea of rest. She dreamed of exquisite spaces of silence, when they would sit cheek to cheek and watch the winter coals shift red in the fire.

But the dumb, unconscious part of Paul was his mother's. He never entirely loved Miriam. It is significant that, whilst he was with the girl, he was ceaselessly active, speculative, analytic; that, if he were silent, Miriam felt as if she had lost him. Often, when he walked without speaking, or sat on the grass beside her, silent for a long time, she asked, in low, timid tones: "What are you thinking about?"

Then he laughed shortly, answering "Nothing."

Or again, she would say: "Why are you sad this evening?"

"Am I sad?" he answered. "Eh well, I'll be gay."

Which answer hurt Miriam inexpressibly. There was part of him which for years she struggled to obtain, and could not.

On the other hand, Paul grew more and more silent with his mother. Yet these silences lacked nothing: there was the same sense of harmony that had always existed between them. When Paul, as a child, had slept with his mother, he had felt that that was rest as perfect as it could be. And still, although there was a growing difference between them, they rested together. Paul yearned for his mother when he was tired. He was delighted that he could get up in the morning and have only his mother with him, before he set out to work. In his adolescence he was irritable, shrinking. To have to talk to his father or to Annie or to Arthur was a disagreeable struggle, at half past six in the morning, whilst to be silent towards them was uncomfortable, almost unbearable. With his mother alone he felt perfectly at ease, in harmony. They rested together during their silences, which is a test of love. In his silences with Miriam, there was always some reticence on his part, and a sense of loneliness on either side.

Nevertheless, the growing intimacy between Paul and Miriam caused an occasional strain between Mrs Morel and her son. To avoid wounding his mother, Paul hid from her many things. He had a passion for writing letters to Miriam, Miriam had a passion for writing letters to him. But Paul felt his mother's hurt as he opened the envelopes in her presence.

It was agreed that Miriam should always address him at Jordan's in Nottingham. This was Paul's first measure of secrecy.

Miriam occasionally came down to see Paul when he happened to have an early evening, which was sometimes on Friday, when his mother was always out at the little market.

> "Jordan's Surgical Appliance Factory
> Nottingham
> Valentine's Day.

Dear Miriam,

I was expecting a letter this morning. There was such a heap of correspondence, but never your narrow writing. On such a day, too, to be disappointed. No wonder the sun came up with a splendid rush, only to be beaten back by clouds. I watched it from the train.

You made a fatal mistake in not coming on Friday. I said to myself 'If Miriam is wise, she'll come tonight.' I was alone—we might have had a lovely conversation—and I should have been so nice for you. You hesitated—and were lost. 'N'importe.'*

I fetched your book-shelves in the driving rain: walked from Kimberley with them. At the time when the drops were rattling on the brown paper covering, they were beating the heart out of you with their tattoos on your umbrella. You were walking from Selston, saying you would never be able to come down, I was coming from Kimberley saying 'Perhaps she'll venture, whether or not.'

Ah well—n'importe!

Your letter was much enjoyed; you really improve—it is almost like reading a revised of myself,* when I peruse a letter from you. Really, I think you develop fast—and with all the quaint self-contradictions of a woman. Besides, you have none of my inflatus, bombast, affectation. I've told you you'll be an authoress yet—oui, vraiment—*

I shall come on Monday—etc."

It will be seen that Paul was a bit of a prig, and women will be inclined to smile pityingly on him. He was nineteen at this time.

It was in this period that Paul began to examine the religion in which he had been brought up. He was, through his mother, of Puritan descent. His mother adhered rigidly to the Independent* faith. Paul, however, with his restless critical soul, could not leave his faith intact. He began round the borders of dogma.

Miriam, for her part, was mediaeval in temperament rather than modern. She was fervent, rhapsodic, what is called intensely spiritual. It was a thousand pities that Paul ever started to batter at her creed.

For him, Nonconformist Christianity as his mother accepted it was a stiff, narrow thing which would not fit his life. Somehow or other, the true Christianity was walled-in, like a monastery, to keep out life. Paul wanted to get out of the four high walls of orthodox, ordinary dogmatic Christianity, and the only way was to break and tear a breach in the enclosure. This he proceeded to do, stimulated towards truth by Miriam. But alas, for her, there was sufficient truth within the high enclosure of uncritical Christianity. She did not mind whether things fitted-in or not. She scarcely knew the world at all, scarcely knew life, to measure it by her beliefs, or to measure her beliefs by the great human experience. It was enough that the security of established religion soothed her, fostered her happiness. And Paul began to destroy her security. She cried out, she was afraid, she warned him.

He wrote in reply to one of her letters, where she had been in trouble because she thought he had hinted that she was a coward:

> "Jordan's—Nottingham
> 20 Sept. 18—

Dear M.,

Your letter to hand, to eye, to mind—but not to heart. You accuse me of an offence which exists only in your imagination. I am no hinter, nor suggester. You surely know me well enough to be certain that if I have a complaint I utter it with much readiness and asperity. Perhaps you apply things I meant for myself—I often abuse myself, incognito, to you—unto yourself: and—what's sauce for the gander is *not* sauce for the goose—hélas. 'One man's meat is another man's poison',* and perhaps I poison you with my meat. It is 'high', I allow. But was I very horrid to you?—and did I say *very* wicked things. You make me worse when you seem horror-struck. Oh dear! Does it really seem terrible when I say the bible-religion is cloth which you cut your coat from to fit you, just as you please—and there's a heap of rag-bag snippings. Or was it because I said you whined after me like a dog that daren't follow its master. Oh dear! I am a pig. I don't know what I say these things for, but you make me mad. And how often shall I tell you not to take anything I say seriously, unless I mark it with three asterisks * * *. One must shy so often at the truth before one can aim straight enough to hit.

Oh, but you are a fidget! Why will you elect to be my guardian-angel? You pester yourself horribly on the behalf of my immortal soul. If I look after my day-to-day, the Lord will look after my immortality. I can trust him, at any rate. It doesn't bother me what sort of immortality it is—or if it's none. What does it matter! Who am I to whine for immortal recognition. I'm not very big compared with the blaze: and if the Lord blows my lighted-match-of-a-soul out into the flame-lot, so that you couldn't get it back individual again not with a spoon nor with chemistry, what does it matter! It's there potentially, if not individually. Pah—my immortal soul!—what do I care about it. But my slippery tomorrows—by Jove! I take care of the pence, and let the Lord look after the pounds.* You say I'm a fearful egotist—but you're egotisticer. You worry what'll happen to *you* in eternity: I don't care what becomes of me, so long as I don't be flippant over here-todays.*

Did I say you take everything from me and give nothing back? I suppose I was disagreeable. Today, at least at this minute, I'm in a lofty frame. As for my knowledge or information or whatever the row is about, you will take it like a bird takes heps* off the hedge—because it's there to take. 'Tis a commodity—"'twas mine, 'tis thine, and will be slave to thousands'.*

But as for allowing me to convince thee—never: I might as well try to melt an iceberg by breathing upon it with my breath. When you doubt me, you say nowt, but you go on doubting. I might as well offer you Mohammedanism as my criticism on religion. Then, if it doesn't affect you, why do you get so mad?

Here is my photo—a worthless reflection. Perhaps the more troublesome original will come round to torment you on Sunday—it depends what turns up. My accursed bicycle is punctured.

I've read half through a volume of Sterne. It's delicious, but how you'd hate it! You'd scorn it. Mother does. She only read the first pages of Tristram Shandy, and she ripped them out.* Mutilation!—etc. etc. etc."

It became Paul's fixed custom to go up to the cottage on Sundays and Mondays, while Miriam would meet him at the station on Friday nights, when the two walked together a long way in the dark country, and Paul arrived home as if by a later train. One evening in August they went far, over Watnall, down towards Strelley Mill. It was ten o'clock as they dipped over the wild hill towards the streams that hid in the bottom of the valley, and very dark. To walk downwards into the treefilled hollow seemed like sinking oneself into thick darkness. Miriam timidly took the young man's arm. That angered him, but he said nothing. Tonight he allowed her. He had pledged himself not to love her. The grief and antagonism of Mrs Morel had grown very great. This girl had slowly absorbed her son's interests, had captured his conscious soul, and would soon turn to herself the deeper, warm stream of his underground life, which had always fed at the mother's springs, and nourished the mother's days. If once Miriam was able to win Paul's sex sympathy and service, then he was lost indeed to his mother. Mrs Morel felt that her life was meaningless once her son was really withdrawn from her. She could have given him up to another woman for passion; she could have borne even that he should love and marry some woman weaker than herself, because then she would not have lost him: but that this intense girl, who had set herself with a fervour almost terrible to win the brilliant, blind-eyed lad—that Miriam, the woman of inaction, the woman of deep, half-swooning rhapsodic dreams, should win the son from her who had fought so heroically all the way through life, was horrible. They were the two different types—the woman who lives to make heroic men, and the woman who exists only to plunge herself into the mystical dark of life. Mrs Morel had lived to make Paul a great man: Miriam lived with hidden intensity, urging herself into the inner experiences of life; and she found Paul who was an adventurer, who could arrive at coast after coast of new knowledge, who could hail and acclaim these new worlds, planting his flag upon them, but who could not possess them: it was for her slow and inarticulate soul to absorb and possess these empires of understanding. She was a mystic, and Paul was her glass.* Often he was too swift and changeable, often his rapidity wearied her, but her soul was insatiable in its desire for experience through him. Strictly, he was an instrument for her. Her passion was of the dreamy, inactive sort. Of active physical passion she would scarcely be capable all her life long: of even love's lust, incapable.

Between her sort, and the active women who live to produce heroes, thinkers, and workers, careless of their own lives, there is an endless antagonism. Mrs Morel and Miriam were both remarkable women, so the struggle between them was tremendous. Miriam was confident, as such women are always confident in their souls: Mrs Morel was passionate, and ready with woman's great resource of sacrifice.

"I would rather bury him than that she should have him," the mother would say to herself, again and again, in the long nights of brooding. "For what would she do but kill him, she would suck the life out of him. Have I borne him for her, just for *her*, in all life. I bore him for God and God's work." Then followed the passionate prayer of the believing woman, a Gethsemane* the mother often suffered for her son.

But Miriam was confident. In her heart of hearts, she said "I shall win him." She laughed at Paul himself: only she was afraid of his mother.

"But in the end," she thought, "I shall win him. She is old."

So Paul let her take his arm, though involuntarily he revolted. There was, again, the mechanical quickening of the blood in the young, inflammable man, and against this, the sickening withdrawal of his mother's part of his soul. Miriam gently laid her hand in his arm, nestled towards him as they descended into the still gloom. Then he hated her.

Always exceedingly quick and observant, he noticed the faint grey gleam of the pond among the trees that were black upon a dark earth. There was just one small, square window shining yellow in the great cradle of the valley. To the right, as he glanced round, he felt a kind of presence above the rim of black wood. He turned again and again. Miriam watched his face.

"What is it?" she murmured huskily.

He did not answer for a moment, but watched the east. The effect of a presence over the wood grew stronger.

"The moon is coming up," he said.

"Where?" she whispered.

He did not answer, so she looked where his face pointed. A radiance, ripe and thrilling slowly floated, mounted over the crest of the far-off trees, that looked like the ridged back of a big newt. The luminous presence increased, seemed to draw nearer, bringing closer the great eastern sky, making the hollow dwindle as if it were a black pouch. The two stood perfectly still, watching. Thicker and thicker the gold radiance approached. Something was certainly coming. Miriam trembled with anticipation. The thing was imminent, gold as an archangel arriving, and as silent. She glanced at Paul: he had that almost sullen look which had characterised him as a child: he watched the sky, forgetting her. She looked in the direction of his gaze.

"Ah!" she cried, and she clung to him. The moon, the very core of the night, the germ of it all, suddenly appeared dazzling over the black edge of the hill. It was a red and burning moon, it was the terrific source of her own emotion. It was herself a million times, as the sea to a cup of water. Thrillingly, with painful inevitability, it rose up, getting larger, more immense and looming, till at last the great disc seemed bigger than the whole night had been. The moon detached itself from the horizon, and immediately space became tremendous, earth a black low thing.

"We will sit down a minute," said Paul.

There was, just off the road, near a ragged row of ancient thorn trees, a large fallen trunk. There they sat, the hill hollowing upward before them, ending on the shore of the deep luminous sky, which all seemed to well out from the floating moon, that still could be seen rising, immense and ruddy. Paul felt as if its immense lustrous face were close, and looked straight into his breast. The two sat in silence, Miriam holding his hand. She would wait for him to speak, then she would get him genuine.

"They say," he began at last, "that it's hurtful towards us."*

"What?" Miriam asked, very low and soft.

"The moon," he answered, in a monotonous, rather dreary voice.

"Why?" she breathed.

He was silent, gripping his fist, holding himself tense. It was one of the great, inflamed moments of his life. Something was being born inside him, as the large rich moon, full facing his open breast, heaved up, smiling, it seemed, a subtle, intimate smile that made him shiver. He panted slightly from parted lips. Something was being born within his soul, and he was torn with pain, yet with ecstasy. Miriam waited a long time for him. Then:

"Why is the moon hurtful to us?" she whispered.

At that moment his hand was hurting her own, by its intense, unre-laxing grasp. But that delighted her deeply. She looked at him with a half-smiling ecstasy. Paul turned to her, saw her large dark eyes glowing near his own. He smiled involuntarily in response to her. Then his face twitched with pain. He held his breath, turned away, looked down at the ground, horribly confused.

"Oh Lord!—Oh Lord!" his heart seemed to be panting.

"Won't you tell me?" she murmured.

Again he turned to her, and his blood heaved over his heart. Twice there passed through him a red flash like lightning, and he was almost stifled in a passionate impulse. But this immediately gave way to the old discordant pain.

"Oh my God—oh my God!" he panted on every breath.

We do not know the power that one soul holds over another, even during absence of the person. In intimacy, there goes on a distinct subconscious life, when soul meets soul, holds converse, bids and is bidden, all unknown. This interior life, this strange unrelaxing clasp of embrace and wrestling, is the terrible fact of marriage. There is marriage of souls, sometimes, where no physical marriage is possible. Such union is usually tragic.

Paul remembered Miriam's question. He leaned back against the trunk of a thorn tree, his wave of passion extinguished. Wan, divorced from the physical, he felt rather like a living spirit, a sort of half-educated angel,* than a lover and a man. He leaned and looked at the moon, till it became the only real thing left, and the moonbeams dipping on the tree-tops quite as substantial as himself.

"I don't know why the moon was always considered hurtful," he said. At the sound of his voice she felt like weeping. "—But they wouldn't, in old days, let their children sleep with faces in moonlight.* I can understand it. The moon sort of soaks the lust of life out of you. Look now—it's a whole world of trooping shadows: dark tall things—trees; a palish thing, rather like sky, which is the earth; mist, white, like a woman, and water, flashing with a laugh for a moment, like a man. Where's the lust of life, the blood, the warm body, the red in it all, in us? None. All gone like day-dew in the moonlight. Pale and black shapes now, the shadows that we are built about. I am built about a shadow;—tonight, I am the shadow—it's the seriousest part of me—the real part—but I ought not to feel like it—because it's simply reaching out to death."

A few times Paul talked thus, in the course of his youth with Miriam. It thrilled her, terrified her, almost stunned her—because he seemed, as he said, not a person but an intellect, a soul, dispassionate. He could never write so: when he remembered, vaguely, the next morning, how he had talked, he was impatient and angry.

"What does she drag it out of me for—I should never be such a fool if it wasn't for her!"

Which was true—he would never have gone through these states save for Miriam. And, in the morning, he hated her for it.

Now, in the evening, she listened, much upset.

"Don't talk so terribly," she pleaded, very softly, at last. He turned and looked at her, smiling. Now he could look at her, look steadily in her eyes till she shrank and shuddered. She fought in despair against that cold, dispassionate, moon-light look of his. It was dreadful to her.

"Put your hat on—you'll take cold," she said, smoothing his hair. Usually, had she put her fingers in his hair, he would have jerked back in a flush of anger. Now he simply allowed her, smiling faintly. His indifference was most cruel. She could not even find the blood in him.

"Your hair is quite cold and damp." she murmured, in the low, communicative voice which an hour earlier would have made him quiver in all his veins.

"It is as thick as thatch," he replied, calmly.

"Ah yes," she said, losing her self-control. She drew her fingers down his face. He turned his head slightly away from her, as if from a leaf that tickled when he was three parts asleep. She was afraid. Her heart sank in acquiescence. There was an intense, dream-filled silence over the hill and the sky and the dark hollow steaming from the pond to the moon. Miriam sat in silent, motionless hysteria. She was too much afraid to show her disturbance.

"We must go," he said suddenly, looking at his watch. "A quarter to eleven—think of mother!"

In an instant, they were striding downhill. He gave her his arm now, for quickness sake, and, light, strong, elastic, he swept her downhill. She was nearly as tall as he, and as heavy, being sumptuously built, but he flung her along as if he were a flexible oar. She would have exulted in the movement, had not its purpose been hostile to her cause. He was anxious to get back to his mother.

At the end of the two meadows he left her. Quickly she climbed the fence, then faced round.

"You won't be too late. I'll see you on Sunday. The grass is wet for your feet—I wish it weren't. Run, will you, and get home warm. Goodbye."

She heard him running down the bank, leap from the stepping stones, and race up the bank again out of earshot. She stood still and listened even after she could hear no more of him. The night seemed very empty to her now.

Already he had forgotten her: that she felt in her soul, though she would never have admitted it, even to herself. She told herself that he resented the maternal authority, that it irked him to be so tied to his mother, that he longed to be with her, Miriam. All of which she firmly believed. But her inner consciousness knew better.

Paul hastened through the wood, that was full of moonlight and tall dark shapes, that smelled of cold bracken and honeysuckle and dew-chilled, acrid oak-leaves. The water glimpsed occasionally below the tree trunks. Nethermere ran alongside, speckled with faint stars: water-fowl cried in loud, mournful fatalism. Far away, over a low hill and the oak trees, was the golden cluster of Eberwich, an immense swarm of gold insects* on the black bush of a hill. Paul hastened down the highway, that was an arcade of dark trees. He passed the colliery, which panted and bustled like a black enormous animal burrowing in the ground, lights burning steadily, showing yellow on the wafts of steam.

It was ten minutes past eleven when Paul opened the door of home. In this new house, there was gas. He blinked hard, blinded by the brilliant light. Glancing swiftly round the room, he saw Annie's blouse thrown across the arm of the sofa: she was gone to bed. His mother, dressed in black, sat in her rocking-chair, bowed over a book. The room was extraordinarily silent. The fire had sunk almost to the bottom of the grate, the brass pendulum of the clock swung fiercely, so that each tick seemed to bruise the air. Paul felt that the very furniture was in a state of suspense. The feeling of coiled, tight emotion was communicated everywhere.

"Is my father in—?" Paul asked, breathless.

Mrs Morel did not raise her head: she had not looked up once.

"—And in bed," she replied.

It was very unusual for Walter Morel to be in and in bed at ten minutes past eleven on Friday, pay-night. Paul wondered.

"Was he drunk?" the lad asked anxiously.

After every question, the mother left a space before replying.

"As usual," she answered at last, very coldly.

Paul could not see his mother's face. It troubled him.

"Was he—was he disagreeable—?" he faltered.

"No."

From this laconic answer, Paul gathered that his mother had been too much put out with *himself* to notice his father's shortcomings. The lad dared not mention the fact of his own lateness—and he was terribly afraid of his mother's silent wrath. If only she would let the night go by without strong emotion—if only she would, like himself, run and take refuge in trivialities—how glad he would be! He did not feel equal to a conflict with his mother; his soul loathed wearily the idea of violent emotions roused at this tired hour.

"Did you buy me a pear?" he asked, rather pitifully. It was his mother's custom to bring him some little favourite morsel from the Friday-evening market.—There was no reply to his question. His mother *had* bought him a pear—this was her thanks.

Paul sighed, began to pull off his boots. He was not particularly hungry, and would rather go to bed than eat, in such an atmosphere. He bowed his head right down as he sat on the stool taking off his boots. There was the cruellest silence ringing in the room at the clock-ticks, startled occasionally by the fierce rustle of a leaf of the book. Paul began to unfasten his collar.

He started, shrank within himself. His mother would not let him go scot-free to bed.

"You don't tell me that you've come from the station at this time," she cried suddenly, scornfully, raising her face to him. His heart beat wildly.

"I've been a walk with Miriam," he said, hiding his face.

"Do you think I didn't know!" she sneered. "Do you think I haven't known these last six weeks!" He started, winced like a culpable creature caught.

"Well, you'd only be horrid if I told you," he said, resentfully excusing himself.

"And must you see her on Fridays as well now—can't you exist five days without her?—it's a poor tale—"

Paul breathed more easily: she would not twit him with deceit or cowardice. He thanked his fates for this generosity, and felt himself able to be angry to answer the lesser charge.

"Well, she comes to meet me—"

This was real cowardice—but not unflattering to the woman it was addressed to.

"She doesn't come without you want her," said Mrs Morel, very scathing.

"She wants more than me—and I let her—" said our hero.

"Oh, don't talk to me!" cried the mother in contempt. "You want her to come, and she comes—what else—" She turned aside in thin, keen scorn. Paul felt his self-respect gone.

"Well if I do, I do then," he replied sullenly.

"Yes,"—he shivered at the new note: "Yes, and I may sit and wait here for you, no matter how tired I may be—"

"It's a wonder my father's in—you know it is—" he cried.

"Well, he *is* in," was the answer.

"And you could go to bed—" Paul protested.

"I shall *not* go to bed—never, never—so don't think it, my boy," she replied.

There was silence. Paul sat on the footstool, his back to the chimney piece, his head ducked down. From under his thick brows he could see as far as the bosom of his mother. She sat still in her rocking-chair, her worn hands mechanically stroking, with a rhythmic, jerked movement, the black sateen of her apron. It was a movement that hurt Paul to see.

"No my boy, it comes to this," said his mother in tones of quiet, bitter despair. "You care nothing for home nor Annie nor me nor any of us now. You only care for Miriam."

"I don't—I don't—I don't care for her—I don't—!"

"Then why do you go with her?" Mrs Morel was quiet and relentless.

"I like to talk to her—but I don't love her—I *don't* love her, not a bit—but I like to talk to her. There's lots of things we talk about that you're not interested in—"

"What things—?" Mrs Morel was so quiet, so cold and hopeless, Paul began to pant. He would die rather than hear his mother sound hopeless.

"Why—music—Schubert—and books—*you* don't care about Herbert Spencer—"*

"No," was the sad reply, "and *you* won't at my age."

"Well, but I do now—and Miriam does—"

"And how do you know," Mrs Morel flashed defiantly, "that I don't care about these things? Do you ever try me—?"

"But you don't, mother, you know you don't," he implored, passionately. "You know you don't care whether a man paints a picture decorative or paints the real living thing through the clothes of the landscape—you know you don't care what *manner* it is."

"How do you know I don't care—do you ever talk to me about it, to try?"

"But it's not that that matters to you, mother, you know it isn't."

"What is it then—what is it then that matters to me—?" she flashed.

He raised his face thoughtfully, trying to think. His lips were lifted off his teeth in pain.

"No," she said. "When you've said and done all, it comes to this: you've got Miriam now, so I may stand aside and let you go, let you have your own way, you've no further use for me."

He looked at her swiftly, his face all distorted with misery. By sympathy of love, it had become to him the most terrible thought in life that his mother should be put aside, in neglect, having no further share in life, she who had been so strong.

"You know it isn't, mother, you know it isn't." She was moved to pity by his cry.

"It looks a great deal like it," she said, brokenly, struggling to retain her sternness. She was an unemotional, undemonstrative woman. But he caught the break.

"No mother—I don't love her a bit—" He had risen, bare throated, ready to go to bed. His mother rose also. "I don't love her," he reiterated, and his soul was sick of Miriam. "I don't love her—I shall never love anybody but you—" There was such a hopelessness and such genuineness about this last protest, that Mrs Morel gave a little cry of pain, and put her arms round his neck. At that moment, she said in her heart, "He shall love her if he wants—she shall have him if he wants her to—" And his mother kissed him fervently, pressed him against her bosom.

He put his arms round the light form of his mother, pressed her close, kissed her cheek and her neck. Then he laid his head on her shoulder, as if he laid it at rest. Again that final test of love—they rested in each other's arms.

A moment or two Mrs Morel remained thus, while both bosoms heaved with after-pain, and both hearts were sore from love.

"You know," she said, musing, appealingly, "I've never had a husband—not really."

And Paul bowed his head, and was silent. Then his mother loosed him. She gave him one long kiss on the brow.

"There," she said, "now go to bed." Her voice was very low, and loving, and protective. "Go to bed, my boy, you'll be so tired in the morning.—I didn't mean to say anything—I didn't—"

"This is best, mother," he said.

"Perhaps I'm selfish—" It was the fear of her heart—but she knew he would contradict her.

"Ha—mother," he laughed, sadly mocking the notion.

"There!" she kissed him, pushed him gently towards the door, "Go to bed, you're tired." He kissed her cheek, which she offered.

"Goodnight mother," he murmured.

He pressed his face among the pillows in a fury of misery. And yet his heart was glad within him also, and his soul peaceful. Nevertheless, he pressed his face hard among the pillows, like a man who has something hard to bear, which he must never lament. Arthur slept undisturbed beside him, his young, full, girl's mouth parted winsomely. Paul looked at his brother. Tears came to his eyes: he must be very protective towards this impetuous, wilful lad. Then he also went to sleep.

On the Sunday Paul went late up to the cottage. Miriam was upstairs, dressing. She did all the work in the house on Sundays, when their girl went home. As she fastened her blouse, Miriam's fingers trembled. She was wondering why Paul was late, and was apprehensive, subconsciously aware, perhaps, of the storm. She stood at her bedroom window fastening her brooch and looking across at the massed oak-trees that shut her in. The honeysuckle berries round the window were just turning red. It gave Miriam a pang to think that the summer was so nearly gone. She pricked her fingers, she was so tremulous.

Hearing the chock of the big white gate, she stood still in suspense. It was a grey day. Paul came through the gate past the end of the farm-buildings. He was just twenty-one years old, moderate in stature, slight. His face was very pale under his darkening hair, and today, Miriam noticed with a shiver, was impassive and cold, the mouth close-shut. As a rule, Paul would ring his bell* and look laughing to the windows. Today he walked straight to the shed.

Miriam came downstairs nervously. She was wearing a new lace blouse which became her wonderfully. At nineteen she was full breasted, and very handsome, with her bowed head, her serious yet healthy face, magnificently coloured, drooped round by fine black curls. Very pensive and immobile, her eyes were startling when once raised, so sensitive, so luminous and full of soul.—Would Paul notice her new blouse?

He sat in the parlour, talking crisp and cleverly to Mrs Revell, who was very fond of him. The cold clearness of his humour made Miriam shrink. She shrank visibly as she entered, and Paul grew more chilly and impersonal. She loved him when he was full of impulsive laughter and interest; in his present state, she dreaded him; he seemed hard and keen, like a weapon.

"Hullo—you are late," she said huskily.

"Am I?" was all his reply, and he went on ironically to describe the people at Jordan's. Mrs Revell laughed very much at him: Mr Revell, an invalid lying on the couch, seemed bored.

"Is it rough riding?" Miriam ventured to say.

"I did not notice it," he returned coldly, and turned rudely again to Mrs Revell, who was not unwilling to help in a lesson to the over-fond girl. Paul noticed the blouse, saw that it suited Miriam: but that only hardened his heart.

The conversation came to an end.

"It is only four o'clock—there is time for you to see my guelder-rose bush before I get tea," Miriam faltered, glancing with appeal to Mrs Revell.

"I will get tea dear," said that lady.

Paul rose, unwillingly complying.

"Very well," he said.

They went in silence over the high hill-meadow to the wood, that was all dark green now.

"Has the wind made you tired?" Miriam asked at last. There was a certain weariness about his deportment, for all its supercilious pride.

"Not in the least," he answered, annoyed by her solicitude, and rather contemptuous.

"Because it's very rough—the wood moans, you can hear it—it must be very rough on the other side."

"You can see from the turn of the leaves, it is a south-west wind. That helps me here," he said.

"You see I don't cycle, so I don't understand," Miriam said humbly.

"Is there need to cycle to understand?" he asked. She bowed her head as she walked beside him.

They passed a trap, a narrow horseshoe hedge of small fir-boughs baited with the guts of an animal. Paul looked at it critically. Miriam, catching his glance, said in a low, rather indignant voice:

"Isn't it ugly—dreadful!"

"Why dreadful?—is it worse than a weasel with its teeth in a rabbit's throat?—one weasel, or many rabbits—which? One or the other must go between the teeth—"

His cruelty was unnecessary. She winced, wept internally, walked almost cringing beside him. They came to the bush of berries.

"See!" she said, and she watched him. Among the handsome, full leaves the crimson berries hung in loaded clusters. Usually Paul would have expanded and flashed his appreciation. Today he stood aloof, eyeing the bush critically and coldly.

"It is very pretty," he said.

"Isn't it a harvest festival?"* she murmured. He smiled, shrugged his shoulders. Going forward, Miriam took a large bunch of berries in her hands. They were heavy, crimson, glistening: they lay sumptuously in her palm. She bent her face, stroked them with her cheek, with her lips, fondled them. He watched her rather angrily.

"Why," he asked, "do you always touch things?"

"But I love to," she replied, afraid.

"I prefer to see them without touching," was his reply, untrue on the whole, though true for the moment. "Why clutch and fondle at things. I prefer more reserve."

She looked at him, full of pain. He was pale, impassive, with a cruel droop of the eyelids. Would she never be able to unbind his better nature?

"You would wheedle the soul out of things," he said.—"I would never wheedle—I would take what I wanted without extravagance of asking—"

He did not know what he was saying. Perhaps he wanted Miriam to rise and conquer his mother in him. There is no telling. Miriam, however, more rhapsodic than perceptive, was confused, lost, stunned.

Over tea, he talked in the same cold, half contemptuous, clever way, that seemed like an insult to Miriam. She washed up the pots. Ordinarily he would help her—today he did not go near the naked-roofed pent-house of a scullery, but read when Mrs Revell left him.

The evening cleared. Right hidden behind the wood was a gold sunset, the glow of which showed on the great bare breast of the hill across the valley.

"Isn't it lovely!" said Miriam. Paul, from being cold and offensive, grew sad. Still he would not allow her to approach.

"Shall we read?" she asked him.

"If you will," he replied.

She went to her shelves, took down Palgrave's "Golden Treasury of Songs and Lyrics."*

"Not that," said Paul.

"Why not?" she inquired in astonishment.

"Prose," he said.

Miriam loved the 'Songs and Lyrics' passionately. Paul had read most of them to her, in his sympathetic manner: he could be so tender, so gentle, so enthusiastic. She could not understand why he wanted prose.

"What?" she asked. "What then?"

"Anything!" He took a volume of Balzac's short stories.* Miriam almost wept for disappointment.

"We will sit on the stack," she said.

He bowed acquiescence.

They went past the lilac trees to the stackyard. The staddle* was laid for the corn-stack, the new hay stood in two great ricks. Just a fragment, solid and brown and woody, remained of the old hay stack. The farmers had been pulling the new stacks, so there was a little heap of loose hay against the standing ruin of last year's harvest. As Miriam and Paul sat down on the new stuff, their backs to the hard brown wall, Trip, the big white bull-terrier of the farm came rushing at them. He knew Miriam thoroughly, but he came gambolling to Paul, putting his great paws on the lad's shoulders, licking him wildly. Then Paul laughed, began to play with the dog.

"No. Oh no!" the man laughed, through shut lips that the dog struggled to reach, "no-no—not kisses, my Tripoli onion—* I forbid thee—" With a quick movement he caught the dog, shut its muzzle between his two hands, then put his mouth between the eyes of the struggling animal, laughing, murmuring. "Be quiet and I'll kiss thee—be quiet—be quiet." He rubbed his cheek on the forehead of the dog, who whined and whimpered to get his nose unmuzzled from the tight, fine hands of the man. Paul let go. Instantly Trip was on him, in an onslaught.

The man was bowled over, lay rolling, trying to shield his face with his arms, while the dog planted paws on his breast, nuzzled to lick his face, his throat. Paul laughed and rolled about with the dog, who was in an ecstasy of affection and play.

Miriam watched them. In his moments of generosity and affection she felt herself kindled by him.

"Why is he never like this with me—why doesn't he play with me, why doesn't he give himself to me in play like that?" she said bitterly to herself.

Trip was sent away; Paul sat up and straightened himself. He resumed at once his old distance with Miriam, and began to read 'Honorine'.

But neither he nor Miriam was interested. At last, she put her hands on the book, and gently took it away. He closed his mouth, looked away over the glowing hills.

"Why are you sad?" she asked falteringly.

"I think I am not sadder than usual," he replied.

"But what is the matter?" she pleaded.

"Nothing!" He was very curt. Nevertheless:

"Nay!" she murmured in remonstrance, grieved by his lack of confidence.

"You had far better not talk," he said, picking up a stick, and poking the earth with it, thrusting, poking in swift blows, as if he would never weary. The movement made Miriam want to cry out.

"But I want to know," she said.

"Eve!" he laughed, ironically.

"It is not fair to me," she murmured.

He thrust, thrust, thrust at the ground with the pointed stick, making a deep wound. He seemed to be thinking hard. His endless tearing of the earth with the stick seemed like madness in her brain who watched him. She gently, but firmly, put her hand on his wrist, and held the weapon.

"Don't!—put it away!" she murmured.

He allowed her to take the stick, then he lay perfectly still. The last state was as bad as the first* for her.

"What is it?" she pleaded softly.

"We had," he said at length, with difficulty, "We had better break off—"

Instantly a shadow darkened the sky, that was thick with light. It felt like a little death to her.

"Why?" she breathed. "What has happened?"

"Nothing has happened—we only realize now and again where we are. It's no good."

She waited in silence, trembling violently.

"It's no good. We agreed for friendship—it's all I'm capable of, by some flaw or other in my make-up—"—he did *not* realize, after all. "I can only give friendship, and the thing overbalances on one side. It's horrid—I hate a toppling balance—let us have done."

"But what has happened?" she gasped.

"Nothing!—I've only happened to look and see where we are."

She bowed her head, thinking that nothing was wrong with their position. She marvelled at the perverse cruelty she got from him. It made her feel sick and blind.

"And what do you want?" she murmured.

"Why—I mustn't come often—that's all. It's no good. It'll only end in calamity. I'm deficient in something. You must have felt it often."

She had, and she guessed what it was, but she would never say. He spoke in dull, miserable tones, and had started beating the ground with a stone. Notwithstanding, his innermost heart exulted, amidst the vague mass of misery, as he broke thus with her.

"But I don't understand," she said, husky and wretched. The night seemed to be turning jangled and hideous as the twilight faded.

"I know—you never will. You'll never believe that I can't—can't physically, no more than fly up like a skylark— —"

"What—?"

"Love you."

He was sorry, and angry, and hard. It was true, he did not understand why he could not love Miriam. He thought, as he said, that it was some defect in his nature, some string missing from his range. They were silent for half an hour. Then he rose, always very quiet and reserved.

"I must go," he said.

"But it's ever so early—it is not nine o'clock."

"I promised to be early."

As he said this, in his curt, final way, Miriam dimly understood what was between them. A woman, she had far more understanding in these matters than he had.

He went, and in bitterness she let him depart. Life seemed ugly, ashy, and cruel to her. She wandered alone in the fields.

And afterwards, it was often thus between them, this hard, cruel thrusting away of her on Paul's side, her pleading and suffering on the other. Paul hated her, was coldly cruel to her, yet could not stay away.

When there happened to come a blank in the Sunday, and he felt at a loose end, he *must* go to the cottage. Then, when he got there, he was strained, cold, distant. For her it was very cruel. He did not understand, being overweening and scornful. He had no idea why he was like it. "I don't *love* her," he said, and this was final for him.

Once, however, towards Christmas, Paul stood behind her as she sang. Mrs Revell played, both young people were singing. But Paul happened to catch sight of Miriam's beautiful face. She looked so submissive and wistful, she looked as if she sung for God, hopeless on earth: her lips opened, glistened with such naïve sadness, like a sorrowful child's, that Paul felt his heart in a grasp of tears. Exercising a great control, he sang on, and chattered. But Miriam, hearing a new softness in his voice, glanced at his eyes. They were dark with grief, and veiled from her. When she went to bed, she wept bitterly. And Paul, dropping down the muddy, steep hill on his bicycle, was blinded with tears. Again and again, he shook the water from his eyes, tried to look at the road. A reckless rider, he dropped down the three leaps of the hill at a sickening pace, the mud flying over him. He struggled to look at the road, but the grief for Miriam was stronger than fear or commonsense. His throat filled up hard, his eyes were blinded again. He rode in a swim of tears, that urged up in spite of him. And for days he could not think of Miriam singing wistfully, like a sad Botticelli angel* singing without the tears gaining mastery over him.

Nevertheless, his attitude remained the same to her: he did not love her, could not love her, ever.

As he walked home sometimes, past Flints' farm, over the wild fields of the hill top, he would look round the great night-landscape and wonder at everything. The horizon went round in an immense sweep, along the brim of the hills, and here and there in the shallow black cup were the golden, fumy patches of villages, and townlets gleaming right against the sky. Over Miriam's quarter alone, all was pitch black; desert country. For the rest, the great black earth was littered with patches of myriad-assembled lights, which showed dark gold on the sky close above. There were black spaces, as if the earth were a black leopard skin with golden spots, while the sky was a paler, more blurred and insignificant a skin, scorched in two places by the great ruddy flare of furnaces too far-off to be seen on the ground.

Paul would lean on the stile on the highest land, before dipping down into the valley, and wonder plaintively why he should have this struggle to defend his little friendship with Miriam from his mother, from Annie,

Arthur, everybody: why all should be struggling against one another, children against their father, father against wife and children: Ah, but his father was dreadful! Remembering, Paul's heart would quicken for his mother again, and he would run down the hill to get home to her, to shelter her, or comfort her, or succour her. Miriam was forgotten: his heart was full towards his mother.

So Miriam lost. For all that, Paul wrote to her very often. In writing he was safe, being then a mere mind. This was as near an approach to a love letter that she got from him.

> "Jordan's—Nottingham
> 10th February 1903.

Dear M.,

I suppose if I do not answer your letter immediately I shall find no time hereafter. Why do you begin with almost an apology to me that you have written. You should think it a great favour to bestow a letter on anyone.

As for you—have you been undergoing another subjective inspection? Perhaps it is as well—but don't be hyper-sensitive: if you are, little things will cast big shadows. I think it is utterly impossible to be *really* frivolous—that you are growing more serious is true, and good especially for you. Yet I should be sorry to see you come round to the more materialistic views, called practical. It is nice to find someone who doesn't say a man is 'worth' his thousands—or his nothing. You know they say this is the age of materialism; of realism, of practicality, and of young men. A world of young men would be all competition—it is nice to find someone who doesn't compete. Try and be practical, frivolous, ephemeral, anything, in so far as it is necessary to understand people and make them like you while they respect you—And after all, we are born to do some good here, in the world, and not in an after-life. So try and be gay, and care about little nothings with a care that is only a pleasure; but do not, do not get an absolute standard of judgment. Sixpence is only worth so much pleasure, for oneself or for somebody else, gone in an hour: it is *not* a little badge of honour for the possessor. To read Homer isn't an atom of merit, except that it makes us more agreeable to other folks, and a bit more radiant in ourselves.—I wish I could read him.*—The best is to be very liberal, to censure cautiously, and to find the good in what is very much bad. You see, Abstraction, Idealism, are apt to scorn those whose eyes are untrained to subtleties, and who are of necessity harsh to fit a workaday world—like a hard hand handling a pick. Someone must hack, and we of the soft hands are apt to wear them as phylacteries.* Be practical & ideal, be realistic & transcendentalistic, be the latter sooner than the former, be both in the ratio as 1:7.

As for la vie, vita, das Leben, Life—I have not yet digested it. (He is twenty one!) I can come at no conclusion: I do not think I can, or will, or would bind myself down to one hard, flat belief. It would be cruel, impossible to give up the Resurrection, yet the Christ-*man* is so much more real, so inspiring. One can feel with a Christ-Man: fancy pitying a God! You see people have such small ideas of the Divine, such indulgent parent notions: they limit him to an Almighty fondler and punisher—which is more terrible than Unitarianism,* as I think they call it. We will let our opinions form gradually, like crystals, the best of which come in the course of ages. A sudden opinion, an immediate belief, is apt to be amorphous and volatile. In patience let us possess our souls.*

I read your letter in a funny conflicting mood. Mr Pappleworth had just asked me to go and telephone a message for him to a friend of his. When I got the man rung up, he said:—'That you, Albert!' whereon I nearly let fall the 'fone in amusement, for he thought I was Mr P. I didn't undeceive him. 'Will you take me some sandwiches?' I said, 'I can't get lunch in town.' 'Right—for the 1.15—right. I say—?'—'Yes!' I said. 'Mrs all right?'—'Oh yes!' I said. 'Didn't twig?' he asked.—'I did her brown,'* I answered. 'Good on yer!' he said.—'It's snowing,' I said. 'Ne'er mind—we'll keep the bitch warm—mustn't let her catch cold. It's the chance of a lifetime with that dog. I say—she'll be all right?'—'Right as houses,' I said. 'Good!' he said. 'One-fifteen then?' I said. 'Right you are, old man. Ta-ta.'—We rang off.

Pappleworth asked me what I was grinning for, and I said etc etc etc."

—The strange thing is that these letters, which must bore a reader to death, only fed the flame of Miriam's passion. She did not mind how he preached to her—in fact, she liked it. They were both very young, and banal things were new, painful, and wonderful to them.

Chapter VIII

CALAMITY

The Morel household was always a small one. Very early William had gone away. He was now in a good position in Birmingham, and earning two hundred and fifty a year, but married to a thriftless wife, a handsome, well dressed, but helpless woman. She was an orphan, daughter of a stockbroker who had died while she was away at school in France. Brought up by an Aunt who had small means, she was elegant, but brainless, and penniless. She adored her husband to distraction. William was big, very vigorous, American in his breeze and bustle, but tainted with Paul's love for philosophising. Often William was on the verge of wretchedness and despair: but he fought it off in action. Mrs Morel despised her daughter-in-law: Lily was afraid of her mother-in-law, disliked her in a mean way. And William, finding his wife a dead weight—she clung to him as if she were a helpless, will-less creature—still turned passionately to his mother for support. Mrs Morel had not lost, would never lose, her eldest son. She loved him dearly, and still extended to him her shelter.

Annie Morel married, when she was twenty three, a young artizan who had saved a couple of hundred pounds. Newcome was steady, very pleasant in his temper, made an admirable husband. He was another, lesser son to Mrs Morel. Annie, inheriting the masterful disposition of the Guylers, her mother's people, was apt to tyrannise over her husband, whom she loved sincerely.

There remained at home, with mother and father, only Paul and Arthur. Arthur was at this time nineteen years of age, Paul being twenty one. The youngest lad had grown tall, was exceedingly graceful. He had dark hair, beautiful, rather moody blue eyes that had handsome lashes, and he had a fresh complexion. From school he won a scholarship at the Nottingham University.* His £65 scholarship paid his fees, his books, and his railway fares, leaving some £30 a year for his maintenance. With this his mother kept him, clothed him, provided him with pocket money and restaurant dinners. He had taken the Intermediate,* and was shortly to sit for his B. A. degree. Highly sensitive and overwrought with study and discord at home, he was irritable in the house, fierce, unrestrained because he had been spoiled in his youth.

When he was twenty one years old, Paul was earning thirty shillings a week. Of this he gave one pound to his mother, for the house: with the rest he clothed himself, paid his railway fares, bought books and paints and amused himself. He did not save anything.

Mrs Morel managed wonderfully. For the last years of his life, he being wasted with drink and low in esteem, Walter Morel's wages were very small. He very, very rarely gave his wife thirty shillings a week, often only sixteen or seventeen. On this and the lads' small money she kept a fairly plentiful house. Her rooms were furnished with an air of distinction. A doctor, a strange clergyman, had only to enter the kitchen to become respectful even to Walter Morel. The room had a certain aristocracy of tone, despite its artizan's furniture: there was a book-case of well-standing books, besides the four shelves with their dark-green serge covers, going nearly to the ceiling, and loaded with school books, an edition of Goethe, of Schiller, of Victor Hugo.* The pictures were prints, not expensive, but large, well mounted, very delicate and pleasing. There were no ornaments save Morel's old brass candlesticks and tobacco jar, with two squat, dark pieces of majolica. Perhaps it was this absence of superfluous ornament that gave Mrs Morel's home its air. At any rate, Paul loved their own house indoors, nor was ever ashamed to take his friends there, poor though it might be. It cost Mrs Morel a great struggle to win back taste and refinement into her home, that had grown so ugly during the bitter, weary times when her children were little. And there was, in her contrivance to get the table refined, something noble, a kind of divine intuition. In the years when she herself had grown despairing, and the children were too tiny to notice, she had let the household get into Walter Morel's ways. They had eaten, like the commonest people, from a bare table, and had had no plates at tea-time, but had put their thick pieces of bread and dripping on the board. As soon, however, as the lads began to grow up, she strove towards restoration of the table. It cost her long hours of trouble to contrive how to buy good table-cloths, new knives, and four-pronged forks* instead of the old, horn-handled things that pricked the mouth with their two points. There were no dessert spoons, no small knives, no small forks, only the barest necessities for eating. Although she scarcely knew how to provide food and clothes, Mrs Morel saved a small sum each week, till she had all that was needful to furnish a table, till she could spread for a meal as it was spread in the houses of her sisters. Her children were unfailingly proud of their table: the doctor's, the clergyman's, they knew by experience, did not look so nice. Mrs Morel was a great woman. "Not with whom you are bred, but with whom you are fed," says Sancho Panza.*

Occasionally, the mother spoke her trouble aloud. On Friday night, when, after reckoning,* her husband had left the wages on the mantelpiece, she would count the money.

"T-t-t-t," she would go rapidly with her tongue. "Twenty one shillings! And his club this week,* five and sixpence—"

She would be talking, partly to herself, partly to Arthur, who sat studying. This constant harassment of insufficient money told on her. It would have worn away a weaker woman. But Mrs Morel kept herself and the home up to pitch, was cheerful, bright, a delightful companion.

"What *am* I to do—what *am* I! Rent, five-and-sixpence, and insurance two shillings, and clubs every week three and sixpence, and gas, and water— —"

"Oh mother don't!" Arthur would cry, unable to bear his mother's tone of angry helplessness. "Oh, shut up, do! How do you think I can study?" The poor lad would be struggling with Vergil's *Bucolics*￼* at the time. "What do you bother for—why don't you let it go?"

"Yes, if I let it go, where would you be?" cried his mother, resentful, yet regretting to have troubled him.

"Well, you bother and whittle* and worry everybody to death, and when you've done it's no better—"

"No," she said, "it isn't. But wait, my lad, till *you* have to make sixpence pay for ninepence, *you'll* worry."

"I'll never *be* like it!" cried the boy.

If Mrs Morel happened to begin her fretting monologue in presence of Paul, this son's eyes would open, his brows knit, in a kind of irritable horror. He was helpless, with a hateful helplessness, before shortage of money. Week after week to know that this struggle to pay for necessaries must recur sent him into a vibrating frenzy.

"And two pairs of boots want soling, and the weather wet as it is—" Mrs Morel would go on. Then Paul cried aloud:

"Oh don't bother about them, mother, don't bother about them! Let them go unsoled."

"Yes, and let you catch your death of cold," she said bitterly.

"All the better—it'll be cheaper," he retorted.

"What—a doctor's bill?" she asked sarcastic.

"No—the insurance money," he replied, brutal, because money, or rather want, is so brutal.

"That's a nice thing to say!" said Mrs Morel, low, indignant. His gambler's spirit, which she discerned better than he himself, troubled her.

And thus she had to refrain from trying to share the economic burden with anybody. The lads, while it was necessary, gave her to the last penny: they could do no more; and they could not be expected to worry with her. She still struggled on alone.

As Paul earned more, the economic stress grew more lenient.

When the income of the household became steadier, Walter Morel was the trouble. As the lads grew up, became more perceptive, more refined, and the household improved in tone, Walter Morel, who steadily deteriorated, showed hideous by contrast. He had drunk till his iron constitution was ruined: ruined by drink and moral despair, both. Now he was very inflammable, fiercely irritable, and in his rage there was a viciousness, a starting back of fear, as there is in the rage of a cowed mongrel. Mrs Morel, afraid for her sons, left him alone to go his own way, very much more than she had done. He, however, was none the better for that. One sore spot he had which was inflamed till it became a kind of madness, namely, the children. He had loved Arthur more than anything on earth, whilst he had valued Paul's affection more than that of anyone else. He would never, all his life long, offend Paul, if he could help it: but there was always a distance between these two. Arthur, however, had loved him, as a child had gone to bed in the afternoons with him, as a boy had worked in the garden with him. Now, however, now that Arthur was the most gentlemanly of all, now that the father could be infinitely proud of his son, there was violent dislike between them.

When Arthur got home from college in the evening, Morel was just coming in from the pit. Arthur had grown up sensitive as a girl. His father would enter in his pit dirt, take off his coat and cap, glouring round the room in an evil temper, because he was tired, in poor health. He did not speak to anyone, no one spoke to him. Morel looked at the table: it was large, heavy, and round. The cloth was fine and white, the tea-china of dark blue willow pattern, there was a bowl of pinkish double primroses in the centre. For Arthur's tea was fruit and cakes. Mother and son were chatting together at the meal. Where did he, the father, come in? At that board there was no place for him.

Mrs Morel rose, took the saucepans from the hob. Morel got hold of the table, dragged it clean away from Arthur, nearer to the fire. The lad flashed up in an instant.

"Can't you leave the table alone?"

"I'm gooin' ter ha'e a bit of warmth while I eat *my* dinner," Morel answered, loudly and coarsely.

"Put a coat on then, you great kid," said Arthur, flushed and indignant at his father's bullying tone.

"I s'll do as I've a mind,"* shouted Morel.

"Will you—you won't then!" flashed Arthur, fiercely. "The house isn't all yours, don't think it."

"Whose is it then?—is it thine, tha snivelling little beggar! I'll smite thee down if tha says another word."

"Will you—but you won't, I tell you," said the lad, his voice vibrating in a low fury. And, with his handsome blue eyes full of hate and scorn, he glared full into the eyes of his father. Morel, under this insolent, hateful gaze of the child, was smothered in his own weakness and degradation. Like a smothered thing, he went mad with fury.

"Goodness me, can we never have a meal in peace," said Mrs Morel, entering. "Arthur, what do you say anything to him for—haven't you learned yet to keep quiet when he's about—!"

Thus she diverted the wrath to herself.

"Yes," cried Morel, in good English, and sneering tremendously. "Teach them not to speak to me—I'm not fit to be spoke to, aren't I?—Am I a dog?"* he suddenly bawled, and banged the table. Arthur started up in a passion—Mrs Morel went into the scullery with a dish. Morel gazed fiercely round—then he dropped his head. He was sober.

There was a silence, save for the slobbering noises of the father's eating: it was a silence of detestation, and as such did its work on the three.

One night Morel came in at half-past ten, tipsy, and in a furious temper because he had lost at dominos in the 'Swan.' Mrs Morel was alone. He sat down heavily, glaring at her like a beast, then said in a peculiar, hideous grating tone.

"What need had you to put that bird-cage in the coalhouse?"

Mrs Morel looked up in astonishment, wondering what he meant. Then she remembered that, three days before, she had removed from the scullery a large, clumsy bird-cage which he had made a year ago for the bird he had now given away. She was almost dumb with astonishment.

"Because it was of no use, and was in the way," she replied coldly.

"It was in your way because *I* made it. *I* had made it, so it was an eyesore to you. You hated the sight of it, and made the lads turn their noses up at it, because *I* made it—"

"Don't be so ridiculous man," she said in disgust. But he raved at her. She had put the children up to despise him, she had put them up to the things they said to him, etc, etc.

Mrs Morel was no psychologist*—which was a pity. She could not even faintly understand the condition of a half-tipsy man, who was boiling with irritation: his liver was so bad. According to the old standards of judgment, he was being wilfully evil: that was how she saw it. Therefore he enraged her.

He lost control and struck her with his fist on the cheek. Arthur came in a moment after. Morel was sitting in a kind of paralysis of irritation, a cruel and pitiable state. The lad looked from one parent to another.

"What's the matter?" he said sharply.

Mrs Morel sniffed, drew herself up coldly, kept her bruised cheek averted. Walter Morel, feeling his blood corrode with fire, as he sat with his arms on his knees, looked up at his son.

"Has he been carrying on?" said the youth to his mother.

"Have nothing to say, and get your supper," said Mrs Morel, giving a sharp, involuntary little sniff of passion, as she did when the woman within her rocked with outrage.

Arthur Morel caught the fierce atmosphere. He looked keenly at his mother, then went deadly pale.

"Has he hit you?" he asked, low and vibrating.

"Never you mind—get your supper and go to bed," said Mrs Morel.

The father glanced up at his son again, wincing all the time, and shrinking till he wished he could be extinguished into nothingness, yet at the same time quivering with rage. Arthur Morel turned to his father. For a moment, he was like Paul; speaking low, and intense:

"You miserable, despicable coward," he said. Then the tears came to his eyes, his lips quivered; lifting both his hands he advanced on his father.

"I could kill you, I could," he cried. "I hate you. Go somewhere else, you nuisance: we can do without you."

"That'll do, Arthur, that'll do," said Mrs Morel. The father sat upright in his chair.

"Are ter stowing it—are ter shutting thy face up—are ter, tha brazen young hound?—"*

"No," cried Arthur. "No—no—no. You're a hateful coward and I can't bear you near me and I wish you'd go. Go and live with your own pals, go and pig with your own scum, you'll be happy. We don't want you here—."

"Arthur, Arthur, stop it at once," cried Mrs Morel with authority.

"If tha says another word, I'll flatten thee out," cried Morel, springing to his feet, bending forward like a boxer about to attack.

"Will you?" cried the youth. "You daren't touch me! You daren't touch me."

"Dursn't I,* dursn't I?" cried Morel, bounding near and thrusting his fist near the boy's nose.

"Get away, you nuisance," cried Arthur, trembling violently. "You stink in my nose."

Mrs Morel had risen and gone to the pair. As Morel let drive, she pushed him back, and dragged the youth by the arm to the door.

"Enough of this, I've had enough of this for one night," she said. "Now you go to bed sir."

At the door, Arthur shook off his mother. He turned to his father, who was clinging to the edge of the table after the wife's thrust.

"When I've finished college," cried the boy, "When I've finished college, in five months, my mother shan't live another day with you. I shall have two pounds a week. Don't you come near us then; I should be thankful never to see you again. And don't you dare to touch *my* mother again—or—"

Before he finished, his father had hurled at him the earthenware bowl of primroses from the table. It smashed on the door-jamb, just beside the boy's head, covering him with water and the winsome, pinky blue flowers.

"You've done a nice thing now!" said Mrs Morel, contemptuously. There was silence in the room after this, whilst Arthur Morel wiped himself dry, and Morel, setting his hands on the table, leaned heavily on them, brooding.

Presently he rose, to stump upstairs to bed.

"You'll be doing something yet that you'll be sorry for, my lord," said Mrs Morel with vibrating gravity to her husband.—"Throwing things about like a mad beast!" she added in contempt.

"I don't care what the hell I do," he shouted.

"No," she said in contempt. "I believe you. But other folk have to suffer."

Morel stumped heavily to bed, picking his way through the broken pieces of earthenware. He was very, very pitiable: but he would have angered an angel from heaven, and all the Morels were hot tempered.

When her husband had gone to bed, Mrs Morel said to the boy, who sat trembling and sick:

"You should *not* say such things—he is your father—"

"What does that matter, if he's a despicable brute?" flashed the boy.

"And you would enrage any man, the things you say. It's not right. You'll understand when you get older, my lad."

"I feel as if I should burst if I lived with him any longer," said Arthur.

"Well," replied Mrs Morel, very sadly, "you won't have to live with him much longer. When you leave college you can go away—like William." It was very bitter for her to have to say this.

"I shan't," he retorted, "unless you come with me. We'll go away from him, you and Paul and I—" He spoke wistfully. She shook her head.

"I shall never leave him—what would become of him?" she said.

"Doesn't matter what becomes of him."

"Yes it does", she said quietly, with that note of quiet certitude and finality, so rarely heard from a man, which closed the conversation.

As she was carrying out the broken fragments Paul came in. He looked at the heap of flowers and pot on the dustpan, at the swimming water near the passage door, at the great splash on the wall. Instantly that tragic side of his life, which usually was completely hidden in light enthusiasms and gaiety, showed. He knit at once into the hateful atmosphere.

"What have you been doing?" he asked.

"Oh never mind, never mind," said Mrs Morel wearily. This condition could not long continue in the family, she felt: and she did not want to be forced to send her sons away, and to live alone with her husband. It would be death to her.

"What has he been doing?" Paul asked sharply of Arthur. Mrs Morel hurried out.

"Hit my mother—going to hit me—threw your bowl of primroses at me."

"And where is he—?"

"In bed."

Paul remained quite still, standing near the table. He was exceedingly pale. Waiting till his mother came in, he turned and looked at her. He went cold as ice when he saw the bruise on her cheek, for some minutes felt like a block of ice, standing paralysed. It was five or six years since his father had struck his mother.

Mrs Morel kept her head bent, and her cheek averted from Paul. She was ashamed, afraid.

"You must foment it, mother," he said, in cold, clear tones. "We'll go to bed, and you must do it at once."

There was silence. Paul fetched a large piece of coal to rake the fire.* He washed his hands. His mother was bringing the bread from the pantry.

"I don't want anything to eat—I've had some sweets," he said.

"You had better have your supper," she remonstrated.

"Not if I don't want it," he replied.

She carried back the food. Arthur took a candle, kissed his mother, and went to bed, shaking the tears from his eyes to try and hide them. Paul brought a flannel and bowl of hot water, which he set on the table, then a box of elder-flower ointment.* He was ready for bed.

"If ever he attempts it, mother, while I'm in, I shall murder him," Paul said, in clear, matter-of-fact tones. "And if he does it while I am out, he shall never sleep under the same roof with us again."

He was very cold and imperious. Mrs Morel was rather afraid of him. When he was kindly again, she would regain her influence. He kissed her on the forehead, and went to bed. Listening, as he undressed, he heard the water trickling from the flannel into the bowl, downstairs in the kitchen: and he heard Arthur in the next room, muffling his weeping, heard his father breathing heavily, asleep.

Then, involuntarily, Paul's mind ran on the various ways of destroying his father. He felt almost a deep, bestial thrill of joy at the thought of strangling him.

"Stop it," he said coldly to himself. "It's disgusting."

Then he ran on to poisons: poison was the best, the feasible way. He discussed all ways, with keen calculation. It seemed to him best to use verdigris.* He had once found an old copper spoon in the cellar, vivid green, like a brilliant fungus. This he had thrown away in horror. "But," his thoughts ran on, "I could put a number of pennies in the cracks under the great stone benches. They would soon go green. Every night I could put just a little in his tin bottle that he takes to work full of tea. Mother rinses it out—he does not. A little, after it is rinsed out, he would not taste in the tea—a little every day."

Paul perfected his plan: he lay awake for hours. If the provocation had remained constant, he would probably have carried it out. But provocation rarely remains constant. In the morning Walter Morel was silent, and tried to efface himself. He cringed for a day or two. Then Paul pitied his father deeply, and suffered agonies of shame to see such degradation of manhood. He would have given a great deal from his own life to restore a little manliness to his father. Morel, never a man of strong moral courage, was now a mere fraction of himself; a terrible, a pitiable, and an exceedingly common sight, is a man gone thus, a fact that youth in its heat and its great expectations finds cruelly hard to accept. There was no longer any war between Mrs and Mr Morel— he was insignificant, a kind of unaccountable animal, sometimes kind, sometimes sad, often disagreeable, surly, occasionally dangerous.

Arthur and his father did not speak to one another for a very long time, an occurrence unusual with the warm-blooded Morels, who were every one of them quick to forgive. There remained between the two an animosity which sank into both their bloods: they were, intrinsically, so much alike. Morel had ceased to remember and feel shame for the blow he had given to his wife, before the discoloration had gone from the bruise. He could not help it—his sense of responsibility was nearly gone. This sense of responsibility, which civilisation cultivates to such degree of fineness, had never been strong in him. But it has its roots in our deepest instincts, and from it are gathered the fruits of all civilisation.

As his examination grew near, the strain on Arthur was very tight. He became exceedingly irritable. Mrs Morel bore it all in silence. Where she loved, she understood marvellously. The lad was tyrannical, and inflammable.

"You must take no notice of him," Mrs Morel continually said to Paul, who flew into wrath at his brother's insults.

"You must take no notice," she said to her husband. "Look how thin he is—do you want him to have brain fever—look at his eyes."

Walter Morel did not want his son to have brain fever. On the spur of the moment, he would have given his life to prevent his having it. But it was another thing to bear his capricious temper.

One day, when Morel was working badly, he met Jerry on his way from work. Jerry, who had left Eberwich three months before, and had been doing well, was taking a week's holiday. Morel had a few drinks with him. But Jerry, inclined now to be cocky, with the drink he gave to Morel gave him also a fair amount of bragging.

"Why, tha looks fair boggered, man—hold thysen up. Come up wi' me ter Yorkshire, if th' missis'll let thee."*

"She'll let me right enough," replied Morel.

"Come on wi' thee then, an' leave 'em to their own hooks. How often has ter owt i' thy pocket—?"

"Why niver," replied Morel, sorely.

"No, an' niver tha will ha'e, while they'n got hold on thee. I'n got five pound ten in my pocket to spend in three days. What's think o' that?* An' there's nobody spits in *my* mouth if I speak— —"

Morel came home primed with injury. They should catch it, the first that made a mug of him. Arthur had finished his tea, sat reading up for his exam.

"It's very evident you've been stopping,"* said Mrs Morel, as Morel lurched against the dresser.

"What the hell's that got to do with you?" he shouted at her, flinging his tin bottle and snap bag on the table. The latter, a dirty calico food-bag, fell on Arthur's book. The young man sent it, with a jerk of contempt, onto the floor.

"Nice behaviour!" said Mrs Morel to her husband. He dragged the table to the fire, though it was midsummer. Arthur, going pale and trembling with rage, dragged it back again. It enraged him to be left sitting before space, his book gone.

"What!" cried Morel, starting to his feet, and bending threateningly over the table. He looked incredibly ugly, the whites of his eyes showing from his black face, his red lips pushed out under the rag of hanging moustache.

"Now then!" cried Mrs Morel in a note of warning. Arthur dropped his eyes, curled his lips in a sneer. Morel sat down again. Mrs Morel went out to pick a few gooseberries in the garden.

Morel, in a fearful temper, did all he could that was irritating. He hawked* and spat in the fire. Arthur, very much overwrought, bore it for a moment, then cried, low and sudden:

"Stop it!"

Morel started, there was such fierce authority in the tone.

"You're there are you?" he sneered at his son. "You mind your books, I s'll mind my own business."

Arthur shrugged his shoulders with contempt.

Morel poured his tea into a saucer, sucked it up with much slobbering. Arthur put his hands over his ears, sat reading with his hands shut tight over his ears. It made his father tremble with rage. Having sharpened the carving knife, Morel hacked off a thick lump of the cold meat. Arthur, looking from under his brows, felt sick at the sight. Then the father proceeded to shovel up peas on his knife, and to thrust them into his mouth. One naked, black arm lay along the clean tablecloth. The great dirty hand seemed near to the boy.

"Eat with your fork," cried Arthur.

"Don't look, if you don't like what I do," shouted Morel.

"I won't," said the lad, quick and low. He snatched up a newspaper, propped it up before the teapot and sugar basin, a screen between himself and his father. Then he put his hands over his ears again. It made Morel boil with rage. However, there was silence between the two. Presently Morel was more than ordinarily disgusting. Arthur started up, the paper fell down.

"Goodness gracious!" cried the lad, "I can't do anything where you are, filthy beast!"

"Go out then," bawled Morel.

Mrs Morel, down the garden, stood still to listen.

"It's you who ought to stop out," cried the son, white to the lips. "You're not fit to live with decent people. You're not fit to live with beasts. I'd rather have a pig in the room than you."

"What—" cried Morel, starting up, his hand closing on something. The last bar of restraint broke.

"Filthy, abominable beast!" cried Arthur, in a white-heat of loathing. "Ah, I wouldn't come near you, I wouldn't touch, Ah, it would make me sick, it makes me sick to have you in the room—"

"Have you done?" yelled Morel. "Have you done."

"No—not while a filthy, stinking thing like you is—"

Morel had sprung up, his chair falling backwards, and had hurled at his son the thing he had in his hand. It was the steel.* Instantly there was a fearful shriek. The boy was flung back on the sofa, there was blood spurting, the steel was stuck in the lad's ear. Mrs Morel, running in, saw her husband crouching forward, immobile, in exactly the position whence he had hurled the steel, whilst Arthur shuddered, writhed convulsively on the sofa.

They came to Paul at Jordans, at ten minutes to eight, just before he was leaving to go home. Mrs Morel had travelled with her son in the miners' ambulance, the long ten miles to Nottingham, to the hospital. In ten minutes Paul was at the hospital. Arthur, starting and giving terrible shrieks, but not recognising anything, was at that moment laid in bed, and doctors were being summoned to consultation. Mrs Morel had helped like a nurse. There was blood on her black skirt—Paul saw it was her working skirt, and her bursten working boots. Now she had nothing more to do, she stood in her small black bonnet, like an image, white and motionless, looking at her wounded son. Paul stood perfectly still for a moment or two, looking at his brother. He wished they were all dead, all the Morels. At that moment he learned that not death, but life, is fearful. We die several times during life, most of us. Paul died distinctly at that moment—as his mother, his father, his brother, all were tasting death.

The doctors came, Mrs Morel must go away. They let her sit in the waiting room. Paul felt all the time that his heart was breaking—but he must do things.

"Listen mother," he said. She did not listen. "Listen!" he said, and he took her hand, looked into her eyes till she was forced to perceive him. Her thin, shut mouth hurt him inexpressibly to see. But he must gain attention from her eyes. For a moment, he was jealous that she did not care for him now—that she had forgotten him.

"Listen mother," he said again, holding and stroking her hand. "Shall I get you a lodging here—just near the hospital?—You won't want to go to Eberwich—?"

Mrs Morel shuddered.

"No," she said, hardly moving her thin, compressed lips; she answered the latter part of the question.

"No. I'll get you a room. Then I'll go home and see to father—eh?"

He spoke gently. She looked at him this time, and there was a glance of her old love. Paul held his breath, held himself still to regain control. He stroked her cheeks, her brow, with his fine fingers, then left her.

There was not much difficulty in getting a room. A quarter of an hour, he was back again. His mother still sat as he had left her. The nurse said she could not see Arthur for some time, nor could they know anything.

"Then come with me," Paul said, "and see your room." She rose quietly.

"You see mother," he said as they went down the cobble-paved street, with the hospital high like precipices on either side, and a little closed-in tunnel-bridge connecting the two walls, high overhead. "You see, the second turning—see, this with the big bush of ivy hanging over the corner wall."

Mrs Morel noted the locality mechanically.

Paul took his mother back, and waited for the doctors' verdict. It was "They did not know." Paul saw the chief.

"I can say nothing with certainty."

Paul looked him in the eyes for a moment.

"And—you've little hope," Paul asked.

The doctor bowed his head. The brother did also.

"Goodnight mother," Paul said, kissing her forehead. He knew Arthur would not recover. "I shall come again early in the morning, and tell you about father." He wanted to be sure his mother did not entertain false hopes. "You'll be able to stay here without bothering about home—I don't suppose—it'll be so very long." His mother gave no sign. Yet Paul, somehow, knew by her mouth that she was wounded deeper. For a moment, he was in trepidation: was it necessary? But he knew Arthur would die. "And I'll send a letter to William—they won't have wired*—it's no good wiring mother!"

"No," she said.

"But kiss me, mother."

She kissed him, looked at him a moment, and her lips quivered. Then she regained her impassivity.

Paul left her. When he got home, he found his father had been taken in charge, was in the lock-up of the police-station. The son was admitted to see his father, and his heart was sore for pity when he saw the man already peaked, quite shrunk.

"How was he?" were Morel's first words, husky and quiet. Morel felt he had no longer any right to anything—must beg to be spoken to. It was very painful.

"I don't know, father," said Paul, drearily. "The doctors had a consultation; they didn't seem to think there was much hope: there might be, of course. You never know."

Morel sunk his head. It was evident from Paul's tone what his opinion was, and Morel had implicit faith in Paul's opinion.

"Shall I try and bail you out, father? I think they'd let me. Shall I? Mother's stopping in Nottingham—Annie will keep house."

"No child," the man replied. "No child, don't you trouble."

"But I *will*, father, if you'd care for me to. I want to do just what you like."

"No child," said the father, pleadingly.

"You'd rather stay here till we see— —"

"Yes child, I think I would."

Paul would have wished the same.

"All right father. I'll come and tell you every day—"

"Do child, if it's not too much trouble—"

"And I'll telephone to the station if anything happens—whether you're here or in Nottingham, I'll come, or I'll telephone—see?"

"Ay."

"Could I bring you anything, father—tobacco?—or a drink?"

"No no—I don't want anything."

Paul took his father's hand. He was sorry for the poor, broken, emotional man; he kissed him on the forehead. Tears began to run down Walter Morel's cheeks.

For ten days Arthur Morel lay in the hospital, in great anguish. His screams were sometimes terrible. Mrs Morel's hair went nearly white in this time. She had no hope.

"Let him go—let him die," she said at last to the doctors. The boy recognised her once or twice, but it was only to cry to her in anguish. Once, on the eighth day, he said:

"It wasn't my father's fault, mother."

When this was told to Walter Morel he was himself in prison-hospital in Nottingham. He wept aloud and unrestrainedly, rather like a dog.

For a fortnight after Arthur's death Morel dared not see his wife.— They buried the lad in the cemetery at Eberwich, on the sunny hill that looks down to the ash-trees of the valley, and over the distant meadows. The tall church* towered up above its trees, half a mile away uphill. In the cemetery field marguerite daisies and red sorrel waved. It was a sweet spot. But to bury a proud young life in, any field is bitter.

For a fortnight after Arthur's death, Walter Morel dared not see his wife. Then she came, and he hid his face among the pillows. She was touched with pity, but nothing moved her deeply now.

Morel was so ill that he could not be tried for four months. Then, such a frail, broken creature he was, the judge expressed his sympathy, and gave him the very minimum penalty. Morel was scarcely in prison at all.

When he came home, he was visibly dying. The will to live had gone. Mrs Morel had a separate room from him, otherwise she was very kind. Everybody was very kind. But life filtered gradually from him. He scarcely went out of doors, scarcely spoke, but wished always to keep in the shadows. As they say, he never looked up.

Within a year he was dead. One could not grieve for that. But when Paul had looked for a time on the dead face of his father, the childish, forlorn, frightened face, he went and hid in his own bed and cried uncontrollably for an hour. Life was so dreadful, and so cruel. It had been very cruel to his father.

Mrs Morel could scarcely believe that this small face, with its big fringed rag of moustache, was the same that had shone in such red and black beauty before her thirty years before.

"They are two different people," she said, which was true. She wept for pity. But it was a relief to be left alone with Paul, when she could rest from life, escape its exigencies for a time before she followed her young son.

They remained in Eberwich: Mrs Morel preferred it. It had been her home for thirty years, she had taken root there. But she moved to a different house, not far away. It was a pleasant five roomed cottage, on the brow of the highest hill,* a little higher even than the church, which from the Breach had seemed such an eminence. The house was some sixty years old, substantially built. The front came on to the road, was common and mean in appearance, but the back was very pleasant. There was a long garden that ran down to a field. Near the door was a square of grass, with a great elder tree and a white lilac tree down one side. Beyond was the vegetable garden, with two or three apple trees. As Mrs Morel sat on the sofa under the big kitchen window, she could look straight ahead, over a few scattered, vivid red-roofed cottages, to the white highway climbing up the hill to Ilkeston four miles away. To the right the townlet of Eberwich crowded, a little below the level of Morel's house, and three fields distant. The church towered up black, the spire pricked brightly into the sky. And beyond, to the north-west, were the heaped hills of Derbyshire usually full of light, or in deep cloud. On a clear day, one could see the high round knoll of Crich,* ten miles as the crow flies, and the sun would glisten on its steep white face, where the limestone is quarried.

Paul felt at last he had a home, here, in this house, that gave so splendidly onto the country. Their other homes had been temporary sorts of places, distasteful for many reasons. This was home. The house had a genuine old character, as if the builder had said: "What I have, I'll have it solid, and thorough, and I'll spend a bit of time over it, to make it ample. I can't have much, but I'll have it good, I'll have it ample, I won't feel mean about it."

Paul liked the house. His trouble was, to get his mother to be interested in it, in anything. All day long he was away, and his mother brooded. Annie was four miles away. When he came home at night, he found his mother sitting waiting, everything ready: but she scarcely noticed his entrance, sat in her rocking-chair, looking into space, and beating lightly with her right hand on the arm of the sofa. He would talk to her, tried in vain to interest her.

"What's the matter, mother?" he said at last, pitifully, because he did not know what else to say. She did not answer.

"What's the matter?" he pleaded.

"You know what's the matter," she answered. He dropped his head despairingly. There was so much to struggle with. She saw him, and rebuked herself.

He did, perhaps, the best thing possible: he fell ill. Then his mother roused herself. She nursed him, she had something vital to do, something to live for. When he was getting better, she was thoroughly tired, and slept at night heavily, as she had not slept for years. Paul saw at last a peacefulness about her that is the equivalent of happiness. They were happy together: it was an afterglow.

"Did I hear you get out of bed?" Mrs Morel would ask with that mock-severe, authoritative tone that is so delicious. Paul laughed, unwilling to confess.

"What did you want?" she asked.

"A book," he confessed.

"That you shall *not* have—give it to me."

And Paul surrendered his book. Yet nothing is sweeter, on either side, than this tyranny of love: the sense of being utterly in the hands of a lover is very sweet to a weak man, whilst to the woman her sense of responsibility is poignant, kindling. They talked a great deal together, of people they knew, of pleasant little things, never of the painful past: sometimes of the future.

"I shan't marry, mother," he said.

"Ah," she smiled roguishly—"an old tale!"

"I'll marry my housekeeper when I'm fifty—you're not much more than fifty now."

"Am I not?" she laughed. "And shall I live to be over eighty then."

"Yes, just to please me, mother."

"Ah, things are not so easily arranged, my boy." A shadow flitted over them both, as they remembered.

"Well mater, we'll arrange just this bit."

She laughed, began to do something for him.

At evening, through the low, large window, came creeping the strange scent of phlox. The half moon, as the night came on, hung glistering white full in Paul's face as he lay.

"I want to sit up a minute mother," he asked.

She looked at him. Even had it been hurtful, she would have allowed him, because his eyes were dark and earnest. She raised him, and together they sat looking out. Far away, the heave of the hill was pale grey in moonlight, the highroad* showing like a pallid cicatrice. The valley between was a great width of darkness, till the corn-land

heaved glistening into sight, approached in the grey glow of the meadows, which ended suddenly at the black and shadowy garden, with its
wrought screen of bean-rows, and, near the house, the intense white
gleam of clumps of phlox.

"I wish, mother," Paul said, "that a man could have a young mother.
It startles me, and makes me feel afraid, when I see your hair white."

She smiled, told him he had better lie down now.

"Not yet, mother. Look how the church dominates the town, gets the
houses under its wing.—* You don't *want* me to be notable—you don't
want me to be great, do you?"

She laughed quickly, catching at his train of thought.

"I don't want you to be anything but happy," she said. Paul, however,
was wise, if unknowing. He did not answer his mother's *words*.

"Because, mother, I think I might be a good painter, and be great,
perhaps. But it would interrupt me: sort of damming up one part of
your life, and letting a lot of the rest wither. Do you want me to bother?"

"*I* want you to bother, my lad!" she exclaimed softly. Yet he knew she
was disappointed. He lay down, and she kissed him, and he determined
to try to be great, though he didn't want to.

He loved to sit up in bed in the morning. Then he could see the
sun swing round the wall, catch at the great stack of red lilies, till they
seemed like a bon-fire of daylight flaring. The cornflowers danced blue,
the poppies, pink and white, fluttered out like butterflies. All the sides
of the houses of Eberwich across the meadows butted their blazing red
walls towards him, glittered their hundreds of chimney-pots, and hid the
shadow somewhere in their depths. As Paul got better he sat under the
elder tree and painted it all. His old, passionate fury for self-expression
revived.

All this while, Paul scarcely thought of Miriam. Occasionally she
came to see him. He was very blind to her. As she sat near him, trembling
with pitiful love, he laughed and chatted pleasantly to her as if she were
a stranger.

"He never speaks to me of the things that trouble him—he only laughs
and is pleasant," Miriam said bitterly to herself as she went away. She
became very moody and passionate. Her father was dead: she had three
hundred pounds of her own.

"I will go away and learn to be a nurse, Miss May," she said to
Mrs Revell.

"A fine nurse you would make, dear—you would drop everything,
you would tremble so."

"I will be a teacher then—"

"And teach what—?"

Miriam could teach nothing, save, perhaps, music. Mrs Revell had given up most of her music-pupils.

"You can have what are left of my girls, dear," said Mrs Revell.

So Miriam became a peripatetic music-teacher, as her governess had been. She could be seen, with her strange swinging stride and her handsome, downcast face, traversing the highroads from village to village, often amongst the crowded groups of miners trailing from work. She was not happy—she was not a born teacher. A dreamer, it was maddening to her to be forced to break into her dreams for the purpose of teaching little girls and boys their scales. It irked her terribly. She was not a great success. Moreover she had none of Miss May's tact and authority. Miss May had made herself respected wherever she was not loved. Miriam roused mistrust in everyone who misunderstood her: and as she was always misunderstood by colliers' and petty tradesmen's wives, she had a poor time of it. What were the women to think of a girl who was deferential, humble, almost pleading towards them, who yet had a haughty contemptuous soul in reserve, whose sudden change to acid coldness was most galling. Among her sisters, the woman who claims her own soul, and who claims the guerdon for her own soul, is as a rule cordially, if secretly hated. The ordinary woman's attitude is—'Let my men-folk think and talk and act, I am content *to be*, I am an underground reservoir for him, whence he draws his sustenance.' Miriam's attitude was—'These men are fools in word and act as well as in soul. Let them subserve *me*, who have understanding.' Between the two types, the women who sacrifice themselves and the women who command sacrifice, there is bitter hostility, founded on some secret sympathy. Miriam was almost universally disliked by women: and to men she was cold. She was lonely, her life was insufficient. She brooded forever on Paul, and on her own soul, which was not receiving just recognition from life. Paul was due to her.

Chapter IX

ATTRACTION

There had come to Jordan's, two years before, a new overseer of the spiral department. Polly left to get married, much to everyone's surprise, for she was thirty-nine years old. The new woman was married, but living apart from her husband. She was a tall, silent blonde, with full strong limbs and small breasts. Her head was bent, her shoulders dropped, not from weakness however, but from a fierce shrinking of reserve. She was silently disliked by the other girls. Her face was pale, impassive, rather heavy round the jaw. When she did raise her eyes, there was a look of sullenness and secrecy in them, as an Italian avenger might look from under the brim of his slouch hat. The other girls said among themselves:

"The way she looks at you!—it makes you shudder." It was the result, however, of extreme self-consciousness, sensitiveness, of feeling of alienity.* She had been brought up by an unwilling aunt. Married, at twenty one, to George Radford, the iron-smith for Jordan, she had spent seven unhappy years. Then she had left her husband, returned to the spiral department, of which Paul was now chief, Mr Pappleworth having set up business for himself. With most of the girls, Frances was exceedingly pleasant, and very lenient. There were never any rows. Yet the place was full of discontent. There was never the least comradeship between the overseer and the workers, to confirm this winning show of friendliness. If Frances hated a girl, and she was prone to contemptuous hate, still she was perfectly amiable towards her: which the other felt as an insult. Towards Fanny, the poor overstrung hunchback, Frances was unfailingly compassionate and gentle, as a result of which Fanny wept in private bitterer tears than Polly's rough tongue ever caused her. The new overseer had been in the place a year, without ever really noticing Paul: he was a flirty boy. For his part, he sometimes found himself watching her handsome, bowed white throat, her glistening yellow hair that she coiled on top of her head. There was something in her he disliked. He was chilly and rather rude to her, feeling that she despised him: but she was so much older and more darkly wise than he. Moreover, all the other girls held him in league against her. Therefore he kept at a cold distance from her. Nevertheless he was deep down angry with her for ignoring him. He would not remain in the same room with her.

George Radford, her husband, still came to the factory, bringing the steels for the trusses, and other metal appliances which he wrought at his forge in another part of the town. He was a large man, of insolent carriage, handsome, not yet thirty years old. Erect, rather heavy, yet indifferent in his bearing, well-dressed, yet negligently, he was difficult to place socially. Something of an artizan, something of the neer-do-well son of a country squire, something large and insolent and brutal, like Henry VIII, showed in his appearance. He would have been very handsome but for the expression of his eyes. Generally dressed in brown, he gave Paul a delightful sense of gold and tawny and brown. His face was of a healthy, golden pallor, his moustache golden brown, his hair dark, his eyes glistening like dark-brown jewels. But his eyelids slouched over his eyes with a brutal leer, his mouth was coarse. None of the girls ever spoke of him to Paul. But Paul knew that Hilda, a girl with a showy figure, fine grey eyes, and the pride of all the devils in her bearing, was at the present Radford's mistress.

Between the two men there was instinctive hostility. The artist in Paul watched Radford with cold, keen criticism. This the other brutally resented.

"Who are yer staring at, yer little sod?" Radford sneered. Paul gave him another look, straight and cold, full in his glistening brown eyes. Then the young man turned away. Radford swore very disgustingly. It affected Paul like a bad smell to hear it. He was, in the words of Radford, "a finicking little swine."

Radford was an illegitimate son, whose mother had been provided for. The old lady, vulgar, still lived with her son in the house attached to the smithy, near the Jews' Burying-Ground, in Sneinton.* She found no fault with George, at least, in his presence. He might drink and go on as he pleased. Once he had been a very skilful player of the flute and piccolo. Frances had accompanied him on the piano at Jordan's Christmas party. Afterwards she had accompanied him at concerts in the town. She was very distant with men, disliking them. Yet she had her splendid throat, and her heavy white arms with small, delicate, but rather reddened hands, often bare. So cold and white, she was; and in spite of this her glances were charged with sorcery, passion that made the man mad for her. They married. She wanted to get poetry, dark fantasy out of the union. He was brutal, vulgar, and lacked repose. She grew to loathe him, at last left him. He hated her. There were no children.

When Paul returned to Jordan's after the death of his brother, everybody was very kind. Miss Jordan, knowing that Paul was fond of painting, made a point of asking him how he progressed in art. The outcome of this was that, upon Miss Jordan's advice, the young man went on Monday and Thursday afternoons to the art school. On Thursday, a slack day, he was given from 3.0 to 5.0 off. He appreciated the generosity of fussy, tyrannical old Jordan, and profited by the lessons.

Frances, forever ready with sympathy, would come in her silent way and take her stand near Paul, would imperceptibly fondle him. Her glances were tender, protective; her voice was very intimate, in spite of the commonplace words; she seemed to lean towards him, as if she too needed sympathy. Paul was very much disturbed. He came to watch her about the room, watch her strong figure bowed over the machine, her neck, powerful and solid-white, always bowed, her straight, heavy arms at repose with the transparent silk of her blouse. Paul had no idea he watched her.

They came to be moderately intimate. She told Paul she would like to see his sketches. He brought several. Some she praised warmly, some she put indifferently aside. That piqued him. She was startled and pleased by his idealised sketches of a colliery. As she looked at him with awakened interest, their eyes met. He felt a great fluttering inside him, was profoundly scared, yet delighted.

She was very self sufficient. If a thing displeased her, no matter what it was, she calmly and indifferently turned aside. If she failed to understand a sketch, or a book Paul gave her, that is, if she merely failed to appreciate them, she said calmly, with a peculiar metallic drawl:

"It doesn't interest me—why should I concern myself with it."

That piqued Paul. He himself would grapple with a thing and spend his efforts on it, to get some meaning from it. This woman insolently, like a Pharisee in soul, walked by.* It maddened Paul: he was furious with her. She smiled.

"I wonder you take so much trouble," she said.

He was continually battling with her.

"I like Miss Jordan," he would say, musingly.

"Do you," she said, quite uninterested.

"You know, she's full of poetry," he said, earnest.

"She doesn't look it," Frances laughed. She was flippant, and Paul was annoyed.

"Because you haven't got eyes to see—you're as blind as a bat to three quarters of the world."

"Am I?" she said, thin-lipped, cuttingly cold.

Paul was furious against her. She smiled. He was such a boy.

She had acquired a certain amount of education, could read French, though in a laboured fashion. Having an immense pride in herself, she was infuriated if anyone suggested that she was stupid.

"You read French, do you?" cried Paul, picking up the *Lettres de Mon Moulin** from the work-bench. Mrs Radford glanced round negligently. She was making an elastic stocking of heliotrope silk, turning the spiral-machine with slow, balanced regularity, occasionally bending down to see her work, or to adjust the needles: then her magnificent white neck, with its glistening yellow down and fine pencils of gold hair shone against the lavender, lustrous silk. She turned a few more rounds, and then stopped.

"What did you say?" she asked, smiling sweetly. Paul's eyes glittered at her insolent indifference to him.

"I did not know you read French," he said, very polite.

"Did you not?" she replied, with a faint, sarcastic smile. He shut his mouth angrily, and watched her. She seemed to scorn the work as she mechanically turned the handle. Yet the hose she made were as nearly perfect as possible.

"You don't like spiral work," he said.

"Oh well, all work is work," she answered, almost with a sneer. He marvelled at her coldness. Whatever he did, he did warmly, infused some of his blood in it. She was astonishing to him.

"What would you prefer to do?" he asked.

She laughed at him, part in contempt, as she said:

"There is so little likelihood of my ever being given a choice, that I haven't wasted time considering."

"Pah!" he said, contemptuous on his side now. "You only say that because you're too proud to own up that you want what you can't get."

"You know me very well," she replied, with a haughty sneer.

"I know you think you're terrific great shakes, and that you live under the eternal insult of working in a factory—" He was very angry, and very rude. She merely turned away from him in disdain. He walked whistling down the room, flirted and laughed wickedly with Hilda.

Later on, he said to himself:

"What was I so impudent to Frances for?" He was rather annoyed with himself, at the same time glad.

"Serve her right—she stinks with silent pride," he said to himself angrily.

For several days he avoided seeing her at all. At last, however, he had to go down and discuss an order with her. Upon the surface of all his wrath and discomfort, he was gay and pleasant as ever.

"You are wearing a flower," he said. "I thought that was against your rule."

"I have no *rule*," she said, gently raising the head of a rather bruised red rose.*

* * * *

her stairs, with her face radiant with a secret. Paul looked at her in astonishment.

"I want you," she said. He was astonished.

"Come on," she coaxed. "Come before you begin of the letters." He went down the half dozen steps into her dry, narrow 'finishing-off' room. Fanny walked before him: her bodice was so short, the waist was under her arm-pits; and her green-black cashmere skirt seemed very long, as she strode with long strides before the young man, himself so graceful. She went to her seat at the far end of the room, where the window opened onto chimney pots. Paul watched her thin hands and her flat red wrists as she excitedly twitched her white apron, which was spread on the bench in front of her. She hesitated.

"You didn't think we'd forget you," she asked, reproachful.

"Why?" he asked. He had forgotten his birthday himself.

"'Why', he says! 'why'! Why, look here!" She pointed to the calender, and he saw, surrounding the big black numbers '21', hundreds of little crosses of black-lead.

"Oh, kisses for my birthday," he laughed. "How did you know?"

"Yes, you want to know, don't you," Fanny mocked, hugely delighted. "There's one from everybody—except Lady Frances—and two from some. But I shan't tell you how many *I* put."

"Oh, I know you're spooney," he teased.

"There you *are* mistaken," she cried, indignant. "I could never be so soft." Her voice was strong and contralto.

"You always pretend to be such a hard-hearted hussy," Paul smiled, speaking caressingly to her. "And you know you're as senti-mental— — —"

"I'd rather be called sentimental than be frozen like foreign meat," she blurted. Paul knew she referred to Frances, and he smiled.

"I hope you don't deal *me* out such squashes," he laughed.

"No, my duck," the hunchback woman answered, lavishly tender. She was thirty eight. "No my duck, because you don't think yourself a fine figure in marble and us common stone. I'm as good as you, aren't I, Paul?" and the question delighted her.

"Nay Fanny, we're not better than one another, good Lord!" he replied.

"But I'm as good as you, aren't I, Paul?" she persisted daringly.

"Yes Fan, you are. It would never occur to me to think of it."

"I thought I'd get here before the others—I don't care if they *are* mad—Now shut your eyes—" she said.

"'And open your mouth, and see what God sends you'," Paul continued, suiting action to words, and expecting a piece of chocolate. He heard the rustle of the apron, and a faint click of metal.

"I'm going to look," he said.

He opened his eyes. Fanny, her long cheeks flushed, her blue eyes shining, was gazing at him. There was a very fine big box of water-colour paints open on the bench before him. He turned pale.

"No Fanny," he said quickly.

"It's from us all," she answered hastily.

"No but— —"

"Are they the right sort?" she asked, rocking herself with delight.

"By Jove—they're the best in the catalogue—"

"But there was two sorts—"

"I like pans better than tubes—I've made up my mind long since to buy these when my ship came in—and here's my ship—"

Fanny was overcome with emotion. She must turn the conversation.

"They was all eager to do it, they all paid their shares, all except the Queen of Sheba."*

The Queen of Sheba was Frances.

"And wouldn't she join?" Paul asked.

"She didn't get the chance—we never told her—we wasn't going to have *her* bossing *this* show. We didn't *want* her to join."

Paul laughed at her, praised the paints. At last he must go. She was very close to him. Suddenly she flung her arms round his neck and kissed him passionately.

"I can give you a kiss today," she said, apologetically. "You've looked so white, it's made my heart ache."

Paul kissed her, and left her. Her arms were so pitifully thin, that his heart ached also.

That day, Frances was staying to dinner. Paul met her as he ran downstairs to wash his hands.

"You have stayed to dinner!" he exclaimed. It was unusual for her.

"Yes—and I seem to have dined on surgical-appliance stock. I *must* go out now, or I shall feel stale and dusty right through."

She lingered. He instantly caught at her wish.

"You are going anywhere?" he asked.

They went together up to the Castle.* Out doors she dressed very plainly, down to ugliness. Indoors she studied her toilet. She walked with quick, light steps alongside Paul, bowing and turning away from him. Dowdy in dress, and drooping, she showed to great disadvantage outdoors: no man would look at her. Paul could scarcely recognise her strong form, that seemed to slumber with power. She looked almost insignificant, drowning her stature in her stoop.

The Castle grounds were very green and fresh. Climbing the precipitous ascent, Paul laughed and chattered, but she was silent, seeming to brood over something. There was scarcely time to go inside the squat, square building that crowns the fine bluff of rock. They leaned upon the wall where the cliff runs sheer down to the Park. Below them, in their holes in the red sandstone, pigeons preened themselves and cooed softly. Away down upon the boulevard at the foot of the rock, tiny trees stood in their own pools of shadow, and tiny people seemed scurrying about in almost ludicrous importance.

"You feel as if you could scoop up the folk like tadpoles, and have a handful of them," said Paul.

She laughed, answering:

"Yes—it is not necessary to get far off in order to see us proportionately. The trees are far more significant."

"Bulk only,"* Paul said.

She laughed cynically.

Away beyond the boulevard, the thin stripes of the metals showed upon the wide scored tracks of the railway, that was crowded round with little stacks of stuff, and fussy with engines. Then the silver string of the canal lay at random among the black heaps. Beyond, the dwellings, very dense on the river flats, looked like black, poisonous herbage, in thick rows and crowded beds, stretching right away, broken now and then by taller plants, right to where the river glistened in a hieroglyph across the country. The steep scarp cliffs across the river looked puny. Great stretches of country, darkened with trees and faintly brightened with corn land, spread towards the haze, where the hills rose blue beyond grey.

"It is comforting," said Mrs Radford, "to think the town goes no further. It is only a *little* sore upon the country yet."

"A little scab," Paul said.

She shivered. She loathed the town. Looking drearily across at the country which was forbidden her, her impassive face pale and hostile, she reminded Paul of one of the bitter, remorseful angels, that had fallen when Satan fell.*

"But the town's all right," said Paul, "It's only temporary. This is the crude, clumsy model we've made, till we find out what the idea is. The town will come all right."

"The optimist by intention!" she smiled, sarcastic.

"Perhaps so. But I don't hate the town. It's only a kid's clumsy effort. We haven't learned to live together yet."

"I doubt we never shall," she replied.

"Are you always like this?" he asked. "Loathing the very clothes you wear, and the words you speak."

"It's only the unnatural things," she smiled. "When things are natural they are beautiful."

"And isn't man natural?" he asked.

"I think not," she said.

"Wasn't Radford natural?" he bluntly asked.

She coloured deeply, looked away from him.

"We will not discuss it," she said coldly.

"All right—But I think he's a bit *too* natural: a bit too near the native beast."

"You can spoil an animal," she said.

"I don't know. He'd be all right in his place. We're only mixed up: seven million stages, from the chimpanzee to me then to the poets and the Christs. Radford suits Hilda."

"I think you have not yet learned respect for another person's feelings," she said, coldly. He laughed.

"I am reprimanded," he said, continuing, "But what does it matter! I think about it—I only say it because I'm interested. And at the present moment, we're 'up above the world so high, like two cherubs in the sky'*—and goodness, if that man was Radford, that strutty little object down there, shouldn't you feel he was little enough to allow discussion?"

The blithe ignorance in which he whistled through her private places disarmed her anger. She smiled at him, inwardly. He was such an interesting, but such a young infant of a boy.

"I shall soon be constrained to call you the 'enfant terrible'," she said, smiling.

"Call me what you like," he replied. "'A rose would smell as sweet etc'."*

The pigeons in the pockets of rock, among the perched bushes, cooed comfortably. To the left, the large church of St. Mary's rose into space, a giantess, to keep close company with the Castle, above the heaped rubble of the town. Mrs Radford smiled brightly as she looked across the country.

"I feel better," she said.

"Thank you," Paul replied. "Great compliment!"

"Oh, little brother!" she laughed.

"Hm! that's snatching back with the left hand what you gave with the right,* and no mistake," Paul said.

She laughed in amusement at him.

"But what was the matter with you?" he asked. "I know you were brooding something special. I can see the stamp of it on your face yet."

"I think I will not tell you," she said.

"All right—hug it," he answered rudely.

She flushed and bit her lip.

"No," she said, "it was the girls."

"What about 'em?" Paul asked.

"They have been plotting something for a week now, and today they seem particularly full of it. All alike, they insult me with their secrecy."

"Do they?" Paul asked in concern.

"I should not mind," she went on, in the metallic, angry tone, "if they did not thrust it into my face, the fact that they have a secret."

"Just like women," said wise Paul.

"It is hateful, their mean gloating," she said intensely.

Paul was silent. He knew what the girls gloated over. He was sorry to be the cause of this new dissention.

"They can have all the secrets in the world," she went on, brooding bitterly. "But they might refrain from glorying in them, and making me feel more alien and alone in hatefulness than ever. It is—it is almost unbearable."

Paul thought for a few minutes. He was much perturbed.

"I will tell you what it's all about," he said, very pale and nervous. "It's my birthday, and they've bought me a fine lot of paints, all the girls. They're jealous of you—."

He felt her stiffen coldly at the word 'jealous.'

"—merely because I sometimes bring you a book," he added slowly. "But—you see—it's only a trifle. Don't bother about it, will you—because—" he laughed brilliantly, "—well—what would they say if they saw us here, in spite of their victory— —!"

She was angry with him for his clumsy reference to their present intimacy. It was almost insolent of him. Yet he was so gentle with her at present, she forgave him, although it cost her an effort.

Their two hands lay on the rough stone parapet of the castle wall. He had inherited from his mother a fineness of mould, so that his hands were rather beautiful. Hers were small, in spite of her large limbs, small, soft, sensitive hands. As Paul looked at them he felt sorry for her. "She is lonely, she is afraid like a child among uncongenial strangers—for all she is so contemptuous of us all," he said to himself. And she felt a longing to be soothed, caressed by *his* hands so strangely blithe and gentle, yet masculine. He was brooding now, staring out over the country with sullen brows. The little, interesting diversity of shapes had vanished from the earth. All that remained was a vast, dark matrix of sorrow and tragedy, the same in all the houses and the river-flats and the people and the birds: they were only shapen differently. And now that the forms seemed to have melted away, there remained only the mass from which all the landscape was composed, a dark mass of struggle and pain. The factory, the girls, his mother, the large uplifted church, the thicket of the town, merged into one atmosphere, dark, brooding and sorrowful, every bit.

"Is that two o'clock striking?" Mrs Radford said in surprise. Paul started, and everything sprang into form, regained its individuality and its forgetfulness, its cheerfulness.

They hurried back to work.

When Paul was in the rush of preparing for the night's post, examining the work up from Fanny's room, which smelt of ironing, the evening postman came in.

"'Mr Paul Morel'," he said smiling, handing Paul a package. "A lady's handwriting! Don't let the girls see it, Sir."

The postman, himself a favourite, was pleased to make fun of the girls' affection for Paul.

It was a volume of Francis Thompson,* with the little note: "You will allow me to send you this, and so spare me my isolation from showing you I also sympathise and wish you well. F. R." Paul flushed hot.

"Good Lord—Mrs Radford! She can't afford it. Good Lord—who ever'd have thought it!"

Paul was suddenly, intensely elated. He seemed to have in his chest and in his belly a consciousness of the woman who had sent him this gift. He could feel the roundness of her fine arms. But he was all in a turbulence of incoherent emotion.

This move on the part of Frances brought them into closer intimacy. The other girls noticed that, when Paul met Mrs Radford, his eyes lifted and gave that peculiar bright greeting which is so significant. Knowing he was unaware, the woman gave no sign, save that occasionally she turned aside her face to hide its secret exultation.

It became their habit to walk out every dinner-time. They talked themselves into a genuine intimacy: Paul had all the rapidity and daring, she her inner ideal and the experience. Gradually, she revealed to him a*

* * *

him mightily. They came keenly to desire each other's company.

"Think!" said Paul, as they came down Standard Hill to go under the old Castle Gateway, then unrestored,* "Think how ripping it would have been to be with Colonel Hutchinson. I should have been a Roundhead* in spite of my fondness for gaiety, because of the intense luxury of having a personal God quite close to one, a God who gave orders. I should have loved it—adventure in God's cause—I should love now to fight against the world—if only there was something to fight against, something you could smite down with a sword, after the psalm was sung. I envy, envy, envy for ever Marston Moor* to the Roundheads. Oh for some adventure—adventure for the sake of one's deepest beliefs."

"I'm afraid you will have to content yourself with the hazards of the spiral ledgers," she said, goading him on.

"Look—the world is discovered from pole to pole: and I should feel it mighty sacrilegious to go hacking at anybody's body: and there's nothing concrete I want very much— —"

"So we're near the millenium," she mocked, as his speech tailed off.

"Good lack!*—Nay, not that. I tell you, there *is* adventure: there's a new, fearful adventure. There's all the underworld to discover: there's the dark continent of the soul. Do you like my phrases? I ought to be in mid-Victoria."

Notes

p. 10, *"Lead Kindly Light"… "There is a green hill far away"*: Hymns by John Henry Newman (1801–90) and C.F. Alexander (1818–95).

p. 10, *"It is finished"*: See John 19:30.

p. 13, *Roger de Coverley*: The name of a popular country dance.

p. 14, *moudiwarp*: Mole (dialect).

p. 16, *worth*: Lawrence added a sentence here: "Gertrude held her head erect, looked straight before her."

p. 24, *Schopenhauer*: The German philosopher Arthur Schopenhauer (1788–1860).

p. 25, *bezzle*: "Squander" (dialect).

p. 26, *pedgilling*: "Struggling to make a living" (dialect).

p. 31, *He would*: Lawrence replaced his original page from the second draft with five pages of revision. As a consequence, twenty-seven lines of the original text are missing at this point.

p. 40, *nesh*: "Delicate, weak" (dialect).

p. 41, *start*: The next page of the third draft is missing following Lawrence's revision in June–July 1912. His replacement page from the final draft is transcribed below:

"What are you doing, clumsy drunken fool?" the mother cried.

"Then you should get the flamin' thing thysen. Tha should get up like other women have to, an' wait on a man."

"Wait on you—wait on you!" she cried. "Yes, I see myself."

"Yis, an' I'll learn thee tha's got to. Wait on *me*, yes, tha sh'lt wait on *me*—"

"Never milord. I'd wait on a dog at the door first."

"What—what?"

He was trying to fit in the drawer. At her last cut, he turned round. His face was crimson, his eyes bloodshot. He stared at her one silent second, in threat.

"P'–h!" she went quickly, in contempt.

He jerked at the drawer in his excitement. It fell, cut sharply on his shin, and on the reflex, he flung it at her.

One of the corners caught her brow as the shallow drawer crashed into the fireplace. She swayed, almost fell stunned from her chair. To her very soul she was sick; yet she clasped the child tightly to her bosom. A few moments elapsed. Then, with an effort, she brought herself to. The baby was crying plaintively. Her left brow was bleeding rather

p. 45, *wormwood… horehound tea*: Popular remedies to cure worms, phlegm and coughs.

p. 47, *the one man cading, the other pulamiting*: One excessively sympathetic, the other excessively self-pitying.

p. 48, *a'most kippered me*: "Almost finished me off" (slang).

p. 48, *a high class fruiterer of Nottingham*: Probably Skinner and Rook on Long Row, Nottingham.

p. 48, *they grand that road*: "They are very good (when cooked) in that way" (dialect).

p. 51, *twig*: "Realize" (slang).

p. 54, *slack*: Small pieces of coal.

p. 55, *busy*: The next page of the third draft does not survive.

p. 59, *Byronic collar*: A stylish open-neck collar, as worn by Lord Byron (1788–1824), as opposed to most men's nightshirts of the 1900s, which were collarless.

p. 59, *rat… stratum*: "Rat" was a general term of abuse until it became more precisely associated in the nineteenth century with strike-breakers and, by extension, with any working-class individuals with questionable morals. The term "stratum" began to be used in the nineteenth century to refer to social class.

p. 59, *brainfever*: Meningitis, almost always fatal in those days.

p. 59, *hasna*: "Has not" (dialect).

p. 59, *Ellen's best*: A reference to a beer brewed by Ellen Wharton, the landlady of the Thorn Tree public house in Eastwood.

p. 59, *Tha*: "You" (dialect).

p. 59, *Durst ter ha'e*: "Dare you have" (dialect).

p. 59, *'er knowed… tha'd better ha'e… canna… it a vittle*: "She knew… you'd better have… can't… it's a victual" (dialect).

p. 60, *nowt but… I durst-na… Tha durs'n't… me 'ead*: "Nothing but… I daren't… you daren't… my head" (dialect).

p. 61, *art bad?… Me 'ead's that wattery*: "Are you feeling bad?… My head is very watery (i.e. dizzy)" (dialect).

p. 62, *caded*: "Treated kindly" (dialect).

p. 62, *mardy*: "Pampered, soft, peevish, whining" (dialect).

p. 63, *gathering*: Boil or abscess.

p. 64, *Dost feel owt like*: "Do you feel all right?" (dialect).

p. 64, *Miss May*: A character based on Fanny Wright (1854–1904), who ended up being omitted from *Sons and Lovers*.

p. 64, *the French strain*: A reference to Lawrence's father's belief that he had a French grandfather.

p. 64, *Arthur*: Sometimes referred to as William or Paul in the manuscript, but always corrected, which perhaps supports the theory that the character is a composite of Lawrence's older brother and himself.

p. 65, *Mr Revell*: This character becomes Mr Heaton in *Sons and Lovers*.

p. 65, *Morven*: A fictionalized version of Moor Green in Eastwood.

p. 65, 52, *The Breach*: The Lawrences lived at 57 The Breach from 1887 to 1891.

p. 65, *collected*: Here used in the sense of "put into order".

p. 65, *Eberwich*: A fictionalized version of Eastwood.

p. 65, *she was with child*: This expression was not in common usage, except in literary or biblical contexts.

p. 66, *like one of God's queens*: The reference is obscure, but the term "queen" has often been used to refer to the Virgin Mary, the goddesses of ancient religions or women of pre-eminent rank in general.

p. 67, *demonstration*: Show of emotion.

p. 67, *neuralgia*: A catch-all term used to refer to pains resulting from tooth decay, sinusitis, blocked ears, shingles, etc.

p. 68, *melancholia*: A medical term at the time, implying that Paul's psychological state is rooted in a biological condition.

p. 68, *hobbing iron... lading-can... fuses*: A "hobbing iron" is an iron anvil used to attach soles to shoes. A "lading-can" is a small tin can used for ladling. Fuses were detonated in the mine to loosen coal.

p. 69, *force little jockey*: "False little rogue" (dialect).

p. 69, *slives*: "Sidles up to" (dialect).

p. 69, *wor*: "Was" (dialect).

p. 70, *owt... again... fair... tanger*: "Anything... against... very much... rogue" (dialect).

p. 70, *Annie... William*: These siblings are based on Lawrence's sister Emily (1882–1962) and brother William Ernest (1878–1901).

p. 70, *Andersen*: Among the many well-known children's stories by Hans Christian Andersen (1805–75) was 'The Ugly Duckling', which is mentioned later in the text.

p. 71, *he'll none catch cold—shall ter*: "He won't catch cold – will you" (dialect).

p. 71, *A dear little girl*: A reference to the poem 'Good Night and Good Morning' by Richard Monckton Milnes, Baron Houghton (1809–85), which begins with the line "A fair little girl sat under a tree".

p. 71, *'ginger' hair*: William is inconsistently described as being "fair haired" on p. 74.

p. 72, *amazons*: Literally "female warriors" from the mythical tribe in Greek legend.

p. 72, *Three Men from Lincolnshire*: A pavement game in which three children, holding hands, dance forwards and backwards a few times with a skipping step, while another child, facing them, asks, "What can you do?" and then has to guess the trades, usually agricultural tasks, which the three mime.

p. 72, *Bacchantes*: "Wild women", from the classical Greek female worshippers of Bacchus, the god of wine.

p. 72, *safe workings... dips... gross... tallows*: "Safe workings" were tunnels in the coalmine where there were no flammable gases. "Dips", or "dip candles", were cheap candles made by repeatedly dipping wicks into melted animal fat. A "gross" is twelve dozen, i.e. 144, and "tallow" was the fat from around the kidneys of sheep and cattle, melted down to make candles.

p. 73, *'Ugly Duckling' and 'Little Folk' stories... glib to a fault*: For 'Ugly Duckling' see third note for p. 70. *Little Folks: The Magazine for Boys and Girls* was a magazine published from 1875 to 1933. Lawrence uses "glib" of Annie less critically later (p. 84), and differently of Mr Staynes (see note for p. 97).

p. 73, *when quite a tiny*: Dialect usage.

p. 73, *sleepers*: Pieces of wood laid in series on the ground to support the rails along which the trucks ran.

p. 74, *The winter of Paul's sixth year*: Lawrence originally wrote, "When he was seven years old", changed it at once to "The winter of Paul's seventh year", and finally revised "seventh" to "sixth".

p. 74, *Nethermere*: Fictional name for Moor Green Reservoir.

p. 75, *vaunter*: It is unclear why Lawrence has chosen this archaic word meaning braggart or praiser.

p. 76, *the mine*: A reference to Moor Green Colliery.

p. 76, *between earth and heaven*: A possible reference to *Hamlet*, Act III, Sc. 1, l. 128: "What should such fellows as I do crawling between heaven and earth?"

p. 76, *the whimsey, or pond, at its foot far below*: A "whimsey" was a steam-driven winding mechanism for raising water and other material to the surface when a mine was being sunk and also when it was in operation; the pond that supplied the water for the stream also became known as a "whimsey".

p. 76, *high road half way between Nottingham and Alfreton*: Nottingham is approximately nine miles south-east and Alfreton is seven miles north-west of Eastwood. The "high road" between them passed through Nuthall and Moor Green, beside Moor Green Reservoir and then north to Underwood.

p. 77, *Ginger*: Apparently based on George Henry Neville (1886–1950).

p. 77, *pasties*: A mocking dialect expression for broad, flat feet, i.e. shaped like pasties.

p. 77, *Lucy Staynes*: The Staynes family was inspired by the local Eastwood family of George Henry Cullen (1845–1915), his wife Lucy (1836–1904) and their children.

p. 78, *Mr Staynes... Mrs Staynes*: See note above.

p. 78, *Miriam*: A character based on Flossie Cullen and Jessie Chambers.

p. 78, *prominent Christian*: George Henry Cullen was secretary of the Congregational Sunday School in Eastwood.

p. 80, *What... down?*: "What have you done to yourself? Have you fallen down?" (dialect).

p. 80, *Grange Farm*: Probably a reference to Newthorpe Grange.

p. 82, *spat on the iron*: In order to test whether it was hot.

p. 82, *a hundred and fifty*: A sum in pounds sterling.

p. 82, *batchy*: "Strange, eccentric" (dialect).

p. 82, *queer*: "Squeamish" (dialect).

p. 84, *His father had married again, and come to live in the Breach*: G.H. Neville's father first married a widow with three children, and they had five sons, of whom G.H. Neville was the second. The family moved to 43 Lynn Croft in 1893–94, while the Lawrences had moved to Walker Street in 1891.

p. 85, *Are ter*: "Are you" (dialect).

p. 88, *down Greenhill Lane to Nethergreen*: Greenhill Lane is a fictional name for Greenhills Road.

p. 88, *market place*: From Eastwood Market Place, derby is twelve miles south-west, Nottingham approximately nine miles south-east and Heanor approximately two miles east.

p. 88, *tod*: "Horse dropping" (dialect).

p. 89, *round scotch*: Normally a "scotch" was a block placed under the wheel of a vehicle to prevent it slipping, but here the block is towed by the wagon and allowed to trail along behind so that it will immediately come into operation when the wagon rolled back onto it.

p. 89, *young clerk in the offices of the Colliery Company*: Lawrence's older brother William Ernest worked as a clerk at the offices of Langley Mill and Aldercar Co-operative Society, before becoming a clerk at the Shipley Colliery Company.

p. 90, *donkey-engine*: A small steam engine used to pump poisonous gases from the mine.

p. 90, *an old Carthusian priory... Annie romanced*: The priory is based on the fifteenth-century Beauvale Priory. See Lawrence's short story 'A Fragment of Stained Glass'.

p. 90, *Abbey Farm. The wood was part of Sherwood forest*: Abbey Farm is a fictional version of Beauvale Manor Farm, and the wood referred to is High Park Wood.

p. 91, *board school... French, German, and a little Latin*: A board school was a local primary school managed by a school board. Lawrence attended the board school in Eastwood, where he learnt French and Latin.

p. 92, *weeping and wailing*: A biblical expression (see Esther 4:3, Jeremiah 9:10, Revelation 18:15 and 19), which could also be found in early English texts such as Langland's *Piers Plowman*.

p. 92, *glegging*: "Peeping" (dialect).

p. 93, *Anthony and Cleopatra*: Probably a reference to Shakespeare's *Antony and Cleopatra* (1606–7).

p. 93, *Indian scalp-lock flying*: Reminiscent of the nickname Lawrence gave his older sister Emily: "Injun Topknot", due to the colour of her hair.

p. 93, *large house in the main-street*: A reference to London House in Eastwood.

p. 94, *Conservative Club*: Lawrence's father was a member of the Conservative Club on Mansfield Road in Eastwood.

p. 95, *the Germans call it 'Golden Rain'*: *Goldregen* is the German word for laburnum.

p. 95, *flower-vawses*: The spelling indicates Mrs Langford's attempt at a "superior" pronunciation.

p. 96, *sat*: Lawrence seems here to mean "turned, by having been sat on".

p. 96, *Bacchic*: One of the many adjectives normally associated with the female worshippers of the classical Greek god of wine, Bacchus.

p. 97, *a glib hour here and there*: The meaning of "glib" here is "easy-going".

p. 99, *passage of pride-in-arms*: Lawrence adapts the expression "passage of arms", which means "war of words".

p. 99, *twaddly*: "Rubbish" (dialect).

p. 100, *parlour*: The "parlour" was the main reception room for visitors in a working-class cottage.

p. 100, *clawks*: "Scratches" (dialect).

p. 103, *the colour of a thrush's egg*: Pale blue.

p. 104, *shelter-mother rôle*: While the meaning is self-evident, the reference or analogy is obscure. Lawrence may be referring to those who ran shelters for vagrants in the nineteenth century.

p. 104, *Lord Nelson*: A public house on Nottingham Road in Eastwood.

p. 105, *galvanic*: Literally, produced by galvanism, which is electricity generated by chemical action. Lawrence appears to mean "full of inner electrical energy" which, by implication, has the power to galvanize others into activity.

p. 106, *she had it so before-hand*: Because of the loss of the opening pages of manuscript, this is the only reference to Bertha Morel's socially superior origins.

p. 106, *line-posts*: Posts to hold washing lines for hanging wet laundry.

p. 106, *like the swine of the parable*: See Matthew 8:32 and Mark 5:13.

p. 106, *black path*: The path would be black from coal dust.

p. 106, *London Pride*: Popular name for the *saxifraga umbrosa* plant, which is long-leafed with small pink-and-white flowers.

p. 107, *gay*: Used in the original sense of "cheerful".

p. 108, *ballad of Uhland… Virgil*: Johann Ludwig Uhland (1781–1862) was a German Romantic poet. In *The White Peacock* Lettie quotes lines of Virgil at George.

p. 110, *he was enraged with Alec*: In his memoir, Neville gives a very different account of his only fight with Lawrence, in which he was easily the victor, although he was surprised by the speed and rage of his opponent.

p. 110, *powdered borax, on charcoal*: Sodium borate, a white powder which was used to test minerals.

p. 110, *flung himself on the antagonist*: Lawrence reworked the structure of this fight scene into his short story 'The Old Adam', as well as into *Sons and Lovers*.

p. 111, *Martha Sharp*: This character becomes Beatrice Wyld in *Sons and Lovers*.

p. 111, *When he was turned thirteen*: The rest of this chapter was rewritten in a similar though expanded version for *Sons and Lovers*.

p. 111, *the Colliery company*: Based on Barber Walker and Company.

p. 112, *Mr Thomas Jordan... 21 Friar Lane*: Based on J.H. Haywood Ltd, the Nottingham firm where Lawrence worked in late 1901, which was located at 9 Castle Gate.

p. 113, *the Castle*: Nottingham Castle, built in 1670, but destroyed in 1831 and restored in 1878.

p. 113, *Fountain*: The Nottingham Drinking Fountain was built in 1865, east of the Castle.

p. 114, *chamois leather*: Originally leather made from the skin of the chamois found in the mountains of Europe, but the term now applies to soft, pliable leather in general.

p. 115, *Did you write this letter?*: Lawrence's application letter was printed in *Young Lorenzo* in 1931, together with the confirmation that his brother Ernest had written a draft for him to copy. In it he claimed to have studied bookkeeping and obtained prizes for Maths, French and German.

p. 118, *finishing the 'spiral' goods*: Photographs of the factory workers and Haywood's catalogue were published in *D.H. Lawrence Review* VII, 1 (Spring 1974), pp. 21–25.

p. 118, *chlorodyne gums*: A popular narcotic and painkiller containing chloroform, morphia, hemp, prussic acid, etc.

p. 119, *He's shaping A.1.*: "He's promising to be first class", after the designation of the top category at Lloyd's Register of shipping.

p. 120, *Miss Dorothy Jordan*: Based on Emily Flintoff Haywood, daughter of the factory owner J.H. Haywood, who was an artist and patron for young artists.

p. 121, *all fond of him*: Neville gives a more ambiguous account of Lawrence's own experience at Haywood's.

p. 122, *Gretchen at the Spinning Wheel*: A scene from Part One of Goethe's *Faust* (1808), containing a poem which was set to music by Schubert.

p. 122, *Rossetti's 'Beata Beatrix'*: Dante Gabriel Rossetti (1828–82) based his painting *Beata Beatrix* painting on Beatrice, Dante Alighieri's love interest and symbol of theology in *The Divine Comedy* and other works.

p. 122, *Rossettian copies of the girl*: One such picture, formerly owned by Emily Flintoff Haywood, is reproduced in *D.H. Lawrence Review* VII, 1 (Spring 1974), Fig. 6.

p. 123, *ticking and tanning and snagging... in a tear*: "Scolding and raging and grumbling... in a rage" (dialect).

p. 124, *'Oh, Flo, why do you go—'*: Published in 1901 with the title 'The Great Motor Car Song', this was a popular song written by the prolific songwriter Frank Dean (1860–1922), under the pseudonym Harry Dacre.

p. 124, *'Ye Banks and Braes O Bonnie Doon'*: Robert Burns (1759–96) wrote this poem (first published in 1792) to fit the tune which is now associated with his words, previously called 'The Caledonian Hunt's Delight'.

p. 125, *Bulwell... furnaces*: Bulwell was originally a village three miles north-west of Nottingham, but was incorporated within the town boundaries from 1877. The furnaces were probably those of the iron works at Bennerley.

p. 125, *Eberwich... Kimberley... Hill-top*: Paul's walk from Kimberley Station to The Breach in Eastwood ("Eberwich") takes him through Hill Top, but Underwood is two miles north of The Breach.

p. 129, *scholarship in the High School at Nottingham*: Lawrence's own experience as a working-class boy at Nottingham High School figures little in his fiction. In *Paul Morel* autobiographical elements are divided between characters, so that Arthur represents the scholarship boy and Paul the artist. Arthur's school experiences are minimal in here, and the significance of character is much reduced in *Sons and Lovers*.

p. 129, *gall of bitterness... abashed by... if of anyone*: "Gall of bitterness" is a reference to Acts 8:23. In Lawrence's original manuscript the passage "abashed by... if anyone" read: "afraid of him. The father had always been afraid of Paul, humble before him, if ever humble."

p. 129, *house newly built on the hill-top*: 3 Walker Street.

p. 130, *Willey Woods... Herod's Cottage*: Willey Woods are located beside Haggs Farm and contain Willey Spring. "Herod's Farm" was the name Lawrence gave to Haggs Farm in *A Collier's Friday Night*.

p. 131, *High Close house*: Based on Lambclose House.

p. 131, *Scotch cattle*: Originally horned, bulls and cows bred in the Highlands of Scotland.

p. 132, *Birnam Wood*: See *Macbeth*, Act IV, Sc. 1, l. 90.

p. 134, *Schubert's songs... 'Du bist wie eine Blume'*: Lawrence is mistaken: the lyric in question was written by Heinrich Heine (1797–1856) and set to music in 1840 by Robert Schumann (1810–56), not Franz Peter Schubert (1797–1828).

p. 137, *Jane Eyre... Rochester*: In the novel *Jane Eyre* (1847) by Charlotte Brontë (1816–55), the young eponymous heroine is employed as a governess in the house of the older Edward Fairfax Rochester, who falls in love with her at the age of forty, after a lifetime of dissipation and an earlier unhappy marriage to Bertha Mason.

p. 139, *'Passover'... 'Tabernacles' remembrance... fiery bush to Moses*: Paul garbles several Old Testament references. The "angel of the Lord appeared" to Moses "in a flame of fire out of the midst of a bush: and [Moses] looked, and, behold, the bush burned with fire, and the bush was not consumed" (Exodus 3:2). God instructed Moses that on the Feast of the Passover, the Israelites should eat lamb and mark their front-door posts with the lambs' blood, so that during the night he would pass over their houses when he killed all the Egyptian first-born living in unmarked houses (Exodus 12:1–30). When Moses had led the Israelites out of Egypt and received God's ten commandments, he built a tabernacle or sanctuary in remembrance of their delivery (Exodus 36–40).

p. 139, *if I was Moses and you Rebecca*: Again Paul seems to be muddling his biblical references: Moses and Rebecca lived far apart in time and place. Rebecca, the daughter of Bethuel (the nephew of Abraham) was wife of Isaac and mother of Esau and Jacob (Genesis 22–49). It was Jacob's son Joseph who brought the Israelites into Egypt, and Moses who, long after Rebecca and Joseph were dead, led them out of Egypt.

p. 140, *blowsy*: Dishevelled, coarse.

p. 141, *dripped, like a Greek ocean, over the edge of the world*: In the classical Greek conception of the world, the ocean constituted the outer edge. The image of the sea dripping over was developed by several English poets.

p. 142, *Lord Tennyson's famous dictum*: Probably a reference to 'Flower in the Crannied Wall' by Alfred Lord Tennyson (1809–92):

> Flower in the crannied wall
> I pluck you out of the crannies,
> I hold you here, root and all, in my hand,
> Little flower – but if I could understand
> What you are, root and all, and all in all,
> I should know what God and man is.

p. 142, *pudeur*: A sense of shame or embarrassment, especially in regard to matters of a sexual nature.

p. 144, *'To be or not to be—'*: See *Hamlet*, Act III, Sc. 1, l. 55.

p. 146, *N'importe*: "It doesn't matter" (French).

p. 146, *a revised of myself*: Lawrence may have accidentally omitted the word "version" after "revised".

p. 146, *oui, vraiment*: "Yes, really" (French).

p. 146, *Independent*: Also known as Congregationalist, a nonconformist church in which each congregation is independent of external authority.

p. 147, *sauce for the goose—hélas… another man's poison*: Proverbial expression about shared likes and dislikes. "Hélas" means "alas" in French.

p. 148, *pence… pounds*: From the proverb recommending thrift: "Take care of the pence and the pounds will look after themselves."

p. 148, *here-todays*: Paul's joke is based on the catchphrase: "Here today and gone tomorrow."

p. 148, *heps*: Rose hips.

p. 148, *'twas mine… thousands*: See *Othello*, Act II, Sc. 3, l. 152.

p. 148, *Tristram Shandy… ripped them out*: The opening pages of the novel *Tristram Shandy* (1760–67) by Laurence Sterne (1713–68) are a satirical depiction of the eponymous protagonist's conception and birth.

p. 149, *mystic… her glass*: This image may have been inspired by Tennyson's 'Lady of Shalott' 46–48 ("And moving through the mirror clear… Shadows of the world appear") and 1 Corinthians 13:11 ("For now we see through a glass darkly").

p. 149, *Gethsemane*: The name of the garden outside the walls of Jerusalem where Jesus prayed all night before he was betrayed, captured and crucified, which can also refer, by extension, to any intense moment of prayer in the face of adversity.

p. 151, *They say… it's hurtful towards us*: It was a common popular superstition that letting the rays of the moon shine through the windows would be harmful to the sleepers and could cause them to lose their senses.

p. 151, *half-educated angel*: See the 'The Cloud' (1820) by Percy Bysshe Shelley (1792–1822): "the beat of [the moon's] unseen feet / Which only the angels hear" (ll. 49–50).

p. 152, *they wouldn't… faces in moonlight*: See first note for p. 151.

p. 153, *immense swarm of gold insects*: See Shelley, 'The Cloud' (cited in second note for p. 151): "[The stars] Like a swarm of golden bees" (l. 54).

p. 156, *Herbert Spencer*: Herbert Spencer (1820–1903) was a famous and influential philosopher, who popularized and expanded the theory of evolution.

p. 158, *ring his bell*: A reference to the small bell, operated by pushing a lever attached to a spring inside, which used to be attached to a bicycle's handlebars.

p. 159, *harvest festival*: A church's autumn service of thanksgiving for the harvest, during which it is decorated with produce, fruit, vegetables, wheat sheaves and flowers.

p. 160, *Palgrave's "Golden Treasury of Songs and Lyrics."*: Francis Turner Palgrave (1824–97) published the reference book *The Golden Treasury of the Best Songs and Lyrical Poems in the English Language* in 1861.

p. 160, *Balzac's short stories*: On the next page, Paul reads from 'Honorine', an 1843 short story by Honoré de Balzac (1799–1850).

p. 160, *staddle*: The bottom layer of a haystack.

p. 160, *Tripoli onion*: This is a pun on the dog's name, Trip. Tripoli onions were common large winter onions.

p. 161, *last state… first*: See Matthew 12:45 and Luke 11:26.

p. 163, *sad Botticelli angel*: A reference to the famous painter Sandro Botticelli (1445–1510).

p. 164, *Homer... I wish I could read him*: Lawrence did not read Greek, but would have had access to the various English translations available since George Chapman (*c*.1559–1634) published *The Iliad* in 1611 and *The Odyssey* in 1614–15.

p. 165, *phylacteries*: Probably used here in the sense of "protective charm worn on the body".

p. 165, *Unitarianism*: Christian sect which denied the Trinity and took God to be a single entity, established in England in 1773 and popular in the early twentieth century for its advanced social doctrines.

p. 165, *In patience... souls*: See John 21:29.

p. 165, *Didn't twig?... did her brown*: "Didn't realize?... defeated her" (slang).

p. 166, *scholarship at the Nottingham University*: The equivalent episode in Lawrence's life, which was much more complicated, was omitted from *Sons and Lovers*.

p. 166, *Intermediate*: From 1906 to 1908, Lawrence took a teacher-training course at University College, Nottingham, but was persuaded to study for an Arts degree, which required for him to take the Intermediate Arts course in London.

p. 167, *an edition of Goethe, of Schiller, of Victor Hugo*: For Goethe, see first note for p. 122. The dramatist and lyric poet Johann Christoph Friedrich von Schiller (1759–1805) was referred to by Lawrence in his essay 'Art and the Individual'. Lawrence read many works by Victor Hugo (1802–85).

p. 167, *four-pronged forks*: During the nineteenth century the wealthy classes began using silver four-pronged forks, while the poor continued to use two-pronged forks.

p. 168, *says Sancho Panza*: In *Don Quixote* (1615) by Miguel de Cervantes Saavedra (1547–1616), Sancho Panza repeats the proverb: "*No con quien naces, sino con quien paces*", which Lawrence interprets to mean that the mother could, by the provision of a civilized table, raise the "breeding" of her children above that of their social circumstance.

p. 168, *reckoning*: Technical term for the division of the week's earnings by a team of miners.

p. 168, *his club that week*: "Benefit clubs" were schemes, contributed to by the miners, which insured against loss of income during illness.

p. 168, *Vergil's Bucolics*: Pastoral poems, also known as *Eclogues* by Virgil (70–19 BC).

p. 168, *whittle*: "Grumble" (dialect).

p. 170, *I'm gooin' ter ha'e... s'll do as I've a mind*: "I'm going to have... shall do as I like" (dialect).

p. 170, *Am I a dog?*: See 1 Samuel 17:43.

p. 171, *psychologist*: The implication that "psychology" would explain Morel's emotions as caused by his liver condition indicates a physiologically based theory of psychology, which probably derives from Lawrence's interest in William James's *The Principles of Psychology* (1890).

p. 171, *Are ter stowing... young hound?*: "Will you be silent – will you shut your mouth – will you, you impertinent young hound" (dialect).

p. 172, *Dursn't I*: "Daren't I" (dialect).

p. 174, *Paul fetched a large piece of coal to rake the fire*: It was common practice to place a large piece of coal on top of an open fire at night to keep it alight till morning.

p. 174, *elder-flower ointment*: This was applied to relieve skin inflammation.

p. 174, *verdigris*: A green rust naturally forming on brass and copper.

p. 175, *Why, tha looks... let thee*: "Hey, you look really exhausted, man – keep your spirits up. Come up with me to Yorkshire, if your wife will let you" (dialect).

p. 176, *Come on wi'... hold on thee. I'n got five pound ten... What's think o' that?*: "Well, *do* come then, and leave them to their own devices. How often have you anything in your pocket?"; "Well never"... "No, and you never will have while they've got hold of you. I've got five pounds and ten shillings... What do you think of that?" (dialect).

p. 176, *stopping*: Pausing for a drink at a public house on the way home.

p. 176, *hawked*: Coughed phlegm up from his throat into his mouth.

p. 177, *steel*: A knife-sharpener in the shape of a tapered and grooved steel rod fitted with a handle. Lawrence's cousin Walter was also killed with a steel.

p. 179, *wired*: Telegraphed.

p. 180, *cemetery... tall church*: Eastwood cemetery was half a mile south of St Mary's Church.

p. 181, *different house… brow of the highest hill*: Based on the Lawrence home, 97 Lynncroft Road.

p. 181, *Crich*: A village nine miles north-west of Eastwood, the highest point of which was a carboniferous limestone quarry.

p. 182, *highroad*: The high road visible from the bedroom of 97 Lynncroft Road was Nottingham Road.

p. 183, *young mother… church dominates… under its wing*: The church referred to here is based on St Mary's Eastwood.

p. 185, *alienity*: A synonym of "alienation", without the political connotations.

p. 186, *Jews' Burying-Ground, in Sneinton*: There is no record of a Jewish graveyard in Sneinton, which is an eastern suburb of Nottingham.

p. 187, *like a Pharisee in soul, walked by*: Lawrence mixes together two New Testament texts. In the parable of the Good Samaritan (Luke 10:30–6), it is famously a "priest" and a "Levite" who "passed by on the other side" refusing to help a man who had been robbed and left lying injured in the road. The parable is told by Christ in answer to a challenge from a "lawyer". However, it is the Pharisees who most often challenge and criticize Christ, and the attitude which is perhaps being attributed Frances is expressed in Luke 18:11: "The Pharisee stood and prayed with himself, God, I thank thee, that I am not as other men are."

p. 188, *Lettres de Mon Moulin*: A reference to a collection of short stories published in 1869 by the French novelist Alphonse Daudet (1840–97).

p. 189, *bruised red rose*: There are two pages missing in the manuscript here, but a lightly revised version of the lost text survives in a separate draft, and is reproduced below without any corrections:

"I have no *rule*," she said, gently raising the head of a rather bruised red rose.

"No; of course; only a preference. But you don't as a rule, I believe, choose to wear the languishing heads of decapitated flowers, on your bosom."

She let fall the flower with a sharp movement.

"This," she said, "is a flower I found in the street."

"Jestam of lost ladies," he said—"I'd hold a conversation with it, if I were you: – 'The Rose and the Tomb.'—Know that poem?"

"I do not," she said.

"I thought you were a French scholar," he mocked. The blood came up in her cheek. She was going to be nasty, but he forestalled her.

"You might learn it," he said, grinning, "and then we'd act it. I'll ventriloquise the rose, and you do the tomb."

"I think," she said, "you should learn manners."

"I will, when it'll profit me anything." He began to lose his head. "And you've enough for two.—And besides, you'd do the tomb so well. Everybody feels as if they want to gleg at the skeleton in your vault."

Now he had lost his head, and gone too far.

"But I beg your pardon," he said, pulling up.

She turned coldly aside. He fled upstairs.

"Paul's sat on a cinder," said the other girls.

In the afternoon he came down. There was a certain weight on his heart, which he wanted to remove. He thought to do it by offering her chocolates.

"Have a choc." he said. "I bought a handful to sweeten me up."

To his great relief, she accepted. He sat on the work-bench beside her machine, twisting a piece of silk round his finger. She loved him for his quick, unexpected movements, like a young animal. His feet swung as he pondered. The sweets lay strewn on the bench. She bent over her machine, grinding rhythmically, then stooping to see the stocking that hung beneath, pulled down the weight. He watched the handsome crouching of her back, and the apron strings curling on the floor.

"There is always about you," he said, "a sort of waiting. Whatever I see you doing, you're not really there, you are waiting—like Penelope when she did her weaving." He could not help a spurt of wickedness. "I'll call you Penelope," he said.

"Would it make any difference?" she said, carefully removing one of her needles.

"That doesn't matter, so long as it pleases me.—Here, I say, you seem to forget I'm your boss. It just occurs to me."

"And what does that mean?" she asked coldly.

"It means I've got a right to boss you."

"Is there anything you want to complain about?"

"Oh, I say, you needn't be nasty," he said angrily.

"I don't know what you want," she said, continuing her task.

"I want you to treat me nicely and respectfully."

"Call you 'Sir', perhaps?" she asked quietly.

"Yes, call me Sir. I should love it."

"Then I wish you would go upstairs, Sir."

His mouth closed, and a frown came on his face. He jumped suddenly down.

"You're too blasted superior for anything," he said.

And he went away to the other girls. He felt he was being angrier than he had any need to be. In fact, he doubted slightly that he was showing off. But if he were, then he would. Clara heard him laughing, in a way she hated, with the girls down the next room.

When he went through the department after the girls had gone, he saw his chocolates lying untouched in front of Clara's machine. He left them. In the morning they were still there. Later on, Minnie, a little brunette they called Pussy, called to him:

"Hey, haven't you got a chocolate for anybody?"

"Sorry Pussy," he replied. "I meant to have offered them, then I went and forgot 'em."

"I think you did," she answered.

"I'll bring you some this afternoon. You don't want them after they've been lying about, do you?"

"Oh, I'm not particular," smiled Pussy.

"Oh no," he said. "They'll be dusty."

He went up to Clara's bench.

"Sorry I left these things littering about," he said.

She flushed scarlet. He gathered them together in his fist. She thought his hand looked cruel as he scooped the sweets together.

"They'll be dirty now," he said. "You should have taken them. I wonder why you didn't. I meant to have told you I wanted you to."

He flung them out of the window, into the yard below. He just glanced at her. She winced violently from his cold eyes.

In the afternoon he brought another packet.

"Will you take some," he said, offering them first to Clara. "These are fresh."

She accepted one, and put it onto the bench.

"Oh, take several, for luck," he said.

She took a couple more, and put them on the bench also. Then she turned in confusion to her work. He went on up the room.

"Here you are Pussy," he said. "Don't be greedy!"

"Are they all for her?" cried the others, rushing up.

"Of course they're not," he said.

The girls clamoured round. Pussy drew back from her mates.

"Come out!" she cried. "I can have first pick, can't I Paul?"

"Be nice with 'em," he said, and went away.

"You *are* a dear," the girls cried.

"Tenpence," he answered. "Quite cheap."

He went past Clara without speaking. She felt the three chocolate creams would burn her if she touched them. It needed all her courage to slip them into the pocket of her apron.

The girls loved him and were afraid of him. He was so nice while he was nice, but if he were offended, so distant, treating them as if they scarcely

212

existed, or not more than the bobbins of thread. And then, if they were impudent, he said quietly: "Do you mind going on with your work, I think you are wasting time."

When he celebrated his twenty third birthday, the house was in trouble. Arthur was just going to be married. His mother was not well. His father, getting an old man, and lame from his accidents, was given a paltry, poor job. Miriam was an eternal reproach. He felt he owed himself to her, yet could not give himself. The house moreover needed his support. He was pulled in all directions. He was not glad it was his birthday. It made him bitter.

He got to work at eight o'clock. Most of the clerks had not turned up. The girls were not due till 8.30. As he was changing his coat, he heard a voice behind him say:

"Paul, Paul, I want you."

It was Fanny, the hunch-back, standing at the top of her stairs, her face radiant with a secret.

p. 190, *Queen of Sheba*: The figure of the Queen of Sheba appears in the Bible and is often associated with pride and self-importance.

p. 191, *the Castle*: See the first note for p. 113.

p. 191, *trees… Bulk only*: An allusion to the poem 'A Pindaric Ode on the Death of Sir H. Morison' by Ben Jonson (1572–1637).

p. 192, *remorseful angels… fell*: See Revelation 12:9 and Milton's *Paradise Lost*.

p. 192, *up above… like two cherubs in the sky*: An adaptation of the 'Twinkle, twinkle little star' nursery rhyme.

p. 193, *A rose would smell as sweet etc*: A quotation from Shakespeare's *Romeo and Juliet* (Act I, Sc. 5, ll. 42–3).

p. 193, *what you gave with the right*: See Matthew 6:3.

p. 194, *Francis Thompson*: A reference to the English poet and ascetic Francis Thompson (1859–1907).

p. 195, *revealed to him a*: The next page of the manuscript is missing.

p. 195, *Castle Gateway, then unrestored*: The Nottingham Castle Gateway into the outer bailey had been almost entirely rebuilt in 1910. This was the place where Charles I raised the standard on 22nd August 1642, thus starting the English Civil War.

p. 195, *Colonel Hutchinson… Roundhead*: A reference to Colonel John Hutchinson, Governor of Nottingham Castle for the Parliamentarian supporters (the "Roundheads") during most of the Civil War (1642–49).

p. 195, *Marston Moor*: The Battle of Marston Moor (2nd July 1644) resulted in an emphatic victory of the Parliamentarians against the Royalists.

p. 195, *Good lack*: An old slang expression meaning "Good Lord".

Extra Material

on

D.H. Lawrence's

Paul Morel

D.H. Lawrence's Life

David Herbert Lawrence was born on 11th September 1885 in *Birth and Early Life* Eastwood, a small colliery town just outside Nottingham. He was the fourth of five children – three brothers and two sisters. His father, and most of his other relatives, were involved in some capacity with work at one of the collieries, including labour at the coalface.

His mother Lydia had once had ambitions to be a teacher, but the poverty of her parents had thwarted her earlier aspirations. However, she still took an interest in reading and in intellectual matters. She tried to contribute to the Lawrence family income by running a small clothes shop from the ground floor of the family house – a financial venture which was never very successful. Lydia tried to encourage all of her children to save money and study, but Arthur, her husband, would go out drinking most evenings, leading to arguments and tension.

The boys in the local school were almost all destined to finish up down the mine, while the girls also would work in the colliery canteens and laundries. However, from an early age the Lawrence children seemed to aim for higher things, and took their school studies extremely seriously. Furthermore, they regularly attended the local Nonconformist Christian chapel, and all took the pledge early in their lives not to touch alcohol.

A major dramatic occurrence in D.H. Lawrence's early life *Bereavement and Illness* was the death in 1901 of his elder brother Ernest from erysipelas. After this traumatic experience, Lawrence developed severe pneumonia and nearly died. This may have been a contributing factor to the tuberculosis and general ill health which dogged his later years, and which finally caused his death.

Teaching Career   Lawrence was at the time reading omnivorously in the local municipal library and at school. In 1902 he became a pupil teacher at a senior school in Eastwood – a common arrangement at the time. Some of the more promising older pupils were given lessons by the headmaster early in the mornings, and then they proceeded to teach the other pupils, usually for nothing or a nominal sum, since the personal tuition they received was meant to constitute their reward. Lawrence's token recompense was £12 per year. He took the opportunity of spending some time each week at what would now be called "teachers' centres" in Nottingham and at Ilkeston in Derbyshire, which ran training courses for other people in his situation living in the area; this led to a huge expansion of his social and intellectual horizons.

After two years as a pupil teacher, Lawrence successfully sat the King's Scholarship Examination in 1904, which gave him entry to a teacher-training college, or even, if he so wished, the opportunity to study for a degree at a university – almost unheard of at the time for anybody from a lower-class background. Interviews with this "working-class boy made good" were subsequently published in the local press and in the national teachers' magazines *The Schoolmaster* and *The Teacher*.

Although success in the examination conferred access to higher education, it gave little financial assistance, and so Lawrence and his family now had to decide whether he should do the degree full-time, supported by his family, or part-time, working to finance himself, as there were no student grants at the time.

It was finally decided he should spend a further year as a pupil teacher at a salary of £50 per year before going to university to do his teacher training. He entered the teacher-training department of Nottingham University in September 1906, but between the scholarship examination and entry to higher education he had started to write. He experimented with poetry, and in 1906 began writing *Laetitia*, the earliest version of his first published novel, *The White Peacock*.

Jessie Chambers   Lawrence was by now spending a considerable amount of time in the company of a young woman he had met some five years earlier, Jessie Chambers. They read together and discussed literature, philosophy and other intellectual subjects. His sisters and mother were worried that this blossoming relationship would be a distraction to "Bert"; they wanted him and Jessie either to get engaged, or meet less frequently. Lawrence took all this to heart, and told Jessie they must cut down the number of their meetings drastically for the time being. She was deeply hurt, and this was the first of numerous occasions on which he treated Jessie, and other women, with seeming insensitivity and selfishness.

At teacher-training college, Lawrence met socialists and freethinkers, and his whole universe expanded. He spent a great deal of time writing and revising his novel. He found the course boring, but ploughed ahead with it and finally gained his teaching certificate in 1908. He also wrote more poetry and experimented with short-story writing. He submitted three stories to a competition in the biggest Nottingham newspaper, and one of these – 'The Prelude' – submitted for him by Jessie Chambers under her own name – won the prize for best story in its category and was printed in the paper. Lawrence also apparently sent some work – possibly one or more essays or sketches – to G.K. Chesterton, then literary editor at the *Daily News* in London, but these were returned with such negative comments that he nearly decided to give up writing altogether. *Early Writing*

Lawrence was still living at home but, under the influence of the new ideas he was encountering at college, he began to react against his narrow upbringing, particularly the world of the Nonconformist chapel his parents attended, and religion in general. Unlike his fellow graduates, Lawrence was prepared to bide his time waiting for a good job to turn up – which might, besides providing him with a reasonable salary, enable him to escape from home. In the meantime he did jobs including farm work and clerking until he obtained a position as a teacher at a boys' school in Croydon, a working-class area of South London, just after his twenty-third birthday.

He started work in London in October 1908 and moved into rooms in a family-run private house nearby. This was the first time he had lived away from home for any extended period, and working at the school proved extremely demanding, as he found it difficult to enforce discipline. However, in his leisure time he went up to central London to attend concerts and plays, and visited art galleries and bookshops. He continued his reading and writing, including further revisions to *Laetitia*. *London*

Lawrence's breakthrough into the literary world came with some of his poems, which he sent initially to Jessie Chambers – still in Nottingham – for comment. Without his knowledge, she submitted them in September 1909 to Ford Madox Hueffer (later known as Ford Madox Ford), the illustrious critic and editor of the recently established radical journal *The English Review*. Hueffer decided to print a few of them and encouraged Lawrence to send him any further work of his, whatever the genre. Hueffer knew all the major London literati, and invited Lawrence to artistic gatherings, where he met, among others, Wells, Yeats and Pound.

Because his journal pursued a radical line, Hueffer was especially interested in promoting Lawrence as an "author from the collieries", and suggested that Lawrence should write about the life of the people he was familiar with. Accordingly, Lawrence's first two plays, written around this period (*A Collier's Friday Night* and *The Widowing of Mrs Holroyd*), were concerned with the life of mining families and partly written in the Nottinghamshire dialect. In December 1910 he sent the manuscript of *Laetitia* to the London publisher Heinemann, accompanied by a letter of recommendation from Hueffer. Heinemann asked for some cuts and alterations – which Lawrence made, including renaming it *The White Peacock* – and accepted it for publication.

Love Life Despite his efforts, Lawrence had failed to forge a physical relationship with any of his various female acquaintances. Around this time, he suggested to his long-time intellectual companion, Jessie Chambers – still living in Nottinghamshire – that they should become lovers. Jessie agreed, but Lawrence did not wish to be tied down by one woman, and the affair was extremely unhappy and bitter. In August 1911 the sexual side of the relationship ended, and two months later Lawrence's mother became seriously unwell, possibly with the first signs of the cancer that would ultimately kill her.

All the following year his mother was in increasingly severe pain, and he was now without Jessie. In this sense of isolation and sadness he embarked on the composition of a new novel, largely drawn from his own experiences at the time. He was at this period re-establishing contact with a friend from his adolescence, Louie Burrows, then living in Leicester. She was apparently not as intellectual as Jessie Chambers, but very loving and fond of Lawrence. Possibly on the rebound from Jessie Chambers, Lawrence proposed marriage to Louie.

Just at this time *The White Peacock* appeared in print, and Lawrence personally put the first copy of it into his mother's hands. His mother would die later that year, on 9th December.

Lawrence's second novel, entitled at this point *The Saga of Siegmund*, was rejected by Heinemann; they suggested numerous revisions and a change of title. Accordingly, Lawrence reworked the novel, which would appear as *The Trespasser* in 1912. At the same time as composing the later stages of *The Saga of Siegmund*, he had started on a third novel, which he planned to entitle *Paul Morel*. By now he had begun to realize his engagement to Louie had been a mistake – since she could not provide the lifelong intellectual companionship he desired – and agonized over ending their relationship. He became very depressed, and in November 1911 developed a severe, near-fatal case of pneumonia – which may have been an early symptom of the lung problems which would plague Lawrence throughout his entire life. He spent a month convalescing at a hotel in Bournemouth, making the final revisions to his second novel and progressing with *Paul Morel*. He gave up teaching on the advice of his doctors and returned to Eastwood in February 1912. There he completely rewrote *Paul Morel* – Jessie Chambers reading all his drafts and making suggestions – while living in his childhood home with his father and two sisters.

It was at this time that one of the major events of Lawrence's life occurred: he met the woman with whom he was to spend most of his life – Frieda Weekley. Née von Richthofen, she was the daughter of minor German aristocrats from the Metz region. She was the wife of the Professor of Modern Languages at Nottingham University, Ernest Weekley, whom she had met and married at the age of nineteen. The couple lived in a respectable suburb of Nottingham with their three children. Lawrence first met her when in March 1912 he came to their house to enquire about the possibility of finding teaching work in Germany. He immediately fell passionately in love with her, even though she was eight years his senior. Since she reciprocated his feelings, he convinced her that she was wasting her best years in her current, comfortable way of life and persuaded her to start a relationship with him.

Frieda

221

In May 1912 *The Trespasser* was published, to reasonably favourable reviews, and on the 12th of the same month Frieda left her husband and travelled with Lawrence to Metz. Ernest Weekley immediately asked for a divorce, stipulating that she should never see the children again. While in Germany staying with her relations, Lawrence made his final revision of *Paul Morel* and sent it off to Heinemann. The publisher rejected it as being poorly written and too sexually explicit. However, Edward Garnett, the reader for Duckworth publishers, assured Lawrence that if, under his guidance, he made a large number of alterations, he would recommend the novel for publication. Lawrence and Frieda undertook a walking tour of Germany, Austria and finally Italy, where they intended to stay for some months as it was much cheaper than Germany and they were short of money.

In Italy, in rooms near Gargnano, on the Lake Garda, Lawrence made the requisite alterations to *Paul Morel*, renaming it *Sons and Lovers* in the process. He sent the novel off to Duckworth and, after further negotiations, the novel was accepted for publication. Lawrence now worked intensively on poems, plays and ideas for possible future novels, finally settling down to a project he provisionally entitled *The Sisters*, which would ultimately, over the next seven years, become *The Rainbow* and *Women in Love*. In June 1913, the couple finally returned to England, since Frieda desperately wanted to see her children again before consenting to a divorce which would forbid her access to them. *Sons and Lovers* had by this time been published to mixed but generally favourable reviews.

Frieda did not succeed in seeing her children, and was threatened with legal action if she attempted to do so again. The couple returned to Italy, this time to Lerici, near La Spezia. There Lawrence produced the first section of a completely revised version of *The Sisters* – which detailed the sexual relationships and emotional development of two sisters, Ella (later Ursula) and Gudrun Brangwen. Having sent this draft to Garnett – who lambasted it as very badly written – Lawrence set about a further revision. However, following the success of *Sons and Lovers*, other publishers were now making overtures to Lawrence, some offering him lucrative contracts for the novel – which by this time had been renamed *The Wedding Ring*. Garnett once again criticized the new version heavily, and in March Lawrence returned to London to negotiate a possible deal with another publisher: Methuen outbid Duckworth and were promised the novel. Finally, in April 1914, Frieda gained her divorce, and Lawrence married her in July of that year. Things seemed to be looking up on all fronts for Lawrence.

Then war broke out and the couple faced enormous problems in returning abroad. The war also hindered the possibility of getting further novels published, since there was a paper shortage, and the entire economy was now geared towards providing for the military effort. Furthermore, Frieda was regarded with suspicion because of her German origin. Lawrence – profoundly disillusioned with the war – felt that the conflict was barbaric and that the entire British national and racial consciousness had been polluted.

War and Rejection

Suddenly Methuen returned the manuscript of *The Wedding Ring*, claiming the subject matter was too risqué, and that publishers' lists were being cut back drastically because of the war. Lawrence and Frieda were once again without money, so they moved to a small cottage in Chesham, Buckinghamshire. He rewrote *The Wedding Ring* between November 1914 and March 1915, splitting the novel into *The Rainbow* and what was ultimately to become *Women in Love*. However, *The Rainbow* became even more sexually explicit than the previously rejected drafts.

During these years, Lawrence had begun to enter new literary circles. Among others he had become acquainted with Lady Ottoline Morrell, the aristocratic society and artistic hostess. At her receptions he met famous intellectuals, such as E.M. Forster and Bertrand Russell. Lawrence's letters from 1914 and 1915 – principally to Russell – show the evolution of his ideas on the best way to live one's life and to develop one's real inner self. At first, Russell was highly impressed by Lawrence, but then became deeply disturbed by what he saw as the authoritarian character of his personality and beliefs, which he later characterized as "leading straight to Auschwitz".

The Rainbow was published in September 1915 and received vicious reviews. Bookstalls and libraries refused to stock it, because of what was perceived to be the pornographic nature of its material. Finally, in November 1915, the police seized all unsold copies and the book was prosecuted in the law courts for obscenity, the magistrates ordering all copies to be

The Rainbow Controversy

destroyed. Although some of Lawrence's artistic entourage protested against this censorship, it was generally the idea of censorship itself they were criticizing: most in fact detested the book as an aesthetic creation.

Move to Cornwall   Lawrence now seriously thought of emigrating permanently to America with Frieda to set up an artists-and-writers' commune in Florida, encouraging their various acquaintances to come and join them. However, Lawrence could only acquire a passport if he declared himself ready to be summoned for military service at any time, which he could not bring himself to do. If they could not leave Britain, they decided to move as far from the centre of war activities in London as they could. Accordingly they hired a cottage in Cornwall, where they lived by growing their own vegetables, settling there in December 1915. In this cottage, Lawrence produced books of poetry and reminiscences of his time in Italy, as well as reviews and other pieces of writing that procured them a very meagre income. Although Lawrence was often ill with colds and pulmonary complaints – perhaps because of the winds from the sea and the moors – both he and Frieda enjoyed the open countryside and often entertained guests from London in their cottage.

Lawrence now began to recast the material left over from *The Wedding Ring*, using that work's original title, *The Sisters*, for the first draft of this reworking. After several revisions the manuscript went through the usual round of publishers, who all rejected it – one even asked if it was really finished. In addition to their reservations about the content, they were probably frightened off by Lawrence's reputation and the police prosecution of *The Rainbow*. Lady Ottoline Morrell had caught a glimpse of the manuscript, thought herself slandered in the person of the novel's society hostess Hermione, and consequently severed all ties with Lawrence.

Because of his weak lungs, Lawrence was rejected for conscription on medical grounds in June 1916, and the locals in Cornwall became suspicious and irritated at this non-combatant writer living with a German wife, and spread rumours that they were spies. They would sometimes be stopped by the coastguard while out on their walks, and return to their cottage to find it had been broken into and searched.

Return to London   In September 1917 they were finally served with a legal order *and Derbyshire*   excluding them from Cornwall altogether, so they moved back

to London, staying in a series of cheap lodgings. In London

Lawrence attempted to settle down to writing his next novel, *Aaron's Rod*, but progress was slow due to their precarious living conditions and the fact that he was at the same time trying to eke out a living by writing poetry, reviews and essays. In May 1918, they moved back to the Midlands – to a cottage in Middleton-by-Wirksworth in Derbyshire – because it was so much cheaper to live there than in the south. Although he was now closer to his family, Lawrence felt himself to be "lost and exiled", sinking into severe depression and growing extremely pessimistic as to his future prospects.

In September 1918 Lawrence was compulsorily examined for military service: by this time the British Army was so desperate for manpower for the war effort that it was willing to conscript almost anybody. He was enlisted for "light non-military duties", a decision which drove him into a fury: "I've done with society and humanity. Labour and military can alike go to hell. Henceforth it is for myself, my own life, I live." He was never actually called up, since war ended in November 1918. In February 1919 he went down with a serious bout of influenza, and nearly died – the disease was then killing millions of people worldwide.

The armistice meant that Lawrence and Frieda could finally *Leaving England* obtain passports, and they decided to abandon England for good. In December 1919 they moved to Capri, and then to Taormina in Sicily. Lawrence now concentrated on his work, *Psychoanalysis and the Unconscious*, followed by his next two novels, *The Lost Girl* and *Mr Noon*. *The Lost Girl* was published in Britain in November 1920 but, because of his reputation, many bookshops again refused to stock it. His publisher demanded both major revisions to this novel and further alterations to *Women in Love*, since the composer Philip Heseltine (better known by his pen name of Peter Warlock) had perceived himself as portrayed and libelled in the novel's character of Julian Halliday.

As a result of all this, the Lawrences grew utterly fed up *Australia and New* with Europe, and decided to renew their attempt at moving *Mexico* to the US, as Lawrence had been invited at this time to set up residence in Taos, a colony of writers and artists in New Mexico. Disillusioned with society, humanity and the artistic life, he and Frieda set off to the States. En route to New Mexico, they spent short periods in Ceylon and New Zealand, and six weeks in Australia, where Lawrence met the Australian writer Mollie Skinner, and collaborated with her in producing *The Boy in the Bush* – probably the least didactic of his novels and the one most similar to an ordinary adventure story. He also began to draft his next novel, *Kangaroo*, also based on Australian life. The couple finally arrived in San Francisco in August 1922, then making their way down to Taos, establishing themselves on a ranch on Lobo Mountain. Lawrence was overwhelmed by the primeval beauty of the landscape opening up around him. At Taos he completed *Kangaroo* and earned a slender living by journalism, reviews and a book of essays on American literature.

Mexico and Return to Europe   In March 1923, Lawrence and Frieda visited Mexico and, by the lake near the settlement of Chapala in the south-west, Lawrence began work on his next novel, *The Plumed Serpent*, which dealt with pagan Mexican religion and political insurrection. Before taking up residence permanently in America, they decided to pay a brief visit to Europe, as Frieda in particular desperately wanted to see both her German and English families again. However, just before they were due to sail, the Lawrences had a huge row, the causes of which are unclear. Frieda sailed to Europe alone, and Lawrence returned to Mexico. It's possible that Frieda may have wanted to return to Europe permanently, whereas Lawrence detested the old Continent so wholeheartedly that he was determined this was going to be his last visit – the shorter the better.

Frieda did not return and, at the end of 1923, he finally wrote to her offering a separation, with the provision of a regular income. She begged him to return to Europe, and other old friends also expressed their desire to see him. Finally in November of that year he set off with the greatest reluctance. He wrote: "I don't want much to go to England – but I suppose it is the next move in the battle which never ends and which I never win." As soon as he reached England, he was confined to bed with a severe cold and, although he visited friends and relations, he declared openly that he now loathed London and the entire country. He once again appealed to friends to come back to America with him and set up an artists-and-writers' commune, but only the artist Dorothy Brett would commit to doing so. At a farewell party, Lawrence drank too much and vomited over the meal table – this traumatic final event in England symbolizing all his loathing for European culture.

Lawrence, Frieda and Dorothy sailed back to the States *Return to America*
in March 1924, and they all moved to a ranch just two miles
away from their previous residence on Lobo Mountain.
Unfortunately, his American publisher now went bankrupt,
depriving him of a great deal of expected royalties. However,
Lawrence at last seemed to have found some slight measure
of happiness there, writing and living the simple life away
from the civilization he so detested. The only major drawback
was that he suffered from serious chest ailments, and began
spitting blood – possibly as a result of the altitude of 2,600
metres. In Autumn 1924 came news that his father had died
at the age of seventy-eight, but he did not return to Europe to
attend the funeral.

In order to complete *The Plumed Serpent*, Lawrence *Tuberculosis*
felt he needed to spend more time in Mexico to imbibe the
atmosphere, so in October he, Frieda and Dorothy travelled
down to Oaxaca, which seemed a warm paradise conducive
to the subject matter of the book and to sustained writing.
However, tensions were now surfacing between Frieda and
Dorothy, and Dorothy returned to America after just ten days.
Lawrence finally finished the book in late January 1925, and
immediately went down with a combination of influenza,
typhoid and malaria which nearly cost him his life. Although
he survived, his lungs were fatally damaged by these illnesses,
and he was finally diagnosed with tuberculosis. He was given
at most two years to live, and decided to return with Frieda
to his ranch in the US. The doctor at the border initially
refused Lawrence re-entry, as he now showed obvious signs
of tuberculosis, a dangerous and contagious disease, but they
were eventually granted a six-month residency.

Once back at the ranch, he recovered somewhat, and began
writing again. In September 1925 – the six months having
expired – the now forty-year-old Lawrence sailed back to
Europe. The couple once again visited Lawrence's family,
Frieda taking the opportunity to see her now adult children,
before moving on through Germany and down to Italy, to a
villa in Spotorno, a Ligurian town on the coast. Lawrence took
up writing again, and started work in 1926 on his final novel,
Lady Chatterley's Lover. Although Lawrence's health was
generally stable, he still had bouts of blood-spitting, and felt
his general condition slowly deteriorating. They then moved
to a villa in Tuscany; Lawrence thought briefly of returning to

227

America, but realized that in his sick state he almost certainly would not be allowed entry, and that the strain of the long journey would exhaust his body still further.

Lady Chatterley's Lover

Lawrence was occupied with completing *Lady Chatterley's Lover* from October 1926 to summer 1928. The manuscript underwent countless radical alterations throughout these months, and during the final stages of revision, Lawrence was writing up to four thousand words a day. Although he had few hopes of its publication, because of its sexually explicit subject matter, he had discovered that it would be possible to publish the novel at his own expense on the Continent. 1,200 copies of the book, which he had arranged to be printed privately in Florence, finally appeared in June 1928. *Lady Chatterley's Lover* was an instant commercial success, and Lawrence for the first time in his life was relatively free from financial worries. After the publication of this novel, he decided to get away from the baking heat of Italy and live for a few months in the Swiss Alps, to see whether the mountain air would improve his condition. Although this change of environment benefited him somewhat, his coughing became more frequent, and he suffered increasingly severe haemorrhages. He tried not to let his illness defeat him, writing in a letter: "I feel so strongly as if my illness weren't really me – I feel perfectly well and all right, in myself. Yet there is this beastly torturing chest superimposed on me, and it's as if there was a demon lived there, triumphing, and extraneous to me." Frieda would later remark that she had never heard him complain about his health.

Last Days

With the money from *Lady Chatterley*, Lawrence and Frieda had some choice about where to live, and they selected a pleasant hotel in Bandol, on the French coast near Toulon. Lawrence tried to write newspaper articles and poems, but he could not undertake any further major projects, as his health was now deteriorating rapidly. He began to compose what would be his final work, *Apocalypse*: its purpose was to offer modern man a kind of psychic recovery of his connections with the old world, by providing a fresh view of humanity's "old, pagan vision" and the "pre-Christian heavens". But his physical condition by now was very poor, and he finally agreed to enter the Ad Astra sanatorium in Vence, near Nice. There he grew very despondent, and decided to discharge himself, as he wanted to die on his own terms. He and Frieda rented a villa in Vence, and hired nurses to look after him. On Sunday

2nd March 1930 his condition worsened considerably; he admitted he needed morphine, and a doctor administered the drug. Lawrence died that evening. Frieda wrote that he was buried "in the little cemetery of Vence which looks over the Mediterranean that he cared so much about". In 1935 his body was exhumed and cremated, and a chapel was erected near his second ranch in the mountains overlooking Taos to house his ashes.

D.H. Lawrence's Works

D.H. Lawrence wrote his first novel, *The White Peacock*, under *The White Peacock* various working titles, between 1906 and 1910. As mentioned above, the London publisher William Heinemann accepted it for publication, and the book came out in 1911. The novel follows a first-person narrator, Cyril Beardsall, who is continually questioning his identity and his place in the world – even at this stage of Lawrence's career, his writing probes the question of the alienation of modern humanity from its natural roots and instincts. The setting is the countryside around Nottingham (Beardsall, incidentally, was the maiden name of Lawrence's mother).

Cyril and his sister Lettie have had a conventional middle-class upbringing: they are cultured and artistic, but they are dissatisfied with their life, and the novel deals with their failure to find genuine love. Cyril courts Emily Saxton, a farmer's daughter, who ends up marrying somebody else, while Lettie, although deeply in love with Emily's brother George, makes a conventional marriage to a narrow-minded man of a much higher social rank. Following this rejection, George marries a pub landlord's daughter, which leaves him unfulfilled, and he becomes an apathetic alcoholic.

There is one further major character, who represents the rejection of modern culture and civilization and embodies the return to nature and the instincts. This is Frank Annable, who had been a student at Cambridge University, before becoming a vicar and marrying a local aristocrat, Lady Crystabel. He has rejected his former life and is now a gamekeeper on a large estate, living in the woods with a second wife and a large family. He is generally disliked by the local men, apparently because, with his animal vitality, he has a great deal of success with their wives. Cyril is attracted by his superb physique and personality, but Annable is found dead at the bottom of a quarry – it is not certain whether he has slipped or been pushed over by a gang of locals. It is interesting to note that, in his very last novel, *Lady Chatterley's Lover*, written around twenty years later, earthiness and return to one's natural instincts are also represented by a gamekeeper who has rejected his middle-class educated background.

George and Lettie therefore are left at the end of the novel feeling that they have not managed to unite their alienated artistic nature with the innate animal instinctive level of their own humanity; neither have they succeeded in bonding at any meaningful level with the members of the human race who are much more attuned with these instincts than they are.

The Trespasser   The follow-up to *The White Peacock*, *The Trespasser*, was composed between March 1910 and February 1912. It was originally to be titled *The Saga of Siegmund*, but was finally published in 1912 as *The Trespasser*. Mainly set on the Isle of Wight, with other scenes in north and south London and Cornwall, the novel centres on Siegmund Macnair, an orchestral musician and music teacher, who is married, with five children, to Beatrice. Despite his domestic comforts, he is restless and gets involved in a relationship with one of his pupils, Helena Verden. The bulk of the novel deals with the week they spend together on the Isle of Wight. The relationship does not work on a physical level: he is passionately attracted to her, but she is very withdrawn. Siegmund, in despair at all the conflicts and tensions in his life, hangs himself, and his wife, for the children's sake, deliberately suppresses all memory of him. But something has died within Helena Verden after this tragedy: she has entered a deep period of emotional stasis, and the novel ends with her new friend and possible future lover, Cecil, trying desperately to arouse her from this state.

Sons and Lovers   Around the same time *The Trespasser* was written, Lawrence
and Paul Morel   was working on another manuscript, provisionally entitled *Paul Morel*, which was completed in 1912 and published as *Sons and Lovers* in 1913. It incorporates numerous elements of Lawrence's life. The "Bestwood" of the novel is the author's home village of Eastwood, and the Morel family bears many resemblances to his own. The novel charts the protagonist Paul Morel's sexual, emotional and intellectual development from his childhood up to the age of twenty-five. The first part of the novel is devoted to a recreation of the early married life and

environment of Paul's parents. Like Lawrence's own family, the father is a miner who drinks, while the mother is intellectual, artistic and well informed; this leads to inevitable arguments. Paul shares his mother's artistic nature and becomes strongly attached to her. Following the early death of his brother from illness, Paul too nearly dies at the age of sixteen and, from then on, the novel concerns Paul's developing emotional and sexual relationships, and his attempt to become independent in all ways from his mother. He has done exceptionally well at school, and wishes to become an artist, but, during the period covered by the novel, works as a clerk at a local factory. At the age of sixteen, he meets his first love, Miriam, who bears many resemblances to Jessie Chambers. They are both passionate about art and ideas, and very much in love, but the sexual side of their relationship is fraught with difficulties. Paul feels he is betraying his mother, while Miriam at first does not want to involve herself in sex outside marriage. Paul constantly tries to force the issue, and Miriam finally acquiesces unwillingly, feeling she is making a great sacrifice for him. This turns out to be a disastrous experience, and Paul ends their relationship. He then enters on a brief and much more fulfilling relationship with an older married woman, but she finally decides to remain faithful to her husband. Near the end of the novel, Paul's mother dies, and he is left on the threshold of his maturity alone, but having become much more aware of his own identity.

Paul Morel, the version published in this volume, includes texts from the second and third of Lawrence's drafts of the novel, which eventually became *Sons and Lovers*. It was published for the first time in the Cambridge Edition of *Paul Morel* (2003), together with other fragmentary manuscripts that have survived from the process of composition, most of them written by Lawrence himself, and some by his friend, Jessie Chambers.

Paul Morel has no ending, because Lawrence never appears to have completed it. He worked at it from approximately mid-March 1911 to April 1912. When *Sons and Lovers* emerged from Lawrence's pen a few months after he had abandoned *Paul Morel*, the whole work had been rewritten from the beginning, then revised, then rewritten from the beginning again. Very little survives of the third draft apart from its first seventy-four pages, but during the transition from the second to the final, fourth version, the novel changed dramatically. Not only did Lawrence jettison many episodes, but he also completely transformed the plot. Therefore *Paul Morel* is a separate, independent piece of fiction, not rivalling *Sons and Lovers* for supremacy, nor subordinated to it like a painter's initial sketch compared with the final canvas. It is a vivid narrative, full of Lawrence's characteristically energetic writing, and also a volatile mixture of light-heartedness and tragedy.

The history of the writing of the manuscripts, and the way the early drafts were dispersed and survived in the fragmentary form, is fascinating, if a little complicated. The context was a period of considerable turbulence and important developments in Lawrence's life.

Some time during the summer of 1910, probably before September, Lawrence drafted a chapter plan for a novel which resembles *Paul Morel* in many respects. He began writing the first manuscript draft in Croydon, probably in October, but seems to have abandoned it by November or December 1910, after completing only a hundred pages, none of which survive. He began the second draft, *Paul Morel*, on about 13th March 1911, and wrote at least 353 pages before he abandoned that, too, around mid-July. Some time in October he sent the unfinished manuscript to Jessie Chambers asking for her advice, and she returned it by 3rd November 1911. Lawrence started again at once, from the beginning, wrote seven opening pages and set them on one side. Immediately he began afresh on what was to be his third draft of *Paul Morel*. He worked away writing onto new paper and discarding the redundant pages of the second draft as he progressed, but he had to stop when he fell ill on about 15th November. His illness was so severe that it radically changed his life. He did not return to the third draft of *Paul Morel* until mid-February 1912, by which time he had left Croydon and was back home in Eastwood. He wrote rapidly and delivered pages to Jessie Chambers for her opinion as he wrote them. He had completed the third draft by 25th March, and Jessie parcelled up the complete manuscript and handed it back to him on 1st April 1912. Inside the parcel he would find some additional pages of critical comments in her handwriting, and her own versions of some of the novel's episodes. She had also written replies and objections in the margins of the manuscript itself and in some places had crossed out Lawrence's sentences and rewritten them.

The extremely convoluted gestation of Lawrence's next novel, *The Rainbow* *The Rainbow*, should be studied with that of the following work, *Women in Love*, since they are both developments of what was originally planned as one novel. *The Rainbow* was published just two years after the commencement of the first draft, in 1913, but the reworking of the later material as a second volume, *Women in Love*, took until 1920. The preliminary drafts were written between March 1913 and August 1915. The first draft, under the provisional title *The Sisters,* was written between March and June 1913. A complete revision, still with the same provisional title, took place between August 1913 and January 1914. This was then substantially revised again, under the new title *The Wedding Ring*, from February to May 1914, and Lawrence finally took the decision to split the material into two books. The first, now known as *The Rainbow*, was put together between November 1914 and March 1915, and published in September 1915. The book portrays the earlier generations of the Nottinghamshire family whose modern members are treated at length in *Women in Love*. The setting is mainly the industrial counties of Nottinghamshire and its neighbour Derbyshire. Tom Brangwen, a young Midlands farmer, marries a Polish exile, Lydia Lensky, in 1867, when he is twenty-eight and she is thirty-four. Lydia is more cultured and intellectual than Tom, and the novel explores firstly the tensions in their marriage, and the way their relationship gradually evolves into a harmonious loving partnership. The couple live with Lydia's daughter, Anna, by her first marriage to a Polish revolutionary. We are shown Anna's development to maturity, until she finally marries Will Brangwen, the son of Tom's brother Alfred. Their stormy marriage is depicted in detail and, although they ultimately achieve some sort of harmony, this is not to the same degree of happiness as Anna's parents, but represents more of a compromise. One of the major differences is in religion: Anna is a "pagan", in that she worships nature and the instinctive physical life, whereas Will is a Christian mystic, hankering after experiences of the eternal and absolute.

The major part of the novel is taken up with the third generation of this family, and mainly describes the life of Will and Anna's daughter, Ursula Brangwen. She is profoundly

233

conscious of her responsibility to form her own personality, and to gain independence from her early upbringing and family; she questions her father's Christianity, and has various relationships, including a lesbian affair. She trains as a student teacher, later becoming a passionate critic of contemporary industrial society and of the alienation of the natural instincts from everyday life. She becomes engaged to a young soldier, Anton Skrebensky, but she gradually opens her eyes to his conventionality and adherence to social norms. She breaks off their relationship and he, unbeknown to her, marries another woman and is posted on military service to India. Ursula discovers she is pregnant by him, and writes to him asking for marriage after all. However, before receiving an answer, she is involved in a traumatic incident while out walking, becomes dangerously ill and suffers a miscarriage. This leads her to a period of epiphany, self-discovery and rebirth; she is delighted when she learns that Skrebensky is already married, realizing that she must wait for the right man "created by God" to come along. She glimpses a rainbow, and has a vision of a new reality for the whole of society, which will enable it to grow once more from its organic roots, and throw off the shackles of industrialization.

Women in Love   When Lawrence had reworked *The Rainbow* to his satisfaction and sent it off to the publisher, he comprehensively recast the remaining material, between April and June 1916, into a new narrative, and resurrected for it the former title *The Sisters*. Between July 1916 and January 1917 this was once again rewritten drastically, and given the new title *Women in Love* (this first version of the novel has since been published as *The First Women in Love*). Unfortunately, by this time *The Rainbow* had been prosecuted for obscenity and all unsold copies withdrawn and destroyed by a legal ruling. Lawrence submitted the manuscript of his new novel to various publishers, including Duckworth, Constable and Secker, and they all rejected it, commenting that, in the present climate of public opinion, with Lawrence's reputation, it would be unpublishable without drastic revision. Furthermore, several of Lawrence's acquaintances who had seen the manuscript claimed to perceive themselves satirized in its text. Accordingly, Lawrence, presumably fearing not only another prosecution for obscenity, but libel suits into the bargain, rethought the entire project, and radically reworked *Women in Love* over the two years between March 1917 and September 1919. The novel was first published in June 1921, and then further significant changes were made to the second edition, to produce *Women in Love* as it is now generally known, following threats of a lawsuit from the composer Peter Warlock, who thought that the portrait of the composer Halliday in the novel was a scurrilous portrayal of him.

The novel traces the adventures of the Ursula Brangwen of *The Rainbow*, now aged twenty-six, and a teacher at a grammar school. She is the lover of Rupert Birkin, an articulate school inspector who has sufficient private means to be able to retire if he so wishes. Ursula's sister Gudrun is twenty-five, has completed a course at art college and teaches at the same school; she is extremely self-confident and dresses in a bright and bohemian fashion. Gudrun's lover is Gerald Crich, who is around thirty, and the son of a wealthy colliery owner. He is handsome, blond, physically active and in charge of the colliery. However, he lacks a sense of any deep meaning in his life, and his relationship with Gudrun runs into the sands because, rather than striving to achieve a mutual unity of their two personalities, he needs constant reassurances of her affections.

The novel may be said to explore love and sexual relationships in both their creative and destructive aspects. Rupert Birkin contains both of these opposites within himself. He despairs of the modern industrial world and of the human race; however, he refuses to surrender to cynicism and apathy, but persists in his belief in personal fulfilment and integration through interpersonal relationships. These relationships will form the bedrock of a new, organic society, not distorted by over-intellectualism or industrialization. Birkin is, in fact, largely a self-portrait of Lawrence, or Lawrence as he liked to view himself at this period. Like Lawrence, he believes that throughout history the human race has either experienced periods of creative progress or of disintegration. With industrialization and the war, the world is currently, according to him, in a "destructive" cycle. Most of the characters throughout the novel display various degrees of over-intellectualism and alienation from the natural world and from their instincts. Birkin is at the beginning of the novel involved in a relationship with the wealthy aristocrat Hermione Roddice, who is described as "a medium for the culture of ideas" – that is, entirely locked up inside her own head, and cut off from her instincts. Not surprisingly, the relationship collapses. However, the liaison between Gerald and Gudrun is purely sensual, and is ultimately just as unfulfilling. In the end, Ursula and Birkin both resign from their jobs, marry and retire to the Continent – presumably having enough money to do so from Rupert's private income. Their relationship appears to be developing into an integrated and harmonious success. However, Gerald and Gudrun's sensual affair has gone off the rails; she has despairingly taken another lover and, in the Austrian Tyrol, he attempts to strangle her and then flees into the snows in a deliberate suicide attempt.

The Lost Girl Eight months before *Women in Love* came off the press, D.H. Lawrence completed *The Lost Girl*, a novel he had begun composing as early as December 1912, and which had also undergone several rewrites and title changes. It was eventually published in November 1920.

The novel traces the history of the main protagonist, Alvina Houghton, the "lost girl" of the title, from the age of twenty-three to thirty-two. She is the daughter of well-to-do tradespeople in Woodhouse, a fictional mining town based on Eastwood. Initially, she is "lost" because she seems destined to end up as an old maid, but subsequently she becomes "lost" to those around her because of her rebellion against her conventional upbringing: she plans to move to Australia with her lover, and then, on being talked out of this, moves to north London to train as a maternity nurse – where she gains first-hand experience of the poverty of the capital's slums. On her return to Woodhouse, she finds that no one can afford to hire her services as a nurse on a private basis, and so abandons the idea of earning a living in this manner for the time being. She toys with the idea of marrying various rich men, but decides they are all too cold and inhuman. At the age of thirty, after her father's death, she joins a travelling theatre group, which contains a number of dark passionate foreigners, whom she feels drawn to but ultimately rejects. Leaving the itinerant actors, she takes up her former occupation as a maternity nurse again and becomes engaged to an older wealthy doctor. However, she breaks off this engagement, marries the Italian Ciccio – who was part of her former theatre group – and moves to the mountains of Italy with him. Ciccio is called up for military service, and the novel ends with Alvina, now pregnant, having to bear and bring up a child alone. She is once more lost in an alien environment from which she feels cut off.

Aaron's Rod, a novel which Lawrence had written between *Aaron's Rod* October 1917 and November 1921, was published in England in 1922. Aaron Sisson is a mine worker and secretary of the local miners' union in Beldover – again modelled on Eastwood – and also a talented musician, principally on the flute and piccolo. He had originally trained to be a teacher, but he ultimately decided he preferred manual labour. At the age of thirty-three, having inherited a substantial amount of money from his recently deceased mother, he leaves his wife and three children well provided for, and sets off to London in a journey of self-discovery. There he becomes an orchestral musician and frequents intellectual and artistic circles. He is seduced by a scheming female acquaintance, but decides that this is not the type of relationship he left his family for. He falls into depression and succumbs to severe physical illness. The writer Rawdon Lilly, a "freak" and "outsider" by his own description, nurses him back to health, and reinforces Aaron's sense of revulsion at modern marriage, and his fear of being entrapped therein. Aaron goes back to see his wife, who not surprisingly is extremely bitter, so he leaves for Italy at an invitation from Rawdon. There he has a passionate relationship with a noble Italian woman, but Aaron once again distances himself from the relationship, because he wants to withdraw still deeper into himself and avoid being tied down. The novel ends with Rawdon helping Aaron to accept his intuition that the "love urge" has been exhausted by civilization, and that the new creative urge now is that of a power surging from the deepest reaches of the soul, which must be used to renew civilization.

As mentioned, from June to July 1922, while he was in *Kangaroo* Australia, Lawrence wrote the bulk of a novel, *Kangaroo*, set around Sydney, which was later published in 1923.

The novel is about Richard Somers and his wife Harriett, who have come to Australia to start a new life after becoming disillusioned with Europe. Their neighbours, Jack and Victoria Callcott, turn out to be members of a clandestine paramilitary organization planning to seize political power by force. Jack offers Somers the chance to become a member, and takes him to see the leader of the movement, Benjamin Cooley, usually referred to as "Kangaroo". Cooley advocates love and brotherhood, but sees this all within a strictly hierarchical model of society controlled by one all-powerful leader. Somers, although in essence sympathetic to his cause, is sceptical and will not commit himself, while Harriett is resentful of her husband's attraction to Kangaroo and the organization. Somers then becomes interested in socialism, but is equally sceptical: Kangaroo's organization is based on love organized through power, whereas the socialists' ideals are based on love for humanity as a generalized and abstract concept, without taking the individual into account. Neither system is what Somers believes he, or humanity in general, needs on a personal level. He is present when the socialists and the right-wingers fight at a rally and numerous men are killed. Kangaroo is wounded, and Somers goes to visit him. Kangaroo asks him once and for all to dedicate himself to the movement, but Somers cannot bring himself to do this. Kangaroo dies, and Somers and his wife start to consider moving to America. Before he leaves, Somers declares that he can only commit himself to nature, to "non-human gods, non-human human being".

The Boy in the Bush   Having met the author Mollie Skinner in Australia, Lawrence collaborated on a novel with her, *The Boy and the Bush*, which was published in 1924. Although both names appear on the title page, the precise degree of participation of either author is unclear. It relates the story of Jack Grant, who arrives in Australia from England in 1882 at the age of eighteen, after having been expelled from school and agricultural college, and having been involved in various other dubious doings. The novel depicts how he becomes a successful sheep farmer and gold miner by his early twenties. There is little of the didacticism and pretentiousness of Lawrence's other novels, and it is in essence an uncomplicated adventure story.

The Plumed Serpent   Lawrence turned to Mexico for the setting of his next novel, *The Plumed Serpent*, which he wrote on location in order to immerse himself fully in the country's atmosphere and accustom himself to the mores of the indigenous population. He completed the novel in 1925 and it was published in England the following year. In *The Plumed Serpent* a revolutionary movement in Mexico intends to overthrow Christianity and re-establish worship of the old gods, such as Quetzalcoatl – the "plumed serpent" of the title. The leaders of this movement even assume the names of these old gods. Kate Leslie, an Irish widow of around forty who is visiting Mexico, is at first impressed by the animal pagan vigour of the organization, but then becomes suspicious of its mysticism and barbarity. The novel simultaneously charts the progress of the movement and Kate's fluctuating sympathies towards it. The movement comes to control large swathes of the country, but Kate grows increasingly alienated by its inhumanity. However, she cannot resist the pagan "soul power" of one of the revolutionary leaders who has named himself Quetzalcoatl, and she agrees to participate in a ritual marriage with him. But even after the ceremony she is profoundly dubious, and at the end of the novel we are left wondering whether the movement will be crushed and whether she will become utterly disillusioned and try to withdraw from it.

Lady Chatterley's Lover was Lawrence's final and most successful major novel. It was written between 1926 and 1928: during this time he completed three separate versions, each of which were subsequently published. The first version, and the only one to appear in Lawrence's lifetime, was privately printed first in Florence in 1928 and then in Paris the following year. In Britain, due to the book's controversial content, it was only published by Secker in a radically expurgated version in February 1932. The first British unexpurgated printing, by Penguin in August 1960, was prosecuted for obscenity; following the collapse of the case, it went on general sale in November of that year, becoming an instant best-seller. A second version of the novel, under the title of *John Thomas and Lady Jane* – which corresponds to the version Lawrence was working on between late 1926 and early 1927 – was first published by Heinemann in 1972. The third version, referred to as *The Second Lady Chatterley's Lover*, uses the text written between December 1927 and January 1928 and was first published by Cambridge University Press in 1993.

The novel is set in Eastwood and other Nottinghamshire towns, as well as Sheffield and Chesterfield – with brief scenes in Venice and London. Its protagonist is Connie Reid, who has had a wealthy, artistic and unconventional upbringing. She and her elder sister Hilda are allowed a great deal of freedom, and both have had sexual affairs by the time they are eighteen. At the beginning of the First World War they settle briefly in London and become part of a coterie of university intellectuals. Hilda marries, and Connie forms an attachment with Clifford Chatterley – a shy and nervous young aristocrat,

Lady Chatterley's Lover

239

who had been studying at Cambridge at the outbreak of war, but then joined the army – marrying him in 1917 when he is home on leave. Clifford is seriously wounded in battle, and becomes sexually impotent. Following the deaths of relatives, he becomes heir to the family title and estate. Clifford is not only impotent, but seriously depressed, and takes up writing as a therapy, eventually becoming a successful author. He plays host to gatherings of literati and other intellectuals, and Connie begins to feel more and more empty, frustrated and peripheral. In 1924, when she is twenty-seven, she sees the gamekeeper Mellors (known as Parkin in the second version) washing his naked body in the woods and feels herself flaming back into life. She and Mellors become lovers, and they both rediscover their deep inner selves and connection with nature. Mellors is in fact an educated man who has rejected his middle-class upbringing to revert to a more meaningful working life. Therefore, though he can discourse on intellectual subjects, and can speak with a refined accent, he prefers to talk in broad dialect, and to project a working-class persona. He too, before he met Connie, had become sad and isolated, disillusioned by the war and the destruction of nature by industrialization. He has previously had various loveless affairs with women, including a now estranged wife. However, his liaison with Connie removes all his encrusted bitterness. Connie becomes pregnant, and at the end of the novel they are both waiting for divorces so that they can marry, live on a farm and start a new life together, sheltered from the artificiality they see around them.

Mr Noon   *Mr Noon* is an unfinished novel in two parts, which Lawrence wrote between 1920 and 1922. Secker posthumously published the first part in 1934, at the end of a collection of Lawrence's short stories, and fifty years later the Cambridge University Press edition appeared, including the very incomplete second part. The novel relates the past life of Gilbert Noon, a science teacher at a school in Nottinghamshire. It is revealed that he came from a working-class background, but proved to be so brilliant at maths, science and music that he gained a scholarship to go to Cambridge University, becoming one of the most outstanding mathematicians of the age. However, due to his somewhat dissipated lifestyle, he did not manage to progress up the academic ladder, and so returned home and became a teacher. He is caught in the act of having sex with

Emmie Bostock, a twenty-three-year-old schoolteacher and, upon her apparently becoming pregnant, he is forced to resign his teaching post. In the second part of the novel Gilbert roams around Germany and elopes with a married woman over the Alps into Italy, where he feels himself to be "reborn" – at which point the fragment ends.

During the course of his life, Lawrence issued twelve volumes *Other Works* of poetry and had scores of poems published in journals. He produced three collections of short stories and six novellas, as well as a large number of stories published in magazines which were not collected during his lifetime. He also wrote seven plays, and his prolific non-fiction includes volumes on psychoanalysis and philosophy, travel sketches and hundreds of reviews and articles for the press.

Select Bibliography

Standard Edition
The authoritative edition of *Paul Morel* is the Cambridge University Press edition, edited by Helen Baron (Cambridge: Cambridge University Press, 2003), which includes extensive annotations.

Biographies:
Aldington, Richard, *Portrait of a Genius, but...: A Biography of D.H. Lawrence* (London: Heinemann, 1950)
Meyers, Jeffrey, *D.H. Lawrence: A Biography* (London: Macmillan, 1990)
Moore, Harry Thornton, *The Priest of Love: A Life of D.H. Lawrence*, 2nd ed. (London: Heinemann, 1974)
Nehls, Edward, ed., *D.H. Lawrence: A Composite Biography* (Madison, WI: University of Wisconsin Press, 1959)
Sagar, Keith, *The Life of D.H. Lawrence: An Illustrated Biography* (London: Eyre Methuen: 1980)
Squires, Michael and Talbot, Lynn K., *Living at the Edge: A Biography of D.H. Lawrence and Frieda von Richthofen* (London: Robert Hale, 2002)
Worthen, John, *D.H. Lawrence: The Early Years 1885–1912* (Cambridge: Cambridge University Press, 1991)
Worthen, John, *D.H. Lawrence: The Life of an Outsider* (London: Allen Lane, 2005)

Additional Background Material:
Boulton, James T., ed., *The Selected Letters of D.H. Lawrence* (Cambridge: Cambridge University Press, 1997)
Miller, Henry, *The World of Lawrence: A Passionate Appreciation* (London: Calder, 1985)
Poplawski, Paul, *D.H. Lawrence: A Reference Companion* (Westport, CT & London: Greenwood Press, 1996)

On the Web:
www.nottingham.ac.uk/mss/online/dhlawrence

Appendix

'Matilda' is the beginning of an unfinished novel which Lawrence wrote at some point between October 1908 and July 1910, when he referred to it in a letter to Louie Burrows. Elements of this fragment were later recast in *Paul Morel* and *Sons and Lovers*.

Some silent emendations and regularizations concerning punctuation have been made by the editor. A full list of emendations, substantive errors and author's manuscript revisions is included in the Textual Apparatus of the Cambridge Edition of *Paul Morel* (2003).

'MATILDA'

Chapter I

I

There is a small cottage off the Addiscombe Road about a mile from East Croydon station. Now it is black and obscure in the blush of advancing pink and plaster houses. A while back it was noticeable as you rode out into Kent, the great elms stretching over its high-pitched roof, the currant bushes straggling towards the gate from its base.

On a Sunday afternoon in January 1860 two men turned in from the highroad to the garden path. One was a man of handsome stature, wearing a frock coat and a chimney-pot felt hat; the other was a short man in wide-awake and clerical garb. It was growing dusk, and a flicker of firelight showed through the small end-window.

Before the men reached the house the door opened. There was a glimpse of a little girl clinging to the latch, then she vanished, and the cleric looked gratefully into the kitchen, full of darkness and fire-glow, at the whiteness of the tablecloth, and the moving shadow of a woman.

"Step forward, Brother," said the taller of the two men, and the cleric entered, followed by his host. The latter glanced behind the door, where the little girl was shrinking, curious but shy.

"What, you young sparrow, what are you hiding for? Come now, shake hands with Mr Coates.—This is Matilda," he added, with a little emphasis on 'this', thus betraying that he had spoken of her to the cleric. She flushed. The plump little parson came forward, patted her head and bent down in front of the child. She held out her hand; Mr Coates took it and kept it, still bending in front of her.

"So this is little Matilda—God bless her! Give me a kiss, little Tilly."

The child drew back. The plump little man sat on his heels coaxing her, but she held firmly away, and tried to withdraw her hand.

"She is a coy little girl," he said, rising, feeling rebuffed.

"Ay—if she thinks you want a thing, you may back your life she won't give it. That's a woman all over."

"Do you think so, Brother?" said Mr Coates, drawing off his overcoat. "Now my experience is that a woman gladly gives what a man asks of her, if he asks in the right spirit."

"Verified by your last bit of experience," replied Robert Wootton. The little cleric would have answered, but the other turned into the kitchen, and said, in something of a grand manner:

"My Wife, Brother."

It was an inopportune moment. The small flurried woman was bending over the hob putting tea from the caddy she held, into the teapot. She started, looked towards the cleric, spilled half her clamp-shell of tea grains into the fender, and, recalled, turned nervously to the teapot. The kettle, perched just in front of the fire, began at that moment to spit, having been furiously on the boil for some moments. Still further flurried, the little woman seized the teapot and poured on the water. The two men waited grandly. When at last the lid was replaced and the teapot clinked on the hob, the little woman gave her attention to the men, even at the last distractedly wiping her hands on her apron.

"My Wife!"

The grandiloquence and the biting sarcasm that accompanied the two words overwhelmed the woman with shame and the parson with confusion.

The little girl had crossed the room unnoticed and stood, illuminated by the fire, at her mother's side. She had her mother's small, svelte figure, and brown, fine, curling hair, but her sagacious brow, her eyes, with their imperious stare, or with their blue concentrated interest, and her close-knit lips were from her father. She was about ten years old. She wore a quaint round apron of roughish linen, bound all round with scarlet turkey-quill. The short sleeves of her frock were of blue cloth, slaty blue suggesting lilacs about to fade; there was a much-puckered frill of the same stuff below her apron. Her stockings were white, and she wore small black shoes. Her arms and her hands were very delicate. She gave an impression of refined exquisiteness bound over with the severity of the little round apron.

Another child, some two years younger than Matilda, had slid out of the great arm-chair at the coming of the two men, and had gone through a door at the back, hiding in front of her two wooden dolls and a cane. The father, as usual had not noticed her; the cleric saw but said nothing. He was a very popular Wesleyan minister. When the child returned, guiltless and serene, he greeted her with warmth, kissed her, praised her black and ruddy beauty, and was flatteringly polite to the mother.

Frances wiped off his kiss, stared at him, and went to gaze at the raisin cake on the table.

The father, always with the air of a man who bends an unwilling dignity, set the lamp on the table and lighted it, revealing and almost immediately waking a brown-haired girl of five, and a baby-girl of two years from the sofa. Ethel, the bonnie, brown-haired child sat up and looked at the stranger. Then she scrambled from the sofa, kicking the baby as she did so, and ran to her father, hanging on to his coat-tails.

"I can say it all, Father," she cried.

"Can you, my duckie? This is my young hussy, Brother! Come on, Scaramouch, let us hear you!"

The child began in a loud voice, with quaint imitation of her father's ironical tone, the curses of Job on his day. Robert Wootton, being a man of overweening pride who has arrived at that phase when he perceives that his life will pass in insignificance, has turned to the Wesleyans, and is just recovering from the bitterness of the knowledge of his own futility, assured by religion that to the grave eternity he is overwhelmingly important. Therefore he is able to appreciate with a kind of sardonic humour the recitation which he has taught his child.

"Let the day perish wherein I was born, and the night in which it was said, 'There is a man child conceived'.

The mother in the scullery suspended her cutting of bread and butter and listened, with the old expression of distress and the mortification of a woman who is of small account to the man she worships. The parson listened, wondered, and disapproved, yet in his soul secretly admitting that he had come upon a race whose native force he must not oppose. Matilda, who sat at the sofa wiping the grey-eyed baby's hands and face with a damp flannel, watched her young sister with some pride. Then her lips tightened, and she turned to the baby, angry with Ethel for her self-confidence and her loud imitation which held the interest of her father and of the stranger. So she arose and went to her mother, and asked her if she had finished the bread and butter, talking subduedly, in contempt of the noise in the kitchen; and her mother answered willingly.

"That is very remarkable, very remarkable," said the little cleric at the end. "You must come and recite for us at the anniversary. Will you? We should like it ever so much, you know. Not that piece; another one, that a little girl can say prettily. You don't like that piece, do you?"

"I think it's a good piece—it is, isn't it Father?"

"It is indeed. But we'll teach you another piece, eh?"

"From the New Testament, Brother," said the clergyman softly. "The words of Our Lord are beautiful on the lips of a babe."

The big, handsome man bowed his head and repented:

"We won't have that one any more, Ethel," he said. "Mr Coates shall choose you one, eh?"

They sat down to table, the four children and the three elders. Annie, the baby, sat in a high chair. The two men talked about St Paul, the rest were silent, the mother only answering "Yes" or "I think so" to the parson's kindly references. Then Frances, crowded between the baby's high chair and her father's arm chair, upset her cup of tea. Instantly her father sent her from the table:

"Go into the scullery, you careless hussy, and stop there. It's every Sunday alike, there's one of 'em makes a mess of everything. Why can't they wait? They've no business to sit down to tea with grown-up folk."

"She hadn't much room, Robert," ventured the mother quietly.

"If there was not much room, why was she here at all? Why were any of them here at all? Why couldn't they wait?"

The clergyman looked at his plate, and the mother talked very gently to the baby. Ethel went on with her tea. From the scullery came the snuffling of the disgraced Frances. Matilda, fragile but erect, sat glaring at her father with blue eyes exactly like his own. He sat gripping the arms of his chair. He was a large man, with a clear fine skin and yellow hair, and eyes at the moment fiercely blue. He felt the child's gaze and looked at her, and, after a moment of defiance, her stare was beaten down. Then he resumed his tea, sucking remorse out of victory. The clergyman chatted amiably to the mother, who hastened to cover this rent in their hospitality with small words of generous deference.

After a while the general cheerfulness was restored. The mother was quite content because she had heard the click of a knife from the scullery, and she knew that Frances was helping herself liberally to the food on the shelf. She smiled, also, thinking what coals of remorse would be heaped on her husband's head when Frances, satisfied, should declare later that she didn't want any tea. Robert Wootton's wife had much humour in her quiet eyes, a humour different from her husband's.

The clergyman sat balancing his teaspoon and wondering what he might say. He had not the courage to address his deacon, and Mary Wootton was preoccupied. So he balanced his teaspoon and wondered and wished the visit ended.

The tea-spoon itself was interesting and perplexing. It was large and heavy, of solid silver, and it was engraved with a monogram "W", not a large sprawling letter, but a small round bit of engraving, flourished with a design which he could not quite understand.

"Robert Wootton," thought the parson, "looks like an aristocrat, and the little girl is quite elegant"—so he addressed himself to Matilda:

"Have you a picture on your spoon?" he asked.

"No, there's only that one" replied the girl.

He tried to draw the child, but she evidently knew nothing except that her grandmother, who lived alone with an old servant in Barrow in Leicestershire, had given the spoons to her mother. No one volunteered to satisfy the clergyman's desire for an aristocratic flavour, so he smiled, and said:

"You looked such a sweet little girl in chapel this morning. I thought you would have talked to me ever so nicely."

"Well," she replied, "I do, don't I?"

"Oh yes. But you don't tell me what you think. I can see little thoughts just coming and peeping out of your eyes, and then when they catch me looking, they draw back and hide themselves, and I never know them."

He accompanied this speech with little dramatic gestures, such as he used when he gave his popular addresses to the children.

"Tell me then what I was thinking," challenged the child, sitting up and smiling, delighted to challenge.

"No," he replied, shaking his head. "I didn't see your thoughts plainly. They peeped and hid themselves. But you were thinking about me."

"Well," she cried, excited, rather confused, enjoying the risks, "what was I thinking about you?"

"You were thinking about me this morning," he hazarded, smiling.

The child's glowing challenge became more intense. She was a born duellist, and, unlike most women, but like all children, she longed keenly to play to the end of the bout, though the weapons were naked.

"Well, and what by that?" she asked.

"That I can't tell you; I want you to tell me."

The parson was very disappointing. She looked at him with disgust, and he beamed back on her. He was a pleasant little man, dark haired and sallow and fat, a man of virtuous desires, or perhaps a man virtuous by lack of desires, something of a prig: at any rate, a very good fellow. Being vain, he was exceedingly curious.

"You must tell me, or I shall think it was something bad."

"Well," she blushed, "it wasn't!"

She hung back, and the little man insisted over and again. At last she was offended. She bridled, and looked him straight in the face:

"I was only wondering if you stood on a stool in the pulpit, and if you might tumble off some time."

"Oh, that's naughty of you," scolded the mother, furtively smiling.

"Matilda, remember whom you're speaking to," commanded her father.

She was angry, and turned to stare at her parent. But she found his blue eyes twinkling; was he not a man of handsome stature, her father—? So she blushed, and hung her head.

"Well now—" said the parson, aggrieved: "That's not a nice question for a little girl to ask, you know. Never mind! Come and give me a kiss, and be forgiven."

She did not move from her chair.

"Won't you give me a kiss?"

She did not answer.

"Surely you owe me one. Come and kiss me, and let us be good friends."

The little man flushed slightly. It piqued him keenly to be set at naught in this fashion. He was generally made much of, but here was a child of ten treating him almost with scorn, in presence of his most scornful of deacons. So he set his teeth, and determined to kiss the child, to save his pride. The mother understood his feeling:

"Don't be silly, child, don't be silly!"

But Matilda would not move.

The exasperated little parson was playing now as if for a great stake: he would *not* be beaten. So he drew from his pocket a small, pearl-handled pocket-knife, a delicate thing.

"There! Come and kiss me and you shall have this knife—that I put in my pocket for a nice little girl," he said, ending with a lie for the parents' sakes.

Matilda looked. It was a dainty knife, and she would love to have it, she could cut such lots of things. Yet she hung back.

"It's got two blades," said the parson. His eyes were getting full of anger, so he looked down. She had brought the situation to breaking point; moreover she wanted the knife, and his offering it was a mark of weakness. As he was so weak, she would kiss him. She went slowly forward and took the knife, hanging her head.

He kissed her a large kiss on the cheek, saying, almost with a gasp of relief:

"That's a good little girl—ever such a nice little girl!"

He patted her head, and she withdrew, retiring to the scullery while he talked to the father. With that subtle understanding of each other's feelings, that tact which alone marks a sensible man from a fool, they went to another topic, never alluding to the kiss. The parson was grateful; he suffered much at the hands of kind fools.

In the scullery Matilda went to the roller towel that hung behind the door and rubbed her cheek. She scrubbed with fury. Licking a clean bit of the towel, she rubbed again and again. Frances, who had eaten and drunk her fill, came to wipe her mouth on the towel. Matilda, in her wrath, glared at her. So the younger girl went out of the little scullery.

"Have you come to finish your tea?" asked the mother innocently.

"I don't want none," she replied.

"But you hardly had a bit—" said the mother. "Come, drink a drop of tea."

"I don't want none," murmured Frances, drawing back. The mother turned and looked at her husband. The reproach of her look made him contract his brows, and falter in his talk with the parson. It was thus his wife combated her overbearing husband. She smiled to herself as she cleared away the pots.

The baby, who had been kept good at the expense of many eatables, now lifted from her chair, went trotting into the scullery. She pulled at Matilda's skirts and dragged her into the house.

"Good Gracious!" exclaimed the mother: "whatever have you been doing at your face."

Matilda turned aside her inflamed cheek.

"She's been spitting on the towel an' rubbin' it—" explained Frances.

There was general silence. The parents wanted to laugh, but they knew the parson was mortally offended. Matilda hated Frances, and when Ethel came trotting round to peer at her red cheek, she was nudged away with ferocity, and went complaining to her mother. But Matilda had the silken comfort of the little pocket-knife in her hand.

When it was time for the cleric and the father to depart again to the service, Matilda went up to the former and gave him her hand.

"Goodnight," she murmured, blushing.

Then she offered him the knife:

"Shall you have it back?"

"Don't you want it?" he said.

She looked at him, shyly. He knew she wanted the knife, and he knew she would kiss him now. So he bent, kindly, and kissed her goodnight.

After that she was fond of him, but among her fondness flourished always an inconspicuous green weed of scorn.

2

Robert Wootton was foreman in an engineering shop in London, a shop where were made difficult machines newly patented. He was a man of capacity, earning about four pounds a week. Though this wage seemed ample to his wife, and though he himself referred to his position proudly, inwardly he was galled by his comparative poverty.

He was the youngest of the Woottons of Nottingham, a family chiefly noted for its decay. They had once held large lands along the Trent, and had been richest among the town's wealthy tanners, in the old years. When the industry of tanning gradually slipped away from the town, the Woottons took up other business.

At the zenith of the tanning, land-owning prosperity, Robert Wootton, great-grandfather of this Robert, had married a daughter of the house of Rutland, a Lady Lydia. Her family had promptly ceased to be aware of her, but she had queened it in state, unconcerned, mistress of her husband, of his magnificent presence and his magnificent temper, of his wealth and city standing, and, at last, of his ten great sons. She was serene and supreme, a splendid autocrat. Not one of her ten sons dared question her. They were great fair fellows: all along the line there was no record of a Wootton with hair darker than a beechnut. That was the range, from red-brown to fair yellow like dry withered sedge. Lady Lydia introduced no new strain of colouring, but her disintegrating influence appeared immediately in the men's characters. The hearty, genial temper of the race was spoiled, but nothing disappeared so remarkably as the astute, aldermanic business-qualities which had kept the Woottons to the front for generations. Three of her sons went to the dogs, as the people said, and their records were lost; four of the others left the Midlands on the breaking-up of the old home; the remaining three, with their shares of the remainder of the family estate, continued in Nottingham. The last of the tanning was given up, and the Woottons entered other industries, in a small way. John Wootton, grandfather of the man whom we are considering, entered the weaving. He declined in fortune very gradually during his lifetime. His fifth son, William, married a Miss Coutts, of Mansfield, and she brought him a thousand pounds, being the daughter of a maltster.

Emma Coutts, like Lady Lydia, came into the family as an invader and a conqueror. She was 'black'; tall, large-boned, and swarthy. Moreover, she was a stern, even a dreadful Wesleyan. William Wootton, a handsome fair man, a very Wootton in appearance, but strangely gentle, submitted wholly to her sway: "Emma, my love," he called her, often entreatingly, very pathetically, as his son Robert remembered him in the later days, a tall, thin, pitiful old man held in his chair by paralysis; "Emma, my love—don't you think the lad might have his way?"

Robert was seventh of nine children; he had a younger sister and brother, and older than he were five brothers, and one sister. Emma Wootton controlled everything, even the business. Her husband was a small lace-manufacturer, and his business-standing was precarious. He wanted to extend, and he wondered whether to take the new machines that were being brought forward. Emma Wootton came down upon him: one of the most influential members of the Wesley Chapel in Bread Street was selling machines, cheap; it was incumbent upon the husband of Emma Wootton to buy from the godly man. The husband of Emma Wootton bought, and eight years afterwards he sat sobbing as if his heart were broken while his machines were sold for fourteen pounds, scrap-iron. He then wound up his business. There was enough money left to produce him an annuity of fifty-five shillings a week. It was a little while before this that the corporation of Nottingham had made burgesses of all the Woottons remaining in the city; of all save William, that is; for Emma found in her Wesleyan conscience something that forbade the acceptance of this dignity, so she refused her husband the burgess-ship, and denied herself and her children and her children's children its privileges and emoluments. But she saved her conscience.

There is a story Robert Wootton once, in his courtship, told to his wife concerning his mother. His sister Lydia, some ten years older than himself, had been known as the "Beauty of Nottingham" in the forties. She was a pure Wootton, with her exquisite clearness of skin, brown-gold hair, cool rather than ruddy, and grey eyes. She appears to have been of wilful, romantic disposition. At any rate, she ran away at seventeen to the convent in the town. It was a great shock to the stern Wesleyan, but "Never mind," she said in her severity, "if she wants to go, I shall not prevent her. But as she makes her bed, she must lie." This was said, however, when the convent doors had closed behind the "Beauty of Nottingham"; if it had been the case of a mooted question, the mother would have spoken differently. The name of the runaway was not mentioned in the household for five weeks. Then the milkman gave to Emma Wootton a scrap of paper along with the basin of milk one morning. He did not stay to be questioned. The paper read, with melodramatic brevity—

"Mother, fetch me."

The resolute woman set down the basin of milk and glared at the paper. Then she went for her bonnet and her shawl.

"I shall be back in less than an hour," she said to her husband, who was helping to clear the breakfast-things away.

"All right, Emma, my love," he replied, his lips unquestioning, his blue eyes full of query. She hastened to the convent and asked to see her daughter. After a while the portress returned again to her:

"The sister is praying, and cannot be disturbed."

"Very well, then I'll wait till she's at liberty."

At the end of ten minutes she knocked again as loudly as she could with the light round knocker.

"I'm here to see my daughter."

"Sister Cecilia is at her devotions."

"It is her mother who asks to see her, tell her that."

"She may not be disturbed."

"I'll wait then."

She was becoming angry. Yet she waited with fierce impatience for fifteen minutes. Then she knocked again. Her answer was:

"We have spoken to Sister Cecilia. She begs that you will leave her, lest you disquiet her peace of soul."

"But I'm going to speak to her . . . "

The wicket was closed, and the woman stood unheeded in the porch. She stiffened her shoulders; she seized the knocker and knocked with all her might but without success. No heed was paid her. Then she went down the steps, and took a large loose cobble-stone from the street. It was the time of riots. With this stone she hammered on the door with all her force, and she was a powerful woman.

"Let me see my daughter, let me see my daughter, or I'll bring the soldiers on you—." She continued to hammer and shout. There was a barracks in Nottingham then. It was the time of riots, and the anti-catholic feeling was still strong. It would be easy to set a mob at the little convent.

The door opened, Lydia Wootton was pushed out, weeping, and the door closed. The mother swept off with her daughter, who had been immured in her cell and locked away from her parent. She was pale and full of distress; she had had to scrub floors and starve, so she told her mother.

254

"Well my lady," answered the black-browed Wesleyan, "I hope it's taught you a lesson. Remember, I shall fetch you back no more."

She had no need. Some time after, Lydia Wootton married and went to live in Birmingham. Her husband ran away and left her. Robert Wootton told no more of the tale to his wife when he was courting her. Perhaps it would have smirched his pride. At any rate, it was the age of virtuous speech between a man of honour and a maid.

Emma Wootton had a rough time. After her husband's failure in business she kept house and nine children on fifty-five shillings a week. William helped her about the house, a man six feet high, once a 'gentleman', now trailing about the house carrying up the coal and swilling the yard. When the paralysis came upon him, he would sit in his round arm-chair and watch her, as she drove the ship of the household single handed against the wind. The boys were very difficult, and she brought them to submission with fierce words of scorn, and threats, and finally the clothes-line looped up in many loops.

"Now Emma, my love—!" William would entreat, with gentle reproach, when he saw her rising like Boadicea to combat her sons. And when she thrashed his young boys with the clothes-line looped up in twenty-five loops, as Robert used to recount, he sat with the tears dropping on his futile knees. Then death came and decently carried him off.

As may be supposed, after such stern and godly upbringing, the boys left home early, and early went to the bad, most of them. Their mother lived on alone. Then she gradually became childish, and one of her sisters came to live with her.

"Ah my soft old mother!" Robert Wootton had said once when listening to the bells pealing from the parish church, "the soft old thing: 'I want to hear the Blid'orth bells, I want to hear the Blid'orth bells ringing'—she used to sit saying that, the old fool." Despite his brutal language, Robert Wootton understood the pathos of the cry. His mother had spent her first sixteen years at Blidworth, a village in the wild country-side near Mansfield. There, among the silent hill-sides famous for black-berries and for bilberries, her God was soft-voiced and comely, not the clawed Yahveh of her later years.

3

Robert Wootton had been apprenticed to the engineering, as they said; that is, to one of the large machine-building shops in the town, where he had learned turning and fitting of the parts of lace-machines. Chiefly, he was a turner. He had fallen in love at twenty with a girl in one of the ware-houses, a creature gloriously shapen, whose contours intoxicated him, and whose grey eyes, glowing deliciously under black lashes, charmed him like magic. Then he had discovered 'she was not as good as she might be', and his mother's son had appeared. He had turned his indignation upon her, and she had laughed. Maddened, he had fetched her a knock upon the lips. She sprang like a devil and beat him wildly on the face. He left her, and she flaunted before him with strange men. People talked about him, which he could not endure, so he went away to America. At the end of a year he came back, converted; but his old mother was too childish to know the supreme joy of these tidings.

At the old Wesley chapel, which had been the hell of his boyhood, and where now he sought heaven, he met Mary Inwood, a meek brown-haired girl who sang very sweetly in the choir. Her father, a stockinger, was the organist at Wesley, and a composer of hymns and anthems and 'voluntaries', pleasant enough pieces, but derivative, insignificant. Gentleness, humility, and disposition to love were family traits. Consequently the family portion was contemptuous or harsh treatment from the well-favoured, and affection from the poor and the needy. Mary Inwood looked down from the choir and saw the young man from America fair and noble, fervent, with the pride of suffering on his lips. So she loved him. She knew his story; she heard him at class-meetings; she sang to him while her father played the flute in the small parlour of a Sunday evening: then she worshipped him. That was her merit, her extreme and self-effacing love for him. They had shortly married and moved south.

She was one of the sweetest women, and she adored him, so magnificent, so proud, and so clever he was. She wished sometimes he would say little gentle things to her; he said nothing but what was eminently sensible. But then, sometimes he held her silently in his arms, and the poignancy of his tenderness brought the tears spilling down from her eyes. That was not often, and only at first. She was a great prattler, and he was impatient, being so much her superior in intellect. She could never, never understand his pride, so she sighed, and left him alone there. He lived quite alone in his incommunicable pride; she never understood that, so she prayed the Lord to cure him of his brutal speech, of his bitterness, and of his scorn for small people like herself. The day came for him to shatter his own Godhead, as it comes to every man beloved.

In her own home in Nottingham Mary Inwood had never been burdened with heavy work. She had helped with the cooking, and had done fine lace-mending. In Robert Wootton's house, after six months she decided she could not afford to have a woman two days a week to work for her. She determined to do everything herself. She would help Robert to save, would there not be the baby—?

When she told him, he answered with a coldness that pained her:

"Well, you please yourself. I suppose other women do their own work."

She never understood to her dying day, that he felt this still another humiliation, that his wife should have to drudge for him. So she thought he did not care for her.

On the Monday she washed all the clothes, even his over-alls, 'swarfed' with machine oil. Consequently she had rubbed the skin off her fingers. When he came home in the evening, and the table was cleared, and he sat down to talk to her a bit, and to read, she came and seated herself on the arm of his chair, and leaned against his shoulder, and, with pretty feminine longing for his pity and his pitiful caresses, she spread out her small hands before him, her fingers all skinned at the knuckles, and said:

"Look, Robert, at my hands, how they're served with washing."

He looked, and turned his head away, and answered harshly, in his tones of slighting contempt:

"What do you want?" he said. "What do you think I married you for? Did you think you were going to be a lady? A working man's wife expects to work. They'll get hard enough."

She had gone away and begun to make baby-clothes, stitching blindly, with the feeling that heaven and earth and everything had collapsed and passed away, and she was left in a desolate space of darkness. He had not spoken to her that evening, and for a week she had gone about her work weeping, forlorn in her dark space. During that time she had taken the soul of her husband, and stripped it of its splendid vestures, as a disillusioned child may strip her beautiful doll that she had thought had come to her wonderfully from the realms of faery, but which she finds is stitched in clumsy imitation of herself. After this, Mary Wootton had loved her husband none the less earnestly, but she had ceased to adore him. She knew that her own mild angel, if it could wheel no terrible flaming sword, was nearer to the hand of God.

Chapter II

As Matilda Wootton grew older, her mother told her of these things, and many others, so that the girl looked at her father with critical eyes. Yet she loved him, and revered him. Reverence, however, runs to swing open the opposite door of hate, and there were times when Matilda hated her father fiercely.

At the age of eighteen she was her mother's friend, confidant, and ally. She helped with the children, and threw her weight on her mother's side to preserve the balance of power.

There were five children younger than herself: four girls, and then a boy. The father rejoiced extravagantly at the appearance of a son. Five girls in succession had dismayed him. He ruled them sternly. But the boy was another matter. It was meet that the girls should serve him, and serve him they did, when they were at home.

Matilda, after having attended a lady's school of mediocre order until her sixteenth year, was established with Miss Laverick. This was a grey smallish woman who kept a little school in South Norwood "for the young children of gentlemen." Matilda Wootton was the second assistant. Her chief duty was to repeat over and over again to the dunces and the refractory who would not submit to Miss Laverick or to Miss Laverick's cousin, who was first assistant:

" 'A', 'A' for 'apple'—round 'O' with a crook; 'a' for 'apple'."

Matilda left home in the morning at 8.15. The men hurrying from Woodside to Norwood Junction would turn to stare at her. She was grown to be a tall girl, thin and flat, but graceful, with dark curls hanging down her back, long swinging tubes of hair, and sometimes, on Sunday, bunches of small curls at the side like brown silken bunches of hops. In her daily passing she had come to know a young man who went up to London by the 8.40. He lived in a rather large house by Woodside Green, and his manners were rather elaborate. She thought him very charming. His dog had rushed from the gate and had danced round her barking as she passed one morning, and he had been very angry with

258

it, and had sent it back home with a yelp, and had apologised. She had blushed and said it didn't matter; she was not afraid of dogs; she liked them: that was how things happened in the romantic sixties. 'Romola' and 'Hereward the Wake' were in the air. The dreadful but wonderful George Eliot formed the subject of conversation during the second month of mornings. It was so daring.

Matilda Wootton said she liked dogs. It was hardly the truth. On the morning when she had said as much to Arthur Murray, she had grave reason to retract. She went straight up the Birchanger Road, and on till she came to a little house in a street off the Portland Road. There she knocked, and after a moment of hesitation, turned the knob and entered.

"Is that you, Matilda?" called a voice from the end of the passage which reminded one of a rabbit-run—

"Vickie has been waiting for you, haven't you Vickie dear? Yes, you have!"

Matilda shrugged her shoulders, and pursuing her narrow way past the sealed doors of the infinitesimal drawing room and dining room, entered the kitchen. There, in the tiny space, a small woman sat at a small table eating a very small egg, and looking up at the door and at Matilda with a remarkable steady stare of her round, dog-like eyes. Although she stared with such fixity, she gave the impression of being incurably timid and self-mistrustful. She affected assertiveness. She had four small knobs of greyish hair and curl-rag on her forehead, and her neck rose out of a sky-blue dressing-gown.

"Vickie has been waiting for you," repeated Miss Laverick. "She thought you couldn't be coming. It's not often her Matilda is late. Vickie was wondering what could be the matter—she could not understand it, not in the least, could you Vickie, my dear one?"

She turned and looked on the rug at her side. There, a fat brown spaniel sat blowing wheezily, and looking up at Miss Laverick as she daintily bit a small piece of bread dipped in her boiled egg. Matilda coloured. She hated Miss Laverick's mean way of talking at her and telling her she was late. Miss Laverick was the meanest and most despicable of creatures, yet she cowed people and trammelled them utterly by talking all round them.

"I think your clock's fast," said Matilda. "I started at the same time."

"My clock!" exclaimed Miss Laverick. "My clock fast! Never! My clock never varies five minutes from week-end to week-end. Do you know, Matilda, I've had that clock over ten years, and it has never sneezed or coughed, it has not turned a hair. No Matilda, it's not my clock. Ask Miss Hayward! Annie dear—!"

Miss Hayward, cousin, house-maid, and first assistant in Miss Laverick's school, came out of the scullery with an iron spoon in her hand. She was cooking the dinner. She was yellow and tasteless, about fifty years old, with the ways and manner and the outlook of a child. Religion alone was left her. Instead of budding, blowing, filling with fruit, ripening, and withering, in the natural course, she was like the outer floret of a guelder-rose, withered years and years ago, yet still hanging like a scrap of yellow rag on the tree.

"Annie dear, do you *ever* remember that clock varying *five* minutes since I had it, dear?"

"I don't indeed! Isn't it remarkable? But not to my knowledge."

"No," Miss Laverick turned to Matilda, who was reduced by this time to a lowest pitch of disgrace—"it is so, Dear. It's not the clock. Don't *you* think it's remarkable, Dear?"

"It is," said Matilda, furious and grudging.

"Yes, it is. Well, take the key, Dear, and poor Vickie is quite ready— aren't you, dear one, quite ready—been waiting and waiting—! Go then with Matilda! Carry him across the road, and over the dirty places, won't you Dear? Take the fifth Chapter of John. I shall not be long. Run along, Vickie—yes, go with Matilda."

Matilda called the dog, which waddled dejectedly after her, thudding clumsily down the hollow sound-box of a passage, causing Miss Laverick to sigh and to exclaim, as she heard the pod! pod! pod!

"Poor dear!"

Matilda banged the door near on Vickie's tail.